W9-BGI-540

TWO OF MASON'S MOST UNUSUAL CASES

—Two Complete Novels in One Volume!

THE CASE OF THE PERJURED PARROT
"One of Mason's best cases"   *—Books*

"Another hit for Erle Stanley Gardner"
     —The New York Times

THE CASE OF THE BEAUTIFUL BEGGAR
"One of the extra good Perry Mason novels . . .
displays Mason in excellent form . . . and the
criminal case is rich in inventive surprises."
     —The New York Times

"When it comes to describing a legal fencing
bout in such a way that the reader follows it
with unabated interest, Erle Stanley Gardner
can give cards and spades to other mystery
writers!"   *—The New York Times*

THE CASE OF THE PERJURED PARROT and
THE CASE OF THE BEAUTIFUL BEGGAR
were originally published by
William Morrow & Company, Inc.

Two Complete Novels by
ERLE STANLEY GARDNER

PERRY MASON

2 in 1

**The Case of
the Perjured Parrot**

**The Case of
the Beautiful Beggar**

PUBLISHED BY POCKET BOOKS NEW YORK

PERRY MASON 2 IN 1

POCKET BOOK edition published July, 1975

The Case of the Perjured Parrot
William Morrow edition published 1939

POCKET BOOK edition published October, 1947
15th printing .... May, 1975

The Case of the Beautiful Beggar
William Morrow edition published 1965

POCKET BOOK edition published January, 1967
3rd printing .... May, 1975

L

This POCKET BOOK edition includes every word contained
in the original, higher-priced editions. It is printed from
brand-new plates made from completely reset, clear, easy-
to-read type. POCKET BOOK editions are published by
POCKET BOOKS, a division of Simon & Schuster, Inc., 630
Fifth Avenue, New York, N.Y. 10020. Trademarks registered
in the United States and other countries.

The Case of
the Perjured Parrot

CAST OF CHARACTERS

The Case of
the Perjured Parrot

CHAPTER ONE

PERRY MASON regarded the pasteboard jacket, labeled "IMPORTANT UNANSWERED CORRESPONDENCE," with uncordial eyes.

Della Street, his secretary, looking as crisply efficient as a nurse in a freshly starched uniform, said with her best Monday-morning air, "I've gone over it carefully, Chief. The letters on top are the ones you simply *have* to answer. I've cleaned out a whole bunch of the correspondence from the bottom."

"From the bottom?" Mason asked. "How did you do that?"

"Well," she confessed, "it's stuff that's been in there too long."

Mason tilted back in his swivel chair, crossed his long legs, assumed his best lawyer manner and said, in mock cross-examination, "Now, let's get this straight, Miss Street. Those were letters which had originally been put in the 'IMPORTANT UNANSWERED' file?"

"Yes."

"And you've gone over that file from time to time, carefully?"

"Yes."

"And eliminated everything which didn't require my personal attention?"

"Yes."

"And yet this morning of Monday, September twelfth, you take out a large number of letters from the bottom of the file?"

"That's right," she admitted, her eyes twinkling.

"How many letters, may I ask?"

"Oh, fifteen or twenty."

"And did you answer those yourself?"

She shook her head, smiling.

"What *did* you do with them?" Mason asked.

"Transferred them to another file."

"What file?"

"The 'LAPSED' file."

Mason chuckled delightedly. "Now *there's* an idea, Della. We simply hold things in the 'IMPORTANT UNANSWERED' file until a lapse of time robs them of their importance, and then we transfer them to the 'LAPSED' file. It eliminates correspondence, saves worry, and gets me away from office routine, which I detest. . . . Incidentally, Della, things which seem frightfully important at the time have a habit of fading into insignificance. Events are like telephone poles, streaming back past the observation platform of a speeding train. They loom large at first, then melt into the distance, becoming so tiny they finally disappear altogether. . . . That's the way with nearly all of the things we think are so vital."

Her eyes were wide and innocent. "Do the telephone poles *really* get smaller, Chief, or do they just appear smaller?"

"Of course, they don't *get* smaller," he said; "it's simply that you're farther away from them. Other telephone poles come in and fill up the foreground. The telephone poles are all the same size. However, as you get farther distant from them they appear to be smaller, and . . ." He broke off abruptly and said, "Wait a minute. You aren't gently trying to point out a fallacy in my argument, are you?"

At her triumphant grin, he made a mock grimace. "I should have known better than to argue with a woman. All right, Simon Legree, get your notebook ready, and we'll write those confounded letters."

He opened the filing jacket, scanned a letter from a prominent firm of lawyers, tossed it across the desk to her, and said, "Write these people that I'm not interested in handling the case, even at twice the fee named. It's just a plain, ordinary murder case. A woman gets tired of her husband, plugs him with a six-gun, and then weeps and wails that he was drunk and trying to beat her up. She lived with him for six years, and seeing him drunk was no novelty. The business about being afraid he was going to kill her doesn't check with the story of the other witnesses."

2

"How much of that," Della Street asked with calm efficiency, "do you want me to put in the letter?"

"Just the part about not wanting to handle the case. . . . Oh, Lord, here's another one. A man, who's swindled a bunch of people into buying worthless stock, wants me to prove that he was within the letter of the law."

Mason slammed the file shut and said, "You know, Della, I wish people would learn to differentiate between the reputable lawyer who represents persons accused of crime, and the criminal lawyer who becomes a silent partner in the profits of crime."

"Just how would you explain the difference?" she asked.

Mason said, "Crime is personal. Evidence of crime is impersonal. I never take a case unless I'm convinced my client was incapable of committing the crime charged. Once I've reached that conclusion, I figure there must be some discrepancy between the evidence and the conclusions the police have drawn from that evidence. I set out to find them."

She laughed. "You sound as though you were more of a detective than a lawyer."

"No," Mason said, "they are two different professions. A detective gathers evidence. He becomes skilled in knowing what to look for, where to find it, and how to get it. A lawyer interprets the evidence after it's been collected. He gradually learns . . ."

He was interrupted by the ringing of the telephone at Della's desk. She answered it, saying, "Hold the line a moment, please," and then, cupping her hand over the mouthpiece, turned to Perry Mason. "Would you be interested in seeing a Mr. Charles Sabin on a matter of the greatest importance? Mr. Sabin says he's willing to pay any consultation fee."

Mason said, "Depends on what he wants. If he has a murder case, I'll listen to him. If he wants me to draw up a chattel mortgage, the answer is 'no.' There isn't enough money in the mint to tempt me to . . . Wait a minute, Della. What's his name?"

"Sabin," she said, "Charles W. Sabin."

"Where is he?"

"In the outer office."

Mason said, "Tell him to wait a few minutes. No, wait a minute. Find out if he's related to Fremont C. Sabin."

Della asked the question over the telephone, and waited for the girl at the information desk in the outer office to relay the inquiry to the visitor. She turned once more to Mason and said, "Yes, he's the son of Mr. Fremont C. Sabin."

"Tell him I'll see him," Mason said. "Tell him he'll have to wait about ten minutes. Go out and meet him, Della. Size him up. Take him into the law library, let him wait there. Bring me the morning newspapers. This, young lady, in case you don't know it, is a Break with a capital 'B.' Okay, get busy . . . Wait a minute, I have one of the newspapers here."

Mason made a dive for the newspaper, sweeping the file of important correspondence over to the far end of the desk, as he hurriedly cleared a space in front of him.

The account of the murder of Fremont C. Sabin occupied much of the front page. There were photographs on the second and third pages. There was a human interest story about his character and personality.

That which was known of the murder was well calculated to stir the imagination. Fremont C. Sabin, eccentric multimillionaire, had virtually retired from the many businesses which bore his name. His son, Charles Sabin, carried on for him. During the past two years the wealthy man had become almost a recluse. At times he would travel in a trailer, stopping in at auto camps, fraternizing with other trailerites, talking politics, exchanging views. None of those with whom he talked had the least inkling that this man, with his shiny business suit, his diffident manner, and his quiet gray eyes, was rated at more than two million dollars.

Or he would disappear for a week or two at a time, prowling around through bookstores, dropping in at libraries, living in a realm of studious abstraction, while he browsed through books.

Librarians invariably classified him as a clerk out of work.

Of late he had been spending much of his time in a

4

mountain cabin, on the pine-clad slope of a rugged range near a brawling stream. Here he would sit on the porch by the hour with a pair of powerful binoculars in his hand, watching the birds, making friends with the chipmunks and squirrels, reading books—asking only to be let alone.

Just touching sixty, he represented a strange figure of a man; one who had wrung from life all that it offered in the way of material success; a man who literally had more money than he knew what to do with. Some of this money he had established in trust funds, but for the most part he did not believe in philanthropy, thinking that the ultimate purpose of life was to develop character; that the more a person came to depend on outside assistance, the more his character was weakened.

The newspaper published an interview with Charles Sabin, the son of the murdered man, giving an insight into his father's character. Mason read it with interest. Sabin had believed that life was a struggle and had purposely been made a struggle; that competition developed character; that victory was of value only as it marked the goal of achievement; that to help someone else toward victory was doing that person an injustice, since victories were progressive.

The elder Sabin had placed something over a million dollars in trust funds for charitable uses, but he had stipulated that the money was to go only to those who had been incapacitated in life's battles: the crippled, the aged, the infirm. To those who could still struggle on, Sabin offered nothing. The privilege of struggling for achievement was the privilege of living, and to take away that right to struggle was equivalent to taking away life itself.

Della Street entered Mason's office as he finished reading that portion of the article.

"Well?" Mason asked.

"He's interesting," she said. "Of course he's taking it pretty hard. It's something of a shock, but there's nothing hysterical about him, and nothing affected about his grief. He's quiet, determined, and very self-controlled."

"How old?" Mason asked.

5

"About thirty-two or thirty-three. Quietly dressed . . . In fact, that's the impression he gives you, of being quiet. His voice is low and well-modulated. His eyes are a very cold blue, and very, very steady, if you get what I mean."

"I think I do," Mason told her. "Rather spare and austere in his appearance?"

"Yes, with high cheekbones and a firm mouth. I think you'll find he does a lot of thinking. He's that type."

Mason said, "All right, let's get some more facts on this murder."

He once more devoted his attention to reading the newspaper, then abruptly said, "There's too much hooey mixed in with this, Della, to give us very much information. I suppose I should get the highlights, because he probably won't want to talk about it."

He returned to the newspaper, skimming salient facts from the account of the murder.

Fishing season in the Grizzly Creek had opened on Tuesday, September sixth. It had been closed until that date by order of the Fish and Game Commission to protect the late season fishing. Fremont C. Sabin had gone to his mountain cabin, ready to take advantage of the first day. Police reconstructed what had happened at that cabin from the circumstantial evidence which remained. He had evidently retired early, setting the alarm for five-thirty in the morning. He had arisen, cooked breakfast, donned his fishing things, and had returned about noon, evidently with a limit of fish. Sometime after that—and the police, from the evidence which had been so far made available, were unable to tell just when—Fremont Sabin had been murdered. Robbery had evidently not been the motive, since a well-filled wallet was found in his pocket. He was still wearing a diamond ring, and a valuable emerald stickpin was found in the drawer of the dresser, near the bed. He had been shot through the heart and at close range by a short-barreled derringer, obsolete in design but deadly in its efficiency.

Sabin's pet parrot, who had of late years accompanied him on nearly all his trips to the mountain cabin, had been left in the room with the body. The murderer had fled.

The mountain cabin was isolated, nearly a hundred yards back from the automobile road which wound its tortuous way up to the pine-timbered cabin. There was not a great deal of traffic on this road, and those people who lived in the neighborhood had learned to leave the wealthy recluse alone.

Day after day such traffic as used the highway passed heedlessly by, while in the cabin back under the trees a screaming parrot kept vigil over the lifeless corpse of his master.

Not until several days after the murder, on Sunday, September eleventh, when fishermen came in large numbers to line the stream, did anyone suspect anything was wrong.

By that time the parrot's shrill, raucous cries, interspersed with harsh profanity, attracted attention.

"Polly wants something to eat. Dammit, Polly wants something to eat. Don't you damn fools know Polly's hungry?"

A neighbor, who owned a nearby cabin, had investigated. Peering through the windows he had seen the parrot, and then had seen something else which made him telephone for the police.

The murderer had evidently had compassion for the bird, but none for the master. The cage door had been left propped open. Someone, apparently the murderer, had left a dish of water on the floor, an abundance of food near the cage. Food remained, but the water dish was dry.

Mason looked up from the newspaper and said to Della Street, "All right, Della, let's have him in."

Charles Sabin shook hands with Perry Mason, glanced at the newspaper on the table, and said, "I hope you are familiar with the facts surrounding my father's death."

Mason nodded, waited until his visitor had seated himself in the overstuffed, black leather chair, and then inquired, "Just what do you want me to do?"

"Quite a few things," Sabin said. "Among others, I want you to see that my father's widow, Helen Watkins

Sabin, doesn't ruin the business. I have reason to believe there's a will leaving the bulk of the estate to me, and, in particular, making me the executor. I can't find that will in searching among his papers. I'm afraid it may be in her possession. She's fully capable of destroying it. I don't want her to act as administratrix of the estate."

"You dislike her?"

"Very much."

"Your father was a widower?"

"Yes."

"When did he marry his present wife?"

"About two years ago."

"Are there any other children?"

"No. His widow has a grown son, however."

"Was this last marriage a success? Was your father happy?"

"No. He was *very* unhappy. He realized he'd been victimized. He would have asked for an annulment, or a divorce, if it hadn't been for his dread of publicity."

"Go on," Mason said. "Tell me just what you want me to do."

"I'm going to put my cards on the table," Charles Sabin told him. "My legal affairs are handled by Cutter, Grayson & Bright. I want you to co-operate with them."

"You mean in the probate of the estate?" Mason asked.

Sabin shook his head. "My father was murdered. I want you to co-operate with the police in bringing that murderer to justice.

"My father's widow is going to require quite a bit of handling. I think it's a job that's beyond the abilities of Cutter, Grayson & Bright. I want you to handle it.

"I am, of course, deeply shocked by what has happened. I was notified yesterday afternoon by the police. It's been very much of an ordeal. I can assure you that no ordinary business matter would have brought me out today."

Mason looked at the lines of suffering etched on the man's face, and said, "I can readily understand that."

"And," Sabin went on, "I realize there are certain

questions you'll want to ask. I'd like to make the interview as brief as possible."

Mason said, "I'll need some sort of authorization to . . ."

Sabin took a wallet from his pocket. "I think I have anticipated your reasonable requirements, Mr. Mason. Here is a retainer check, together with a letter stating that you are acting as my lawyer and are to have access to any and all of the property left by my father."

Mason took the letter and check. "I see," he said, "that you are a methodical man."

"I try to be," Sabin told him. "The check will be in the nature of a retainer. Do you consider it adequate?"

"It's more than adequate," Mason said, smiling. "It's generous."

Sabin inclined his head. "I've followed your career with a great deal of interest, Mr. Mason. I think you have exceptional legal ability and an uncanny deductive skill. I want to avail myself of both."

"Thanks," the lawyer said. "If I'm going to be of any value to you, Mr. Sabin, I'll want an absolutely free hand."

"In what respect?" Sabin asked.

"I want to be free to do just as I please in the matter. If the police should charge someone with the crime, I want the privilege of representing that person. In other words, I want to clear up the crime in my own way."

"Why do you ask that?" Sabin said. "Surely I'm paying you enough . . ."

"It isn't that," Mason told him, "but if you've followed my cases, you'll note that most of them have been cleared up in the courtroom. I can suspect the guilty, but about the only way I can really prove my point is by cross-examining witnesses."

"I see your point," Sabin conceded. "I think it's entirely reasonable."

"And," Mason said, "I'll want to know all of the salient facts, everything which you can give me that will be of assistance."

Sabin settled back in the chair. He spoke calmly, almost disinterestedly. "There are two or three things to be taken into consideration in getting a perspective on my

9

father's life. One of them was the fact that he and my mother were very happily married. My mother was a wonderful woman. She had a loyalty which was unsurpassed, and a complete lack of nervousness. During all her married life, there was literally never an unkind word spoken, simply because she never allowed herself to develop any of those emotional reflexes, which so frequently make people want to bicker with those whom they love, or with whom they come in constant association.

Naturally, my father came to judge every woman by *her* standards. After her death, he was exceedingly lonely. His present wife was employed in the capacity of housekeeper. She was shrewd, scheming, deadly, designing, avaricious, grasping. She set about to insinuate herself into his affections. She did so deliberately. My father had never had any experience with women of her kind. He was temperamentally unfitted to deal with her in the first place, or even to comprehend her character. As a result, he permitted himself to be hypnotized into marriage. He has, of course, been desperately unhappy."

"Where is Mrs. Sabin now?" Mason asked. "I believe the paper mentioned something about her being on a tour."

"Yes, she left on a round-the-world cruise about two and a half months ago. She was located by wireless on a ship which left the Panama Canal yesterday. A plane has been chartered to meet her at one of the Central American ports, and she should arrive here tomorrow morning."

"And she will try to take charge?" Mason asked.

"Very completely," Sabin said, in a voice which spoke volumes.

"Of course, as a son," Mason said, "you have certain rights."

Sabin said wearily, "One of the reasons that I have set aside my grief in order to come to you at this time, Mr. Mason, is that whatever you do should be well started before she arrives. She is a very competent woman, and a very ruthless adversary."

"I see," Mason said.

"She has a son by a former marriage, Steven Watkins,"

Sabin went on. "I have sometimes referred to him as his mother's stool pigeon. He has developed conscious affability as an asset. He has the technique of a politician, the character of a rattl snake. He has been East for some time, and took the plane from New York to connect with the plane that will pick up his mother in Central America. They will arrive together."

"How old is he?" Mason asked.

"Twenty-six. His mother managed to put him through college. He looks on an education only as a magic formula, which should enable him to go through life without work. As a young man he advocated a share-the-wealth philosophy as something which would reward him for living without making it necessary for him to engage in competitive work. After his mother married my father, she was able to wheedle him into giving her large sums of money which were squandered upon Steve with a lavish hand. He has reacted just as one would expect him to under the circumstances. He is now extremely contemptuous of what he refers to as the 'common herd.'"

"Have *you,*" Mason asked, "any idea of who murdered your father?"

"None whatever. If I did have, I would try to dismiss it from my mind. I don't want to even think of anyone whom I know in that connection until I have proof. And when I have proof, Mr. Mason, I want the law to take its course."

"Did your father have any enemies?"

"No. Except . . . there are two things which I think you should know about, Mr. Mason. One of them, the police know, the other, they don't."

"What are they?" Mason asked.

"It was not mentioned in the newspapers," Sabin said, "but in the cabin were certain intimate articles of feminine wearing apparel. *I* think those clothes were left there by the murderer, simply to swing public sympathy toward the widow."

"What else?" Mason asked. "You mentioned something which the police didn't know about. Was that . . ."

Sabin said, "This is something which may be significant, Mr. Mason. I believe you have read in the newspapers of my father's attachment for his parrot."

Mason nodded.

"Casanova was a present given to my father by his brother three or four years ago. His brother's a great parrot fancier, and Dad became very much attached to the bird. It was with him frequently . . . And the parrot which was found in the cabin with my father's body, and which the police and everyone else have assumed to be Casanova, is, in fact, *not my father's parrot.*"

Mason's eyes showed keen interest. "You're certain?" he asked.

"Absolutely certain."

"May I ask how you know?"

"In the first place," Sabin said, "the parrot in the cabin is given to profanity, particularly in connection with requests for food. Casanova had never learned to swear."

"Perhaps," Mason said, "a change of environment would have been responsible for that. You know, a parrot can pick up . . ."

"Moreover," Sabin said, "—and you'll pardon me if I interrupt you, Mr. Mason, because I am about to mention a point which is irrefutable—Casanova had one claw missing, a claw on his right foot. This parrot does not."

Mason frowned. "But why the devil," he asked, "should anyone want to substitute parrots?"

"The only reason I can think of," Sabin said, "is that the parrot is more important than would at first seem to be the case. I am quite certain that Casanova was with my father in the mountain cabin when my father was murdered. He, perhaps, saw something, or heard something, so he was removed and another parrot substituted. My father returned home on Friday, September second, long enough to pick up Casanova. We hadn't expected him until Monday, September fifth."

"But it would have been so much simpler and easier for the murderer to have killed the parrot," Mason said.

"I realize that," Sabin replied, "and I know that my theory is bizarre. Nevertheless, it is the only explanation I have been able to make in my own mind."

"Why," Mason asked, "didn't you tell the police about this?"

Sabin shook his head. This time there was no attempt to disguise the weariness in his eyes or his voice. "I have come to realize," he said, "that it is absolutely impossible for the police to keep matters from the newspapers, and I don't have any great confidence in the ability of the police to solve a crime such as this. I think you will find that it has very deep ramifications, Mr. Mason. I've told the police no more than was absolutely necessary. I have not volunteered information. I am giving this information to you. I would suggest that you keep it from the police. Let them build up their own case."

And Sabin indicated that he had told everything he knew by getting to his feet and extending his hand. "Thank you very much, Mr. Mason," he said. "I'll rest a lot easier in knowing that the matter is in your hands."

CHAPTER TWO

MASON, pacing back and forth across his office, jerked out comments. Paul Drake, head of the Drake Detective Agency, his tall form draped crosswise across the over-stuffed leather chair, made notes in a leather-backed notebook.

"That substituted parrot," Mason said, "is a clue which we have in advance of the police. . . . It's a profane parrot. . . . Later on, we're going to find out why the murderer wanted to substitute parrots. Right now, we're going to try and trace the profane parrot, which should be easy. . . . We can't hope to compete with the police, so we'll ignore the commonplace factors."

"How about the pink silk nightie?" Paul Drake asked, in his slow, drawling voice. "Do we do anything about that?"

"Not a thing," Mason said. "That's something the police are working on tooth and nail. . . . How much do you know about the case, Paul?"

"Not very much more than what I've read in the papers," Drake said, "but one of my friends, who's in the newspaper game, was asking me something about weapons."

"What did he want to know?" Mason asked.

"Something about the murder gun."

"What about the gun?"

"It's some sort of a trick weapon," Drake said. "One of those short-barreled guns, with a trigger which folds back out of the way. It's small enough to be carried anywhere."

"What caliber?"

"A forty-one."

"Try and find out about ammunition for it," Mason said. "See if the shells are carried in stock . . . No, forget it. The police will do all that. You stick to parrots, Paul. Cover all pet stores. Find out about parrot sales during the last week or two."

Paul Drake, whose efficiency as a detective depended in large part upon the fact that he looked so completely innocuous, closed his leather-backed notebook and dropped it into his pocket. He surveyed Perry Mason with slightly protruding eyes, the expression of which was habitually masked by a glassy film.

"How far do you want me to check up on Mrs. Sabin and the son, Perry?" he asked.

"Everything you can find out," Mason said.

Drake checked off the points on his fingers. "Let's see now, if I have everything straight. Get the dope on the widow and Steve Watkins. Cover the bird stores and find out about the profane parrot. Get all the information I can about the mountain cabin and what happened up there. Get photographs of the interior, and . . . How about the exterior, Perry, do you want them?"

"No," Mason said, "I'm going to drive up there, Paul, and give it the once-over. The only photographs I want are those which were taken when the police discovered the body."

"On my way," Drake told him, sliding out of the chair.

"And incidentally," Mason said, as the detective was

halfway to the door, "here's another hunch. Let's suppose the murderer substituted parrots, then what became of Casanova?"

"I'll bite," Drake said, with a grin, "what do you do with a parrot? Make a parrot pie, or do you broil 'em on toast?"

Mason said, "You put them in cages and listen to them talk."

"No, really!" Drake exclaimed in mock surprise. "You don't tell me."

Mason said, "Get it through that droopy mind of yours that I'm not joking. That's *exactly* what you do with a parrot, and whoever took Casanova, may have done it because he wanted to listen to something Casanova had to say."

"That," Drake admitted, "is a thought."

"Moreover," Mason went on, "the murderer probably has moved into a new neighborhood. You might make a check on any new parrots."

"What do you want me to do?" Drake asked. "Take a bird census, or put a bird bath on the roof and watch for parrots . . . My God, Perry, have a heart! How the devil can a man find a new parrot?"

"I think," Mason told him, "you'll find there aren't so many parrots. They're a noisy pet, and they aren't particularly apartment pets. People who have parrots are apt to live in the suburbs. Parrots are something of a nuisance as far as neighbors are concerned. I think there's a city ordinance on parrots in apartments. I have an idea you may find something from talking to pet stores. Trace the sale of new cages. Find out people who have been inquiring about the care and feeding of parrots. And incidentally, Paul, remember there's a pet store here in the block. Karl Helmold, the chap who runs it, is a client of mine. He'll probably have some trade lists, which will give you the names of the larger pet stores in the vicinity, and he may be able to tell you quite a bit about parrots. Put every available operative on the job."

"Okay," Drake said. "I'll be on my way."

Mason nodded to Della Street. "Come on, Della, let's go take a look at that cabin."

The road wound up the sides of the long canyon, turning and twisting on itself like a snake in pain. Through the windshield Mason caught occasional glimpses of purple mountains. Below, a threadlike stream tumbled whitely over granite boulders. Back of the car the heat haze of the valley country showed as a gaseous blanket, heavy, oppressive, shimmering.

It was dry up here, and the air was impregnated with scent which oozed from the tips of pine needles. It was hot, too, but the dry balsam-laden heat was kind to the nostrils. High overhead the southern California sky was so blue that it almost seemed black in contrast with the bright sunlight which beat down upon the sheer granite ridges where there was not enough soil to support trees.

They came to a shaded turn in the road, where a spring trickled into a natural basin, then overflowed, to spill through a culvert into a stream which plunged into the dark obscurity of tangled greenery.

Mason stopped the car and said, "We'll let the motor cool, and have a drink of mountain water. . . . Hello, here comes a police car."

He pointed down the side of the mountain to where a section of the road showed almost directly below them. A car, winding its laborious way up the long ascent, showed glinting red from a police spotlight fastened on the upper right-hand corner of the windshield.

"Do we try to beat them up?" Della Street asked.

Mason, stretching his long legs, sucked in deep breaths of the dry mountain air, and said, "No. We'll wait and follow. It will save time locating the cabin."

They drank the cool water, bending over the rock basin to place pursed lips against the limpid surface of the little pool. Gradually, above the sound of the wind sighing through the eloquent pines, came the grinding of a motor, whining in gear as it labored up the steep ascent.

As the car came into sight around the turn, Mason said, "I believe it's our old friend, Sergeant Holcomb, from headquarters. . . . Now, why should *he* be interested in a murder case which took place outside of the city . . . He's stopping."

The car veered abruptly from the paved highway to

come to a stop on the shaded parking space at the side of the road. A big man, who wore a broad-brimmed black Stetson, was the first to emerge. He was followed, a moment later, by Sergeant Holcomb of the Metropolitan Police.

Holcomb walked truculently across to Mason. "What the devil are *you* doing *here?*" he asked.

Mason said, "Odd, Sergeant, but I was thinking the same about you."

Sergeant Holcomb said, "I'm helping out Sheriff Barnes. He telephoned in for assistance, and the police loaned me to him. Shake hands with Perry Mason, Sheriff."

The sheriff, a big man in the late fifties, who moved with slow efficiency, swung out a bronzed hand which engulfed Mason's fingers. Mason introduced Della Street, and then produced the letter which Charles Sabin had given him. The Sheriff was impressed.

Sergeant Holcomb glanced from the letter to Mason. There was suspicion in his eyes, as well as in his voice. "Sabin employed you?"

"Yes."

"And gave you this letter?"

"Yes."

"Just what does he want you to do?"

"He wants me to co-operate with the police."

Sergeant Holcomb's laugh was sarcastic. "That's the best one I've heard in twenty years. Perry Mason co-operating with the police! You co-operate with the police just like the Republicans co-operate with the Democrats."

Mason turned to the sheriff. "Just because a lawyer represents innocent defendants doesn't mean he's opposed to the authorities," he said quietly.

"The hell it doesn't!" Sergeant Holcomb interpolated. "You've always been against the police."

"On the contrary," Mason told him, "I've helped solve quite a few murder cases."

"You've always managed to get *your* clients acquitted," Sergeant Holcomb pointed out.

"Exactly," Mason said. "It happened that the police were trying to convict innocent parties. It remained for me to prove my clients innocent by finding the real murderers."

Sergeant Holcomb flushed, stepped forward, and started to say something, but Sheriff Barnes interposed what was apparently an unintentional shoulder. "Now listen, boys," he said, "there's nothing to argue about. I'm the sheriff of this county. This thing is just a little bit high-powered for me. I ain't got the facilities to make an investigation on this the way I'd like to, and I asked the city police to loan me a man who could help out with fingerprint work, and give me some suggestions. As far as I'm concerned, I'm going to be glad of any assistance I can get, and I don't care who gives it. I've read about some of Mason's cases in the newspapers. To my mind, when a lawyer proves his client innocent of crime by showing that someone else is guilty, he's done society a darn good turn, and the police have no kick coming."

"Well," Sergeant Holcomb said to the sheriff, "it's *your* funeral. His methods are enough to give you gray hairs."

Sheriff Barnes tilted back the sombrero and ran his fingers through sweat-moistened hair. "I've got gray hairs now," he said. "How about it, Mason, you going up?"

"I'll follow you," Mason told him. "You know the way?"

"Sure, I was up there nearly all day yesterday."

"How much has been touched?" Mason asked.

"Not a thing. We've taken the body out, and cleaned out the remains of a string of fish, which had gone pretty bad. Of course, we took the parrot. Aside from that, we ain't touched a thing, except to go over everything for fingerprints."

"Find any?" Mason asked.

"Quite a few," the sheriff admitted noncommittally.

Sergeant Holcomb said abruptly, "Well, Sheriff, let's get going. Mason can follow us."

The road crossed a ridge, debouched onto a plateau. Here and there were little clearings, cabins nestled back against the trees. Up near the upper end of the plateau, when they were within a few hundred feet of the stream which came roaring down from a mountain canyon,

Sheriff Barnes abruptly signaled for a right-hand turn. He swung into a dirt road, carpeted with pine needles, which ran back to a cabin so skillfully blended with the trees that it seemed almost to be the work of nature rather than of man.

Mason exclaimed, "Look at that cabin, Della! It certainly is a beautiful setting!"

A bluejay, resenting their intrusion, launched himself downward from the top of one of the pine trees, screeching his raucous, *"Thief . . . thief . . . thief."*

Mason swung the car into the shaded area back of the cabin and parked it. Sheriff Barnes crossed over and said, "I'm going to ask you to be careful not to touch anything, Mr. Mason, and I think Miss Street had better wait outside."

Mason nodded acquiescence.

A tall, rangy man who moved with the easy grace of a mountain dweller emerged from the shadows and touched his somewhat battered hat to the sheriff. "Everything's okay, Sheriff," he said.

Sheriff Barnes took a key from his pocket, unlocked the padlock on the door, and said by way of introduction, "This is Fred Waner. He lives up here. I've had him guarding the cabin."

The sheriff opened the door. "Now, let's try not to walk around any more than is necessary. You, Sergeant, know what to do." Mason glanced into the mountain cabin with its big fireplace, plain pine table, hand-hewn rafters. A neatly made bed with snowy linen was in startling contrast to the seed-littered floor. Mud-stained rubber boots stood, sagging limply; above them was a jointed fly rod.

Sergeant Holcomb said, "My advice, Sheriff, would be to let Mr. Mason look around without touching anything, and then leave. *We* can't do anything as long as he's here."

"Why not?" Sheriff Barnes said.

Sergeant Holcomb flushed. "For various reasons. One of them is that before you get done, this man is going to be on the other side of the fence. He's going to be opposing you, he's going to be trying to tear down the case you're building up against the murderer. The more you expose your methods to him, the more he has an opportunity to tear you to pieces on the witness stand."

Sheriff Barnes said doggedly, "That's all right. If anybody's going to be hung for murder on my say-so, I want it to be after a case is built up which can't be torn down."

"I'd like to see as much as you care to show me," Mason said to the sheriff. "I take it, that chalk outline on the floor represents where the body was found when it was first discovered."

"Yes, that's right. The gun was found over there about ten feet away, where you'll notice the outline in chalk."

"Is it possible that Mr. Sabin could have shot himself?" Mason asked.

"Absolutely impossible according to the testimony of the doctors. What's more, the gun had been wiped free of fingerprints. Sabin wasn't wearing gloves. If he'd shot himself, he'd have left some fingerprints on the gun."

Mason, frowning thoughtfully, said, "Then the murderer didn't even want it to look like suicide."

"How so?" the sheriff asked.

"He could very easily have placed the gun nearer the body. He could have wiped off his own fingerprints, and pressed the weapon into the hand of the dead man."

"That's logical," the sheriff said.

"And," Mason went on, "the murderer must have wanted the officers to find the gun."

"Baloney," Sergeant Holcomb said. "The murderer simply didn't want the officers to find the gun *on him*. That's the way all clever murderers do. As soon as they commit a crime, they drop the rod. They don't even keep it with them long enough to find some place to hide it. The gun can hang them. They shoot it and drop it."

"All right," Mason said, smiling, "you win. They shoot it and drop it. What else, Sheriff?"

"The parrot cage was over here on the floor," the sheriff said, "and the door was propped open with a little stick so the parrot could walk out whenever he wanted to."

"Or walk in, whenever it had been out?" Mason asked.

"Well, yes. That's a thought."

"And how long do you think the parrot had been here without food or water, Sheriff?"

"He'd had plenty of food. The water had dried up in the pan. See that agateware pan over there? Well, that had evidently been left pretty well filled with water, but the water had dried out—what the parrot hadn't had to drink. You can see little spots of rust on the bottom which show where the last few drops evaporated."

"The body then," Mason said, "must have been here for some time before it was discovered."

"The murder," Sheriff Barnes asserted, "took place some time on Tuesday, the sixth of September. It took place probably right around eleven o'clock in the morning."

"How do you figure that?" Mason asked. "Or do you object to telling me?"

"Not at all," the sheriff said. "The fishing season in this entire district opened on September sixth. The Fish and Game Commission wanted to have an area for fall fishing which hadn't been all fished out. So they picked out certain streams which they kept closed until later on in the season. This was one of the last. The season opened here on September sixth.

"Now then, Sabin was a funny chap. He had places that he went and things that he did, and we haven't found out all of 'em yet. We know some of them. He had a trailer and he'd drive around at trailer camps, sit and whittle and talk with people, just finding out that way what was going on in the world. Sometimes he'd take an old suit of shiny clothes and go prowl around libraries for a week or two . . ."

"Yes, I read all about that in the newspaper," Mason interrupted.

"Well," the sheriff went on, "he told his son and Richard Waid, his secretary, that he was going to be home on Monday the fifth to pick up his fishing things. He'd been away on a little trip. They don't know just where, but he surprised them by coming home on Friday the second. He took his fishing tackle, picked up his parrot, and came up here. It seems he was putting across a big deal in New

York, and had told his secretary to charter a plane and be ready to fly East when he gave the word. The secretary waited at the airport all Monday afternoon. He had a plane in readiness. About ten o'clock on the night of the fifth, the call came through. Waid says that Sabin seemed in wonderful spirits. He said everything was okay, that Waid was to jump in his plane and get to New York at once."

"He was talking from the cabin here?" Mason asked.

"No, he wasn't. He told Waid the telephone here had gone dead so he'd had to go to a pay station. He didn't say where, and Waid didn't think to ask him. Of course, at the time, it didn't seem particularly important. Waid was in a hurry to get started to New York."

"You've talked with Waid?" Mason asked.

"On the long distance telephone," the sheriff said. "He was still in New York."

"Did he tell the nature of the business?" Mason asked.

"No, he said it was something important and highly confidential. That was all he'd say."

"Waid, I take it, had a chartered plane?" Mason asked.

The sheriff grinned and said, "It looks as though Waid may have cut a corner there. Steve Watkins, who's the son of Sabin's wife by a former marriage, is quite a flyer. He's got a fast plane and likes to fly around the country. I take it Sabin didn't care much for Steve and wouldn't have liked it if he'd known Waid was going to fly back to New York with Steve; but Steve wanted to make the trip and needed the money, so Waid arranged to pay him the charter price and Steve Watkins flew him back."

"What time did they leave?"

"At ten minutes past ten, the night of Monday the fifth," the sheriff said. "Just to make sure, I checked up with the records of the airport."

"And what time did Sabin call Waid?"

"Waid says it wasn't more than ten minutes before he took off. He thinks it was right around ten o'clock."

"He recognized Sabin's voice?" Mason asked.

"Yes, and said Sabin seemed very pleased about something. He told Waid he'd closed the deal and to start at once. He said there'd been a little delay because the telephone here was out of order. He'd had to drive down to a pay station, but he said he was driving right back to the cabin and would be at the cabin for two or three days, that in case Waid encountered any difficulties he was to telephone."

"And Waid didn't telephone?"

"No, because everything went through like clockwork, and Sabin had only told him to telephone in case something went wrong."

Mason said thoughtfully. "Well, let's see then. He was alive at ten o'clock on the evening of Monday, September fifth. Did anyone else see him or talk with him after that?"

"No," the sheriff said. "That's the last time we actually *know* he was alive. From there on, we have to figure evidence. The fishing season opened on Tuesday the sixth. Over there's an alarm clock which had run down. It stopped at two forty-seven. The alarm was set at five-thirty."

"The alarm run down too?" Mason asked.

"Uh-huh."

The telephone bell shattered the silence. The sheriff said, "Excuse me," and scooped up the receiver. He listened a moment, then said, "All right, hold the line," and turned to Mason. "It's for you," he said.

Mason took the receiver and heard Paul Drake's voice at the other end of the line. "Hello, Perry. I took a chance on calling you there. Are you where you can talk?"

"No," Mason said.

"But you can listen all right?"

"Yes. Go ahead. What is it?"

"I think I've found your murderer—at any rate, I've got a lead on that profane parrot, and a swell description of the man that bought him."

"Where?"

"At San Molinas."

"Keep talking," Mason told him.

"A man by the name of Arthur Gibbs runs a pet shop in San Molinas. It's known as the Fifth Avenue Pet Shop.

On Friday the second, a seedy-looking chap came in to buy a parrot in a hurry. Gibbs remembers it, because the man didn't seem to care anything about the parrot except its appearance. Gibbs sold him this profane parrot. He thinks the man didn't know about its habit of cussing . . . I think you'd better talk with Gibbs, Mason."

"Any details?" Mason asked.

"I've got a swell description."

"Does it fit anyone?" Mason inquired.

"No one so far as I can tell," Drake said. ". . . Tell you what I'll do, Perry. I'll go to the Plaza Hotel and wait in the lobby. You get down here as soon as you can. If it's after five-thirty, I'll arrange with Gibbs to wait."

Mason said, "That'll be fine," and hung up the telephone to face the coldly suspicious eyes of Sergeant Holcomb.

Sheriff Barnes, apparently not noticing the interruption, said, "When we broke in here, we found a creel filled with fish. We boxed it up in an air-tight container and sent it to the police laboratory in the city. They report that the creel contained a limit of fish which had been cleaned and wrapped in leaves but hadn't been given a final washing. We've found the remains of his breakfast—a couple of eggs and some bacon rinds. We've found the remains of his lunch—canned beans. The body was clothed in slippers, slacks, and a light sweater. That leather coat there was on the back of the chair. Those are his fishing boots over there with mud on them. There's his fly rod and flies on the table, just as he'd left them when he came in.

"Now, I figure he was killed right around eleven o'clock on the morning of Tuesday the sixth. Would you like to know how I figure it?"

"Very much indeed," Mason said.

Sergeant Holcomb turned on his heel and walked away, showing his silent disgust.

Sheriff Barnes said, "Well, I ain't had much experience in murder cases, but I know how to figure probabilities. I've been in the forest service, and I've worked cattle, and I know how to read trail. I don't know whether the same kind of reasoning will work in a murder case or not, but I don't see why it wouldn't. Anyway, here's the way I figure

24

it. Sabin got up at five-thirty because that's when the alarm went off. He had breakfast of bacon and eggs. He went out fishing. He caught a limit. He got back here, and he was tired and hungry. He didn't even bother to wash the fish and put them in the icebox. He took off his boots, chucked the creel of fish over there, went out into the kitchen and cooked himself some canned beans. There was some coffee in the pot—probably still left from breakfast. He warmed that up.

"The next thing he'd have done was to have given the fish a good washing and put them in the icebox. He was murdered right after lunch and before he'd had a chance to do that. I fixed the time at around eleven o'clock."

"Why not later?" Mason asked.

"Oh, yes," the sheriff said, "I overlooked that. The sun gets on the cabin here about half past ten or eleven and it starts to get warm. It's off the cabin by four o'clock in the afternoon, and it gets cold right away. During the middle of the day it's hot. During the nights it's cold. So I figured he was murdered after it had warmed up and before it had cooled off, but not during the middle of the day when it was real hot. If it had been real cold, he'd have had his coat on and would have lit the fire over there in the fireplace. You see, it's all laid. If it had been real hot, he wouldn't have been wearing his sweater."

"Nice going," Mason said approvingly. "Have you made any experiments to find out how long it takes the alarm clock to run down after it's wound up?"

"I wired the factory," the sheriff said. "They say from around thirty to thirty-six hours, depending on the condition of the clock and how long it's been used.

"Now, here's another thing, Mr. Mason. Whoever killed Sabin was a kindhearted, considerate sort of a guy. Anyway, that's the way I figure it."

He tilted back his hat and scratched the thick hair back of his ears in a characteristic gesture. "Now, you may think it sounds kind of funny for a man to say that about a murderer, but that's the way I figure it just the same. This man had something against Sabin. He wanted to kill him, but he didn't want to kill the parrot. He figured it was apt to be some time before Sabin's body was discovered, and he arranged so the parrot wouldn't starve to death in the meantime.

"Now that makes it look as though the murderer had some powerful reason for wanting Sabin out of the way. It wasn't robbery and it wasn't just sheer cussedness. The murderer was kindhearted. . . if you get what I mean."

"I think I do," Mason said with a smile. "And thank you very much, Sheriff. I won't intrude on you and Sergeant Holcomb longer. I think I understand the situation. I'll walk around the outside of the cabin a couple of times and give it the once-over. I certainly appreciate your courtesy and . . ."

He broke off as someone knocked on the cabin door.

Sheriff Barnes opened the door. A blond, studious-appearing young man in the early thirties peered owlishly from behind horn-rimmed spectacles. "Sheriff Barnes?" he inquired.

"You're Waid?" the sheriff asked.

"Yes."

Sheriff Barnes shook hands. "This is Sergeant Holcomb," he said, "and this is Mr. Mason."

Waid shook hands with each in turn. "I've followed your instructions to the letter, Sheriff," he said. "I got off the plane at Las Vegas. I traveled under an assumed name. I've ditched all the newspaper reporters and . . ."

"Just a minute," Sergeant Holcomb interrupted. "Don't do any talking right now, Waid. Mr. Mason is a lawyer, not an officer. *He's just leaving.*"

Waid suddenly turned to regard Perry Mason with wide eyes. "You're Perry Mason, the lawyer," he said. "Pardon me for not recognizing the name. I've read of your cases, Mr. Mason. I was particularly interested in that one where you acquitted . . ."

"Mason is leaving," Sergeant Holcomb interrupted, "and we'd prefer that you didn't talk with *anyone,* Waid, until you tell us your story."

Waid lapsed into silence with an amused smile flickering at the corners of his mouth.

Mason said, "I'll talk with you some other time, Waid. I'm representing Charles Sabin. Does he know you're here?"

Sergeant Holcomb stepped firmly forward. "That," he said, "is all. There's the door, Mason. Don't let us detain you."

"I won't," Mason assured him with a grin. "The atmosphere here is just a trifle stuffy—or don't you think so, Sergeant?"

Sergeant Holcomb's only retort was to slam the door as Mason stepped out into the glare of the mountain sunlight.

Della Street was seated on the running board of the automobile, making friends with some half-dozen chipmunks. The little animals came almost to her fingertips before turning to scamper away to the comparative safety of a dead pine log, where they chattered their spirits up before slowly creeping back, to approach within a matter of inches. Up in the pine tree above her head a bluejay, apparently thinking she was feeding the chipmunks, fluttered nervously from limb to limb, dropping ever lower, cocking his head from side to side, muttering low throaty squawks of protest at being excluded from the feast—a strange combination of impudence and diffidence.

"Hello, Chief," she said. "Who's the new arrival?"

"Waid, the secretary," Mason replied. "He has something to tell them. That's why they came up here to the cabin. They wanted to meet Waid where no newspaper men would be around . . . And Paul Drake's telephoned he has something hot in San Molinas."

"How about Waid?" she asked. "Going to wait and see if he'll talk, Chief?"

"No. We'll rush to San Molinas. Sergeant Holcomb will warn Waid not to tell me whatever it is he knows, but Charles Sabin will get it out of him later, and then we'll find out. Come on, tell your friends good-by and let's go."

He climbed in behind the steering wheel, started the car, and drove slowly down the driveway which led from the cabin. Once or twice he stopped to look overhead in the branches of the pine tree. "That bluejay," he said, laughing, "is still following us. I wonder if there isn't something I could find to feed him."

"There's some peanut brittle in a bag in the glove

compartment," Della Street said. "You might break a peanut out of that."

"Let's try," Mason said.

He opened the glove compartment, and Della pulled out a paper bag. "Here are a couple of loose peanuts in the bottom of the bag," she told him, and poured them into Mason's cupped hand.

He stood on the running board, held his hands up above his head so that the bluejay could see the shelled peanuts. The jay fluttered noisily from branch to branch, swooped down until he was almost even with Mason's shoulder, then, becoming frightened at his own temerity, zoomed upward with a startled squawk. Twice he repeated this maneuver. The third time, he perched on Mason's hand long enough to grab one of the peanuts in his beak before jumping up, to flutter into the branches of the tree overhead.

Mason, laughing, said, "Gosh, Della, I think I want to do this when *I'm* ready to retire. How nice it would be to have a cabin where you could make friends with . . ."

"What is it, Chief?" she asked, as he broke off abruptly.

Without answering her, Mason strode over to the pine tree in which the bluejay was perched. The jay, thinking he was being pursued, fled into the dark retreat of the forest, his startled squawk being superseded by cries of *"Treason!"* which merged into a more raucous and continuous vituperation of the man who had betrayed his confidence. Della Street, sliding across the seat, her feet pointed at the open door, gave herself impetus by a boost from the steering wheel, and slid to the ground with a quick flash of shapely legs. She ran across to where Mason was standing.

"What is it, Chief?"

Mason said, slowly, "That wire, Della."

"What about it . . . I don't see any . . . Oh, yes . . . . Well, what is it, Chief?"

"I don't know," Mason said. "It isn't an aerial, but you can see the way it's been concealed. It runs along the branch of that limb and is taped to the upper side of it. Then it hits the tree trunk, runs along the tree trunk until it comes to that other limb, goes up through that, runs into this tree, then crosses over to that grove . . . Drive the car outside and park it on the highway, Della. I'm going to take a look."

"What do you think it is, Chief?"

"It looks," he told her, "as though someone had been tapping Fremont Sabin's telephone."

"Gosh, Chief!" she exclaimed. "Isn't *that* something?"

He nodded, but said nothing. He was already walking along under the trees, following the course of the wire so cleverly concealed as to be invisible to any save the most alert observer.

Della Street parked the car on the highway, climbed through a fence, and took a short cut through the pine thicket to join him. A hundred yards away an unpainted cabin was so inconspicuous among the trees that it seemed as much a part of the scenery as the surrounding rocks.

"I think that's the place we're looking for," Mason said, "but we'll trace the wire and find out."

"What do we do when we get there?" she asked.

"It depends," Mason told her. "You'd better stay back, Della, so you can get the sheriff, if the party gets rough."

"Let me stay with you, Chief," she pleaded.

"No," he told her. "Stay back there. If you hear any commotion, beat it for Sabin's cabin as fast as you can, and bring the sheriff."

Mason followed the wire to the place where it abruptly left the protection of the trees to loop itself around insulators just below the eaves of the unpainted cabin. At this point it had been arranged so that it looked very much like the aerial of a wireless set. Mason circled the cabin twice, keeping in the concealment of the dense shadows as much as possible.

Della Street, anxiously watching him from a point some fifty yards distant, moved slowly toward him.

"It's all right," he called to her. "We're going to notify the sheriff." He joined her and they walked back to the cabin where Fred Waner emerged apparently from nowhere to bar their way.

"I want to see the sheriff again," Mason told him.

"All right. You wait here. I'll tell the sheriff you're here."

Waner went to the door of the cabin and called the sheriff. A moment later Sheriff Barnes came out to see what was wanted. When he saw Mason, his face clouded with suspicion. "I thought you'd gone," he said pointedly.

"I started," Mason told him, "and came back. If you can step this way, Sheriff, I think I have something important to show you."

Sergeant Holcomb came to the door of the cabin to stand just behind the sheriff. "What is it?" he asked.

"Something to show the sheriff," Mason replied.

Sergeant Holcomb said grimly, "Mason, if this is a trap to distract our attention, I'll . . ."

"I don't care whether *your* attention's distracted or not," Mason interrupted. "*I'm* talking to the sheriff."

Sergeant Holcomb said to Waner, "Waner, you stay here with Mr. Waid. Don't let him leave. Don't let anyone talk with him. Don't let him touch anything. Do you understand?"

Waner nodded.

"You can count on my co-operation, Sergeant," Waid said with cold formality. "After all, you know, I'm not a criminal. I'm trying to co-operate with you."

"I understand that," Holcomb said, "but whenever Perry Mason. . ."

"What do you have to show us, Mason?" Sheriff Barnes interrupted.

Mason said, "This way, please."

He led the way down the road to where the wire had been tapped under the telephone line. Sergeant Holcomb and the sheriff followed along a few steps behind. "See that?" he asked, pointing upward.

"What?" the sheriff asked.

"That wire."

"It's a telephone wire," Sergeant Holcomb snorted. "What the devil did you think it was, Mason?"

"I'm not talking about that wire," Mason said. "I'm talking about the one which leads off from it. See where it

30

goes through that pine tree where the needles come over and . . ."

"By George, you're right!" the sheriff said. "There *is* a wire!"

"All right," Mason said, "now that you see where the wire is cut in, I'll show you where it runs to," and he led the way over to where he could point out the unpainted cabin, concealed in the trees.

Sergeant Holcomb asked suspiciously, "How did you happen to notice that wire, Mason?"

"I was feeding a bluejay," Mason said. "He took a peanut from my hand, then hopped up in that tree and sat on the limb which carries the wire."

"I see," Holcomb observed in a tone which showed his complete and utter disbelief, "and you just *happened* to see the wire while you were standing under the tree staring up at the bluejay to whom you'd just given a peanut. Is that right?"

"That's right."

"You wanted to see how he'd digest the peanut, I suppose?"

"No, I had another peanut I was going to give him," Mason said patiently. "I wanted him to come down and take it out of my hand."

Sergeant Holcomb said to Sheriff Barnes, "I don't know what his game is, but if Perry Mason is walking down the road feeding peanuts to bluejays, you can gamble there's something back of it. He knew darn well that wire was there, all the time. Otherwise, he'd never have found it."

Sheriff Barnes stared moodily at the cabin. "Keep away," he said, as though entirely oblivious of their conversation. "I'm going into that cabin. Sergeant, if any shooting starts, I leave it to you to back me up."

Quietly, calmly, he approached the door of the cabin, pounded with peremptory knuckles, then lowering his shoulder, smashed his weight against the door. At his third lunge the door gave way and shot backward on its hinges. Sheriff Barnes stepped into the half darkness of the interior to find that Perry Mason was right on his

31

heels, while Sergeant Holcomb was behind Mason, holding his gun in readiness.

"It's all right," the sheriff called, "there's no one here . . . You, Mason, shouldn't have taken chances like that."

Mason made no reply. He was staring in frowning contemplation at the array of paraphernalia on the inside of the room. What looked like half of a piece of baggage proved to be a radio amplifier. The whole outfit had been neatly tailored so that, when it was fitted together, it was impossible to distinguish between it and any ordinary piece of baggage. There were headphones, elaborate recording devices, a pencil and pad of paper. A partially smoked cigarette was lying on the edge of a pine table. The cigarette, apparently forgotten, had charred through the wood of the table top. A fine layer of dust had settled over it, as well as over everything else in the room.

"Evidently," the sheriff said, "he ain't been here for quite a spell. But when he left, he lit out in a hurry. He even forgot his cigarette."

"How did you know this was here?" Sergeant Holcomb demanded of Perry Mason, his voice harsh in its implied accusation.

Mason shrugged his shoulders and turned away.

Sheriff Barnes stopped him as he started to walk out. "Say, just a minute, Mason," he said in a quiet tone which was, nevertheless, charged with authority.

Mason stopped.

"Did you know this line had been tapped, Mason?"

"Frankly, Sheriff, I didn't."

"How did you discover it?"

"Just as I told you."

Sheriff Barnes still appeared dubious. Sergeant Holcomb made no attempt to disguise the contemptuous disbelief on his face.

"Did you," Sheriff Barnes asked, "know that Fremont C. Sabin had been back of an attempt to expose organized vice and graft in the Metropolitan Police?"

"Good heavens, no!" Mason said.

Sergeant Holcomb, his face almost a brick-red, said, "I didn't give you that information to be bandied around, Sheriff."

Barnes said, without taking his eyes from Mason, "I'm not bandying it around. You've probably read, Mason, of the confidential advices which the Grand Jury have been receiving, advices which have caused it to start an inquiry against some persons who are prominent politically."

"I've heard something about it," Mason admitted cautiously.

"And you knew that some private citizen was back of this campaign to get information?"

"I'd heard something of the sort."

"Did you have any idea that that person was Fremont C. Sabin?"

Mason said, "Sheriff, I can assure you I didn't have any idea who the person was."

"That's all," Sheriff Barnes said. "I just wanted to be sure, Mason."

"Thanks," Mason said, and walked out, leaving them alone in the cabin.

CHAPTER THREE

PAUL DRAKE was waiting for Mason in the lobby of the Plaza Hotel in San Molinas. He looked at his watch and said, "You're late, Perry, but Gibbs is waiting for us."

Mason said, "Before we go around there, Paul, has anybody else been trying to get in touch with Gibbs?"

"I don't think so. Why?"

"Do you know?"

"No I don't. I hung around there until about an hour ago and then came over here to wait in the hotel. I've been rather expecting you to drive in any time during the last hour."

Mason said, "I was delayed up there because we found that Sabin's line was tapped."

"His line was tapped?"

"Yes. The line into the cabin. The tapping plant may not have been used lately. On the other hand, someone may have been listening in on your conversation with me.

Here's something else. Sabin is the man who's been furnishing finances to the citizens' committee which has been investigating vice conditions and transmitting information on graft to the Grand Jury."

Drake gave a low whistle. "If that's the case," he said, "there were probably anywhere from a hundred to a hundred and fifty people who would have murdered him without batting an eyelash."

"Well, that angle's up to the police. It's too big for us to cover," Mason said.

"You're the boss," Drake said. "We'll go down and talk with Gibbs. He has a swell description of the man who bought the parrot."

"He's certain about the parrot?"

"Yes," Drake said. "I'll let you talk with him, but it's a cinch. He says the man looked a little seedy," Drake continued, "but then, Perry, that's about what you could expect. If any of the vice interests had decided to bump Sabin off, they'd have hired a down-and-outer to do the job, or else would have had a mobster put on the act."

"Would this man know the fellow who bought the parrot if he saw him again?"

"I'll say he would."

"Okay," Mason said, "let's go."

Della Street was waiting in the car at the curb, with the motor running. She said, "Hello, Paul," and handed Mason a newspaper. "Here's the latest afternoon newspaper, Chief, just in from the city. Do you want me to drive?"

"Yes."

"Where is it, Paul?" she asked.

"Straight down this street for three blocks, then turn to the right for two blocks, and swing to the left. It's on a side street, halfway in the block. You should be able to find a parking place in front."

"Okay," she said, and snapped the car into gear. As she slid the big machine out into traffic, Mason opened the newspaper and said, "There probably won't be anything much in here."

"How do they fix the time of death so accurately," Drake asked, "if they didn't find the body for so long?"

"It's quite a story," Mason told him. "Depends on some deduction by the sheriff. He's rather a level-headed chap. I'll tell you about it when we have more time."

He skimmed through the contents of the paper while Della Street drove with swift competency to the pet store.

Mason and Drake alighted. "Want me to stay here, Chief?" Della asked.

"You'd better," Drake said. "You're parked in front of a fireplug. Keep the motor running. We probably won't be long."

Mason handed her the newspaper. "Brush up on current events while we learn about parrots; and quit eating that peanut brittle. It'll spoil your appetite for dinner."

She chuckled. "I was getting along fine until you made me think of that candy; but you're going to have to buy Paul and me dinner on the expense account, Chief, so my loss of appetite may be a blessing in disguise."

They were grinning as they entered the pet store.

Arthur Gibbs was a thin, bald-headed individual with eyes the color of a faded blue shirt which had been left too long on the clothesline. "Hello," he said in a calm, well-modulated voice. "I was just getting ready to close up. I'd about given you up."

"This is Perry Mason," Paul Drake introduced.

Mason extended his hand. Gibbs gave him a bony, long-fingered hand which seemed completely lacking in initiative. As Mason released it, he said, "I suppose you want to know about that parrot."

Mason nodded.

"Well, it's just like I told you," Gibbs said to Paul Drake.

"Never mind what you told me," Paul Drake said. "I want Mr. Mason to get it firsthand. Just go ahead and tell him about it."

"Well, we sold this parrot on the . . ."

"Before you go into that," Drake interrupted, "tell Mr. Mason how you identify the parrot."

"Well," Gibbs said, "of course, I'm just acting on an assumption there. You're asking me about a parrot that cussed whenever it wanted something to eat. I trained a parrot to do that stunt."

"What was the idea?" Mason asked.

"It's just a stunt," Gibbs explained. "Occasionally, you'll find people who think it's smart to have a parrot that cusses. Usually they get tired of them before they've had them a long while, but when they first hear a bird swear, it's quite a novelty."

"And you deliberately train them to swear?" Mason asked.

"Sure. Sometimes a bird will pick up an expression or a sentence just from hearing it once, but for the most part, you have to drill sounds into 'em. Of course, we don't train them to do any real lurid cussing; just a few 'damns' and 'hells' do the trick. People get such a kick out of hearing a parrot cut loose with a good salty line of talk instead of the usual stereotyped 'Polly wants-a-cracker,' they'll buy a bird on the spot."

"All right. When did you sell this bird?"

"Friday, the second of September."

"At what time?"

"Around two or three o'clock in the afternoon, I think it was."

"Tell me about the man who bought it."

"Well, he wore spectacles and had sort of tired eyes. His clothes didn't look any too good, and he looked . . . sort of discouraged . . . no, not discouraged either. Ever since I talked with Mr. Drake about him, I've been trying to think more clearly so I can describe him. He didn't look unhappy. . . . In fact, he seemed to be a man who knew what he was doing and was living his own life in his own way and getting some happiness out of it. He certainly didn't seem to have much money. His suit was shiny, and his elbows were worn almost through, but I will say this for him—he was clean."

"How old?" Mason asked.

"Around fifty-seven or fifty-eight, somewhere around in there."

"Clean-shaven?"

"Yes, he had wide cheekbones and pretty straight lips.

He was about as tall as you are, but he didn't weigh quite as much."

"What was his complexion? Pale or ruddy?" Mason asked.

"He looked like some sort of a rancher," the man said. "He'd been out of doors quite a bit, I think."

"Did he seem nervous or excited?"

"No, he didn't seem as though he'd ever get excited over anything, just calm and quiet. Said he wanted to buy a parrot, and he gave me a description of the sort of bird he wanted to buy."

"What do you mean when you say 'description'?" Mason asked.

"Oh, he told me the breed and size and age."

"Did you have any other birds beside this?"

"No, this was the only one I had that would fit the description."

"Did he hear the bird talk?"

"No, he didn't. That's a funny thing. He just seemed to want a parrot of a certain appearance. He didn't seem to care much about anything else. He took a look at the bird, asked me the price, and said he'd take it."

"Did he buy a cage at the same time?"

"Yes, of course. He took the parrot with him."

"And he was driving a car?"

"That's the thing I can't remember," Gibbs said, frowning. "I can't remember whether I took the cage out to the car or whether he did. I have an impression that he was driving a car, but I didn't pay too much attention to it. If he did have a car, it was just the ordinary sort of a car you'd associate with a man of that type, nothing to attract attention or to impress itself on my memory."

"Did he talk like an educated man?" Mason asked.

"Well, there was something quiet about the way he talked, and he had a peculiar way of looking at you while he was talking . . . looking right straight through you without seeming to be trying to do it. Some people just stare at you, and some seem to try to look holes through you, but this fellow just had a quiet way of . . ."

"Wait a minute," Mason interrupted. "Would you know the man if you saw his picture?"

"Yes, I think I would. I know I'd recognize him if I saw him, and I think I'd recognize the picture if it was a good picture."

Mason said, "Just a minute."

He walked out to where Della Street was sitting in the car. He pulled out his penknife and said, "Going to have to cut your paper to pieces, Della."

"Making dolls?" she asked.

"Making mysteries," he told her, and ran his knife around the border of the newspaper photograph of Fremont C. Sabin. He took it back into the pet store, unfolded the photograph, and said, "Is this, by any chance, the man who bought the parrot?"

Gibbs became excited. "That's the fellow," he said, "that's the man all right. That's a good picture of him; those high cheekbones and that strong, firm mouth."

Mason folded the newspaper photograph and pushed it down in his pocket. He and Drake exchanged significant glances.

"Who was it?" Gibbs asked. "Has his picture been in the paper recently?"

"Just a man who liked parrots," Mason said casually. "Let's wait until after a while to talk about *him*. Now, I want to get some information. Have there been any new parrots sold around here that you know of, recently?"

"I gave everything I had to Mr. Drake," Gibbs said. "But when Mr. Drake was asking me about parrot food this afternoon, and whether I'd had any inquiries from any new people about how to take care of parrots, I couldn't think of any at the time; but after Mr. Drake had left, I happened to remember Helen Monteith."

"And who's Helen Monteith?" Mason asked.

"She's the librarian over at the city library, and a mighty nice girl. Seems to me I read about her being engaged to be married a short time ago. She came in a week or so ago to buy some parrot food and asked me questions about taking care of parrots."

"How long ago?"

"Oh, a week or so. . . . Let me see, yes, it's been a little more than a week, maybe ten days."

"Did she tell you that she'd bought a parrot?"

38

"No, she didn't; just asked some questions about parrots."

"Did you ask her why she wanted to know?"

"I may have. I can't remember now. The whole thing is kind of fuzzy in my memory. You know how it is; a man doesn't think very much about all of those little transactions. Thinking back on it now, I can remember that at the time I wondered whether she'd been in the city and bought a parrot in there. . . . Come to think of it, I guess I didn't ask her any questions at all, just gave her what she wanted."

"Do you have her address?"

"I can find it in the phone book," Gibbs said.

"Don't bother," Mason said, "we'll look it up. You'd better shut up shop and go home. . . . She's listed in the telephone book, is she?"

"I think so. If she isn't, it's a cinch she's listed in the city directory. Here, let me look her up."

Gibbs ran the pages of a thick, blue book through his long, listless fingers, then said, "Here it is, 219 East Wilmington Street. You go out Main Street ten blocks and come to a wide street. That's Washington. The next street on the other side is Wilmington. Turn to the right and go for two blocks, and you'll be right near the place."

Mason said, "Thanks. I wonder if we can compensate you in any way for your trouble. . . ."

"Not at all," Gibbs said. "I'm glad to do it."

"Well, we certainly appreciate it."

"You don't know whether we'd find Miss Monteith at the library now, or whether she'd be at her residence, do you?" Drake asked.

Before the man could answer, Mason said, "I don't think that angle is particularly important, Paul. After all, it's just a matter of someone asking a casual question. Good Lord, if we're going to try to run down everyone who orders parrot food, we'll be working on this thing for a year." He turned to Gibbs with a smile and said, "It looked as though we were on the track of something, but the way it's turning out now, I guess it doesn't amount to much."

He took Paul Drake's arm and led him to the door.

When they were out on the sidewalk, Drake said, "What was the idea, Perry? He might have given us a little more information."

"Not much more," Mason said, "and I don't want to let him think we consider this as being too important. Later on he's going to read his afternoon newspaper. Then, if he thinks we struck a hot trail, he'll tell the police, and . . ."

"That's right," Drake interrupted. "I'd overlooked that."

"What luck?" Della Street asked.

"Plenty," Mason said, "but whether it's good, bad, or indifferent is more than we know yet. Swing over to Main Street and run out until after you've passed Washington, then turn to the right on the next block. We'll tell you where to stop."

She touched two fingers of her right hand to the abbreviated rim of her tilted hat. "Aye, aye, sir," she said, and started the car.

"We don't want to try the library first?" Drake asked. "It's probably nearer."

"No," Mason said. "A woman wouldn't keep a parrot in a library. She'd keep it in her home."

"Do you think she's keeping a parrot?"

"I wouldn't be surprised. I'll tell you more about it within the next ten or fifteen minutes."

Della Street swung the car skillfully through the late afternoon traffic. Drake, with his head pushed outside the car, reading street signs, said, "That's Washington, Della, the next is the one we want."

"There's no sign on this corner," Della said as she slowed the car.

"I think it's the corner we want," Mason told her. "Go ahead and make the turn anyway. . . . Good Lord, I don't know why it is that a city will go to all sorts of trouble and expense to attract tourists and strangers with advertising, and then act on the assumption that only the natives, who know every street in the city, are going to be looking for residences. It wouldn't cost much to put up a sign big enough to read on every street intersection of any importance. . . . This is it, Della, pull in to the curb."

The house was a small California bungalow which

dated back to an era of older and cheaper buildings. The outside consisted of redwood boards with strips of batten nailed across the cracks. Back of the house was a small garage, the doors of which stood open, disclosing an interior which was evidently used as a wood-shed and store-house.

As Mason got out of the car, a parrot squawked in a high, shrill voice. "Hello, hello. Come in and sit down."

Mason grinned at Drake. "Well," he said, "I guess we've found *a* parrot."

"There he is," Della Street said, "in a cage on the screen porch."

"Do we go to the front door and interview Helen Monteith?" Drake asked

"No," Mason said, "We go to the back door and interview the parrot."

He walked directly across the strip of dry grass which had evidently been a lawn at one time, until lack of care and the long Southern California dry spell had forced it to give up the struggle for existence. The parrot, in a bell-shaped cage on the screen porch, executed a peculiar double shuffle on the round perch of the cage. His feet fairly streaked back and forth in excitement as he squawked, "Come in and sit down. Come in and sit down. Hello, hello. Come in and sit down."

Mason said, "Hello, Polly," and went up close to the screen.

"Hello, Polly," the bird replied.

Mason pointed at the parrot. "Oh, oh," he said.

"What?" Drake asked.

"Look at the right foot. One of the toes is gone," Mason said.

The parrot, as though mocking him, burst into high, shrill laughter; then, evidently in high good humor, preened his glossy, green feathers, smoothing them carefully between the upper hooked beak and the surface of the black-coated tongue. Abruptly, the bird turned its wicked glittering eyes on Perry Mason. It ruffled its feathers as though showing great excitement and suddenly squawked, "Put down that gun, Helen! Don't shoot! *Squawk. Squawk.* My God, you've shot me!"

41

The parrot paused and cocked its head on one side as though seeking by a survey of the three startled faces lined up in front of the screen to estimate the sensation its words had produced.

"Good Lord," Drake said. "Do you suppose . . ."

He broke off as a woman's voice said, "Good evening. What was it you wanted, please?"

They turned to see a matronly woman with broad, capable shoulders staring curiously at them.

"I'm looking for a Miss Monteith," Mason said. "Does she live here?"

The woman inquired, with just a trace of reproof in her voice, "Have you been to the front door?"

"No, we haven't," Mason admitted. "We parked the car out here at the curb and saw the garage was empty. . . . Then I became attracted by the parrot. I'm interested in parrots."

"May I ask your name?"

"Mason," the lawyer told her, "Mr. Mason, and may I inquire yours?"

"I'm Mrs. Winters. I'm Helen Monteith's next-door neighbor, only her name isn't Monteith any more."

"It isn't?"

"No. She was married almost two weeks ago . . . a man by the name of Wallman, George Wallman, a book-keeper."

"Do you," Mason asked, "happen to know how long she's had the parrot?"

"I believe the parrot was a present from her husband. She's had it for almost two weeks. Did you have some business with Mrs. Wallman?"

"Just wanted to see her and ask her a few questions," Mason said with his most disarming manner, and as Mrs. Winters looked at the other two as though expecting an introduction, Mason detached himself from the group and took her to one side where he could lower his voice in confidence. Della Street, interpreting his tactics, touched Paul Drake with her elbow, and they walked back to the automobile, got in and sat down.

Mason asked, "How long has Mrs. Wallman been gone, Mrs. Winters?"

42

"About half or three quarters of an hour, I guess."

"You don't know where she went or when she expects to be back, do you?"

"No, I don't. She came home in an awful hurry and ran across the lawn to the house. I don't think she was in the house over two or three minutes, then she came tearing out and got her car out of the garage."

"Didn't she drive up in her own car?" Mason asked.

"No, she doesn't usually take her car to work with her. It's only eight or ten blocks and, when it's nice, she walks to work."

"How did she come home?" Mason asked her.

"In a taxi. I don't know what she intends to do about the parrot. She didn't say a word to me about giving him food or water. I guess there's plenty in the cage to last him over night, but I don't know how long she intends to be gone. . . . I must close those garage doors for her. She never leaves them open when she takes the car out, but today she didn't stop for anything, just backed the car out of the garage, and went a-kiting down the street."

"Probably had a date in the city for a theater or something," Mason said. "Perhaps she was meeting her husband. . . . I take it her husband wasn't with her."

"No. I believe he's out somewhere looking for work—he comes and goes. She spent the weekend with him somewhere I know, because I had to keep the parrot for her."

"Her husband's out of work?" Mason asked.

"Yes."

"Quite a few people are these days," Mason told her, "but I suppose a young man who has plenty of vitality and stick-to-it-iveness can . . ."

"But he isn't young," Mrs. Winters interrupted, with the air of one who could be led to say more if properly encouraged.

"Why, I gathered she was a young woman," Mason said. "Of course, I haven't met her personally, but . . ."

"Well, it depends on what you call young. She's in the early thirties. The man she married must be twenty years older than she is. I guess he's steady enough and nice enough and all that, but what in the world a young

43

woman wants to go and tie herself up for, with a man old enough to be her father . . . There, I mustn't go gossiping. I suppose it's none of *my* business. After all, *she* married him, *I* didn't. I made up my mind when she introduced him to me that I wasn't going to say a word to her about his age. I figure it's just none of my business, and I'm a great body to mind my own business. . . . May I ask what you want to see Mrs. Wallman about?"

Mason said, "I wanted to see Mrs. Wallman, but I also wanted to see her husband. You don't know where I could reach him, do you?"

Her eyes glittered with suspicion. "I thought," she said, "you didn't know she was married."

"I didn't," Mason admitted, "when I came here, but now that I've found it out, I'm quite anxious to see her husband. I . . . I might have a job for him."

"There's a lot of younger men out of jobs these days," Mrs. Winters said. "I don't know what Helen was thinking of, taking on a man like that to support, because that's just what it's going to amount to. I guess he's a nice, quiet, respectable man and all that, but after all he's out of work, and if you ask me, his clothes show it. I *would* think Helen'd get him a new suit of clothes. She lives simple enough and they do say as how she has quite a little put by for a rainy day."

Mason's eyes narrowed in thoughtful speculation. Abruptly he fished in his vest pocket with his thumb and forefinger and took out the folded newspaper picture of Fremont C. Sabin. "Is there any chance," he asked, showing Mrs. Winters the picture, "that this photograph is of her husband?"

Mrs. Winters carefully adjusted her glasses, took the newsprint picture from Mason, and held it up so that the western light fell full upon it.

In the automobile, Paul Drake and Della Street watched breathlessly.

An expression of surprise came over Mrs. Winters' face. "Land sakes, yes," she said. "That's the man, just as natural as life. I'd know him anywhere. Good Lord, what's George Wallman done to get *his* picture in the newspapers?"

Mason retrieved the picture. "Look here, Mrs. Winters," he said, "it's vitally important that I find Mrs. Wallman at once and . . ."

"Oh, you want to see *Mrs.* Wallman now. Is that it?"

"Either Mr. or Mrs.," Mason said. "Since she was the last one you've seen, perhaps you could tell me where I'd be able to find her."

"I'm sure I don't know. She might have gone to visit her sister. Her sister's a school teacher in Edenglade."

"Is her sister married?" Mason asked.

"No, she's never been married."

"Then her name is Monteith?"

"Yes, Sarah Monteith. She's a couple of years older than Helen, but she looks about fifteen years older. She's painfully correct in her ways. She takes life too seriously and . . ."

"You don't know of any other relatives?" Mason asked.

"No."

"And no other place where she would have gone?"

"No."

Mason terminated the interview by raising his hat with elaborate politeness. "Well, Mrs. Winters," he said, "I certainly thank you for your co-operation. I'm sorry that I bothered you. After all, I guess I'll have to plan on seeing Mrs. Wallman some other time."

He turned back toward the car.

"You can leave a message with me," Mrs. Winters said. "I'll see that she gets it and . . . but . . ."

"I'm afraid I'll have to see her personally," Mason said, jumping into the car and signaling for Della Street to drive on.

"Put down that gun, Helen!" the parrot on the porch screamed. "Don't shoot! *Squawk. Squawk.* My God, you've shot me!"

Della Street lurched the car into motion.

Mason said, "Okay, Paul, find her. Get out and start using the telephone. Spread operatives all over the country. Get a description of her car and the license number from the Motor Vehicle Department or from the Assessor's Office or wherever you can. Try the sister in Edenglade."

"Where are you going?" Drake asked.

"I'm heading for Sabin's place in town," Mason told him. "I think the chances are about even that she's headed there, and I want to beat her to it if I can."

"What do I do with her if I find her?" Drake asked.

"Put her where no one can talk with her until after I do."

"That," Drake said, "is something of a large order, Perry."

"Oh, shucks," Mason told him, "don't be so squeamish. Put her in a sanitarium somewhere as suffering from a nervous breakdown."

"She's probably upset," Drake told him, "but we'd have quite a job making the nervous breakdown business stick."

"Not if she realized the full significance of what that parrot's saying, you wouldn't," Mason said grimly.

CHAPTER FOUR

MASON guided his car in close to the curb and glanced across the street at the lighted house. "Certainly is big enough," he said to Della Street. "No wonder the old man got lonely living there."

He had slid out from behind the wheel and was standing at the curb, locking the car door, when Della Street said, "I think this is one of Paul Drake's men coming."

Mason looked up to see a man emerge from the shadows, glance at the license plate on the automobile, then cut across the beam of illumination from the headlights.

"Shall I put the lights out, Chief?" Della Street asked.

"Please," he told her.

The light switch clicked the surroundings into darkness. The man approached Mason and said, "You're Mason, aren't you?"

"Yes," Mason told him. "What is it?"

"I'm from the Drake agency. The old woman and her son got in on the plane this afternoon. They came directly here. Another operative is tailing them. They're inside now, and there's a hell of a row going on."

Mason looked across at the huge house silhouetted against the night sky, its windows glowing in subdued brilliance through the drapes.

"Well," he said, grinning, "I may as well go on in and join the fight."

The operative said, "The boss telephoned for us to be on the lookout for a car with license number 1V-1302. I saw you drive up and thought maybe that was the bus I was looking for."

Mason said, "No, that's probably Helen Monteith's car. She lives in San Molinas, and she may come to the house here. I want to see her just as soon as we can . . ."

He broke off as a car swung around the corner, and headlights cast moving shadows along the street.

"I'll see who this is," the detective said. "Probably some more relatives coming in to join the family row."

He walked around the rear of Mason's machine, then came running back and said, "That's the license number the boss told us to be on the lookout for. Do you want it?"

Mason's answer was to start running for the place where the car was being backed into a vacant space at the curb. By the time the young woman who was driving it had switched off her headlights and stepped from the car, Mason was abreast of her.

"I want to talk with you, Miss Monteith," he said.

"Who are you?" she asked sharply.

"Mason is the name," he said. "I'm a lawyer, representing Charles Sabin."

"What do you want with me?"

"I want to talk with you."

"What about?"

"About Fremont C. Sabin."

"I don't think I have anything to say."

"Don't be silly," Mason told her. "The thing has gone so far now it's entirely out of your hands."

47

"What do you mean?"

"I mean that the newspaper men are on the job. It isn't going to take *them* long to find out that you claim to have gone through a marriage ceremony with Fremont C. Sabin, who was going under the name of George Wallman. After they've gone that far, they'll find out that Sabin's parrot, Casanova, is on the screen porch of your house in San Molinas, and that since the murder he's been saying, 'Drop that gun, Helen. . . . Don't shoot. . . . My God, you've shot me.' "

She was tall enough so that she needed to raise her eyes only slightly to meet the lawyer's. She was slender enough to be easy and graceful in her motions, and her posture indicated a self-reliance and ability to reach decisions quickly, and put them into rapid execution.

"How," she asked, apparently without batting an eyelash, "did *you* find out all this?"

"By using the same methods the police and the newspapermen will use," Mason said.

"Very well," she told him quietly, "I'll talk. What do you want to know?"

"Everything," he said.

"Do you," she asked, "want to talk in my car, or in the house?"

"In my car," Mason told her, "if you don't mind."

He cupped his hand under her elbow, escorted her back to his automobile, introduced Della Street, and placed Helen Monteith beside him in the front seat.

"I want you to understand," Helen Monteith said, "that I've done nothing wrong—nothing of which I am ashamed."

"I understand," Mason told her.

He could see her profile outlined against the illumination which filtered in through the car windows. Her manner was quick, alert, intelligent; her voice was well controlled. She evidently had ample speaking range to make her voice expressive when she chose, yet she resorted to no tricks of emphasis or expression to win sympathy. She spoke rapidly, and managed to convey the impression that, regardless of what her personal feelings in the matter might be, she was keeping her emotions entirely divorced

48

from those events which she considered it necessary to report.

"I'm a librarian," she said, "employed in the San Molinas library. For various reasons, I have never married. My position gives me at once an opportunity to cultivate a taste for the best in literature, and to learn something of character. I have nothing in common with the younger set who find alcoholic stimulation the necessary prerequisite to any attempt at conversation or enjoyment.

"I first met the man whom I now know as Fremont C. Sabin about two months ago. He entered the library, asked for books dealing with certain economic subjects. He told me he never read newspapers because they were merely a recital of crimes and political propaganda. He read news magazines for his general information, was interested in history, economics, science and biographies. He read some of the best fiction. His questions and comments were unusually intelligent, and the man impressed me. I realized, of course, that he was much older than I, and, quite apparently, was out of work. His clothes were well-kept, but had seen far better days. I'm dwelling on this because I want you to understand the situation."

Mason nodded.

"He told me his name was George Wallman; that he had been employed as a grocery clerk, had saved a little money, and purchased a store of his own; that, after making a living out of it for several years, he found himself forced out of business by a combination of unfortunate circumstances. His original capital was gone. He had tried to get work and was unable to find any because, as he had been so frequently told, not only were there no jobs, but in the event there had been, employers would prefer to fill them with younger men."

"You had no inkling of his real identity?" Mason asked.

"None whatever."

"Do you know why he chose to assume this fictitious personality?" Mason asked.

"Yes," she said shortly.

"Why?"

"I realize now," she said, "that, in the first place, the

man was married; in the second place, he was wealthy. He was trying to protect himself from an unpleasant wife on the one hand, and avaricious gold-diggers or blackmailers on the other."

"And apparently, somewhere in the process, he messed up your life pretty well," Mason said sympathetically.

She turned on him, not in anger, but with quick resentment. "That," she said, "shows that you didn't know George . . . Mr. Sabin."

"It's a fact, isn't it?" Mason asked.

She shook her head. "I don't know what the complete explanation is," she said, "but you can rest assured that when all the facts are uncovered, his reasons will have been good ones."

"And you feel no bitterness?" the lawyer inquired.

"None whatever," she said, and for a moment there was a wistful note in her voice. "The happiest two months of my life were in the period following my meeting with Mr. Sabin. All of this tragedy has hit me a terrific blow. . . . However, you're not interested in my grief."

"I'm trying to understand," he said gently.

"That's virtually all there is to it," she said; "I had some money which I'd saved from my salary. I recognized, of course, that it was hopeless for a man in the late fifties, who had no particular skill in any profession, and no regular trade, to get employment. I told him that I would back him in starting a grocery store in San Molinas. He looked the town over, but finally came to the conclusion that it wouldn't be possible to make a go of things there. So then I told him to pick his place."

"Then what?" Mason asked.

"Then," she said, "he went out to look the territory over."

"You heard from him?" Mason asked.

"Letters, yes."

"What did he say in his letters?"

"He was rather vague about matters pertaining to business," she said; "his letters were—mostly personal. We had been married less than a week when he left." She turned suddenly to face Mason and said, "And regardless of what else may transpire, he loved me."

She said it simply, without dramatic emphasis, without allowing her personal grief to intrude upon the statement. It was merely a statement of facts made as a calm assertion by one who knows whereof she speaks.

Mason nodded silent acquiescence.

"The first intimation I had," she said, "was . . . was . . . this afternoon, when I picked up the afternoon paper and saw his picture as Fremont C. Sabin, the man who had been murdered."

"You recognized him at once?"

"Yes. There had been certain things which hadn't been exactly . . . consistent with the character he had assumed. Since our marriage, I had found myself watching him with a vague uneasiness, because the man simply didn't fit into the character of a failure. He was a man who couldn't have failed at anything in life; he had too much quiet force of character, too much intelligence, too much native shrewdness; and he seemed too reluctant to touch any of my money. He kept putting that off, saying that he had a little money of his own saved up, and that we'd use that to live on until it was gone, and then he'd take mine."

"But you didn't suspect that he really had great wealth?" Mason asked.

"No," she said, "I hadn't crystallized any of the doubts in my mind into even being doubts. They were simply little things which remained lodged in my memory, and then, when I saw his picture in the paper, and read the account of his death, those things all clicked into place. I'd been prepared for it in a way when I read in the morning paper about the mountain cabin . . . and saw the photographs of that cabin."

"Of course," Mason said, "you'd been without letters for the past week?"

"On the contrary," she said, "I had received a letter from him only this Saturday, the tenth. It had been mailed from Santa Delbarra. He said he was negotiating for a lease on what seemed to be an ideal storeroom. He seemed to be very enthusiastic, and said he hoped to be back within a few days."

"I presume," Mason said, "you aren't entirely familiar with his handwriting, and . . ."

51

"I feel quite certain," she said, "that the writing is that of Mr. Sabin . . . or George Wallman, as I knew him."

"But," Mason said, "the evidence shows that the body was lying in that cabin—you'll forgive me for being brutally frank, Miss Monteith, but it's necessary—the evidence shows that he was murdered on September sixth."

"Can't you understand?" she said wearily. "He was testing my love. He wanted to keep in the character of Wallman until he knew I loved *him* and wasn't after money. He wasn't looking for any lease. He planted these letters and left them to be mailed from various places on different dates."

"You have that last letter?" Mason asked.

"Yes."

"May I see it?"

She made as though to open her purse, then shook her head and said, "No."

"Why not?"

"The letter is personal," she said. "I understand that, to a certain extent, my privacy must of necessity be invaded by authorities making an investigation, but I am not going to surrender his letters, unless it becomes absolutely imperative."

"It's going to become imperative," Mason said. "If he left letters with someone to be mailed at various times and places, that someone may have been the last person to have seen him alive."

She remained silent.

"When were you married?" Mason asked.

"August twenty-seventh."

"Where?"

She hesitated a moment, then tilted her chin and said, "We crossed the border into Mexico and were married there."

"May I ask why?"

"George . . . Mr. Sabin said that for certain reasons he preferred to be married there . . . and . . ."

"Yes?" Mason prompted as she stopped.

"We were to be married again," she said, "in Santa Delbarra."

"Why there?"

"He . . . he intimated that his former wife had secured a divorce, that the interlocutory decree had not yet become final, and there might be some doubt as to the validity of the marriage. He said that it would . . . After all, Mr. Mason, this is something of a private matter."

"It is in part," Mason said, "and in part it isn't."

"Well, you can look at it in this way. I knew at the time I married him that the marriage was of doubtful legality. I considered it as a . . . as a gesture to the conventions. I understood that it would be followed with a second and more legal marriage that was to have taken place very shortly."

"Then you thought your first marriage was illegal?"

"No," she said, "I thought that it was legal . . . Well, when I say it was of doubtful legality, I mean that it was a marriage which would have been illegal if it had been performed in this country. . . . That's rather difficult to explain . . . and I don't know that I care to try."

"How about the parrot?" Mason asked.

"My hus— Mr. Sabin had always wanted a parrot."

"I understand that. How long had the parrot been with you?"

"Mr. Sabin brought him home on Friday, the second, I believe it was. It was two days before he left."

Mason stared in frowning contemplation at the determined profile. "Did you," he asked, "know that Mr. Sabin purchased this parrot in San Molinas?"

"Yes."

"What's the parrot's name?"

"Casanova."

"Did you read about the parrot which was found in the mountain cabin?"

"Yes."

"Do you know anything about that parrot?"

"No."

Mason frowned and said, "You know, Miss Monteith, this just doesn't make sense."

"I understand that," she admitted readily enough. "That's why I think it's a mistake to try and judge Mr.

53

Sabin by what has happened. It means we simply haven't all the facts."

"Do you know anything about that mountain cabin?" Mason asked.

"Yes, of course, we spent our honeymoon there. My hus— Mr. Sabin said that he knew the owner of the cabin, and had arranged to borrow it for a few days. Looking back on it now I can realize how absurd it was to think that this man who claimed to be out of a job and . . . Oh, well, he had his reasons for doing what he did, and I respect those reasons."

Mason started to say something, then checked himself and frowned thoughtfully for several silent seconds. "How long were you at the cabin?" he asked at length.

"We just stayed there over the weekend. I had to be back on my job Monday night."

"You were married in Mexico, and then drove to the cabin?"

"Yes."

"And did your husband seem to know his way around the cabin pretty well—that is, be familiar with it?"

"Oh, yes, he told me that he'd spent a month there once."

"Did he tell you the name of the man who owned the cabin?"

"No."

"And you made no attempt to find out?"

"No."

"You were married on the twenty-seventh of August?"

"Yes."

"And you arrived at the cabin on the evening of the twenty-seventh?"

"No, the morning of the twenty-eighth. It was too long a drive to make that first night."

"You left some clothes there?"

"Yes."

"Did you do that deliberately?"

"Yes, we left rather hurriedly. One of the neighbors came to call, and Mr. Sabin didn't want to see him. I suppose he didn't want the neighbor to know about me—

or was afraid I'd learn his real identity through the neighbor. Anyway, he didn't answer the door, and then we hurried into the car and left. Mr. Sabin told me that no one else would be using the cabin, and that we'd return sometime within the next month."

"During the time you were there in the cabin, did Mr. Sabin use the telephone?"

"He put through two calls."

"Do you know whom the calls were to? Did you listen to the conversation?"

"No."

"Do you have any idea who might have killed him, any inkling whatever as to . . ."

"Not the slightest."

"And I don't suppose," Mason went on casually, "that you know anything about the weapon with which the murder was committed?"

"Yes," she said unexpectedly, "I do."

"You do?"

"Yes."

"What about it?" Mason asked.

"That weapon," she said slowly, "is part of a collection at the San Molinas Public Library."

"There's a collection of guns there?"

"Yes, there's a museum in one room, in connection with the library—that is, it isn't exactly operated in connection with the library, but it was presented to the city, and, under an arrangement with the library committee, the librarian has charge of the room. The janitor, who takes care of the library, does janitor work, and . . ."

"Who took this gun from the collection?"

"I did."

"Why?"

"My husband asked me to. He . . . No, I don't think I'm going to talk about that, Mr. Mason."

"To whom did you give this gun?"

"I think we'll just skip everything about the gun."

"When did you first know your husband was really Fremont C. Sabin?"

"This morning, when I saw the picture of the cabin in the paper . . . well, I suspected it then. I didn't know what to do. I just waited, hoping against hope. Then the afternoon papers published his picture. Then I knew."

Mason asked abruptly, "Just what do you have to gain in a financial way?"

"What do you mean?"

"Was there any will, any policy of insurance, any . . ."

"No, of course not," she interrupted.

Mason stared thoughtfully at her. "What are your plans?" he asked.

"I'm going in and meet Mr. Sabin's son. I'm going to explain the circumstances to him."

"His wife is in there now," Mason said.

"You mean Fremont C. Sabin's wife?"

"Yes."

She bit her lip, then sat silently digesting that bit of information.

Mason said gently, "You know, Miss Monteith, the authorities are not going to understand how that gun happened to be one to which you had access . . . Look here, you didn't find out, by any chance, who he was, and find out about his wife, and get angry because . . ."

"You mean and kill him?" she interrupted.

"Yes," Mason said.

"The very thought is absurd! I loved him. I have never loved any man . . ." she broke off.

"He was," Mason pointed out, "considerably older than you."

"And wiser," she said, "and gentler, and more considerate, and . . . You have no idea how grand he was; contrasted with the young men whom I meet around the library—the fresh ones who try to take me out, the stupid ones, the ones who have lost all ambition . . ." Her voice trailed away into silence.

Mason turned to Della Street. "Della," he said, "I want you to take Miss Monteith with you. I want you to keep her some place where she won't be annoyed by newspapermen, do you understand?"

"I think I do," Della Street said quietly from the back seat, and her voice sounded as though she had been crying.

"I don't want to go anywhere," Miss Monteith said. "I

understand that I'm in for a disagreeable ordeal. The only thing I can do is face it."

"Do you want to meet Mrs. Sabin?" Mason asked. "I understand that she's rather disagreeable."

"No," Helen Monteith said shortly.

Mason said, "Miss Monteith, I think the developments of the next few hours may make a great deal of difference. Right at present the police haven't identified that murder weapon; that is, they haven't found out where it came from. When they do . . . well, you're going to be arrested, that's all."

"You mean and charged with murder?"

"You'll be booked on suspicion of murder."

"But that's absurd."

"It isn't absurd, looking at it from the police viewpoint," Mason said. "It isn't even absurd looking at it from any common-sense reconstruction of the evidence."

She was silent for a few seconds, thinking over what he had said, then she turned to him and asked, "Just whom do you represent?"

"Charles Sabin."

"And what are you trying to do?"

Mason said, "Among other things, I'm trying to clear up this murder case. I'm trying to find out what happened."

"What is your interest in me?"

"You," Mason told her, "are in a spot. My training has been to sympathize with the underdog and fight for him."

"But I'm not an underdog."

"You will be by the time that family gets done with you," Mason told her grimly.

"You want me to run away?"

"No, that's exactly what I *don't* want. If the situation hasn't clarified itself by tomorrow, we'll . . . well, we'll cross that bridge when we come to it."

She reached her decision. "Very well," she said, "I'll go."

Mason said to Della Street, "You'll go in her car, Della."

"Shall I communicate with you, Chief?" she asked.

"No," Mason said. "There are some things I want to find out, and other things I don't want to know anything about."

"I get you, Chief," she said. "Come on, Miss Monteith. We haven't any time to waste around here."

Mason stood on the curb, watching the car, until the tail-light became a red pin-point in the distance. Then he turned toward the huge, gloomy house with its somber atmosphere of massive respectability.

CHAPTER FIVE

RICHARD WAID, the secretary, opened the door in response to Mason's ring. His face showed his relief at seeing the lawyer. "C.W. has been trying to get you on the phone," he said. "I've been calling every few minutes."

"Something wrong?" Mason inquired.

"Mrs. Sabin is home—the widow."

"Has that resulted in complications?" the lawyer asked.

"I'll say it has. Listen, you can hear them in there now."

Richard Waid stood slightly to one side, and the sound of a woman's excited voice came pouring through the doorway. The words were undistinguishable, but there could be no mistaking the harsh, rasping sound of the voice itself.

"Well," Mason said, "perhaps I'd better join in the fight."

"I wish you would," Waid said, and then, after a moment, "It may be that you can tone her down a bit."

"Does she have a lawyer?" Mason asked.

"Not yet. She's threatening to hire all the lawyers in the city."

"Threatening?" Mason inquired.

"Yes," Waid said shortly, and as he led the way into the living room, added, "And that's putting it mildly."

Charles Sabin got to his feet at once, as Mason entered. He came forward to grasp the lawyer's hand, with evident relief. "You must be a mind reader, Mr. Mason," he said. "I've been trying to get you for the last half hour."

He turned and said, "Helen, let me present Perry Mason. Mrs. Helen Watkins Sabin, Mr. Mason."

Mason bowed. "I am pleased to meet you, Mrs. Sabin."

She glared at him as though he had been an insect impaled with a pin and mounted on a wall board. "Humph!" she said.

She was heavy, but there was nothing flabby about her heaviness. Her body was hard beef, and her eyes held the arrogant steadiness of a person who is accustomed to put others on the defensive and keep them there.

"And her son, Mr. Watkins, Mr. Mason."

Watkins came forward to take Mason's hand in a firm, cordial grasp. His eyes sought those of the lawyer, and his voice as he said, "I'm *very* glad to meet you, Mr. Mason," lent emphasis to his words. "I've been reading so much about you, from time to time, that it's a real pleasure to meet you in the flesh. I was particularly interested in the newspaper accounts of the trial of that case involving the murder of the insurance man."

"Thank you very much," Mason said, letting his eyes take in the bulging forehead, the well-rounded cheeks, the steady blue eyes, and the fit of the well-pressed flannels.

"I've had quite a trip," Steve Watkins said by way of explanation. "I flew from New York down to Central America to pick up mother, and came back with her. Haven't even tubbed yet."

"Did you fly your own plane?" Mason asked.

"No, I didn't, although I do quite a bit of flying. But my job wasn't exactly tuned up for a long flight. I went on a passenger plane to Mexico City, and then chartered a private plane down and back. We had another plane fly down to wait for us in Mexico City."

"You *have* had quite a trip," Mason agreed.

Mrs. Sabin said, "Never mind the personal amenities, Steve. I see no occasion to waste time trying to meet Mr.

Mason on friendly terms. You know perfectly well he's going to try to knife us. We may just as well start our fight and get it over with."

"Fight?" Mason asked.

She pushed forward her chin aggressively and said, "I said 'fight.' *You* should know what the word means."

"And what," Mason asked, "are we going to fight about?"

"Don't beat around the bush," she said, "it isn't like you—not from all I've heard, and I don't want to be disappointed in you. Charles has employed you to see that I'm jockeyed out of my rights as Fremont's wife. I don't intend to be jockeyed."

Mason said, "Perhaps in the circumstances, Mrs. Sabin, if you retained your attorney, and let me discuss matters with him . . ."

"I'll do that when I get good and ready," she said. "I don't need any lawyer—not right now. When I need one I'll get one."

Steve Watkins said, "Just a minute, Moms, Uncle Charles only said that . . ."

"Shut up," Mrs. Sabin snapped, "I'm running this. I heard what Charles said. All right, Mr. Mason, what have you to say for yourself?"

Mason dropped into a chair, crossed his long legs, grinned across at Charles Sabin, and said nothing.

"All right, then, *I'll* say something. I've told Charles Sabin, and now I'm telling you. I know only too well that Charles has resented me ever since I married into this family. If I had told Fremont one half of the things that I've had to put up with, Fremont would have had Charles on the carpet. He wouldn't have stood for it for a minute. Regardless of what Charles may think, Fremont loved me. Charles was so afraid that some of the property was going to get away from him, that he was completely blinded by prejudice. As a matter of fact, if he'd been disposed to be fair with me, I might have been fair with him now. As it is, I'm in the saddle, and I'm going to do the driving. Do you understand, Mr. Mason?"

"Perhaps," Mason said, lighting a cigarette, "you could explain a little more clearly, Mrs. Sabin."

"Very well, I will explain clearly. I'm Fremont's widow. I *think* there's a will leaving the bulk of his property to me. He told me he was making such a will. If there is a will I'm the executrix of it; if there isn't, I'm entitled to letters of administration. In any event, I am going to be in charge of the estate, and I don't want any interference from any of the relatives."

"You haven't the will with you?" Mason asked.

"Certainly not. I'm not in the habit of carrying my husband's wills around with me. I presume it's in his papers somewhere, unless Charles has destroyed it. And in case you don't know it, Mr. Mason, Charles Sabin is perfectly capable of doing just that."

Mason said, "Can't we leave the personalities out of it, Mrs. Sabin?"

She stared defiantly at him, and said simply, "No."

Richard Waid started to say something, then checked himself.

Mason said, "Look here, Mrs. Sabin, I want to ask you a personal question. Hadn't you and Mr. Sabin separated?"

"What do you mean by that?"

"Just what I say. Hadn't you separated, hadn't you decided that you were not going to live together any longer as man and wife? Wasn't your trip around the world in accordance with such an understanding?"

"Absolutely not, that's ridiculous."

"Didn't you have an agreement with Mr. Sabin by which you were to get a divorce?"

"Absolutely not."

Waid said, "Really, Mr. Mason, I . . ."

He broke off as Mrs. Sabin glowered at him.

The telephone rang, and Waid said, "I'll answer it."

Mason turned to Charles Sabin and said significantly, "I have recently come into the possession of certain information, Mr. Sabin, which leads me to believe that your father had every reason to believe that by Monday, the fifth of this month, Mrs. Sabin would have obtained a divorce. I can't interpret the information I have received in any other light."

"That's a defamation of character," Mrs. Sabin said belligerently.

Mason kept his eyes on Charles Sabin. "Do you," he asked, "know anything about that?"

Sabin shook his head.

Mason turned back to Mrs. Sabin. "When were you in Paris, Mrs. Sabin?"

"That's none of your business."

"Did you get a divorce while you were in Paris?"

"Most certainly not!"

"Because," Mason went on, "if you did, I'll find out about it sooner or later, and I'm warning you now that I'm going to look for evidence that will . . ."

"Bosh," she said.

Richard Waid, who had been standing in the door near the hallway in which the telephone was located, came striding into the room and said, "Well, it isn't bosh, it's absolute fact."

"What do you know about it?" Mason asked.

Waid came into the room, met Mrs. Sabin's eyes, and turned to Charles Sabin. "I know everything about it. Look here, Mr. Sabin, I realize there's going to be a family fight. I know enough of Mrs. Sabin's character to know that it's going to be a free-for-all. As she pointed out to me, within a few minutes after she arrived, I can best safeguard my interests by keeping my mouth shut and keeping out of it. But my conscience won't let me do that."

"You and your conscience," Mrs. Sabin said, her voice rising shrilly. "You're nothing but a paid 'yesman.' My husband had completely lost confidence in you. You may not know it, but he was getting ready to discharge you. He . . ."

"Mrs. Sabin," Waid interrupted, "didn't go around the world, at all."

"She didn't?" Mason asked.

"No," Waid said, "that was just a stall to fool the newspaper reporters so she could get a divorce without any publicity. She boarded a round-the-world boat. She only went as far as Honolulu. Then she took the Clipper back, and established a residence at Reno. She obtained a divorce there. All this was done under Mr. Sabin's direction. She was to receive one hundred thousand dollars in cash when she furnished Mr. Sabin with evidence that she had received her divorce. Then she was to fly to New York, pick up a round-the-world boat, come back through the Panama Canal, and then let Mr. Sabin, at such time as he thought best, announce the divorce. That was the agreement between them."

Mrs. Sabin said with cold finality, "Richard, I warned you to keep your mouth shut about that."

Waid said, "I didn't tell the sheriff because I felt it wasn't up to me to discuss Mr. Sabin's business. I didn't tell Mr. Charles Sabin because Mrs. Sabin told me that it would be to my own good to keep my mouth shut. She said that if I co-operated with her, she'd co-operate with me once she got in the saddle."

"The question," Mason said, "is whether this divorce was actually obtained."

Mrs. Sabin settled back in her chair. "Very well," she said to Richard Waid. "This is your party. Go ahead and furnish the entertainment."

Waid said, "I will. The facts in this case are bound to come out sooner or later, anyway. Fremont C. Sabin had been unhappy for some time. He and his wife had been virtually separated. He wanted his freedom; his wife wanted a cash settlement.

"For some reason, Mr. Sabin wanted to have the matter remain a closely guarded secret. He didn't trust any of his regular attorneys with the matter, but went to a man by the name of C. William Desmond. I don't know whether any of you gentlemen know him."

"I know of him," Mason said, "a very reputable attorney. Go ahead, Waid. Tell me what happened."

Waid said, "An agreement was reached by which Mrs. Sabin agreed to get a divorce in Reno. When she presented a certified copy of the divorce decree to Mr. Sabin, he was to pay her the sum of one hundred thousand dollars in cash. It was stipulated as part of the agreement that there was to be absolutely no publicity, and that the responsibility was up to Mrs. Sabin to arrange the matter in such a way that the newspapers would not get hold of it."

"Then she didn't go around the world, after all?" Mason asked.

"No, of course not. As I told you, she went only as far as Honolulu, took the Clipper ship back, established a six weeks' residence in Reno, secured a decree of divorce, and went to New York. That was what Mr. Sabin telephoned to me about on the evening of the fifth. He said that everything was arranged and Mrs. Sabin was to meet me in New York with the decree of divorce. As I've already explained to the officers, Steve was waiting at the airport with his plane all tuned up and ready. I stepped in and we took off for New York. We arrived in New York on the afternoon of the sixth. I went directly to the bankers to whom Mr. Sabin had directed me, and also to the firm of solicitors who represented Mr. Sabin in New York. I wanted them to check over the certified decree of divorce before I paid over the money."

"They did so?" Mason asked.

"Yes."

"And when did you pay the money?"

"I paid that on the evening of Wednesday, the seventh, at a New York hotel."

"How was it paid?"

"In cash."

"Certified check or currency or . . ."

"Cash," Waid said. "It was paid in one hundred bills of one thousand dollars each. That was the way Mrs. Sabin wanted it."

"You have a receipt from her?" Mason asked.

"Yes, of course."

"And how about the certified copy of the decree of divorce?"

"I have that."

"Why," Charles Sabin asked, "didn't you tell me about this before, Richard?"

"I wanted to wait until Mr. Mason was here."

Mason turned to Mrs. Sabin. "How about it, Mrs. Sabin? Is this correct?" he asked.

"This is Waid's party," she said. "Let him go ahead

with the entertainment. He's played his first number, now let's have an encore."

"Fortunately," Waid said, "I insisted on the money being paid in the presence of witnesses. I thought that perhaps she was getting ready to pull one of her fast ones."

"Let's see the certified copy of the decree of divorce," Mason said.

Waid took from his pocket a folded paper.

"You should have delivered this to *me,*" Charles Sabin said.

"I'm sorry," Waid apologized, "but Mr. Sabin's instructions were that I was to keep the decree of divorce and deliver it to no one except himself. I was not, under any circumstances, to mention it to anyone. The nature of the business which took me to New York was to be so confidential that no one, save his New York counselors, was to know anything about it. He particularly cautioned me against saying anything to you. I realize now, of course, that the situation is changed. Either you or Mrs. Sabin is going to be in charge of the entire estate, and my employment—if it continues—is going to be subject to your instructions.

"Mrs. Sabin has taken particular pains to tell me that she's going to be in the saddle and that if I say anything to anybody, I'll suffer for it."

Mason reached out and took the folded paper from Waid's hand. Sabin crossed over to look over the lawyer's shoulder.

"This," Mason said, as he examined the printed form with the certification attached to it, "appears to be in proper form."

"It was passed on by the New York lawyers," Waid said.

Mrs. Sabin chuckled.

Sabin said, "In that event this woman isn't my father's widow. As I take it, Mr. Mason, under those circumstances she isn't entitled to share in any part of the estate—that is, unless there's a specific devise or bequest in a will."

Mrs. Sabin's chuckle became harsh, mocking laughter.

"Your lawyer isn't saying anything," she said. "You overplayed your hand, Charles; you killed him too soon."

"*I* killed him!" Charles Sabin exclaimed.

"You heard what I said."

"Moms," Steve Watkins pleaded, "please be careful of what you say."

"I'm more than careful," she said, "I'm truthful. Go ahead, Mr. Mason, why don't you tell them the bad news."

Mason glanced up to confront Sabin's troubled eyes.

"What's the matter?" Charles Sabin asked. "Isn't the decree good?"

Waid said, "It has to be good. The New York lawyers passed on it. A hundred thousand dollars was paid on the strength of that decree."

Mason said quietly, "You'll notice, gentlemen, that the decree of divorce was granted on Tuesday the sixth. There's nothing on here to show at what time on the sixth the decree was rendered."

"What does that have to do with it?" Sabin asked.

"Simply this," Mason said. "If Fremont C. Sabin was killed *before* Mrs. Sabin was divorced, the divorce was inoperative. She became his widow immediately upon his death. You can't get a divorce from a dead man."

And the silence which followed was broken by Mrs. Sabin's shrill laughter. "I tell you, Charles, you killed him too soon."

Slowly, Charles Sabin crossed the room to sit down in his chair.

"But," Mason went on, "in the event your father was killed *after* the divorce decree was granted, the situation is different."

"He was killed in the morning," Mrs. Sabin said positively, "after he'd returned from a fishing trip. Richard Waid has gone over all the facts with me in a preliminary conference. Those facts can't be changed and can't be distorted . . . because I'm going to see to it that no one changes them."

Mason said, "There are several factors involved in fixing the time, Mrs. Sabin."

"And that," she said, "is where I come in. I'm going to

see that none of the evidence is tampered with. My husband met his death before noon on the sixth. I didn't get my divorce until four-thirty in the afternoon."

"Of course, the decree of divorce doesn't show at what time during the day the decree was granted," Mason said.

"Well, I guess my testimony amounts to something, doesn't it?" she snapped. "I know when I got the divorce. What's more, I'll get a letter from the lawyer who represented me in Reno."

Charles Sabin looked at Mason with worried eyes. "The evidence," he said, "shows my father met his death some time before noon, probably around eleven o'clock."

Mrs. Sabin said nothing, but rocked back and forth, triumphantly, in the big rocking chair.

Charles Sabin turned to her savagely. "You have been rather free with your accusations directed at me," he said, "but what were *you* doing about that time? If anyone had a motive for killing him, you did."

Her smile was expansive. "Don't let your anger get the best of you, Charles," she said. "It's bad for your blood pressure. You know what the doctor told you. . . . You see, Charles, I was in Reno getting my divorce. Court was called at two o'clock, and I had to wait two hours and a half before my case came up. I'm afraid you'll have to find a pretty big loophole in that alibi to pin the crime on me—or don't you think so?"

Mason said, "I'm going to tell you something which hasn't as yet been made public. The authorities at San Molinas will probably discover it shortly. In the meantime, the facts happen to be in my possession. I think you all should know them."

"I don't care what facts you have," Mrs. Sabin said. "You're not going to bluff me."

"I'm not bluffing anybody," Mason told her. "Fremont C. Sabin crossed over into Mexico and went through a marriage ceremony with a librarian from San Molinas. Her name is Helen Monteith. It has generally been supposed that the parrot which was found in the cabin, with the body, was Casanova, the parrot to which Mr. Sabin was very much attached. As a matter of fact, for reasons which I haven't been able to uncover as yet, Mr. Sabin purchased another parrot in San Molinas and left Casanova with Helen Monteith. Casanova remained with Helen Monteith from Friday, the second, until today."

Mrs. Sabin got to her feet. "Well," she said, "I don't see that this concerns *me*, and I don't think we have anything further to gain here. You, Richard Waid, are going to be sorry that you betrayed my interests and violated my instructions. I suppose now I've got to go to a lot of trouble making affidavits as to when that divorce decree was actually granted. . . . So my husband has a bigamous wife, has he? Well, well, well! Come, Steve, we'll go and leave these gentlemen to themselves. As soon as I've gone, they'll try to find evidence which will show that Fremont wasn't killed until the evening of Tuesday the sixth. In order to do that, it's quite possible they'll try to tamper with the evidence. I think, Steve, that it will be wise for us to retain a lawyer. We have our own interests to protect."

She swept from the room. Steve Watkins, following her, turned to make some fumbling attempt to comply with conventions. "Pleased to have met you, Mr. Mason," he said, and to Charles Sabin, "You understand how things are with me, Uncle Charles."

When they had left the room, Charles Sabin said, "I think that woman has the most irritating personality of any woman I have ever encountered. How about it, Mr. Mason? Do I have to sit quietly by and let her accuse me of murdering my father?"

"What would you *like* to do?" Mason asked.

"I'd like to tell her just what I think of her. I'd like to let her know that she isn't fooling me for a minute, that she's simply a shrewd, gold-digging, fortune-hunting . . ."

"That wouldn't do you any good," Mason interrupted. "You'd tell her what you thought of her. She'd tell you what she thought of you. I take it, Mr. Sabin, you haven't had a great deal of experience in giving people what is colloquially known as a piece of your mind, have you?"

"No, sir," Sabin admitted.

Mason said, "Well, she evidently has. When it comes to

an exchange of personal vituperation, she'd quite probably have you beaten before you started. If you want to fight her, there's only one way to fight."

"What's that?" Sabin asked, his voice showing his interest.

"That is to hit her where she least expects to be hit. There's only one way to fight, and that's to win. Never attack *where* the other man is expecting it, *when* the other man is expecting it. That's where he's prepared his strongest defense."

"Well," Sabin demanded, "where can we attack her where she hasn't her defenses organized?"

"That," Mason said, "remains to be seen."

"Why," Sabin asked, "should my father have gone to all these elaborate preparations to insure secrecy about that divorce? I can understand, of course, that my father didn't like publicity. He wanted to avoid all publicity as much as possible. Some things are inevitable. When a man gets divorced, it's necessary for the world to know he's divorced."

"I think," Mason said, "that your father probably had some reasons for wanting to keep his picture out of the newspaper at that particular time, although it's rather hard to tell."

Sabin thought for a moment. "You mean that he was already courting this other girl, and didn't want her to know who he was?"

Richard Waid said, "If you'll pardon me, I think I can clear that situation up. I happen to know that Fremont C. Sabin was rather . . . er . . . gun-shy about women, after his experience with the present Mrs. Sabin . . . Well, I feel quite certain that if he had wanted to marry again, he would have taken every possible precaution to see that he wasn't getting a gold-digger."

Charles Sabin frowned. "The thing," he said, "gets more and more complicated. Of course, my father had a horror of publicity. I gather that the plans for this divorce were made before he met this young woman in San Molinas, but probably he was just trying to avoid reporters. What's all this about the parrot, Mr. Mason?"

"You mean Casanova?"

"Yes."

"Apparently," Mason said, "for reasons best known to himself, your father decided to put Casanova in a safe place for a while, and take another parrot with him to the mountain cabin."

"Good heavens, why?" Sabin asked. "The *parrot* wasn't in any danger, was he?"

Mason shrugged his shoulders and said, "We haven't all the facts available as yet."

"If you'll permit me to make a suggestion," Waid said, "it seems that the parrot most decidedly was *not* in any danger. The person who murdered Mr. Sabin was especially solicitous about the welfare of the parrot."

Mason said, *"Peculiarly* solicitous, would be a better word, Waid . . . Well, I must be going. I have quite a few irons in the fire. You'll hear from me later on."

Sabin followed him to the door. "I'm particularly anxious to have this cleared up, Mr. Mason."

Mason grinned. "So am I," he said. "I'll have photostatic copies made of this divorce decree and then we'll chase down the court records."

CHAPTER SIX

MASON was two blocks from the office building which contained his office and that of the Drake Detective Agency, when his car was suddenly enveloped in the red glare of a police spotlight. A siren screamed him over to the curb.

Mason stopped his car and frowned across at the police automobile being driven by Sergeant Holcomb. "Well," he asked, "what's the excitement?"

Holcomb said, "A couple of gentlemen want to talk with you, Mason."

Sheriff Barnes opened the door in the rear of the car, and was followed by a closely coupled man, some ten years younger, who pushed his way across to Mason's car, and instantly assumed the conversational lead. "You're Mason?" he demanded.

Mason nodded.

"I'm Raymond Sprague, the district attorney from San Molinas."

"Glad to know you," Mason told him.

"We want to talk with you."

"What about?" Mason asked.

"About Helen Monteith."

"What about her?" Mason inquired.

"Where is she?"

"I don't know," Mason told him.

Sheriff Barnes said, "We'd better go some place where we can talk it over."

"My office is within a couple of blocks," Mason pointed out.

"And the Drake Detective Agency is in the same building, isn't it?" Sprague inquired.

"Yes."

"You were on your way there?" Sprague asked.

"Does it," Mason inquired, "make any particular difference?"

"I think it does," Sprague told him.

"Well, of course," Mason remarked, "I have no means of knowing just what you have in mind."

"That isn't answering my question," Sprague said.

"Were you asking a question?"

Sheriff Barnes interposed. "Now, wait a minute, Ray," he said. "That's not getting us anywhere," and, with a significant glance toward the curious pedestrians, who had gathered on the sidewalk, "It isn't doing the case any good. Let's go up to Mason's office."

Mason kicked out the clutch and snapped the car into low gear. "I'll see you there," he said.

The others jumped into the police car, followed closely behind, until Mason had parked his machine. They rode up in the elevator with him and entered his private office. When Mason had switched on the lights and closed the door, Sergeant Holcomb said, "Don't say I didn't warn you birds about this guy."

71

"You didn't warn me," Raymond Sprague said, "you warned the sheriff."

"Just what," Mason asked, "is the beef about?"

"What have you done with Helen Monteith?"

"Nothing," Mason said.

"We think differently," Sprague announced.

"Suppose you tell me what you think," Mason said.

"You've had Helen Monteith take a powder."

Mason faced them, his feet spread far apart, his shoulders squared, his hands thrust into the side pockets of his coat. "All right," he said, "let's get this straight. I'm representing Helen Monteith. I'm also representing Charles Sabin. I'm trying to solve the murder of Fremont C. Sabin. I'm being paid money by my clients for doing just that. You gentlemen are being paid money by your county for solving the same murder I'm trying to solve. Naturally, you're going to solve it your way, and, by the same token, I intend to solve it mine."

"We want to question Helen Monteith," Sprague said.

Mason met his eyes squarely. "Go ahead and question her, then."

"Where is she?"

Mason pulled his cigarette case from his pocket and said, "I've told you once I don't know. You're running this show, I'm not."

"You wouldn't want me to charge you with being an accessory after the fact, would you?" Sprague asked ominously.

"I don't give a damn what you charge me with," Mason told him. "Only, if you want to talk law, remember that I can't be an accessory after the fact, unless I give aid to the murderer. Now then, do you intend to claim that Helen Monteith is the one who committed the murder?"

Sprague flushed and said, "Yes."

Sheriff Barnes interposed a drawling comment. "Now wait a minute, Ray, let's not get our cart before our horse."

"I know what I'm doing," Sprague said.

Mason turned to Sheriff Barnes and said, "I think you and I can get along, Sheriff."

"I'm not so certain," Barnes said, pulling a sack of tobacco from his pocket, and spilling rattling grains to the surface of a brown cigarette paper. "You have quite a bit to explain before I'll give you my confidence again."

"What, for instance?" Mason asked.

"I thought you were going to co-operate with me."

"I am," Mason told him, "to the extent that I intend to find out who murdered Fremont C. Sabin."

"We want to find out, too."

"I know you do. You use your methods. I'll use mine."

"We don't like having those methods interfered with."

"I can understand that," Mason told him.

Sprague said, "Don't waste words talking with him."

"If you birds want to charge him with compounding a felony, or being an accessory after the fact," Sergeant Holcomb said, "I'll take him into custody with the greatest of pleasure."

Mason struck a match and held it to Sheriff Barnes' cigarette, then lit his own. The conversation came to an abrupt standstill. After a few moments Mason said to Sprague, "Are you going to take him up on that, Sprague?"

"I think I am," Sprague snapped, "but I'm going to get some evidence first."

"I don't think you'll find much here in my office," Mason pointed out.

Holcomb said, "I'll take him down to headquarters, if you fellows say the word."

Sheriff Barnes turned to face them. "Now listen," he said, "you boys have been kicking me around because I gave Mason a break. I still don't see any reason why we should be stampeded into going off half cocked. Personally, I'm not going to get antagonistic until I find out a few things." He turned to Mason and said, "Did you know that the gun which killed Fremont C. Sabin was taken from a collection at the public library in San Molinas?"

"What if it was?" Mason asked.

"And the librarian, Helen Monteith, went through a marriage ceremony with a man who gave the name of George Wallman, and whom neighbors identify absolutely as being Fremont C. Sabin?"

"Go ahead," Sergeant Holcomb said sarcastically, "give him all the information you have, and when he gets done he'll laugh at you."

"On the contrary," Mason said, "I'm very much inclined to co-operate. Having gone that far, I presume you gentlemen have noticed that the caged parrot on the screen porch of Helen Monteith's little bungalow is Casanova, the parrot owned by Fremont C. Sabin, and that the parrot which was found in the mountain cabin is a parrot which Sabin had recently purchased from the Fifth Avenue Pet Shop in San Molinas?"

Sheriff Barnes' eyes widened for a moment, then narrowed. "You're giving us the straight goods on that?" he asked.

"Absolutely," Mason said.

"He's drawing a red herring across the trail," Sergeant Holcomb said disgustedly.

"If you knew all of that," Raymond Sprague said, "and *then* hid Helen Monteith where we couldn't question her, I think I *will* charge you with being an accessory."

"Go ahead," Mason invited. "As I remember the law, you'll have to charge that I concealed a principal in a felony case, with the intent that such principal might avoid or escape from arrest, trial, conviction or punishment, having knowledge that said principal had committed such felony, or had been charged with such felony. Now then, as I gather it, to date Helen Monteith hasn't been charged with the commission of any felony."

"No, she hasn't," Barnes admitted.

"And *I* don't think she has committed any felony," Mason said.

"Well, I do," Sprague told him.

"A mere difference of opinion," Mason observed; and then turned once more to Sheriff Barnes. "It may interest you to know, Sheriff," he said, "that the parrot in the cage on Helen Monteith's porch keeps saying, 'Put down that gun, Helen . . . don't shoot . . . My God, you've shot me.' "

The sheriff's face showed his interest. "How do you account for that?" he asked.

"I don't," Mason said. "Of course, the obvious way to account for it is that the parrot was present when someone named Helen threatened someone with a gun, and then, after being told to drop the gun, fired a shot, which took effect. However, the shooting took place, not in Helen Monteith's bungalow, but in a mountain cabin some miles away, while, apparently, the parrot on Helen Monteith's porch wasn't present at the shooting."

"Just what are you getting at?" Sheriff Barnes inquired.

"I'm trying to co-operate with you," Mason told him.

"Well, we don't want your co-operation," Sprague told him. "It's quite evident to me that you've gathered a great deal of information from questioning Helen Monteith. Now, I'm going to give you twenty-four hours to produce her. In the event you fail to do so, I'm going to have you brought before the Grand Jury at San Molinas."

"Better make it twelve hours," Sergeant Holcomb suggested.

Sprague hesitated a moment, then looked at his watch and said, "You have her in San Molinas for questioning before the Grand Jury by noon tomorrow. Otherwise, you'll take the consequences."

He nodded to Sergeant Holcomb, and they started for the door. Mason caught Sheriff Barnes' eye and said, "Going, Sheriff, or do *you* want to stay?"

Sheriff Barnes dropped easily into the overstuffed leather chair and said, "Don't go just yet, Ray."

"We're not getting anywhere here," Sprague objected.

"I am," the sheriff said, puffing calmly at his cigarette.

Mason seated himself on one corner of his big office desk. Sprague hesitated a moment, then walked across to a chair. Sergeant Holcomb, making no attempt to conceal his disgust, stood by the door leading to the corridor.

Mason said to Sheriff Barnes, "Rather a peculiar situation developed out at Sabin's house. It seems that Mrs.

Sabin and Fremont C. Sabin entered into an agreement by which she was to pretend to take a round-the-world trip, double back by Clipper ship to the coast, go to Reno, establish a residence, and get a divorce, taking pains to avoid any publicity whatsoever. Having done that, she was to receive, in full payment of any claims she might have as the wife of Fremont C. Sabin, the sum of one hundred thousand dollars in cash."

"She wasn't in Reno. She was on a boat coming through the Panama Canal, when we located her," Sprague said. "That Reno business is some sort of a pipe dream."

"Perhaps it is," Mason admitted, "but Richard Waid met her in New York on Wednesday the seventh. She gave him a certified copy of a decree of divorce, and he gave her one hundred thousand dollars, and holds her receipt for it. That's the important business which took him to New York."

"What are you getting at, Mason?" Sheriff Barnes asked.

"Simply this," Mason said. "The decree was dated on Tuesday the sixth. If a divorce decree was granted *before* Sabin was murdered, his widow received one hundred thousand dollars after his death, in accordance with an agreement which had been entered into. But, if Sabin was murdered *before* the divorce decree was granted, then the divorce decree was invalid, Mrs. Sabin has received one hundred thousand dollars in cash, and is also entitled to take a share of the estate as the surviving widow of the decedent. That's rather an interesting, and somewhat complicated, legal point, gentlemen."

Sergeant Holcomb said wearily, "Listen. Helen Monteith married Sabin. She didn't know he was married. She thought his name was Wallman, but she went up to that cabin with him. We traced those clothes through the laundry mark. They were hers. She'd found out he was married. She figured he'd been taking her for a ride. She made up her mind she was going to call for a showdown. She wanted a gun, and she wanted one right away. She couldn't get into a store to get a gun, but there was a collection of weapons in the library. She had a key to that collection. She picked out a gun, intending to return it to the collection. Perhaps she only wanted to run a bluff, I don't know. Perhaps it was self-defense. I don't know and I don't care. But she took that gun up to the cabin and killed Fremont C. Sabin.

"She ran to Mason to represent her. He's found out stuff which he could only have found out after having talked with her. She told her sister she was going to Sabin's residence and talk with the son. Apparently, she never showed up at the residence. Mason was there. He went out there with his secretary. He comes back alone. Where's his secretary? Where's Helen Monteith?

"You start questioning him, and he starts drawing Mrs. Sabin across the trail as a red herring. He'll get you more red herrings as fast as you fall for them."

A peculiar knock sounded on the corridor door. Mason slid to his feet, walked across the office, and opened the door. Paul Drake, on the threshold, said, "Well, Perry, I've . . ." and broke off as he saw the people gathered in the room.

"Come in, Paul," Mason said. "You know Sergeant Holcomb, of course, and this is Sheriff Barnes of San Molinas, and Raymond Sprague, the district attorney of San Molinas. What have you found out?"

"Do you," Drake asked, "want me to report here?"

"Sure," Mason told him.

"Well, I've been burning up the long distance telephone and getting operatives on the job. As nearly as I can tell right now, Mrs. Sabin sailed to Honolulu, took the Clipper ship back from Honolulu, went to Reno, and stayed at the Silver City Bungalows, establishing a residence under the name of Helen W. Sabin. At the end of six weeks she probably filed suit for divorce against Fremont C. Sabin, but I can't get into the courthouse records until tomorrow morning. On the evening of Wednesday the seventh, Mrs. Sabin was in New York. She sailed from New York at midnight."

"Then she was in Reno until when?" Mason asked of the detective.

"As nearly as we can find out, she took the plane from

Reno on the evening of Tuesday the sixth and arrived in New York on the seventh."

"Then the divorce decree must have been granted the morning of the sixth," Raymond Sprague said.

"It would look that way," Drake told him.

Sprague nodded and said, "She must have been in court on the sixth."

"What are you getting at?" Sheriff Barnes inquired.

"I'm just checking up," Sprague told him. "Mason has defeated his own purpose."

"How do you mean?" Barnes asked.

"Simply this," Sprague said. "Mason's trying to distract our attention from Helen Monteith by dangling Mrs. Sabin in front of our noses, but if she was in court in Reno, she could hardly have been killing her husband in a mountain cabin in San Molinas County at one and the same time. Regardless of what other things the woman may have done, she couldn't have been concerned in the murder."

Mason stretched his arms above his head and sucked in a prodigious yawn. "Well, gentlemen," he observed, "at least *I'm* putting *my* cards on the table."

Raymond Sprague walked across to the door. "I think," he said, "we're fully capable of making our own investigations. As far as you're concerned, Mason, you heard my ultimatum. You either have Helen Monteith before the Grand Jury at San Molinas at twelve o'clock tomorrow, or *you'll* go before the Grand Jury."

Sheriff Barnes was the last to leave the office. He seemed reluctant to go. In the corridor he said in an undertone, "Aren't you acting a bit hasty, Ray?"

The district attorney's answer was a rumbling undertone, drowned by the slamming of the door.

Mason grinned at Paul Drake and said, "Well, Paul, that's that."

"Are you keeping Helen Monteith out of sight somewhere?" Drake asked.

Mason smiled at him and said, "I don't have the slightest idea, Paul, where Helen Monteith is."

"My man reported that you picked her up out at Sabin's residence, and that she and Della Street drove off in her car."

Mason said, "I trust the man who made that report to you won't do any talking to outsiders, Paul."

"He won't," Drake said. "What are you going to do about having her before the Grand Jury in San Molinas, Perry?"

"I can't get her there," Mason said. "I don't know where she is."

"Della does."

"I don't know were Della is."

"Well," Drake told him, "it's your funeral."

"How about that wire tapping?" Mason asked. "What have you found out about it?"

"Not a darned thing," Drake confessed. "And the more I dig into it, the less I know."

"Some of the gambling element," Mason asked, "wanting to get a line on what's happening in this vice crusade?"

"Not a chance," Drake told him.

"Why not?"

"The gamblers aren't worried."

"Why?"

"Because they aren't. They're too strongly entrenched."

"That Citizens' Committee was digging up a lot of evidence," Mason said.

"Not evidence that would convict anybody of anything. Just evidence that gives rise to a lot of suspicion. Gamblers, and all forms of organized vice, figure on that stuff, Perry. Every so often there's a clean-up and a shakedown. Some of the small fry try to fight back. They struggle against the stream. The big fish don't; they just drift along with the current and wait for the police to clear things up."

"The police?" Mason asked.

"Sure," Drake said. "Figure this, Perry. Whenever there's a recognized vice district, or open gambling, there's police graft. That doesn't mean all of the policemen are in on it. It means *some* of the policemen are, and it means some of the higher-ups are. Whenever there's a squawk, the big shots in the vice game simply sit back and say to their cronies on the police force, 'Okay, you birds tell us when it's safe to open up again. In the meantime, we're both losing income, so you'd better hurry.' "

"Then you don't think the big-shot gamblers were trying to listen in on Sabin's telephone conversations?"

"Not one chance in a hundred. They just pulled in their horns and took a vacation . . . To tell you the truth, Perry, it looks more like a private job to me."

"You mean private detectives?"

"Yes."

"Employed by whom?" Mason asked.

"Mrs. Sabin, on a hunch," Drake told him. "Taken by and large, Perry, that woman doesn't seem to me to be exactly dumb."

"No," Mason admitted, "her mother didn't raise many foolish children . . . You have your car, Paul?"

"Yes. Why?"

"I have a job for you."

"What is it?"

"You're going with me," Mason told him, "and we're making a rush trip to San Molinas."

"What for?" Drake wanted to know.

"We're going to steal a parrot," Mason said.

"Steal a parrot?"

"That's what I said."

"You mean Casanova?"

"Yes."

"What the devil do you want with *him?*"

Mason said, "Get right down to brass tacks, Paul, and what do you have? You have a case which entirely revolves around a parrot. Casanova is the key clew to the whole affair. Notice that whoever killed Sabin was particularly solicitous about the welfare of the parrot."

"You mean that it was someone who loved the parrot, or was tender-hearted about birds in general?"

Mason said, "I don't know yet exactly *what* the reason was. However, I'm commencing to have an idea. Notice, moreover, Paul, that lately Casanova says, 'Put down that gun, Helen . . . don't shoot . . . My God, you've shot me.' "

"Meaning that Casanova must have been the parrot

which was present when the shots were fired?" Drake asked. "And that whoever committed the murder took Casanova away, and subsequently substituted another parrot?"

"Why," Mason asked, "would a murderer do that?"

"To tell you the truth, Perry, I don't know. That parrot angle sounds goofy to me."

"Well," Mason said, "any explanation which has been offered to me so far sounds goofy; but my best hunch is that that parrot offers the key to the situation. Now, Helen Monteith isn't home. The sheriff and the district attorney of San Molinas County are wandering around here trying to chase down developments at this end, with the help of Sergeant Holcomb. It *should* be an excellent time to raid San Molinas."

"If they catch you cutting corners in that county, you're going to jail," Drake warned.

"I know it," Mason admitted, grinning, "and that's why I don't want to be caught cutting corners. If you have your car here, let's go."

"You going to lift cage and all?" Drake asked.

"Uh-huh," Mason said, "and I'm going to put another parrot in place of the one that's there."

He picked up his telephone, dialed a number, and after a moment said, "Hello, Helmold, this is Perry Mason, the lawyer. I'd like to get you to run down to your pet store and open the place up. I want to buy a parrot."

CHAPTER SEVEN

THE parrot, in the back of the car, squawked from time to time slumberous noises of parrot protest as the lurching of the car forced him to fight for his balance.

Drake, at the wheel, seemed particularly pessimistic as to the probable outcome of their mission, while Mason, settled comfortably back against the cushions, smoked cigarettes and stared in meditative silence at the unwinding ribbon of moonlit road which flashed past beneath the headlights of the speeding car.

"Don't overlook the fact that Reno isn't so very far away—not by airplane," Drake said. "If Mrs. Sabin was in Reno, and *if* she was the one who employed private detectives to tap Sabin's telephone line, then you'd better forget this Monteith woman."

"How much do you charge for tapping telephone wires?" Mason asked.

Drake was sufficiently startled to take his eyes momentarily from the road. *"Me?"* he asked.

"Uh-huh."

Drake said, "Listen, Perry, I'll do darn near anything for you, but tapping a telephone line is a felony in this state. I'm certainly not going to do *that* for you."

"That's what I figured," Mason observed.

"What're you getting at?" Drake wanted to know.

"Simply this, Paul; those telephone lines were tapped. *You* don't think the gamblers did it. It doesn't look as though the police did it. You think a private detective agency did it. It's my guess a detective agency would think twice before it went in for wire-tapping."

"Some of 'em would," Drake said, "some of 'em wouldn't. There are some chaps in this game who would do anything for money. However, I get your point, Perry, and you *may* be right. Remember this, that most of the wire-tapping these days is done by the police."

"Why the police?" Mason asked.

"Oh, I don't know. Of course, they figure that laws don't apply to them. You'd be surprised to know how extensively they do tap telephone lines and listen in on conversations. It's almost a matter of investigative routine."

"Well, it's an interesting subject for speculation," Mason agreed. "If the telephone lines were tapped by the police, Sergeant Holcomb must have known about it. And if that's the case, the police must have records of the conversations which took place over that telephone . . . You check up on those divorce records first thing in the morning, Paul."

"I'm going to," Drake said. "I have two men waiting in

Reno. They're going through the records just as soon as they become available."

They drove for several miles in thoughtful silence, until a sign announced the city limits of San Molinas.

"Want to go directly to Helen Monteith's house?" Drake asked.

"Make certain we're not being followed," Mason said, sliding around in the seat so he could look through the back window.

"I've been checking pretty carefully on that," Drake told him.

"Well, make a figure eight, just for the sake of being absolutely certain," Mason said.

When Drake had completed the maneuver, Mason nodded his satisfaction. "Okay, Paul, drive right to the bungalow."

"That's rather a snoopy neighbor," Drake observed thoughtfully. "We'd better switch out the lights a block or so before we get to the house . . . How about parking a few doors away, Perry?"

"No," Mason said, "I want to make it fast. You can drive around the block once, and I'll size up the situation, then switch off your lights, and swing in to the curb as near the screen porch as you can make it . . . I hope this damned parrot doesn't squawk when I start moving him."

"I thought parrots slept at night," Drake said.

"They do," Mason told him. "But when they're being dragged around the country in automobiles, they get nervous—and I don't know how much of a squawk Casanova will make when I steal *him*."

Drake said, "Now listen, Perry, let's be reasonable about this thing. If anything goes wrong, don't get pigheaded and keep trying to make the switch. I'll be all ready to make a getaway. For God's sake, drop that parrot and make a run for it."

"I don't think anything will go wrong," Mason told him, "—not unless the house is being watched, and we should be able to find that out by swinging around the block."

"Well, we'll know in a minute," Drake said, turning the

wheel sharply to the left. "We're within two blocks of the place now."

He ran two blocks and swung once more to the left. Mason sized up the bungalow as they glided past. "The house is dark," he said. "There are lights in the house next door, and lights across the street. The screen porch looks easy."

Drake said, "Maybe you think it won't be a relief to me when this is over, Perry."

He circled the block, swung in to the curb, with lights out and motor off.

Mason glided out of the car, the cage and the parrot in his hand, and vanished into the shadows. He found it a simple matter to cut the screen, snap back the catch on the screen door and effect an entrance to the porch. The parrot he had brought with him was restive, moving about on the perch in the cage, but Casanova, apparently drugged with sleep, barely stirred when Mason gently lowered the cage from its hook, and substituted the cage he had brought with him.

A few moments later, Mason had deposited Casanova in the back of the automobile. "Okay, Paul," he said.

Drake needed no signal. He lurched the car into motion, just as the door of the adjoining house opened and the ample figure of Mrs. Winters stood framed in the doorway.

As Paul Drake skidded around the corner, with the lights out, the parrot in the back of the car mumbled sleepily, "My God, you've shot me."

CHAPTER EIGHT

MASON unlocked the door of his private office, and then suddenly stood motionless, staring in surprise at Della Street.

"You!" he exclaimed.

"None other," she told him, blinking back tears. "I guess you'll have to get a new secretary, Chief."

"What's the matter, Della?" he asked, coming toward her solicitously.

She started to cry then, and he slid his arm around her shoulders, patting her reassuringly. "What happened?" he asked.

"That t-t-t-two-timing little d-d-d-devil," she said.

"Who?" Mason asked.

"That librarian, Helen Monteith."

"What about her, Della?"

"She slipped one over on me."

"Come on over here; sit down and tell me about it," Mason said.

"Oh, Chief, I'm so d-d-darned sorry I let you down!"

"How do you figure you let me down, Della? Perhaps you didn't let me down as much as you think."

"Yes, I did too. You told me to keep her where no one could find her, and . . ."

"What happened?" Mason asked. "Did they find her, or did she take a run-out powder?"

"She took a p-p-p-powder."

"All right, how did it happen?"

Della Street dabbed at her eyes with a lace-bordered handkerchief. "Gosh, Chief, I hate to be a b-b-bawl-baby," she said. ". . . Believe it or not, this is the first tear I've shed. . . . I could have wrung her neck with my bare hands. . . . She started in and told me a story that tore my heart inside out."

"What was the story?" Mason asked, his face without expression.

"It was the story of her romance," Della said. "She told it. . . . Oh, Chief, you'd have to be a woman to understand. . . . It was all about her life. She'd been romantically inclined when she was young. There'd been a high school, puppy-love affair, which had been pretty serious with her. . . . But it hadn't been so serious with the boy . . . that is, it had at the time, Chief. I don't know if you can get the sketch, I can't tell it to you the way she told it to me.

"This boy was just an awfully nice boy. She made me see him just the way she saw him—a nice, clean, decent chap, with something of the mystic, or spiritual, in him . . . something that a woman really wants in every man she loves, and this was a real love affair.

"Then the boy went away to get a job, so he could make enough money to marry her, and she was all thrilled with pride. And then, after a few months, he came back, and . . ."

". . . And he was in love with someone else?" Mason asked as she hesitated.

"No, it wasn't that," Della said. "He was still in love with her, but he'd become sort of smart-alecky. He looked on her as something of a conquest. He wasn't in such a hurry to get married, and he'd been running around with a crowd of boys that thought it wasn't smart to have ideals. They had a sophisticated attitude, and . . . well, I'll never forget the way she described it. She said the acid of their pseudo-realism had eaten the gold off his character and left just the base metal beneath."

"So then what happened?" Mason asked.

"Then she naturally became bitter—toward men and toward love. At a time when most girls were seeing the world through rose-tinted spectacles, she was embittered and disillusioned. She didn't care too much for dances, and parties, and things, and gradually became more and more interested in books. She said she formed her friendships among books; that books didn't tease you along until they'd won your friendship, and then suddenly reverse themselves and slap you in the face.

"Along about that time, she acquired the reputation of being narrow-minded and strait-laced, and a poor sport. It started in with a few fellows whose vanity was insulted because she wouldn't drink bathtub gin, and neck. They advertised her as an awful pill, and gradually that reputation stuck to her. Remember, Chief, she was in a small town. It's pretty hard for people to really see each other in a small town. They only see the reputation which has been built up by a lot of word-of-mouth advertising."

"Was that the way she described it?" Mason asked.

Della Street nodded.

"All right, go ahead. Then what happened?"

"Then, when she'd just about given up any idea of

romance, along came Fremont Sabin. He was kindly and gentle, he wasn't greedy. He had a philosophy of life which saw the beautiful side of everything. In other words, Chief, as nearly as I can explain it, there was something of the idealism in this man that she had worshiped in this boy with whom she'd been in love. But, whereas the boy had the ideals of youth, and they weren't strongly enough entrenched in him to withstand the cynicism and cheap worldly wisdom of his associates, this man had battled his way through every disillusionment life had to offer, and won his idealism as an achievement, as an ultimate goal. His ideals stood for something—they were carefully thought out. They'd stood the test of time."

"I guess," Mason said thoughtfully, "Fremont C. Sabin was really a wonderful character."

"Apparently he was, Chief. Of course, he played an awful trick on her, but . . ."

"I'm not so certain he did," Mason said. "We can look at the thing from Sabin's viewpoint, and see just what he was trying to do. When you get the whole picture in its proper perspective, and in the light of some new evidence we've uncovered, it's quite consistent with his character."

"Can you tell me about this new evidence, Chief?"

"No, you tell me about Helen Monteith first."

"Well, this man started coming to the library. She knew him only as Wallman, a man who was out of work, a man who had no particular trade, and no particular cause to feel friendly toward the world; yet he did. He was interested in books on philosophy and social reform, and he was particularly interested in his fellowmen. He'd sit in the library, sometimes at night, apparently reading a book, but in reality studying the men who were seated around him. And then, whenever he had an opportunity, he'd get acquainted, in an unostentatious manner, and listen. He was always listening.

"Naturally, Helen Monteith, as a librarian, watched him and became interested in him. He started talking to her. Apparently, he had quite a knack of drawing people out, and he got her to tell him a great deal about herself before she realized how much she actually was telling him. And then she fell in love. Because the man was older than she, and because she hadn't been anticipating anything of the sort, romance sneaked up on her and caught her unaware. She was madly in love with him before she even realized she *was* in love. And then when she found out that he loved her . . . Well, Chief, as she told me about it, she said it felt as though her soul was singing all the time."

"She must have something of a gift for expression," Mason said, his eyes narrowing slightly.

"No, Chief, it wasn't an act she was putting on. She was absolutely sincere. She loves to talk about it, because it was such a beautiful thing with her. Despite the shock of the tragedy, and all the disillusionment which has come with finding out he was married, she's still happy and philosophical about it all. She feels that she finally found happiness in her life. The happiness didn't last, but she doesn't seem to feel bitter about that, but, instead, is grateful for the measure of happiness she did have. Of course, when she read the morning paper about the murder, about how Sabin would go around using an assumed name, studying people, browsing in libraries . . . Well, of course, that made her suspicious. Then she saw the photograph of this mountain cabin and recognized it. But she fought against her fears, trying to convince herself against her better judgment. . . . And then the afternoon paper carried the picture of Sabin, and her worst fears were confirmed."

"Then you don't think she killed him?" Mason asked.

"Absolutely not," she said. "She couldn't . . . Well . . ."

"Why the doubt?" Mason asked, as her voice trailed off into silence.

"Well," Della said, "there is this side to her character. If she had thought that he had been going to do something to hurt her . . . If she had thought that his ideals were going to . . . well, not exactly his ideals, either, Chief, but if she had thought that there was something about him which was counterfeit, I think she'd have killed him, in order to keep from discovering it, if you know what I mean."

"I think I do," Mason told her. "Go on, what happened?"

"Well, I took her to a little hotel. I went to some precautions to make certain we couldn't be traced by the police. I gathered that was what you wanted. I got some baggage out of my apartment, and we registered as two sisters from Topeka, Kansas. I asked the clerk a lot of questions that tourists would ordinarily ask, and I think I completely sold him on the idea.

"We had a corner room, in the back, with twin beds and a bath, and quietly, in such a manner that she wouldn't notice what I was doing, I locked the door from the inside and put the key in my purse.

"Well, we sat down and talked, and she told me all about her romance, and about everything which had happened. I guess we talked for three or four hours. I know it was long after midnight when we went to bed; and I guess it was about five o'clock this morning when she woke me up, shaking me and telling me she couldn't get the door open. She was fully dressed, and seemed very much upset.

"I asked her why she wanted to get the door open, and she said she had to go back to San Molinas, that she simply *had* to. There was something she'd forgotten.

"I told her she couldn't go back. She said she must, and we had quite an argument. Finally, she said she was going to telephone the hotel and have someone come up to open the door. Then I got hard with her."

"What did you tell her?" Mason asked.

"I told her that you were sacrificing a great deal to help her, and that she was giving you a double-cross; that she was in danger, and that the police would catch her and charge her with murder; that her romance would be written up by every sob sister in the tabloid newspaper game; that she'd be dragged through courts, and the pitiless white light of searching and unfavorable publicity would beat upon her. . . . I told her everything I could think of. I talked like a lawyer working on a jury."

"What happened?"

"She still wanted to go," Della Street said; "so then I told her that the minute she walked out of that door, you were finished with her, you wouldn't protect her in any way; that she was going to have to obey your orders, and stay there, until I could get in touch with you. She wanted to know when I could get in touch with you, and I told her I didn't know, not until after you got to the office at around nine-thirty; that I could get Paul Drake to give you a message. She wanted me to call your apartment directly, and I told her absolutely nothing doing, because I was afraid the police would be plugged in on your line, and because I thought you didn't want to know where she was, or have anything to do with her disappearance.

"Well, she thought that over for a while and decided it was reasonable. She said that was all right, she'd wait until nine-thirty, but made me promise, solemnly, that I'd try and get in touch with you then. She undressed and went back to bed, and said she was sorry she'd made such a scene. It took me about half an hour to get composed enough to drop off to sleep again. . . . And I woke up, and she was gone. . . . She'd deliberately planned that business about giving in just so she could double-cross me."

"She'd taken the key out of your purse?" Mason asked.

"Of course not," Della Street said. "I had that purse tucked under my pillow slip. She couldn't have possibly got that key without waking me up. She went down the fire escape. The window was open."

"You don't know what time she went?" Mason asked.

"No."

"What time did you wake up?"

"Not until after eight o'clock," she said. "I was pretty tired, and I figured we wouldn't have anything to do except be waiting, so I sort of set my mental alarm clock for around eight o'clock. I woke up and lay there for a while, thinking she was over on the other bed, and being grateful that she'd calmed down. I slipped out quietly from between the covers, so as not to awaken her, and started to tiptoe to the bathroom, and then looked over my shoulder, and saw that her bed looked rather strange. I went over for another look. She'd pulled the old stunt of wadding up some blankets and a pillow, and putting them under the covers, to make it look as though someone was asleep in the bed. . . . Well, Chief, that's all there is to it."

Mason held her close to him. "Don't worry, Della," he said. "You certainly did all anyone could have done. . . . Where did she go, do you know?"

"I think she was headed back for San Molinas."

"If she goes there," Mason said, "she'll put her neck in a noose."

"Well, I think she's done it. She's probably there by this time."

"What did you do," Mason asked, "when you found she was gone?"

"I telephoned Paul Drake's office right away and told them to get in touch with you. I tried to locate you myself, but couldn't find you anywhere."

"I went uptown for breakfast, and then stopped in at a barber shop," Mason told her.

"Well," she said, "I think Paul Drake's on the job. I finally got him personally, and explained to him what had happened, and told him to have his men in San Molinas try and pick her up and keep her out of sight."

"What did Drake say?" Mason asked.

"Drake," she said with a wan smile, "didn't seem over-ly enthusiastic. I guess I caught him before he'd had his morning coffee. He seemed to think that he'd be dragged up before the Grand Jury in San Molinas if he tried anything like that."

"Did you sell *him* on the idea?" Mason asked.

"I sold him," she said grimly, "but I had to get pretty tough with him, in order to do it. He . . ." She broke off, as Drake's code knock sounded on the door, and said, "There he is now."

Mason nodded to her, and she crossed the office toward the door, then turned and said, "My eyes are a sight; let him in, will you, and let me go splash some cold water on my face?"

Mason nodded. As she glided through the door into the law library, Mason opened the corridor door. "Hi, Paul," he said.

Drake's shoulders were slumped forward, his manner lugubrious. "H'lo, Perry," he said, walking across to the big leather chair, and sliding into it sideways in his favorite position.

"What's new?" Mason asked.

"Plenty," Drake said.

"Good, bad, or indifferent?" Mason asked.

"It depends on what you consider indifferent," Drake said, mustering a slow grin. "To begin with, Perry, your certified copy of the divorce decree is an absolute forgery, and *that* was a damned clever stroke of genius, good enough for a cool one hundred thousand bucks."

"You're certain?" Mason asked.

"Absolutely certain. Mrs. Sabin probably had some Reno lawyer helping her, but we'll never find out who it was, of course, because it's a slick scheme of obtaining money under false pretenses. They had the regular printed blanks all in proper form, the signature of the clerk, and the deputy, and quite apparently they managed to get a genuine imprint of the court seal. That *could* have been done, the clerk admits, by sneaking around behind the counter sometime when he was occupied, but they don't let every Tom, Dick and Harry go behind the counter; so, evidently, it was pretty carefully worked out in advance."

"Then there wasn't any case of Sabin *vs.* Sabin ever filed?"

"No."

"That," Mason said, "was clever. If it hadn't been for this murder, no one would ever have detected that forgery. A certified copy of a decree of divorce is accepted at face value everywhere. Unless there's some question of the pleadings, no one ever thinks of going back to look at the court records. What a sweet job that was. A cool hundred thousand, and still his legal wife! Of course, there's the forgery angle and obtaining money under false pretenses; but if it hadn't been for this murder, no one would ever have tumbled to it."

"Even as it is, she's doing pretty well for herself," Drake said. "She's the legal widow, and, as such, entitled to step in and take charge."

"All right," Mason said, "we'll skip that for a while. What's this about Helen Monteith?"

Drake made a wry grimace and said, "I wish you'd wash your own dirty linen, Perry."

"Why?" Mason asked.

"It's bad enough to *hold* your coat while you cut the legal corners," Drake said, "but when I find myself suddenly wished into the position of *wearing* your coat, it doesn't go over so big."

Mason grinned, offered a desk humidor to the detective, and helped himself to a cigarette. "Go on," he said, lighting up, "give me the works."

"Della called the agency about quarter past eight this morning, and was in an awful lather," Drake said. "She wanted to get in touch with me, and wanted to get in touch with you, and wanted operatives to watch for Helen Monteith in San Molinas. My agency got in touch with me, and I telephoned Della at the number she'd left. She was registered under the name of Edith Fontayne. She told me all about Helen Monteith taking a run-out powder, and how you wanted her kept away from the police, and for me to beat it down to San Molinas and pick her up, and keep her hidden out.

"I told her to get in touch with you.

"She said she didn't know where you were. I told her I'd try and find you, and that was every damn thing I *would* do. My gosh, here I was remonstrating with you last night about the chances *you* were taking in holding a fugitive from justice away from the sheriff and the district attorney, and then all of a sudden Della proposes that I stick *my* neck out on the same proposition. It was so hot that even you had to play it so you didn't know where she was. . . ."

"What did you finally do?" Mason interrupted.

"Do?" Drake groaned. "What the devil *could* I do? I did exactly what she wanted. My God, Perry, I've always been friendly with Della, and it's been sort of a give-and-take, informal relationship. I always felt she was my friend, but when I told her I had to draw the line some place, she became a regular little hellcat over the wire. She told me that if I wanted your business, I was to take care of it the way you wanted; that I should know damn well you wouldn't leave me out on the end of a limb, and that you'd never made a foolish move yet; that you wanted Helen Monteith kept away from the police, and . . ."

"Never mind what she told you," Mason said, grinning, "what did you do?"

"Took my medicine like a little man, got my operatives in San Molinas on the telephone, and told them to get out to Helen Monteith's house; to grab her as soon as she showed up, and rush her back to the city; to kidnap her, if they had to, or do anything else that was necessary. My operatives started arguing with me, and I had to read the riot act to them, and told them I'd take the responsibility."

"Well," Mason said, "where's Helen Monteith now?"

"In jail," Drake said gloomily.

"How come?"

"My operatives didn't get the message in time. She'd got out to the house about half an hour before they did. Evidently, the police had left word with Mrs. Winters to let them know as soon as Helen Monteith showed up. The sheriff and the district attorney went out there on the run. They nabbed Helen. She'd been killing parrots, burning papers, and trying to find some place to hide a box of forty-one caliber cartridges. . . . You can figure where that puts *her*."

"How about the parrot-killing?" Mason asked with interest.

"She went home and killed the parrot," Drake said. "Snickasneed its head off with a butcher knife—made a nice clean job of it, too."

"As *soon* as she got home?" Mason asked.

"I reckon so. The sheriff didn't tumble to it for a little while. They caught her red-handed with the forty-one caliber shells and stuff she'd been burning in the fireplace. The sheriff went to quite a bit of trouble trying to get something out of the ashes, but about all he could tell was she'd been burning paper. They hustled her out to jail and telephoned in for a technical man from the homicide squad here, to see what could be done about reconstructing the papers. . . . Sergeant Holcomb has been working hand and glove with 'em, you know."

"I know," Mason said. "What did she say about the forty-one caliber shells? Does she admit buying them?"

"I don't know," Drake said. "They hustled her off to jail, and that's all anyone knows."

"When did they find out about the parrot?"

"Not so very long ago," Drake said. "Sergeant Holcomb's men apparently discovered *that* when they went through the house. . . ."

"Wait a minute," Mason interpolated. "Couldn't the parrot have been killed *after* Helen Monteith was arrested?"

"Not a chance," Drake said; "they put the place under guard right after they'd pinched her. That was so no one could get in and remove any evidence. I think your friend, Helen Watkins Sabin, may have been back of that move. I understand they're going through the house with a magnifying glass, looking for additional evidence. They found out about the parrot, and my man telephoned in a report about fifteen minutes ago. . . . Perry, why the devil do you suppose she killed that parrot?"

"The murder of a parrot," Mason said, with his eyes twinkling, "is somewhat similar to the murder of a human being; that is, a person must look for a motive. Having found a motive, there must then be opportunity, and . . ."

"Nix on it, nix on it," Drake interrupted. "Cut the comedy, Perry. *You* know damn well why she killed that parrot. Now, *I* want to know why."

"What makes you think I know?" Mason asked.

"Phooey!" Drake exclaimed, "don't take me for such a simp. She wanted the parrot out of the way, and you wanted the parrot preserved as evidence of something or other. You knew she was going to kill that parrot if she had a chance, so you had Della keep Helen Monteith out of the way long enough for us to go down and substitute parrots. I suppose it was because of the cracks the parrot's making about 'Drop that gun, Helen' and 'My God, you've shot me,' but I still don't see why she didn't kill the parrot before, instead of waiting until she had to climb down a fire escape to do the parrot-butchering. . . . I admit that I thought last night you were trying to keep Helen Monteith concealed from the authorities, and I thought so this morning when Della Street rang up. I didn't realize until just now that what you were really trying to do was to keep her away from that parrot."

"Well," Mason said, "now that the parrot's dead, we might as well . . ."

"But the parrot isn't dead," Drake interrupted. "You have the parrot. I suppose that the parrot is a witness to something or other—probably the murder—but damned if I see how he could have been. Tell me, Perry, could a parrot be used as a witness in a court of justice?"

"I don't know," Mason said. "It's an interesting point, Paul. I'm afraid the oath couldn't be administered to a parrot. In other words, he *might* commit perjury."

Drake glanced sidelong at Mason and said, "Go ahead and joke all you want to, brother. I suppose if you don't want to tell me, there's nothing I can do to make you."

"What else do you know?" Mason asked, abruptly changing the subject.

"Oh, a few things," Drake said. "I've had a bunch of men working all night. I've been trying to find out as much as I could about that wire-tapping up there at the cabin. You know, it occurred to me, Perry, that I might find out something about the calls which had been listened in on, by getting a copy of the telephone bill. You see, that cabin line is on a local exchange, but Sabin wouldn't have been interested in maintaining a telephone to call any of his neighbors. All of his contacts were in the city, and, of course, they'd have to be handled as long distance calls."

"A good idea," Mason said. "You deserve credit for that, Paul."

"Credit, hell," Drake said lugubriously. "I deserve cash for it. When you get the bill, it's going to floor you, Perry. I've got men working on overlapping nine-hour shifts, and I've got 'em scattered all over the country."

"That's fine," Mason said. "How did you get the telephone bill, Paul?"

"One of the men took a chance," Drake said, "went down to the telephone office, said he was a 'detective,' and, because of the murder, wanted service discontinued on the telephone, and wanted to pay the bill. The girl in the local telephone office fell for it, and handed him the bill. He insisted on checking all the long distance charges."

"What did you find?" Mason asked.

"A few calls to his residence, here in the city," Drake said. "Those were evidently calls where he'd talked with his secretary. Several of them had been station-to-station calls, and quite a few of them had been for Richard Waid personally. But the interesting things, Perry, are the person-to-person Reno calls."

"The Reno calls?" Mason asked.

"Yes. Apparently he was in almost daily telephone communication with his wife in Reno."

"What about?" Mason asked.

"You've got me on that," Drake said. "Probably trying to make certain that the divorce was going through according to schedule, and that she'd be in New York with a certified copy of the decree."

Della Street, her face freshly powdered, eyes showing but little trace of tears, bustled busily into the office, and appeared surprised to see Paul Drake. "Hi, Paul," she said.

"Don't you 'Hi, Paul' me, you baggage," Drake grumbled. "Of all the high-pressure stuff I ever had handed me . . ."

She came over to where he was sitting on the chair, and put her hand on his arm. "Don't be such an old grouch-face," she laughed.

"Grouch-face nothing," he told her. "You put it up to me cold-turkey that I either had to go in for kidnapping or lose Mason's business."

"Well, Paul," she said, "I was trying to do what the Chief wanted—that is, what I thought he'd want under the circumstances."

Drake said to Mason, "You're bad enough. This girl is twice that bad."

Mason grinned at Della. "Don't talk with him this morning, Della, he's suffering from an ingrowing disposition."

"Did he get Helen Monteith?" she asked.

"No, the officers did," Mason told her.

"Oh!" she exclaimed in startled dismay.

"It's all right, Della," Mason said. "Ring up Sabin's residence, get Richard Waid or Charles Sabin, whichever one is available; say that I'd like to see both of them at the office at their earliest convenience."

He turned back to Paul Drake. "Have your men found out anything about where those forty-one caliber shells were bought, Paul?"

"Not *where* they were bought," Drake said, "but by this time the police sure have found out *who* bought 'em."

Mason dismissed it with a gesture. "Concentrate for a while on the Reno end of things, Paul. Find out as much as you can about what Mrs. Sabin did in Reno, and get me copies of the long distance telephone bill."

"Okay," Drake said, sliding from the chair, "and remember this, Perry Mason, the next time you duck out because things are getting too hot for *you* to handle, *I'm* going to duck out too. Being a stooge is all right, but being pushed up into the front-line trenches just when the machine guns start rattling, is a gray horse of another color."

CHAPTER NINE

IT WAS shortly after eleven when Charles W. Sabin and Richard Waid reached Mason's office. Mason wasted but little time in preliminaries. "I have some news," he said, "which may be of interest to you. As I told you last night, I had located Casanova. He was in the possession of a Helen Monteith, whom Fremont C. Sabin apparently married under the name of George Wallman. The parrot in her house was killed sometime either last night or early this morning. The theory of the police is that Helen Monteith killed him. The parrot had been saying re-

peatedly, 'Put down that gun, Helen . . . don't shoot. . . .
My God, you've shot me.'

"Now then," Mason went on, glancing from one to the
other, "does that mean anything to you?"

"It must mean the parrot was present at the time my
father was murdered," Sabin said. "Then Helen must
have . . . but which Helen?"

"But another parrot was found in the cabin," Mason
pointed out.

"Perhaps the murderer switched parrots," Waid ven-
tured.

Charles Sabin said, "Before we discuss that, I have
something of prime importance to take up with you."

"Go ahead," Mason told him, "we'll let the parrot
wait."

"I've found a will," Sabin announced.

"Where?"

"You remember it was disclosed that C. William Desmond acted as attorney for my father in connection with
certain matters pertaining to the divorce settlement. That
was news to me; I hadn't heard of it. It wasn't until Waid
told me that I knew anything about it.

"However, it seems that my father didn't care to have
Cutter, Grayson & Bright represent him in connection
with the divorce matter."

"And he had Desmond draw up a will at the same time
he made the property settlement agreement?" Mason
asked.

"Yes."

"What was the will?" Mason wanted to know.

Charles Sabin took a leather-backed notebook from his
pocket, and said, "I have made a copy of so much of the
provisions as relate to the distribution of his property. It
reads as follows:

" 'Because I have this day entered into an agreement
with my wife, Helen Watkins Sabin, by which it is agreed
and understood that she is to receive the sum of one
hundred thousand dollars in cash from me, by way of a
complete property settlement, and which said sum is to be
paid on the completion of divorce proceedings, and the

99

delivery of a certified copy of a final decree of divorce, I direct that, in the event I should die before said sum of one hundred thousand dollars is paid to my said wife, Helen Watkins Sabin, that then, and in such event, my said wife is to receive, from such estate as I may leave, the sum of one hundred thousand dollars in cash. In the event, however, said sum of cash has so been paid to the said Helen Watkins Sabin prior to the time of my death, I then intentionally make no other provision for her in this, my will, because the said sum of one hundred thousand dollars is ample to provide for her, and adequately compensate her for any claims she may have on my bounty, or to my estate.

" 'All of the rest, residue, and remainder of my estate, real, personal, or mixed, I give, devise, and bequeath, share and share alike, to my beloved son, Charles W. Sabin, who has, for years, maintained a commendable patience toward the vagaries of an eccentric man, who has ceased to regard the dollar as the ultimate goal of human endeavor, and to my beloved brother, Arthur George Sabin, who will probably not care to be made the object of my bounty.' "

Sabin glanced up from the notebook. "Suppose Dad died before the divorce was granted, does that," he asked, "have any effect on his will?"

"No," Mason said. "The way the will is drawn, Helen Watkins Sabin is completely washed up. Tell me about this brother."

"I don't know very much about Uncle Arthur," Charles Sabin said. "I have never seen him, but I understand, generally, he's something of an eccentric. I know that after Dad became wealthy, he offered Uncle Arthur an opportunity to come into the business, and Uncle Arthur indignantly refused it. After that, Dad visited him and became very much impressed with Uncle Arthur's philosophy of life. I think that something of my father's detachment from active business was due to the influence of Uncle Arthur, and I think that's what he means in his will. . . . Of course, you understand, Mr. Mason, that I want to make some independent provision for my father's widow?"

"You mean Helen Watkins Sabin?" Mason asked in surprise.

"No, I mean Helen Monteith, or Helen Wallman, or whatever her legal name is. Somehow, I regard her as being my father's widow, and much more entitled to recognition, as such, than the fortune hunter who hypnotized Dad into matrimony. Incidentally, Mr. Mason, Wallman is a family name. My own middle name is Wallman. That's probably why my father used it."

"Well," Mason said, "as it happens, Helen Monteith, as we may as well call her, is in custody in San Molinas. The authorities intend to charge her with the murder of your father."

Sabin said, "That's one of the things I want to talk with you about, Mr. Mason. I want to ask you, fairly and frankly, if *you* think she murdered my father."

Mason said, "I'm virtually certain that she didn't murder him, but there's some circumstantial evidence which she's going to have a hard time explaining away—in fact, she may never be able to do it, unless we uncover the real murderer."

"What evidence, for instance?" Sabin asked.

"In the first place," Mason said, "she has motivation. She'd been tricked into a bigamous marriage. Men have been killed for less than that. She had opportunity; and what's more, she had the weapon.

"That's the worst of circumstantial evidence. The prosecuting attorney has at his command all the facilities of organized investigation. He uncovers facts. He selects only those which, in his opinion, are significant. Once he's come to the conclusion the defendant is guilty, the only facts he considers significant are those which point to the guilt of the defendant. That's why circumstantial evidence is such a liar. Facts themselves are meaningless. It's only the interpretation we give those facts which counts."

"We've had some significant facts develop out at the house," Waid said, glancing across at Charles Sabin. "Did you intend to tell Mr. Mason about Mrs. Sabin and Steve?"

Sabin said, "Thank you, Richard, for calling it to my attention. After you left last night, Mr. Mason, Steve Watkins and his mother were in the mother's room in deep consultation. They left the house about midnight and haven't returned since. They didn't leave any word where they were going, and we haven't been able to locate them. The coroner at San Molinas had called an inquest for eight o'clock this evening, and the funeral is scheduled for tomorrow at two o'clock. Having Mrs. Sabin missing is, of course, embarrassing to the family. I consider her departure evidence of shocking bad taste."

Mason looked across at Waid. "Did you tell Sheriff Barnes and Sergeant Holcomb anything about this business you were transacting for Mr. Sabin in New York?"

"No, I only told them what I considered entered into the case. On this other matter, I didn't tell a soul until last night. Mrs. Sabin had browbeaten me into silence."

"You told the sheriff about receiving a telephone call from Mr. Sabin at ten o'clock at night?"

"Yes, of course. I felt that entered into the case and wasn't betraying any confidence."

"Did Mr. Sabin seem in good spirits when you talked with him?"

"In excellent spirits. I don't think I've ever heard his voice sound happier. Looking back on it now, of course, I can understand. He'd just received word that Mrs. Sabin was going to get the divorce decree the next day, and that gave him the chance to remarry Miss Monteith. Mrs. Sabin had evidently telephoned him and told him that the divorce was going through."

"Did you know that he was spending some time in San Molinas?" Mason asked.

"Yes, I did," Waid admitted. "I knew he was there quite a bit of the time. He telephoned to me several times from San Molinas."

"I knew that also," Charles Sabin interposed. "I didn't know what he was doing there, but Dad was peculiar that way. You know, he'd go into a community, completely lose his identity, take an assumed name, and just mingle with people."

"Have you any idea why he did it?" Mason asked. "That is, was he after anything in particular?"

"As to that, I couldn't say," Charles Sabin said. "Of course, in considering father's character, you must take into consideration certain things. He'd been a highly successful business man, as we judge standards of success; that is, he had amassed a comfortable fortune. He had nothing to gain by adding to his material wealth. I think he was, therefore, thoroughly ripe for some new suggestion. It happened to come through Uncle Arthur. Uncle Arthur lived somewhere in Kansas—at least he did two or three years ago, when father visited him; and I know that his philosophies made a profound impression on Dad. After Dad returned, he said that we were all too greedy; that we worshiped the dollar as the goal of our success; that it was a false goal; that man should concentrate more on trying to develop his character.

"You might be interested in his economic philosophy, Mr. Mason. He believed men attached too much importance to money as such. He believed a dollar represented a token of work performed, that men were given these tokens to hold until they needed the product of work performed by some other man, that anyone who tried to get a token without giving his best work in return was an economic counterfeiter. He felt that most of our depression troubles had been caused by a universal desire to get as many tokens as possible in return for as little work as possible—that too many men were trying to get lots of tokens without doing *any* work. He said men should cease to think in terms of tokens and think, instead, only in terms of work performed as conscientiously as possible."

"Just how did he figure the depression was caused, in terms of tokens?" Mason asked, interested.

"By greed," Sabin said. "Everyone was gambling, trying to get tokens without work. Then afterward, when tokens ceased to represent honest work, men hated to part with them. A man who had performed slipshod work in return for a token hated to part with that token in exchange for the products of slipshod labor on the part of another laborer. In other words, the token itself came to mean more than what it could be exchanged for—or people thought it did, because too many people had become economic counterfeiters."

"That's interesting," Mason said. "By the way, how many people lived in the house?"

"Only two of us, Mr. Waid and I."

"Servants?"

"One housekeeper is all. After Mrs. Sabin left for her world tour, we closed up virtually all the house, and let the servants go. I didn't realize why that was done at the time, but, of course, I understand now that Dad knew Helen Watkins Sabin wouldn't return, and was intending to close up the house."

"And the parrot?" Mason asked. "Did your father take the parrot with him on his trips?"

"Most of the time the parrot was with Dad. There were times when he left it home—with Mrs. Sabin, mostly. Incidentally, Mrs. Sabin was very much attached to the parrot."

Mason turned to Waid. "Did Steve have any motive for murder, any hatred of Mr. Sabin?"

"Steve himself *couldn't* have murdered Mr. Sabin," Waid said positively. "I know that Mr. Sabin was alive at ten o'clock Monday night, the fifth of September. Steve and I left for New York right after I'd received that telephone call. We didn't arrive in New York until late Tuesday afternoon. You see, there's a four-hour time difference, what with the difference in sun time and the additional hour of daylight saving time."

Mason said, "The certified decree of divorce, which Mrs. Sabin handed you in New York, was a forgery."

"Was *what?*" Waid exclaimed, startled.

"A forgery," Mason repeated.

"Look here, Mr. Mason, that decree was passed on by Mr. Sabin's New York attorneys."

"It was perfectly legal *in form,*" Mason admitted. "In fact, it was all worked out to the last detail, even the name of the clerk and the deputy. A very clever forgery—but nevertheless the document was forged."

"How did you find that out?" Sabin asked, highly excited.

Mason said, "I made it my business to investigate the court records. I gave a photostatic copy of the decree to a detective who flew to Reno. The case was purportedly a default matter, and handled in a routine manner. Much to my surprise, when I investigated, I found that there were no court records of any divorce."

"Good heavens," Charles Sabin said, "what did she expect to gain by that? She must have known she'd be discovered."

"On the other hand," Mason said, "under ordinary circumstances, no one would ever look back at a certified copy of a divorce decree. It would have been rather a safe forgery."

"But why did she want to rely on a forged document?" Sabin asked.

"I don't know," Mason told him. "There are several guesses. One of them is that there's some question as to the validity of her marriage to your father."

"But why should that have kept her from filing suit for divorce?" Waid asked.

"Because," Mason said, "regardless of the optimistic ideas of Fremont C. Sabin, there was bound to have been publicity. Newspapers keep highly trained investigators stationed at Reno for the purpose of scrutinizing divorce actions. They're particularly anxious to find out if any of the movie celebrities slip over to Reno for the purpose of getting a divorce under their true names, and without disclosing their Hollywood identities. Now if, perhaps, Helen Watkins Sabin had another husband living, from whom she'd never been divorced . . . well, she wouldn't have dared to risk the publicity. There was a hundred thousand dollars at stake—and that's a considerable stake."

Sabin said, "If there's anything illegal about that first marriage, then how about the marriage ceremony my father went through with Helen Monteith in Mexico?"

"Now," Mason said, with a grin, "you're getting into the *real* legal problem."

"What's the answer?" Sabin asked.

"That," Mason told him, "depends very much on what we can find out by examining Helen Watkins Sabin on the witness stand. Suppose, Mr. Sabin, you attend the inquest at San Molinas tonight. I think the sheriff will be broadminded enough to see that a complete investigation is made. Some interesting facts should be uncovered."

The telephone on Mason's unlisted private wire buzzed sharply. Mason picked up the receiver to hear Paul Drake's voice saying, "Are you busy right now, Perry?"

"Yes."

"Anyone there in connection with this case?"

"Yes."

"I think," Drake said, "you'd better arrange to meet me outside the office."

"That won't be necessary," Mason said. "The clients who are in the office are just finishing up their business. I'll see you in just a moment or two."

He hung up the telephone and extended his hand to Sabin. "I'm glad to learn about that will," he said.

"And you'll let us know if anything new . . . well, if you . . . I mean if you hear anything about Helen Watkins Sabin, let me know what she's doing, will you?"

"She's probably keeping under cover," Mason told him, "until she can find out what's going to be done about that forged decree of divorce."

"Not that woman," Charles Sabin said. "You'll never get *her* on the defensive. She's busy somewhere right now, stirring up a whole mess of trouble for us."

Mason ushered them out through the exit door. "Well," he said, with a smile, "at least she's energetic."

As his visitors turned the corner in the corridor, Mason stood in the door, waiting for Drake. The detective appeared within a matter of seconds. "Coast clear?" he asked.

"The coast is clear," Mason told him, ushering him into the room. "I've just had a session with Charles Sabin and Richard Waid, the secretary. What do you know, Paul?"

"You wanted the long distance telephone calls which had been put in from the cabin," Drake said. "Well, I've had men breaking down numbers into names. Here's what we find. The last call of which there's any record came through on the afternoon of Monday the fifth at about four o'clock. Now as I understand it, the secretary says that when Sabin called him at ten o'clock, he reported the telephone at the cabin was out of order. Is that right?"

Mason nodded.

"Well," Drake said, "if the telephone was out of order, Sabin couldn't put in any calls and couldn't send out any calls. Do you get what I mean?"

"No, I don't," Mason told him. "Go on and spill it."

"Well," Drake said. "Something happened to cause Sabin to send Waid to New York. We don't know what that something was. We don't know where the pay station was that Sabin telephoned from, but in all probability it was the nearest one to the cabin. We can tell more when we check up on calls; but suppose that it was twenty minutes or half an hour away from the cabin."

"What are you getting at?" Mason asked.

"Simply this," Drake said. "If the telephone was out of order from four o'clock on, and Sabin telephoned Waid to go to New York, Sabin must have received some information between the hours of four o'clock in the afternoon and probably nine-thirty at night which convinced him that Mrs. Sabin would be in New York on the evening of Wednesday the seventh to surrender a certified copy of the divorce decree and pick up the money.

"Now then how did he get that information? If the telephone was out of order, he couldn't have received it over the telephone. He evidently didn't have it at four o'clock. In other words, Perry, that information *must* have been obtained from someone who came to the cabin."

"Or sent Sabin a message," Mason said. "That's a good point, Paul. Of course, we don't *know* that the telephone went out of commission immediately after four o'clock."

"No," Drake said. "We don't, but on the other hand it's hardly probable that the telephone would have been in commission when Sabin received word that the divorce was going through all right and then gone out of commission as soon as he tried to telephone the news to Waid—which would have been immediately afterwards."

"You forget," Mason pointed out, his eyes narrowing

into thoughtful slits, "that the telephone line was tapped."

"By George, I do at that!" Drake exclaimed.

"Anything may happen on a tapped line," Mason said. "The wire-tappers could have thrown the telephone out of commission at a moment's notice, and may have done so."

"What would have been their object?" Drake asked.

"That," Mason said, "remains to be discovered."

"Well," Drake told him, "I thought you might be particularly interested in that four o'clock call because of what had happened."

"I am," Mason said. "Whom was it to?"

"To Randolph Bolding, the examiner of questioned documents."

Mason frowned. "Why the devil did Sabin want to ring up a handwriting expert?" he asked.

"You don't suppose he'd had a look at that certified decree of divorce and figured it was a forgery?" Drake asked.

"No," Mason said. "The decree wasn't dated until the sixth. If he'd seen it on the fifth, he'd have known it was a forgery."

"That's right," Drake admitted.

"Have you talked with Bolding?" Mason asked.

"One of my operatives did," Drake said, grinning, "and Bolding threw him out on his ear. Said that anything which had transpired between him and Sabin was a professional confidence. So I thought perhaps you'd better go down there, Perry, and talk him into being a good dog."

Mason reached for his hat. "On my way," he said.

CHAPTER TEN

RANDOLPH BOLDING had carefully cultivated an expression of what Mason had once described to a jury as "synthetic, professional gravity." His every move was calculated to impress any audience he might have with the fact that he was one of the leading exponents of an exact science.

He bowed from the hips. "How do you do, Mr. Mason," he said.

Mason walked on into the private office and sat down. Bolding carefully closed the door, seated himself behind the huge desk, smoothed down his vest, mechanically adjusted papers on the blotter, giving his visitor an opportunity to look at the enlarged photomicros of questioned signatures which adorned the walls.

Mason said abruptly, "You were doing some work for Fremont C. Sabin, Bolding?"

Bolding raised his eyes. They were bulging, moist eyes which held no expression. "I prefer not to answer that question."

"Why?"

"My relations with my clients are professional secrets— just as yours are."

Mason said, "I'm representing Charles Sabin."

"That means nothing to me," Bolding said.

"As Fremont C. Sabin's heir, Charles Sabin is entitled to any information you have."

"I think not."

"To whom *will* you communicate this information?"

"To no one."

Mason crossed his long legs and settled back in the chair. "Charles Sabin," he said, "wanted me to tell you that he thought your bill was too high."

The handwriting expert blinked his moist eyes several times in rapid succession. "But I haven't submitted one yet," he said.

"I know; but Sabin thinks it's too high."

"Well, what's that got to do with it?"

"Sabin," Mason said, "will probably be the executor of the estate."

"But how can he say my bill is too high when he doesn't know how much it is?"

Mason shrugged his shoulders. "That," he said, "is something you'll have to take up with Sabin. Of course, you know how it is, Bolding. If an executor approves the charge against the estate, it goes right through. If he doesn't approve it, then you have to bring suit to establish your claim. In case you don't know it, it's a long way to Tipperary."

Bolding gazed down at the blotter on his desk for several thoughtful seconds.

Mason stretched, yawned prodigiously, and said, "Well, I guess I'll be going. I've got lots of work to do."

"Wait a minute," Bolding said, as Mason rose to start toward the door. "That attitude isn't fair."

"Probably not," Mason agreed carelessly. "However, Sabin is my client and that's what he says. You understand how it is dealing with clients, Bolding. We have to follow our client's wishes and instructions."

"But it's so manifestly unfair," Bolding protested.

"I don't think it is," Mason said.

"You don't?"

"No."

"Why not?"

"Because," Mason told him, "you aren't submitting a bill to Fremont C. Sabin for anything you did for him personally, you're submitting a bill to the estate for things which were done to conserve the property during Sabin's lifetime . . . at least, I suppose that's the theory of it."

"That's the theory of it," Bolding agreed.

"Well," Mason said, "you haven't conserved anything."

Bolding flushed. "I can't help it if a man dies before he carries out his plans."

"No," Mason observed, "I daresay you can't. However, that would seem to be your loss, not ours. You've lost a client."

"But under the law, I'm entitled to recover compensation for my services. A thousand dollars is a most reasonable charge."

"Go right ahead," Mason told him, "and recover your compensation. I was simply giving you a friendly tip that Sabin thinks your charges are too high. He'll probably bring in a couple of the other experts, who have been waiting to take a rap at you, and have them testify that your fees are outrageous."

"Are you trying to blackmail me?" Bolding asked.

"Just warning you," Mason said.

"What do you want?"

"Me?" Mason asked, surprised. "Why *I* don't want anything."

"What does Sabin want?"

"I don't know," Mason told him. "You'll be getting in touch with Sabin when you present your bill. You can ask him then."

"I'll ask him nothing."

"Okay by me," Mason said. "Sabin thinks your charges are plain robbery. He says that whatever you did, you did for Mr. Sabin and not for the estate."

"I am doing it for the estate."

"I don't see how," Mason said.

"You'd have to understand what it was all about in order to see that," Bolding said.

"Doubtless," Mason admitted, "if I knew all the facts, I'd feel differently about it. Doubtless, if Sabin knew all the facts, he'd feel differently about it. You see, he doesn't know all the facts, and there's no likelihood he'll learn them—in time to do the estate any good."

"You're putting me in a very difficult position, Mason," Bolding said irritably.

Mason's voice showed surprise. "I am? Why, I thought you'd put yourself in it."

Bolding pushed back his swivel chair, crossed over to a steel filing case, unlocked the catch and angrily jerked the steel drawer open. "Oh, all right," he said, "if you're going to act that way about it."

Bolding opened the files and spread papers out on the desk. "Richard Waid," he said, "was Fremont C. Sabin's secretary. He held Sabin's power of attorney and had authority to sign checks up to five thousand dollars. Checks over five thousand dollars had to be signed by Sabin. I have in this file sixteen thousand five hundred dollars in forged checks. The checks are three in number, each is over five thousand in amount, and each purports to have been signed by Sabin. The forgeries were so clever the bank cashed them."

"How were they discovered?" Mason asked.

"Sabin discovered them when he audited his bank account."

"Why didn't Waid discover them?"

"Because Sabin had the habit of issuing checks from time to time without advising his secretary."

"Did Waid finally learn of these checks?"

"No, Mr. Sabin wanted it kept a closely guarded secret, because he thought it was a family matter."

"Just what," Mason asked, "do you mean by that?"

Bolding said, "Perhaps I can quote from Mr. Sabin's letter to me, and it will explain matters more clearly." He picked up a typewritten letter, turned over the first page and read from the second page:

" 'I suppose it will be difficult for you to detect any handwriting characteristics of the forger from the signature itself. However, it occurs to me that the payees are probably fictitious, that the endorsements on the back of the check will give you something on which to work. I am, therefore, enclosing herewith, in addition to the checks, a letter written to me by Steven Watkins. Inasmuch as this young man is the son of my wife, you can appreciate the importance of regarding the entire matter as most confidential. Under no circumstances must there be any newspaper publicity. The bank is sworn to secrecy. I am saying nothing at this end. Therefore, if there should be any disclosure, I will know that it was brought about through an indiscretion on your part.

" 'As soon as you have arrived at an opinion, please advise me by telephone. I will be in my mountain cabin at least by Monday, the fifth, and will remain there for several days.' "

"What conclusions did you reach?" Mason asked.

"The checks are clever forgeries. They are free-hand forgeries; that is, the signatures were dashed off at high speed by a competent and daring forger. There are no tremors in the signatures. The signatures were not traced. There is no evidence of the painfully laborious handwriting of the slow, clumsy forger who must rely upon tracing. Such signatures look quite all right to the naked eye, but under the microscope look quite different from the smooth, fast-flowing lines of a quickly executed signature such as these."

"I understand," Mason said.

"The forged signature *may* be the work of Steven Watkins, the young man whose handwriting was sent me by Mr. Sabin. I don't know. I am inclined to think the endorsements, however, were not made by young Watkins. In fact, they have all the earmarks of being genuine signatures, although they *may* have been fictitious."

"How were the checks cashed?"

"They were put through various banks for collection, in each instance by a person who opened an account, let it remain for a week or two, and then drew out the entire balance. The references, addresses, etc., in each instance were fabricated."

"And you don't think Watkins did it?"

"To be frank," Bolding said, "I do not . . . That is, the endorsements on the checks. As to the forgery of the signature, I cannot say."

"Did you so advise Mr. Sabin?"

"Yes."

"When?"

"On Friday, the second of September. He was in the city and called on me for a brief conference."

"Then what?" Mason asked.

"He said he would think it over and let me know."

"Did he?"

"Yes."

"When?"

"About four o'clock on Monday, September fifth. It was a holiday, but I happened to be in my office. Sabin caught me here on a long distance telephone call."

"Did he say where he was?"

"He said he was in his mountain cabin."

"What did he say?"

"He said, he'd been thinking over the matter of those forgeries and said he was sending me other handwriting specimens in a letter which he would mail that afternoon."

"Did you ever receive the letter?" Mason asked.

"No."

"Then you gather that he didn't mail it?"

"I think that's a reasonable inference."

"Do you know why he didn't mail it?"

"No. He may have changed his mind; he may have postponed it, or he may have entered into some transaction . . . perhaps some property settlement . . . which was conditioned upon the fact . . . Well, you may draw your own conclusions."

"What gives you that idea?" Mason asked.

"Certain circumstances which I am not at liberty to divulge."

Mason said, "Under the circumstances, Bolding, it would seem that your services have been of the greatest value to the estate. I would advise the executor to honor your bill."

Bolding said, without enthusiasm, "Thank you."

Mason said, "If you're in need of money, I might advance the money myself from my personal account and take payment of your claim in the regular course of administration."

Bolding said, "That would be most acceptable."

"Your bill was a thousand dollars?" Mason asked.

"Fifteen hundred," Bolding said.

"I would, of course, want to take possession of the documents in the case on behalf of the administrator," Mason said.

"That's understood."

Mason pulled out his checkbook, wrote a check for fifteen hundred dollars, scribbled an assignment of Bolding's bill on the back of the check, and passed it across to Bolding. "Your endorsement on the back of the check," he said, "will at once constitute a receipt for the amount of the money and an assignment of your claim against the estate."

"Thank you," Bolding said. He pocketed the check, took an envelope from the desk drawer, placed the checks and letters in it, and handed the envelope across to the lawyer. Then he arose, went to the door of the private office and held it open.

Mason heard the rapid, nervous *click . . . click . . .*

click of the high heels on a woman's shoes. He stepped back so that he was concealed behind the jamb of the door as he heard Helen Watkins Sabin say, "I bet you didn't think I was going to come back with the cash, did you, Mr. Bolding? Well, here it is, one thousand dollars, ten one-hundred-dollar bills. Now, if you'll give me a receipt, I'll take the documents and . . ."

Bolding said, "You'll pardon me, Mrs. Sabin, but would you mind going around to the other office. I have a client here."

"Oh, well," she said, "your client can go right on out. He doesn't need to mind me. You were standing there in the door to usher him out, so you can just usher me in."

She swept past Bolding into the office, and then suddenly whirled to face Perry Mason.

"You!" she said.

Mason bowed.

"What are you doing here?" she asked.

"Collecting evidence," Mason told her.

"Evidence of what?"

"Evidence of what may have been a motive for the murder of Fremont C. Sabin."

"Bosh," she said. "Mr. Bolding doesn't have any such evidence."

"You are familiar with what he has then?" Mason asked.

"I didn't come here to be cross-examined," she said. "I have some business to transact with Mr. Bolding, and I don't care to have you present at my conversation."

"Very well," Mason said, and bowed himself out into the corridor.

He had just reached the elevator when he heard a door open and close with a violent bang. He heard running feet in the corridor and turned to find Mrs. Sabin bearing down upon him with ominous purpose.

"You got those papers from Bolding," she charged.

"Indeed," Mason said.

"You boosted the ante five hundred dollars and took those documents. Well, you can't get away with it. You have no right to them. I'm Fremont's widow. I'm entitled to everything in the estate. Give me those papers at once."

"There is some doubt," Mason told her, "about just who will be settling up the estate. There is even some doubt about your being Fremont Sabin's widow."

"You tangle with me," she said, "and you'll be sorry. I want those papers, and I'm going to get them. You can save time by turning them over to me now."

"But I see no reason to save time," Mason told her, smiling coldly. "*I'm* not in a hurry."

Her eyes glittered with the intensity of her feeling. "You," she said, "are going to try to frame something on Steve. You can't make it stick. I'm warning you."

"Frame what on him?" Mason asked.

"You know perfectly well. Those forgeries."

Mason said, "I'm not framing anything on anybody. I'm simply taking charge of evidence."

"Well, you have no right to take charge of it. I'll take charge of it myself."

"Oh, no," Mason said, "I couldn't think of letting you do that. You might lose the forged checks. After all, this is rather a trying and exciting time, Mrs. Sabin. *If* you should mislay these checks and couldn't find them again, it would give the forger altogether too much of a break—particularly when we consider that the forger is, in all probability, the murderer."

"Bosh!" she said. "Helen Monteith murdered him! I found out all about her. However, I suppose you're quite capable of dragging Steve into it in order to save her, aren't you?"

Mason smiled and said, "Quite."

"Are you going to give me those checks?"

"No."

"You'll wish you had."

"By the way," Mason observed amiably, "the inquest is to be held tonight in San Molinas. I believe the sheriff has a subpoena for you, and . . ."

She stamped her foot. "It's just the same as larceny. I think there's a law covering that. All property belonging to the decedent . . ."

"Is a forged check property?" Mason asked.

"Well, I want them anyway."

"I gathered you did," Mason observed affably.

"Oh!" she exclaimed. "You . . . you . . . you . . ."

She launched herself at him, clawing at the envelope in the inside pocket of his coat. Mason pushed her easily aside and said, "That isn't going to get you anywhere, Mrs. Sabin."

A red light flashed as an elevator cage slid to a stop. Mason entered. "Coming, ma'am?" the elevator man asked Mrs. Sabin.

"No," she said, and turned on her heel to stride belligerently back toward the office of Randolph Bolding.

Mason rode down in the elevator and drove at once to a branch post office. He carefully sealed the envelope containing the forged checks and the various letters and addressed the envelope to Sheriff Barnes at San Molinas. He then placed postage stamps on the letter and dropped it in the mailchute.

CHAPTER ELEVEN

PERRY MASON, Della Street and Paul Drake rode three abreast in the front seat of Mason's car. The parrot was in the rear of the car, the cage partially covered with a lap robe.

Drake, looking at his wrist watch, said, "You're going to get there plenty early, Perry."

Mason said, "I want to talk with the sheriff and with Helen Monteith."

As Mason guided the car clear of the city traffic and hit the open highway, Drake said, "Well, it looks as though you had the right hunch on this divorce business, Perry. There's a pretty good chance Helen Watkins never was divorced from Rufus Watkins. We've found a witness who says Helen Watkins told her that she hadn't been divorced. That was two weeks before she started working for Fremont C. Sabin."

"Don't you suppose she got a divorce afterwards?" Mason inquired.

"I don't know, Perry, but I'm inclined to think she

didn't. You see, she was a resident of California. She couldn't leave in order to establish a residence elsewhere. If she'd secured a California divorce, she'd have had to wait a year for the interlocutory decree to become final, before she could have married again. That didn't suit her purpose at all. She had her hooks out for Sabin before she'd been working there three weeks."

"How about Rufus Watkins?" Mason asked. "Don't you suppose she could have arranged with him to get a divorce?"

"That," Drake said, "is the rub. She *may* have done so, but it looks as though she didn't do anything until after she'd married Sabin, and by that time Rufus was in a position to do a little fancy blackmail."

"Is that surmise?" Mason asked. "Or do you have some evidence to support it?"

"I can't tell just yet," Drake told him, "but it looks very much as though we had some evidence to support it. We got a tip that Helen Watkins Sabin's bank account showed quite a few checks payable to a Rufus W. Smith. We're trying to verify that, and find out about this Rufus W. Smith. We know that he answers the general description of Rufus Watkins, but we haven't as yet definitely established that they are one and the same."

Mason said, "That's good work, Paul. That gives us something to go on."

"Of course, Perry, there's quite a bit of stuff shaping up against Helen Monteith," Drake pointed out. "I understand, now, they've found a witness who saw her in the vicinity of the cabin about noon on the sixth."

"That," Mason admitted, "would be bad."

"Well, it may be just rumor," Drake said. "My operative in San Molinas picked it up."

Mason said, "We're going to go and see the sheriff as soon as we get there. He may be willing to put the cards on the table."

Della Street said, "Chief, she simply *can't* be guilty of murder. She *really* loved him."

"I know," Mason said, "but she certainly left a lot of circumstantial evidence hanging around loose . . . Incidentally, there's a nice legal point involved. If she actually *is* the widow of Fremont C. Sabin, then she inherits a share of his property, because the will is invalid as to her."

"How so?" Drake asked.

"A will," Mason said, "is revoked by the subsequent marriage of the testator. On the other hand, a will in which he makes no provision for his wife, and in which it appears that the omission was not intentional, is also subject to attack. The farther we go into this thing, Paul, the more possibilities it has."

They drove for several miles in thoughtful silence, then suddenly, from the back seat, came the hoarse voice of the parrot: "Put down that gun, Helen! Don't shoot! *Squawk. Squawk.* My God, you've shot me!"

Drake said, "We have two suspects in this case, both of them named Helen. Perry, if you introduce that parrot in evidence to show that Helen Watkins Sabin fired the shot, the district attorney will turn your own evidence against you to show that Helen Monteith did it."

Mason grinned, "That parrot may make a better witness than you think, Paul."

Sheriff Barnes had an office in the south wing of the old courthouse. Afternoon sunlight, beating through the windows, illuminated battered furniture, a floor covered with linoleum, which, in several spots, had been completely worn through. Bulletin boards on the wall were adorned with printed circulars of persons wanted for crime. Across from these posters, and on the wall on the opposite side of the room, were glass-framed display cases, in which various lethal weapons, which had figured in historic murder cases in the county, were on display.

Sheriff Barnes sat behind the old-fashioned roll-topped desk, in a dilapidated swivel chair, which squeaked monotonously as he teetered back and forth.

While Perry Mason talked, the sheriff slipped a plug of tobacco from his pants pocket, opened a knife, the blade of which had been rubbed thin through many sharpenings, and cut off a corner of moist, black tobacco.

When Mason had finished, the sheriff was silent for a few moments, rolling the tobacco over the edge of his tongue; then he shifted his steady, thoughtful eyes to the lawyer and said, "Those are all the facts you have?"

"That's a general summary of everything," Mason told him. "My cards are on the table."

"You shouldn't have done that about the telephone bill," the sheriff said to Paul Drake. "We had some trouble getting a duplicate telephone bill. It delayed things for us a little while."

"I'm sorry," Mason told him, "it was my fault. I'm assuming the responsibility."

The sheriff swung his weight slowly back and forth in the creaking chair. "What conclusions are you drawing?" he asked of Mason.

Mason said, "I don't think I'm ready to draw any conclusions yet. I'd like to wait until after the inquest."

"Think you could draw some then?"

"I think I could," Mason told him, "if I were permitted to question the witnesses."

"That's sort of up to the coroner, ain't it?" the sheriff asked.

"Yes," Mason said, "but it occurs to me the coroner might do what you suggested would be in the best interests of justice."

"I suppose he'd have to ask the district attorney about what he should do," the sheriff remarked musingly.

"In that event," Mason said, "we're sunk. That's why I said I didn't want to form any opinion from the evidence. Once a man forms an opinion, he starts interpreting facts in the light of that belief. He ceases to be an impartial judge of facts. That's what's happened to Raymond Sprague. He's come to the conclusion that I'm opposed to justice; that my tactics must necessarily be opposed to justice; that, therefore, he can best serve the ends of justice by blocking me at every turn. He's also come to the conclusion that Helen Monteith is guilty of murder; therefore, he interprets all the facts in the light of that belief."

"Ain't that being a little harsh on Sprague?" the sheriff asked.

"I don't think so," Mason replied. "After all he's only human."

The sheriff munched on his tobacco, then slowly nodded and said, "One of the things I've got against this state is the way they measure the efficiency of a district attorney. The state keeps records of the criminal trials in the different counties. They gauge the efficiency of the district attorneys by the percentage of convictions they secure in cases tried. Now that ain't right. If I was keeping a district attorney's record, I'd give him more points for finding out somebody was innocent, and not prosecuting that person, than I would for getting a conviction just because he'd gone into court."

Paul Drake started to say something, but Mason warned him to silence with a gesture.

"Of course," Sheriff Barnes went on, "Raymond Sprague has his record to consider. Sprague is a good boy, he wants to get some advancement politically. He knows that when he comes up for office, no matter what he runs for, people are going to look at his record as district attorney.

"Now, I'm different. I'm sheriff, and that's all I want to be—just sheriff. I know that I have a lot of power to use, and I want to use it fair and square to everyone. I don't want to have anyone convicted that ain't guilty."

"Under those circumstances," Mason said, "don't you think it would be more fair, all around, to have the guilt or innocence determined at the coroner's inquest tonight? Then, perhaps, it wouldn't be necessary to take the matter before a jury. If Helen Monteith *isn't* innocent, the prosecution has everything to gain by having me put all my facts before the coroner's jury. If she *is* innocent, then the prosecution has everything to gain by not being put in the position of going into court on a big case, and having the jury return a verdict of not guilty."

"Of course," the sheriff said, "if we was going to do that down at the coroner's inquest, we couldn't have a lot of objections and things; we'd have to scoot right along and hit the high spots. You couldn't make a lot of objections to questions and all that sort of stuff."

"I wouldn't," Mason promised.

"Well," the sheriff said, "I'll see what I can do."

"I'd prefer," Mason told him, "that you didn't try to do

anything with Sprague. In other words, I don't want to tip my hand to Sprague. I'm putting my cards on the table with you."

"Nope," the sheriff said, "I'm co-operating with the district attorney; the district attorney has to know everything about it. Maybe he'll be willing to give you a break. Maybe he won't. I'm telling you, fair and square, if he agrees to let you talk it'll be because he'll want to give you lots of rope and watch you hang yourself."

"That suits me," Mason said. "All I want is the rope."

"You'd have to be kinda tactful," the sheriff said. "Sprague wouldn't like it if it appeared you was bringing out all the evidence."

"I can appreciate that," Mason said. "I'd try to let it appear I was co-operating with the district attorney; whether I can really co-operate or not, depends upon how Sprague looks at it."

Sheriff Barnes looked out the window. The afternoon sunlight etched the lines of his bronzed countenance, showed the silver strands in his hair. He held his lips pursed for ten thoughtful seconds before seeking the relief of a cuspidor.

"Well," he said, "we'll see what we can do. As I understand it, all you want is to see that all the evidence gets before that coroner's jury."

"That's all," Mason said, "and I'd like to do it in such a way the coroner's jury would feel I was trying to assist the coroner. As I've mentioned before, when people get fixed beliefs, they interpret everything in the light of those beliefs. Take politics, for instance. We can look back at past events, and the deadly significance of those events seems so plain that we don't see how people could possibly have overlooked them. Yet millions of voters, at the time, saw those facts and warped their significance so that they supported erroneous political beliefs.

"The same is true of the things which are happening at present. A few years from now we'll look back in wonder that people failed to see the deadly significance of signs on the political horizon. Twenty years from now even the most stupid high school student can appreciate the importance of those signs and the results which must inevitably have followed. But right now we have some twenty-five million who think another. And both sides believe they're correctly interpreting the facts."

The sheriff came to an upright position, while the chair gave forth one long, last, protesting squeak, which made Della Street wince. "Well," he said, "I'll let you know in an hour or so. I'll have to talk with the coroner and the district attorney. Personally, Mason, I'm for you. I ain't running the prosecution, but I am running the department of criminal investigation. There's been a murder committed in my county. I'm going to do everything I can to find out who committed that murder. I think you're prejudiced because you think Helen Monteith is innocent, whereas I think she's guilty. Naturally, you're trying to protect your client. On the other hand, you've had a lot more experience with big murder cases than I have. I ain't going to let you lead me around by the nose, but I am going to take any help you have to offer, and be mighty darned glad to get it.

"And now you want to see Helen Monteith?"

Mason nodded.

"All right," the sheriff said, "you'll have to come over to the jail, and only you can see her. You'll have to leave the others behind."

Mason entered the cement-floored office of the jail as Sheriff Barnes swung back the heavy iron door. The atmosphere was permeated with the sickly sweet odor of jail disinfectant, with the psychic emanations from scores of dispirited derelicts. It exerted a strangely depressing influence upon one who had not become immune to it.

"She's in the detention ward," the sheriff said, "and the detention ward's over on that side. The matron's the jailer's wife. I'll have to get her and bring her down. You can go in that room and wait."

Mason entered the little office and waited some five minutes before the jailer's wife escorted Helen Monteith into the room.

"Well," she said, as she dropped into a chair, "what do you want?"

"I want to help you, if I can," Mason told her.

"I'm afraid you can't. I seem to have put my foot in it all the way along the line."

The matron said, "I'll stand just outside the door here, and . . ."

"Go ahead and close the door," the sheriff told her. "Let them talk in private."

When the door had swung shut Mason said, "Tell me about it."

Helen Monteith seemed fatigued to the point of spiritual and mental exhaustion. "Oh, what's the use," she said. ". . . I guess I was just too happy, that's all . . . The bottom dropped out of everything. By the time this is over, my job will be gone. The only man I ever really loved is dead. They're accusing me of murdering him, and . . . and . . ." She blinked back tears and said, "No, I'm not going to cry. It's all right. When a woman reaches my age, crying is just a sign of self-sympathy, and I don't intend to give in to myself."

"Why did you leave Della Street?" Mason asked.

"Because," she said, in that same dispirited tone of voice, "I wanted to go back and burn the letters I'd received from . . . *from my husband,*" she said, with a trace of defiance in her voice.

Mason said, "He may really have been your legal husband, after all. There's some doubt as to the validity of his marriage to Helen Watkins. If you'll help, we may be able to do something."

"There's nothing you can do," she said wearily. "They have the cards all stacked against me. I didn't tell you the worst thing against me."

"What?" Mason asked.

"I went up to that mountain cabin Tuesday, the sixth."

"Why?" Mason asked.

"Just sentiment," she said. "No one will believe me, no one would ever understand. I suppose you'd have to be in love to get my viewpoint anyway, and probably it has to be a love which comes after you've had one complete and utter disillusionment. Anyway, I went up there just because I'd been so happy there. I just wanted to go up and bask in the smell of the woods, in the sunshine and the aura of peace and tranquillity which surrounds the place. The chipmunks were so friendly, the bluejays so impudently inquisitive . . . I wanted to live over in my mind the happiness I'd had."

"Why didn't you tell that to the officers?"

"I just didn't want to be made to appear ridiculous. It's the same thing you have to contend with in love letters. They seem sacred and tender when you read them, but when they are read in court, they sound simply ghastly."

"Someone saw you up there?"

"Yes, I was arrested for speeding. That is, the traffic officer says I was speeding. Personally, I think he just wanted to round out his day's quota of arrests. It was a steep curve, and he claimed there was a limit of fifteen miles, and I was going twenty-five . . . Anyway, he took the number of my car, and gave me a traffic ticket to sign, and I signed it. They found out about that, and that puts me on the spot."

"And how about the gun?" Mason asked.

"My husband asked me to get that gun for him."

"Did he say why?"

"No. He rang me up at the library and asked me if there wasn't a gun in the collection which would shoot. I told him I didn't know, but I supposed so. He said he'd seen a derringer in there, which he thought was in pretty good shape, and thought we could get shells for it. He asked me to get the gun and get some shells for it. He said he only wanted it for a few days, and then I could put it back."

"Didn't that request seem rather unreasonable?" Mason asked.

"Of course not. I was in love," she said simply, as one might talk of a happy home life before it had been completely destroyed by some catastrophe.

"So you went back home in order to burn up the letters?"

"Yes."

"Wasn't it to hide the shells?"

"No."

"But you did try to hide the shells?"

"After I got there, I decided it would be a good plan to get rid of them."

"And the parrot?" Mason asked. "Did you kill the parrot?"

"Good heavens, no! Why should I want to kill the parrot?"

"You probably noticed," Mason said, "that the parrot kept repeating, 'Put down that gun, Helen . . . don't shoot . . . My God, you've shot me.' "

"Well, you can't blame that on me," she said. "My husband purchased that parrot at a pet store on Friday the second. I'm not responsible for anything a parrot says. What's more, that parrot never was anywhere near that cabin."

Sudden tears flooded her eyes. "I can't believe, I simply *can't* believe that he ever intended to do anything which wasn't for my complete happiness. Oh, God, *why* did he have to die. He was so gentle and kind and considerate and had such a wonderful character."

Mason crossed over to her and placed his hand on her shoulder. "Take it easy," he said, "save your nerves as much as you can. You're going through an ordeal tonight before the coroner's jury."

"What do you want me to do?" she asked, choking back sobs. "T-t-tell them I refuse to answer questions? I understand that's what the b-b-best lawyers tell c-c-clients who are accused of m-m-murder."

Mason said, "On the contrary, you're going to go on that witness stand and answer all their questions. No matter how they hurl accusations at you, or how they try to browbeat you, you're going to keep your head and simply tell the truth. It's going to be an ordeal, but you're going to emerge with flying colors."

"That isn't the attitude you adopted last night," she said. "Then you were trying to keep me away from the police."

"Not the police," Mason said. "I was trying to keep you away from a parrot killer."

"What do you mean?"

"I thought," Mason said, "that it was well within the bounds of possibility that someone would try to kill the parrot at your house. If you were there and heard the intruder . . . Well, whoever killed that parrot had already committed one murder. One more or less wouldn't have made a great deal of difference."

"But how did you know someone was going to try and kill the parrot?"

"It was just a hunch," Mason said. ". . . Think you can go through with it tonight?"

"I'll try," she promised.

"All right," Mason told her. "Let's cheer up; let's get this feeling of hopelessness completely licked."

"I'll try to stick out my chin and take it," she told him. "Just a few days ago I thought I was the happiest woman in the world. Now, if I dared to let myself start sympathizing with myself, I'd feel I was the most miserable. It's quite a comedown."

"I know it is," Mason sympathized.

"I've lost the man I loved, and I'm accused of murder on top of that."

"That accusation isn't going to last very long," Mason said.

She managed to smile, tilted her chin up a bit. "All right, let's go."

CHAPTER TWELVE

ANDY TEMPLET, the coroner, having acquired some reputation as a practical philosopher, refused to be stampeded by the flattering preparations which the press had made for reporting the inquest. He stood calmly and at ease while press photographers snapped pictures of his kindly, twinkling eyes and the whimsical smile about his mouth. Having called the inquest to order and selected his jury, he made a brief speech in which there was no attempt at grandiose eloquence.

"Now, folks," he said, "we've got to determine the cause of death in this case. In other words, we've got to find out how this man died. And if somebody killed him, and we know who that someone was, we can say so. If we don't know, we hadn't better try to fix the responsibility. We aren't here to try anyone for anything. We're just trying to determine how Fremont C. Sabin met his death, up in his mountain cabin.

"Now, the coroner has charge of inquests. Most of the time he lets the district attorney ask questions, when the district attorney wants to, but that doesn't mean the district attorney runs the inquest. It simply means the district attorney is here to help us, and, in a case of this kind, he's here to try and uncover facts which will help him convict the murderer. The sheriff is also an interested party, and the sheriff has a lawyer here, Mr. Perry Mason. Mr. Mason is representing the heirs—that is, one of the heirs. Mr. Mason wants to find out how the murder was committed. Mr. Mason is also representing Helen Monteith.

"I want everybody to understand that we ain't going to have any monkeyshines, and we ain't going to have any oratory, or long-winded objections. We're going to move right along with this thing, and if I get my order of proof all cockeyed, that's my responsibility. I don't want anybody to point out anything except facts. I don't want anybody to try and get the witnesses rattled.

"Now, I'm going to start out asking questions. When I get done I'll let the district attorney ask questions, and I'll let Perry Mason ask questions, and the jurors can ask questions. But let's get down to brass tacks and keep moving. Do you all understand?"

"I understand," Perry Mason said.

The district attorney said, "Of course, the coroner's idea of what is a technicality may differ from mine, in which event . . ."

". . . In which event," the coroner interrupted, "what *I think* is going to be what counts. I'm just a plain, common, ordinary citizen. I've tried to get a coroner's jury of plain, common, ordinary citizens. The object back of this proof is to give the coroner's jury a chance to figure what happened. We haven't got a jury of lawyers. We've got a jury of citizens. I think I know what they want. . . . Anyway, I know what *I* want."

Andy Templet stilled the titter which ran over the

courtroom and said, "I think we'd better have the neighbor who discovered the body, first."

Fred Waner came forward and was sworn. He gave his name, address, and occupation.

The coroner said, "You found the body, didn't you, Mr. Waner?"

"Yes."

"Where?"

"In his mountain cabin, up in Grizzly Flats."

"He owned a cabin up there?"

"Yes, that's right."

"Now, I've got some pictures here. We'll connect them up later, but they're pictures of the cabin. You take a look at them and tell me if that's the cabin."

"Yes, that's right. Those are pictures of the cabin."

"All right. You found the body there. When was it?"

"It was Sunday, September eleventh."

"About what time?"

"Around three or four o'clock in the afternoon."

"What happened?"

"Well, I was coming along the road, driving up to my place, and got to wondering whether Sabin had got in for the fishing. I hadn't seen him, but he usually managed to get in when they opened up the fishing in Grizzly Creek, so I stopped the car to take a look at the house, and heard the parrot screaming something awful. So I says to myself, 'Well, he's there if his parrot is there,' so I drove up to the house. The shutters were all down the way it is when the place is closed up, and the garage was closed and locked, and I thought, 'Shucks, I've made a mistake, there ain't anyone home.' So I started to drive away, and then I heard this parrot again."

"What was the parrot saying?" the coroner asked.

Waner grinned and said, "The parrot was cussing a blue streak; he wanted something to eat."

"So what did you do?"

"Well, I got to wondering if Sabin had maybe left the parrot there without being there himself. I figured maybe he'd gone fishing, but if he had, I didn't see why he'd pull all the shutters down; so I got out and looked around. Well, the garage was locked, but I could get the doors open a crack, just enough to see that Sabin's car was in there, so then I went around to the door and knocked, and didn't get any answer, and finally, thinking maybe something was wrong, pried open one of the shutters and looked inside. This parrot was screaming all the time, and, looking inside, I saw a man's hand lying on the floor. So then I got the window up and got inside. I saw right away that the man had been dead for quite a while. There was some food for the parrot on the floor, and a pan that had held water, but the water was all gone. I went right over to the telephone and telephoned you. I didn't touch anything."

"Then what did you do?"

"Then I got out into the fresh air, and left the place closed up until you got there," the witness said.

"I don't think there's any need to ask this man any more questions, is there?" the coroner asked.

The district attorney said, "I'd like to ask one question, just for the sake of fixing the jurisdictional fact. The body was that of Fremont C. Sabin?"

"Yes, it was pretty far gone, but it was Sabin, all right."

"How long have you known Fremont C. Sabin?"

"Five years."

"I think that's all," the district attorney said.

"Just one more question," the coroner said. "Nothing was touched until I got there, was it, Waner?"

"Absolutely nothing, except the telephone."

"And the sheriff came up there with me, didn't he?"

"Yes, that's right."

"Well, we'll hear from the sheriff," the coroner said.

Sheriff Barnes eased himself into the witness chair, crossed his legs, and settled back at his ease. "Now, Sheriff," the coroner said, "suppose you tell us just what you found when we went up there to Sabin's cabin."

"Well, the body was lying on the floor, on its left side. The left arm was stretched out, and the fingers clenched. The right arm was lying across the body. Things were pretty bad in there. We opened all the windows and got as much air in as we could . . . looking over the windows before we opened them, of course, to make certain they were locked on the inside, and there weren't any evidences that they'd been tampered with.

"There was a spring lock on the door, and that lock was closed, so whoever did the killing, walked out and pulled the door shut behind him. We got the parrot back in the cage, and closed the cage. It had been propped open with a notched pine stick. I took some chalk and traced the position of the body on the floor, and traced the position of the gun, and then the coroner went through the clothes, and then we had a photographer take a few pictures of the body, as it was lying on the floor."

"You've got prints of those pictures with you?" the coroner asked.

"Yes, here they are," the sheriff said, and produced some photographs. The coroner, taking possession of them, said, "All right, I'll hand all these over to the jury a little later. Let's find out, now, what happened."

"Well, after we moved the body and got the place aired out," the sheriff said, "we started looking things over. I'll start with the kitchen. There was a garbage pail in the kitchen; in the garbage pail were the shells of two eggs, and some bacon rind, a piece of stale toast, badly burnt on one side, and a small can of pork and beans, which had been opened. On the gas stove—he had a pressure gas outfit up there—was a frying pan in which some pork and beans had been warmed up quite a while ago. The pan was all dry, and the beans had crusted all around the sides. There was still some coffee, and a lot of coffee grounds, in the pot on the stove. There was a knife and fork and a plate in the sink. There'd been beans eaten out of the plate. In the icebox was part of a roll of butter, a bottle of cream, and a couple of packages of cheese which hadn't been opened. There was a locker with a lot of canned goods, and a bread box, which had half a loaf of bread in it, and a bag with a couple of dozen assorted cookies.

"In the main room there was a table on which was a jointed fly rod, a book of flies, and a creel, in which was a mess of fish. Those fish had evidently been there about as long as the body. We made a box to put the creel in, got the box as nearly airtight as possible, and put the whole thing in and nailed it up, without touching the contents. Then we checked on the gun and found it was a forty-one caliber derringer, with discharged shells in each of the two barrels. The body had two bullet holes just below the heart, and, from the position of the bullet holes, we figured that both barrels of the gun had been fired at once.

"There were some rubber boots near the table, and there was dried mud on the boots; an alarm clock was on the table near the bed. It had stopped at two forty-seven; the alarm had been set for five-thirty; both the alarm and the clock had run down. The body was clothed in a pair of slacks, a shirt and sweater. There were wool socks and slippers on the feet.

"There was a telephone line running out of the cabin, and the next day, when Perry Mason and Sergeant Holcomb were helping me make an investigation, we found that the telephone line had been tapped. Whoever had done the tapping had established a headquarters in a cabin about three hundred and fifty yards from the Sabin cabin. It had evidently been an old, abandoned cabin, which had been fixed up and repaired when the wire-tapping apparatus was installed. We found evidences that whoever had been in the place had left hurriedly. There was a cigarette on the table, which had evidently been freshly lit, and then burnt down to ashes. The dust indicated that the place hadn't been used for a week or so."

"Did Helen Monteith make any statement to you about that gun?" the coroner asked.

"Yes, she did," the sheriff said. "That was only to-day."

"Now, just a moment," the district attorney inquired. "Was that statement made as a free and voluntary statement, and without any promises or inducements of any kind having been offered to her?"

"That's right," the sheriff said. "You asked her if she'd ever seen the gun before, and she said she had. She said she'd taken it at the request of her husband, and bought some shells for it; that she'd given him the gun and shells on Saturday, the third of September."

"Did she say who her husband was?" the district attorney inquired.

"Yes, she said the man she referred to as her husband was Fremont C. Sabin."

"Any questions anyone wants to ask of the sheriff?" the coroner inquired.

"No questions," Mason said.

"I think that's all for the moment," the district attorney said.

The coroner said, "I'm going to call Helen Monteith to the witness stand." He turned to the coroner's jury and said, "I don't suppose Mr. Mason will want his client to make any statement at this time. She'll probably decline to answer any questions, because she's being held in the detention ward on the suspicion of murder, but I'm going to at least get the records straight by letting you gentlemen take a look at her and hearing what she says when she refuses to answer."

Helen Monteith came forward, was sworn, and took the witness stand.

Mason said to the coroner, "Contrary to what you apparently expect, I am not advising Miss Monteith to refuse to answer questions. In fact, I am going to suggest that Miss Monteith turn to the jury and tell her story in her own way."

Helen Monteith faced the jury. There was extreme weariness in her manner, but also a certain defiance, and a certain pride. She told of the man who had entered the library, making her acquaintance, an acquaintance which ripened into friendship, and then into love. She told of their marriage; of the weekend honeymoon spent in the cabin in the mountains. Bit by bit she reconstructed the romance for the jury, and the shock which she had experienced when she had learned of the tragic aftermath.

Raymond Sprague fairly lunged at her, in his eagerness to cross-examine. "You took that gun from the museum exhibit?"

"Yes."

"Why did you do it?"

"My husband asked me for a gun."

"Why didn't you buy a gun?"

"He told me he needed one right away, and that, under the law, no store would deliver one for a period of three days after he'd ordered it."

"Did he say why he wanted the gun?"

"No."

"You knew it was stealing to take that gun?"

"I wasn't stealing it, I was borrowing it."

"Oh, Sabin promised to return it, did he?"

"Yes."

"And you want this jury to understand that Fremont C. Sabin deliberately asked you to steal the gun, with which he was killed, from a collection?"

Mason said, "Don't answer that, Miss Monteith. You just testify to facts. I think the jury will understand you, all right."

Sprague turned savagely to Mason and said, "I thought we weren't going to have any technicalities."

"We aren't," Mason assured him smilingly.

"That's a technical objection."

"It isn't an objection at all," Mason said. "It's simply an instruction to my client not to answer the question."

"I demand that she answer it," the district attorney said to the coroner.

The coroner said, "I think you can question Miss Monteith just about facts, Mr. Sprague. Don't ask her what she wants the jury to understand."

Sprague, flushing, said, "How about that parrot?"

"You mean Casanova?"

"Yes."

"Mr. Sabin bought it . . . that is, that's what I understood."

"When?"

"On Friday, the second of September."

"What did he say when he brought the parrot home?"

"Simply said that he'd always wanted a parrot, and that he'd bought one."

"And you kept that parrot with you after that?"

"Yes."

"Where were you on Sunday, the fourth of September?"

"I was with my husband."

"Where?"

"At Santa Delbarra."

"You registered in a hotel there?"

"Yes."

"Under what name?"

"As Mrs. George Wallman, of course."

"And Fremont C. Sabin was the George Wallman who was there with you?"

"Yes."

"And did he have this gun there at that time?"

"I guess so. I don't know. I didn't see it."

"Did he say anything about going up to this cabin for the opening of the fishing season?"

"Of course not. He was leading me to believe he was a poor man, looking for work. He told me that Monday was a holiday, but he had some people he wanted to see anyway—so I went home Monday."

"That was the fifth?"

"Yes."

"Where were you on Tuesday, the sixth?"

"I was in the library part of the day, and . . . and part of the day I drove up to the cabin."

"Oh, you were up at this cabin on Tuesday, the sixth?"

"Yes, that's what I said."

"And what did you do up there?"

"Simply drove around and looked at it."

"And what time was that?"

"About eleven o'clock in the morning."

"What was the condition of the cabin at the time?"

"It looked just like it had when I'd last left it."

"Were the shutters down?"

"Yes."

"Just the same as is shown in that photograph?"

"Yes."

"Did you hear a parrot?"

"No."

"The cabin seemed deserted?"

"Yes."

"Did you notice whether there was any car in the garage?"

"No."

"What did you do?"

"Just drove around there for a while, and then left."

"Why did you go up there?"

"I went up to . . . well, simply to see the place. I had some time off, and I wanted to take a drive, and I thought that was a nice drive."

"It was quite a long drive, wasn't it?"

"Yes."

"Now, you understand that the evidence points to the fact that Fremont C. Sabin was killed at approximately ten-thirty or eleven o'clock on the morning of September sixth?"

"Yes," she said.

"And that he arrived at the cabin on the afternoon of Monday, September fifth?"

"Yes."

"And did you want the coroner's jury to understand that you found the cabin with the shutters closed, saw no evidence of any occupancy, heard nothing of a parrot, and did not see Mr. Sabin at that time?"

"That's right. I found the cabin just as I have described, and I did not see Mr. Sabin. I had no idea he was there. I thought he was in Santa Delbarra, looking for a location for a grocery store."

Mason said, "I think this witness has given all the information which she has to impart. I think any further questions are in the nature of a cross-examination, and argumentative. There is no new information being elicited. I will advise the coroner and the district attorney that, unless some new phase of the case is gone into, I'm going to advise the witness not to answer any more questions."

"I'll open up a new phase of the case," the district attorney said threateningly. "Who killed that parrot which was kept in your house?"

"I don't know."

"This parrot was brought home to you on Friday, the second?"

"That's right."

"And on Saturday, the third, you left with your husband?"

"No, my husband left on Saturday afternoon and went to Santa Delbarra. Monday was a holiday. I drove up to Santa Delbarra Sunday, and spent Sunday night and Monday morning with him in the hotel. I returned Monday night to San Molinas. My next-door neighbor, Mrs. Winters, had been keeping the parrot. I arrived too late in the evening to call for it. The next day, Tuesday, the sixth, I didn't have to be at the library until three o'clock in the afternoon. I wanted to be away from people. I got up early in the morning, and drove to the cabin, and returned in time to go directly to the library at three o'clock."

"Isn't it a fact," the district attorney persisted, "that you returned to your house at an early hour this morning for the purpose, among other things, of killing the parrot which was in the house, the parrot which your next-door neighbor, Mrs. Winters, had kept while you spent your so-called honeymoon with the person whom you have referred to as your husband, in this mountain cabin?"

"That is not a fact. I didn't even know the parrot was dead until the sheriff told me."

The district attorney said, "I think perhaps I can refresh your recollection upon this subject, Miss Monteith."

He turned and nodded to his deputy, a young man who was standing near the doorway. The deputy stepped outside long enough to pick up a bundle covered with cloth, then hurried down the aisle, past the rows of twisted-necked spectators, to deliver the bundle to Sprague.

District Attorney Sprague dramatically whipped away the cloth. A gasp sounded from the spectators as they saw what the cloth had concealed—a bloodstained parrot cage, on the floor of which lay the stiff body of a dead parrot, its head completely severed.

"That," the district attorney said dramatically, "is *your* handiwork, isn't it, Miss Monteith?"

She swayed slightly in the witness chair. "I feel giddy," she said. ". . . Please take that away . . . The blood . . ."

The district attorney turned to the spectators and announced triumphantly, "The killer quails when confronted with evidence of her . . ."

"She does no such thing," Mason roared, getting to his feet and striding belligerently toward Sprague. "This young woman has been subject to inhuman treatment. Within the short space of twenty-four hours, she has learned that the man whom she loved, and whom she regarded as her husband, was killed. No sympathy was offered her in her hour of bereavement. Instead of sympathy being extended, she was dragged out into the pitiless glare of publicity and . . ."

"Are you making a speech?" the district attorney interrupted.

Mason said, "No, I'm finishing yours."

"I'm perfectly capable of finishing my own," the district attorney shouted.

"You try to finish that speech *you* started," Mason told him, "and you'll . . ."

The coroner's gavel banged. The sheriff, jumping from his seat, came striding forward.

"We're going to have order," the coroner said.

"You can have it from me," Mason told him, "if you keep the district attorney from making speeches. The facts of the matter are that this young woman, who has been subjected to a nerve strain well calculated to make her hysterical, is suddenly confronted with a gruesome, gory spectacle. Her natural repugnance is interpreted by the district attorney as an indication of guilt. That's his privilege. But when he starts making a speech about it . . ."

"I didn't make a speech about it," the district attorney said.

"Well," the coroner observed, "we're going to have no more speeches made by either side. The coroner is inclined to feel that it's asking pretty much of any young woman to have a gruesome spectacle like this suddenly thrust in front of her."

"It was done," Mason said, "purely as a grandstand,

purely for the purpose of capitalizing on Miss Monteith's overwrought condition."

"I had no such intention," the district attorney said.

"What did you have in mind?" the coroner asked.

"I merely wanted to identify the parrot as being the one which had been given to her by her husband on Friday, September second."

"He can do that," Mason said, "without throwing all this blood-stained paraphernalia in her lap."

"I don't need any suggestions from you," Sprague said.

The sheriff stepped forward. "If the coroner wants to make any rulings," he said drily, "I'm here to enforce them."

"The coroner is going to make a ruling," Andy Templet announced. "The coroner is going to rule that there'll be no more personalities exchanged between counsel. The coroner's also going to rule that there'll be no more sudden and dramatic production of blood-stained garments, bird cages, or dead birds."

"But I only wanted to identify the parrot," the district attorney insisted.

"I heard you the first time," the coroner told him, "and I hope you heard the coroner. Now, let's proceed with the inquest."

"That's all," the diistrict attorney said.

"May I ask a question?" Mason inquired.

The coroner nodded assent.

Mason stepped forward and said in a low, kindly voice, "I don't wish to subject your nerves to any undue strain, Miss Monteith, but I'm going to ask you to try and bring yourself to look at this parrot. I'm going to ask you to study it carefully, and I'm going to ask you whether this *is* the parrot which your husband brought home to you."

Helen Monteith made an effort at self-control. She turned and looked down at the lifeless parrot in the cage, then quickly averted her head. "I c-c-can't," she said, in a quavering voice, "but the parrot my husband brought home had one claw missing. I think it was from his right foot. My husband said he'd caught the foot in a rat trap, and . . ."

"*This* parrot has no claws missing," Mason said.

"Then it isn't the same parrot."

"Just a moment," Mason said; "I'm going to ask you to make another identification."

He nodded a signal to Paul Drake, who, in turn, passed the word to an operative who was waiting in the corridor. The operative came through the door carrying a caged parrot.

Amid a silence so tense that the steps of the detective could be heard as he walked down the carpeted aisle, the caged parrot suddenly broke into shrill laughter.

Helen Monteith's lips quivered. Apparently she was restraining herself from hysteria by a supreme effort.

Mason took the caged parrot from the operative. "Hush, Polly," he said.

The parrot twisted its head first to one side, then the other, leered about him at the courtroom with twinkling, wicked little eyes; then, as Mason set the cage on the table, the bird hooked its beak on the cross-wires of the cage, and completely circled it, walking over the top, head downward, to return to the perch as though proud of the accomplishment.

"Nice Polly," Mason said.

The parrot shuffled its feet on the perch.

Helen Monteith turned to regard the parrot. "Why," she said, "that's Casanova. . . . The sheriff told me he'd been killed."

The parrot, tucking its head slightly to one side, said in a low, throaty voice, "Come in and sit down, won't you? Come in and sit down, take that chair . . . *Squawk* . . . *Squawk* . . . Put down that gun, Helen . . . don't shoot . . . *Squawk* . . . *Squawk* . . . My God, you've shot me."

The spectators stared wide-eyed at the drama of the parrot apparently accusing the witness.

"*That's* Casanova!" Helen Monteith exclaimed.

The district attorney said dramatically, "I want the words of this parrot in the record. The parrot is accusing the witness. I want the record to show it."

Mason regarded the district attorney with a half smile twisting his lips. "Do I understand," he inquired, "that you're adopting this parrot as your witness?"

"The parrot has made a statement. I want it in the record," the district attorney insisted.

"But the parrot hasn't been sworn as a witness," Mason observed.

The district attorney appealed to the coroner. "The parrot has made a statement. It was a plainly audible statement."

"I would like to know," Mason said, "whether the district attorney is making the parrot his witness."

"I'm not talking about witnesses," Sprague countered. "I'm talking about parrots. This parrot made a statement. I want it in the record."

"If the parrot is to be a witness," Mason said, "I should have *some* right of cross-examination."

"Well," the coroner ruled, "a parrot can't be a witness, but the parrot *did* say something. What those words were can be put in the record for what they're worth. I think the coroner's jury understands the situation thoroughly. I never did believe in putting things in a record and then striking them out. When jurors hear things, they've heard them, and that's that. Now, go on with the inquest."

"I think that's all the questions I have," Mason said.

"That's all," Sprague said, "except . . . wait a minute. . . . Miss Monteith, if this parrot is Casanova, then where did the parrot come from that was killed?"

"I don't know," she said.

"It was in your house."

"I can't help that."

"You must have had something to do with it."

"I didn't."

"But you're certain this is Casanova?"

"Yes. I can identify him by that claw that's missing, and by what he said about dropping the gun."

"Oh, you've heard *that* before, have you?"

"Yes. My husband commented on it when he brought the bird home with him."

The district attorney said, "Miss Monteith, I'm not satisfied that your violent emotional reaction when this dead parrot was brought before you is purely the result of a nervous condition. Now, I'm going to insist that you look closely at this parrot and . . ."

Mason got to his feet and said, "You don't need to look at that parrot, Miss Monteith."

Sprague flushed and said, "I insist that she does."

"And I insist that she doesn't," Mason said. "Miss Monteith is not going to answer any more questions. She's been a witness. She's under a great emotional strain. I think the jury will understand my position as her attorney in announcing that she has now completed her testimony. She has given the district attorney and the coroner an opportunity to ask her all reasonable questions. I am not going to have the examination unduly prolonged."

"He can't do that," Sprague said to the coroner.

"I've already done it," Mason told him.

The coroner said, "I don't know whether he can or not, but I know that this young woman is nervous. I don't think you're making proper allowance for that condition, Sprague. Under ordinary circumstances, a widow is given condolences and sympathy. She's particularly spared from any nerve shock. This witness certainly has been subjected to a series of trying experiences during the last twenty-four hours. As far as the coroner is concerned, she's going to be excused. We're trying to complete this inquest at one sitting. I'm getting facts, that's all. And I want to keep moving. You'll have plenty of opportunity to ask her questions before the Grand Jury, and on the witness stand . . . I'm going to ask Mrs. Helen Watkins Sabin to come forward as a witness."

"She ain't here," the sheriff said.

"Where is she?"

"I don't know, I haven't been able to serve a subpoena on her."

"How about Steven Watkins?"

"The same with him."

"Is Waid here, the secretary?"

"Yes. He's been subpoenaed and is here."

"Well, let's hear from Sergeant Holcomb," the coroner said. "Sergeant Holcomb, come forward and be sworn, please."

Sergeant Holcomb took the witness stand. The coroner said, "Now, you're a sergeant on the homicide squad of the Metropolitan Police, aren't you, Sergeant, and you know all about the investigation of murder cases, and the scientific method of apprehending criminals?"

"That's right," Sergeant Holcomb admitted.

"Now you got this box with the creel of fish in it, that Sheriff Barnes sent in?"

"Yes, that was received at the technical laboratory of the police department. We had previously received a telephone call from Sheriff Barnes about it."

"What did you find out about the fish?" the coroner asked.

"We made some tests," Sergeant Holcomb said. "I didn't make the tests myself, but I was present when they were made, and know what the experts found."

"What did they find?"

"They found that there had been a limit of fish in the creel; that the fish were, of course, badly decomposed, but, as nearly as could be ascertained, the fish had been cleaned and wrapped in willow leaves. They had not been washed after being wrapped in willow leaves."

"And you went up to the cabin with Sheriff Barnes the next day?"

"That's right. Sheriff Barnes wanted me to see the cabin, and we were to meet Richard Waid there. He was coming on from New York by plane, and we wanted to meet him in a place where our first conversation wouldn't be interrupted by newspaper reporters."

"All right, go on," the coroner said.

"Well," Holcomb observed, "we went to the cabin. We met Mr. Mason on the road up to the cabin. Richard Waid came while we were there at the cabin."

"What did you find at the cabin, in the line of physical conditions?" the coroner asked.

"Just about the same as has been described."

"At this time," the coroner said, "I think the jury had better take a look at all of these photographs, because I'm going to ask Sergeant Holcomb some questions about them."

The coroner waited while the photographs were passed around to the jurors, then turned back to Sergeant Holcomb.

"Sergeant Holcomb," he said, "I want to give the

members of this jury the benefit of your experience. I want you to tell them what the various things in that cabin indicate."

The coroner glanced down at Perry Mason and said, "I suppose you may object that this is a conclusion of the witness, but it seems to me this man has had a lot of experience, and I don't know why he shouldn't . . ."

"Not at all," Mason said. "I think it's a very wise question. I think it's a perfectly proper way of getting at the ultimate facts of the case."

Sergeant Holcomb shifted himself to an easier position in the witness chair, gazed impressively at the jury, and said, "Helen Monteith killed Fremont C. Sabin. There are dozens of things which would be sufficient to establish an absolutely ironclad case against her, before any jury. First, she had motive. Sabin had married her under an assumed name; he had placed her in the position of being a bigamous wife. He had lied to her, tricked her, and deceived her. When she found out that the man she had married was Fremont C. Sabin, and that Sabin had a wife very much alive at the moment, she shot him. She probably didn't intend to shoot him when she went to the cabin. Our experience has been that, in emotional murders of this nature, a woman frequently takes a gun for the purpose of threatening a man, for the purpose of frightening him, or for the purpose of making him believe that she isn't to be trifled with; then, having pointed the gun at him, it's a simple matter to pull the trigger, an almost unconscious reflex, a momentary surrender to emotion. The effects, of course, are disastrous.

"Second, Helen Monteith had the murder weapon in her possession. Her statement that she gave it to her husband is, of course, absurd on the face of it. The crime could not have been suicide. The man didn't move from the time he fell to the floor. The gun was found some distance away, and was *wiped clean of fingerprints*.

"Third, she admits having been present at the cabin at the exact moment Sabin was murdered. She, therefore, combines motive, means and opportunity."

"How do you fix that exact moment of the murder?" the coroner asked.

"It's a matter of making correct deductions from circumstantial evidence," Sergeant Holcomb said.

"Just a minute," Mason interrupted. "Wouldn't it be better to let the sergeant tell the jury the various factors which control the time element in this case, and let the jurors judge for themselves?"

"I don't know," the coroner admitted. "I'm trying to expedite matters as much as possible."

Sergeant Holcomb said, "It would be absolutely foolish to resort to any such procedure. The interpretation of circumstantial evidence is something which calls for a highly specialized training. There are some things from which even the layman can make logical deductions, but on a complicated matter it requires years of experience. I have had that experience, and I am properly qualified to interpret the evidence for the jury. Therefore, I say that Fremont C. Sabin met his death sometime between ten o'clock in the morning and around noon, on Tuesday, the sixth day of September."

"Now, just explain to the jury how you interpret the evidence so as to fix the time," the coroner said.

"First, we go back to known facts, and reason from them," Sergeant Holcomb said. "We know that Fremont C. Sabin intended to go to his cabin on Monday, the fifth, in order to take advantage of the opening of fishing season on the sixth. We know that he actually did go there; we know that he was alive at ten o'clock in the evening of the fifth, because he talked with his secretary on the telephone. We know that he went to bed, that he wound the alarm clock and set the alarm. We know that the alarm went off at five-thirty. We know that he arose, went out, and caught a limit of fish. It is problematical how long it would take him to catch a limit, but, in discussing fishing conditions with other anglers on the creek, it would seem that with the utmost good fortune he could not possibly have caught a limit before nine-thirty o'clock. He returned to the cabin, then, at between ten and eleven in the morning. He had already had a breakfast, two eggs, probably scrambled, some bacon and some coffee. He was once more hungry. He opened a can of beans, warmed those up and ate them. He did this before he even bothered to put his fish in the icebox. He left his fish in the creel, intending to put them in the icebox as soon as he had washed them. But he was hungry enough to want to finish with his lunch before he put the fish away. In the ordinary course of things, he would have put those fish away immediately after he had eaten, probably before he had even washed his dishes. He didn't do that."

"Why don't you place the time as being later than noon?" the coroner asked.

"Those are the little things," Sergeant Holcomb said, with very evident pride, "which a trained investigator notices, and which others don't. Now, the body was clothed in a light sweater and slacks. From the observations which I made on the temperature in that cabin, I found that it varies quite sharply. The shade is such that the sun doesn't get on the roof good until after eleven o'clock. Thereafter it heats up very rapidly until about four o'clock, when once more shade strikes the roof, and it cools off quite rapidly thereafter, becoming cold at night.

"Now, there was a fire laid in the fireplace. That fire hadn't been lit, which shows that it wasn't late enough in the evening for it to have become cold. From noon until around four in the afternoon, it would have been too hot for a person to have been comfortable in a sweater. The records show that the fifth, sixth and seventh were three very warm days—that is, it was warm during the daytime. Up there at that elevation it cooled off quite rapidly at night. It was necessary to have a fire in the evening, in order to keep from being uncomfortably cool. That cabin, you understand, is just a mountain cabin, rather light in construction, and not insulated against conditions of temperature, as a house in the city would be."

"I see," the coroner remarked approvingly. "Then you feel that Mr. Sabin must have returned and had his second breakfast—or lunch—before the sun got on the roof?"

"That's right."

"I think that covers the situation very comprehensively," the coroner said.

"May I ask a question or two?" Mason inquired.

"Certainly."

"How do you know," Mason asked, "that Mr. Sabin didn't meet his death, say, for instance, on Wednesday, the seventh, instead of on the sixth?"

"Partially, from the condition of the body," Sergeant Holcomb said. "The body had been there at least six days. Probably, seven. In the heat and closeness of the room, decomposition had been quite rapid. Moreover, there's another reason. The decedent had had a breakfast of bacon and eggs. Mr. Sabin was an enthusiastic fisherman. He went up to the cabin for the purpose of being there on the opening morning of fishing season. It is inconceivable that he would have gone fishing on that first morning and not caught at least *some* fish. If he had caught them, there would have been evidences that he'd eaten them for breakfast the next morning instead of bacon and eggs. There were no remains of fish anywhere in the garbage pail, nor in the garbage pit in the back of the house, to which the contents of the garbage pail were transferred each day."

And Sergeant Holcomb smiled at the jury, as much as to say, "That shows how easy it is to avoid a lawyer's trap."

"Very well," Mason said, "Let's look at it from another angle. The fire was laid in the fireplace, but hadn't been lit, is that right?"

"Yes."

"Now, it's rather chilly there in the mornings?"

"Quite chilly."

"And at night?"

"Yes."

"Now, according to your theory, the alarm went off at five-thirty, and Mr. Sabin got up to go fishing, is that right?"

"Yes."

"And cooked himself rather a sketchy breakfast?"

"A hasty breakfast, you could call it," Sergeant Holcomb said. "When a person gets up at five-thirty in the morning on the opening day of the season, he's anxious to get out and get the fish."

"I see," Mason said. "Now, when Mr. Sabin came back from his fishing trip, he was in very much of a hurry to get something to eat. We may assume that the first thing he did when he entered the house, and immediately after removing his boots, was to get himself something to eat. Next in order of importance would have been washing the fish and putting them in the icebox. Is that right?"

"That's right."

"Yet, according to your theory," Mason said, "after he got back, he took enough time to lay the fire in the fireplace, all ready for lighting, before he even took care of his fish."

Sergeant Holcomb's face clouded for a moment, then he said, "No, he must have done that the night before." Having thought a minute, he added, triumphantly, "Of course, he did it the night before. He didn't have any occasion for a fire in the morning: it was cold when he got up, but he went right out in the kitchen and cooked his breakfast, and then went out fishing."

"Exactly," Mason said. "But he had reason for a fire the night before, I believe."

"What do you mean?"

"In other words," Mason said, "we know that he was at the cabin at four o'clock on the afternoon of Monday, the fifth. We can surmise that he remained at the cabin until shortly before ten o'clock in the evening, when he went out to place a phone call. If it was cold Monday evening, why didn't he light a fire?"

"He did," Sergeant Holcomb said. "He must have. There's no evidence to show that he didn't."

"Exactly," Mason went on. "But when the body was found, a fresh fire was laid in the fireplace. Now, according to your theory, he either laid that fire Monday night, in a grate that had just been used—or else he laid it the next day, after he got back from fishing. That is, he took time to lay the fire before he even took care of his fish. Does that seem logical to you?"

Sergeant Holcomb hesitated a moment, then said, "Well, that's one of those little things. That doesn't cut so much ice. Lots of times you'll find little things which are more or less inconsistent with the general interpretation of evidence."

"I see," Mason said. "And when you encounter such little things, what do you do, Sergeant?"

"You just ignore 'em," Sergeant Holcomb said.

"And how many such little things have you ignored in reaching your conclusion that Fremont C. Sabin was murdered by Helen Monteith?"

"That's the only one," Sergeant Holcomb said.

"Very well, let's look at the evidence from a slightly different angle. Take the alarm clock, for instance. The alarm was run down, was it not?"

"Yes."

"And where was this alarm clock placed?"

"On the shelf by the bed—or rather on a little table by the bed."

"Quite close to the sleeper?"

"Yes."

"Within easy reaching distance?"

"Yes."

"And, by the way," Mason said, "the bed was made, is that right?"

"Yes."

"In other words, then, after getting up in the morning, at five-thirty, to go fishing, Mr. Sabin stopped long enough to lay a fire in the fireplace, long enough to make his bed, long enough to wash his breakfast dishes?"

Sergeant Holcomb said, "Well, it wouldn't take a man so very long to make his bed."

"By the way," Mason inquired, "did you notice whether there were clean sheets on the bed?"

"Yes, there were."

"Then, he not only must have made the bed, but must have changed the sheets. Did you find the soiled linen anywhere in the cabin, Sergeant?"

"I don't remember," Sergeant Holcomb said.

"There are no laundry facilities there. The soiled laundry is taken down in Mr. Sabin's car and laundered in the city, and returned to the cabin from time to time?"

"I believe that's right, yes."

"Then what became of the soiled sheets?" Mason asked.

"I don't know," Sergeant Holcomb said irritably. "You can't always connect up all these little things."

"Exactly," Mason said. "Now, let's get back to the alarm clock, Sergeant. The alarm was entirely run down?"

"That's right."

"The clock had a shut-off on it, by which the alarm could be shut off while it was sounding?"

"Yes, of course, all good clocks have that."

"Yes; and this was a good clock?"

"Yes."

"Yet the alarm had not been shut off?"

"I didn't notice . . . well, no, I guess not. It was completely run down."

"Yes," Mason said. "Now, is it your experience, Sergeant, as an expert interpreter of circumstantial evidence, that a sleeper permits an alarm to run entirely down before shutting it off?"

"Some people sleep more soundly than others," Sergeant Holcomb said.

"Exactly," Mason agreed, "but when a man is aroused by an alarm clock, his first natural reflex is to turn off the alarm—that is, if the alarm is within reaching distance, isn't that right?"

"Well, you can't always figure that way," Sergeant Holcomb said, his face slowly darkening in color. "Some people go back to sleep after they shut off an alarm, so they deliberately put the alarm clock where they can't get at it."

"I understand that," Mason said, "but in this case the alarm was placed within easy reach of the sleeper, apparently for the purpose of enabling the sleeper to shut off the alarm clock just as soon as it had wakened him, isn't that right?"

"Yes, I guess so."

"But that wasn't done?"

"Well, some persons sleep sounder than others."

"You mean that he wasn't wakened until after the alarm had run down?"

"Yes."

"But *after* an alarm runs down, it ceases to make any sound, does it not, Sergeant?"

"Oh, all that stuff isn't getting you anywhere," Sergeant Holcomb said. "The alarm was run down. He certainly got up. He didn't lie there and sleep, did he? He got up and went out and caught a limit of fish. Maybe the alarm ran down and didn't wake him up, and he woke up half an hour later, with a start, realizing that he'd overslept."

"And then," Mason said with a smile, "despite that realization, he paused to get himself breakfast, washed the breakfast dishes, made the bed, changed the sheets on the bed, laid the fire in the fireplace, and took the soiled bedclothes in his car down to the city to be laundered. Then he drove back to go fishing."

Sergeant Holcomb said, "All that stuff is absurd."

"Why is it absurd?" Mason asked.

Sergeant Holcomb sat in seething silence.

Mason said, "Well, Sergeant, since you seem to be unable to answer that question, let's get back to the alarm clock. As I remember it, you made some experiments with similar alarm clocks, didn't you, to find out how long it would take them to run down?"

"We made experiments with that same alarm clock," the sergeant said. "We made experiments with other alarm clocks and we wired the manufacturer."

"What did you find out?" Mason asked.

"According to the manufacturer, the alarm clocks would run down thirty to thirty-six hours after they'd been completely wound. According to an experiment we made with that clock, it ran down in thirty-two hours and twenty minutes after it was wound."

"In that case," Mason said, "the alarm clock must have been wound about twenty minutes after six o'clock, is that right?"

"Well, what's wrong with that?"

"Nothing," Mason said. "I'm simply asking you to interpret the evidence for the benefit of the jury, which is the thing you set out to do, Sergeant."

"Well, all right, then the clock was wound at twenty minutes past six. What of it?"

"Would you say at twenty minutes past six in the morning, or at twenty minutes past six in the evening?" Mason asked.

"In the evening," Sergeant Holcomb said. "The alarm went off at five-thirty. He wouldn't have wound the alarm clock in the morning, and if he had, he'd have wound up the alarm again. It was wound up at six-twenty in the evening."

"That's fine," Mason said, "that's exactly the point I'm making, Sergeant. Now, you have examined the long distance telephone bills covering calls which were put in from that cabin?"

"I have."

"And you found, did you not, that the last call listed was one which was placed at four o'clock in the afternoon, on Monday, the fifth of September, to Randolph Bolding, examiner of questioned documents?"

"That's right."

"And you talked with Mr. Bolding about that call?"

"Yes."

"Did Mr. Bolding know Mr. Sabin personally?"

"Yes."

"And did you ask him whether he recognized Mr. Sabin's voice?"

"Yes, I did. He knew it was Sabin with whom he was talking. He'd done some work for Sabin before."

"And Sabin asked him about some conclusions he had reached on some checks which had been given him?"

"Yes."

"And Bolding told him that, of course, the checks were forgeries; that he hadn't yet decided whether the endorsements on the back were in the same handwriting as the specimen which had been furnished him. And didn't he say he was inclined to think they were not?"

"Yes, I gathered that."

"And what else did Mr. Sabin say?"

"Mr. Sabin said he was going to send him another envelope, containing half a dozen more specimens of handwriting from five or six different people."

152

"Was that envelope received by Mr. Bolding?"

"It was not."

"Therefore, Mr. Sabin never had an opportunity to mail that letter?"

"So it would seem."

"Now, let us return for the moment to the identity of the murderer. We now understand that Mr. Sabin suspected Steve Watkins of having forged checks in a very large amount. A handwriting expert was checking Watkins' handwriting. Now, if Watkins had been guilty, what's more natural than for him to have tried to silence Mr. Sabin's lips by murder?"

Sergeant Holcomb's lips curled in a sneer. "Simply because," he said, "Watkins has a perfect alibi. Watkins left in an airplane, in the presence of a reputable witness, shortly after ten o'clock on the night of Monday the fifth, for New York. Every moment of his time is accounted for."

"Exactly," Mason said, "*If* we act on the assumption that Fremont C. Sabin was murdered on Tuesday, the sixth, but the trouble with your reasoning, Sergeant, is that there is nothing to indicate he was not murdered on the fifth."

"On the fifth?" Sergeant Holcomb exclaimed. "Impossible. The fishing season didn't open until the sixth, and Fremont Sabin would never have fished before the season opened."

"No," Mason said, "I daresay he wouldn't. I believe it's a misdemeanor, isn't it, Sergeant?"

"Yes."

"And murder is a felony?"

Sergeant Holcomb disdained to answer the question.

"Therefore," Mason said, "a murderer would have no conscientious scruples whatever against catching a limit of fish on the day before the season opened. Now, Sergeant, can you kindly tell the coroner, and this jury, what there is about your reasoning any stronger than a string of fish?"

Sergeant Holcomb stared at Perry Mason with startled eyes.

"In other words," Mason said, "having arrived at the

conclusion Helen Monteith murdered Fremont C. Sabin at eleven o'clock in the morning, on Tuesday, the sixth of September, you have interpreted all the evidence on the premises to support your conclusions; but a fair and impartial appraisement indicates that Fremont C. Sabin was murdered sometime around four o'clock in the afternoon of Monday, September the fifth, and that the murderer, knowing that it would be some time before the body was discovered, took steps to throw the police off the track and manufacture a perfect alibi by the simple expedient of going down to the stream, catching a limit of fish, the afternoon before the season opened, and leaving those fish in the creel.

"And in order to justify that conclusion, Sergeant, you don't have to disregard any 'insignificant' details. In other words, there were fresh sheets on the bed, because the bed had not been slept in. The alarm clock ran down at two forty-seven because the murderer left the cabin at approximately six-twenty o'clock in the afternoon, at which time he wound the alarm clock, after having carefully planted all the other bits of evidence. The reason the alarm which went off at five-thirty the next morning wasn't shut off is because the only occupant of that cabin was dead. And the reason the murderer was so solicitous about the welfare of the parrot was that he wanted the parrot to perjure itself by reciting the lines which the murderer had been at some pains to teach it—'Put down that gun, Helen . . . don't shoot. . . . My God, you've shot me.' The fire was laid in the fireplace because Sabin hadn't had reason to light it that afternoon. He was wearing a sweater because the sun had just got off the roof and it was cooling off, but he was murdered before it had become cool enough to light the fire.

"Sabin let the murderer in, because the murderer was someone whom he knew, yet Sabin had reason to believe he was in some danger. He had secured a gun from his wife, in order to protect himself. The murderer also had a gun which he intended to use, but after he entered the cabin he saw this derringer lying on the table near the bed, and he immediately realized the advantage of killing

Sabin with that gun rather than with the one he'd brought. The murderer had only to pick it up and shoot. Now then, Sergeant, will you kindly tell me what is wrong with that theory? Will you kindly interpret *any* of the evidence to indicate that it is erroneous, and will you please explain to the jury why your whole fine-spun thread of accusation depends on nothing stronger than a string of fish?"

Sergeant Holcomb squirmed uncomfortably in his chair, then blurted out, "Well, I don't believe Steve Watkins did it. That's just an out you've thought of to protect Helen Monteith."

"But what's wrong with that theory?" Mason asked.

"Everything," Sergeant Holcomb asserted.

"Point out one single inconsistency between it and the known facts."

Sergeant Holcomb suddenly started to laugh. "How," he demanded, "could Sabin have been killed at four o'clock in the *afternoon* of Monday, the fifth of September, and yet call his secretary on the long distance telephone, at ten o'clock in the *evening* of the fifth, and tell him everything was okay?"

"He couldn't," Mason admitted, "for the very good reason that he didn't."

"Well, that shoots your theory full of holes," Sergeant Holcomb announced triumphantly. ". . . Er . . . that is . . ."

"Exactly," Mason said; "as you have so suddenly realized, Sergeant, Richard Waid is the murderer."

Sheriff Barnes jumped to his feet. "Where's Richard Waid?" he asked.

The spectators exchanged blank glances. Two of the people near the door said, "If he was that young chap who was sitting in this chair, he got up and went out about two minutes ago."

The coroner said suddenly, "I'm going to adjourn this inquest for half an hour."

A hubbub of excited voices filled the room where the inquest was being held; chairs overturned as those nearest the door went rushing out pell-mell to the sidewalk. Sheriff Barnes, calling to one of his deputies, said, "Get on the teletype, watch every road out of town, get the city police to call all cars."

Mason turned to Helen Monteith and grinned. "That," he said, "I fancy, will be about all."

CHAPTER THIRTEEN

MASON sat in Sheriff Barnes' office, waiting patiently for the formalities incident to the release of Helen Monteith, who sat, as one in a daze, in a chair by the door.

Sheriff Barnes, pausing intermittently to check on telephone reports which were pouring in, tried to readjust the situation in his mind, through questions which he asked of Mason.

"I don't see yet just how you figured it," he said.

"Very simple," Mason told him. "The murderer must have been someone who had access to the parrot, someone who had planned the murder for a long time; someone who intended to pin the crime on Helen Watkins Sabin, since he probably knew nothing of Helen Monteith. Since he knew Sabin usually took the parrot with him when he went to the cabin on the opening of the fishing season, this person, who must have been someone residing in the house, started in educating the parrot to say, 'Drop that gun, Helen . . , don't shoot. . . . My God, you've shot me!' The whole crime had been carefully planned. Sabin was due to appear on Monday, the fifth, pick up the parrot, and go to the cabin for his fishing. The murderer had his plans all arranged, even to his manufactured alibi.

"And then, Sabin upset plans somewhat by appearing on the second and picking up the parrot. Taking the parrot with him, he heard the bird suddenly spring his new lines—'Drop that gun, Helen . . . don't shoot. . . . My God, you've shot me!'

"Probably no one will ever know just what happened after that, but Sabin either felt that his life was in danger, or else Casanova's repeated statements got on his nerves. He wanted to have a parrot around him, either because he liked parrots, or because in some way he wanted to fool the potential murderer—and I'm frank to confess that this substitution of the parrots has me guessing, and I won't rest until I've found out—if I ever can—just what was back of it.

"This much we do know: Sabin became alarmed. He switched parrots and got Miss Monteith to get a gun for him. Despite those precautions, he was murdered. The murderer naturally assumed that the parrot in the cage was Casanova, and took excellent steps to see that it didn't die before Sabin's body was discovered.

"Sabin, in the meantime, thought that he was getting a divorce—that is, he thought his wife was getting one. He thought that he would soon be free to follow up the bigamous marriage ceremony in Mexico with a perfectly legal marriage ceremony elsewhere.

"Waid, lying in wait in the cabin, in which he had ensconced himself so that he could overhear all the telephone conversations which took place over Sabin's telephone, was waiting for the proper moment to strike."

"Why was he so anxious to hear the telephone conversations?" the sheriff inquired.

"Because the success of his entire plan depended upon leaving in an airplane with Steve Watkins, at such a time that it would apparently give him an alibi. The only excuse they had to do this was the appointment Sabin had made to pay over a hundred thousand dollars to his wife in New York. He knew that Sabin was in constant telephone communication with his wife in Reno. Therefore, he had to be certain that nothing went wrong.

"While he was listening on the telephone, he heard Sabin put in a call for Bolding, the examiner of questioned documents, realized suddenly that if Sabin sent Bolding the specimens of handwriting of all the persons with whom he'd had business dealings, those handwriting specimens would include some of his own; that the handwriting expert would break down the endorsements on the back of those forged checks, and brand him as a forger. He realized, suddenly, that whatever he was to do had to be done swiftly. I think he had intended to wait until eight o'clock before committing the murder. He had his string of fish already caught, the evidence all ready to plant. Then, that telephone call came through. He knew that he had to get to Sabin before those documents went into the mail, so he jumped up and ran out of the cabin without even pausing to pick up the cigarette he had laid down on the table when he heard the telephone call come through."

"Why didn't you tip us off so we could grab Waid?" the sheriff grumbled.

Mason said, "Because the evidence would be materially strengthened by having Waid become panic-stricken, and make a sudden disappearance. Flight, in itself, is an evidence of guilt. You can see that Waid was panic-stricken. As soon as he realized he had murdered the wrong parrot, he knew how deadly the evidence of the parrot would be, because it would prove conclusively that the parrot didn't learn his speech by hearing the excited last words of Fremont C. Sabin, but had been carefully coached to repeat those words by someone who had access to it; and Waid was the only one, outside of Fremont Sabin, and the son Charles, who had access to the parrot. You will note that Steve Watkins didn't live in the house, and Mrs. Sabin had been away for six weeks.

"Of all the persons who had a complete alibi, the parrot was the one who had the best. The parrot was not at the scene of the shooting. That was attested to by Mrs. Winters. Therefore, the parrot couldn't have learned his speech from hearing Sabin say those words. I felt it was quite possible that Sabin's murderer might be in the room last night when I disclosed the switch in parrots. Charles Sabin had known of it for some time. The information came as news to Mrs. Sabin, Steve and Waid—I saw to that. . . . So Waid decided the only thing for him to do was to kill the parrot. He didn't know that other persons had heard the parrot's comments. You see, that's the trouble with teaching a parrot something to say: you never can tell how often he'll say it, or when he'll say it.

"But Waid had all the breaks in one way. He hadn't intended to pin the crime on Helen Monteith. It's probable that he knew nothing of Helen Monteith. He had intended to pin the crime on Helen Watkins Sabin. Imagine his consternation when he found that Helen Watkins Sabin had an alibi; that she had been in court in Reno when the murder was supposed to have been committed. Then, he suddenly realized there was an excellent opportunity to pin the crime on Helen Monteith, but he had to get that parrot out of the way. And then his confidence suddenly returned when he learned that the decree of divorce had been forged, and that Mrs. Sabin didn't have an alibi after all.

"Once having placed the time of the murder accurately, and disregarding the evidence of the string of fish to which Sergeant Holcomb attached such great importance, it became obvious that Sabin was not alive at ten o'clock on the evening of Monday, the fifth. Therefore, Waid's statement that he had talked with Sabin over the telephone must have been false."

Helen Monteith said, "Well, I hope they hang him! He killed one of the best men who ever lived. You've no idea how unselfish and considerate Mr. Sabin was. He thought of everything, no detail was too small to escape him. Nothing which would go for my comfort was overlooked."

"I can readily appreciate that," Mason said soberly. "Everything that he did ... Wait a minute ..."

He stopped abruptly.

"What's the matter?" the sheriff asked.

Mason said excitedly, "That will! He really executed that after he'd married you. Yet he didn't make any provision in it for you. He provided for everyone else."

"Yes," she said.

"Why didn't he provide for you?" Mason asked.

"I don't know. He would have had some good reason. I didn't want money, anyway. I wanted him."

Mason said, "That's the angle to this case I can't understand. Fremont Sabin made his will at the time he was negotiating that property settlement with his wife."

"What's wrong with that?" Sheriff Barnes asked.

Mason said, "It just doesn't fit into the picture. He makes provision for every one of the objects of his affection, but he doesn't make any provision whatever for Helen Monteith."

"That was because he didn't have any reason to," the sheriff said. "He'd married her in Mexico, and he was going to marry her again, later on. We know now that the reason for all this was that he was waiting for Helen Watkins Sabin to get her divorce. Naturally, he didn't expect to die in the meantime."

Mason said, "No, that doesn't cover it. The businessman doesn't make his will because he *expects* to die, but to take effect when he *does* die. He covers every possible eventuality. Notice that the will specifically provided for the payment of money to Helen Watkins Sabin in the event he died before the divorce decree had been granted and the money paid. In other words, she, having made a good faith attempt to carry out the agreement, was to be protected, regardless of what might happen to Sabin. That shows his essential fairness. Yet, he made no provision for Helen Monteith."

Helen Monteith said, "I didn't want him to. I'm not dependent on him for anything. I'm making my own living. I . . ."

Suddenly Mason got to his feet and started pacing the floor. Once or twice he made little gestures with his fingers as though checking off points against some mental inventory he was taking. Abruptly he turned to Della Street. "Della," he said, "go get the car. Fill it up with oil and gas, and bring it down to the front door. We're going to take a ride."

He turned to Sheriff Barnes and said, "Sheriff, I'd consider it as a personal favor if you'd expedite all the formalities as much as possible. Cut all the red tape you can. I want to get Helen Monteith out of here at once."

The sheriff studied him from beneath leveled eyebrows. "You think she's in some danger here?" he asked.

Mason didn't answer the question. He turned to Helen Monteith. "Do you suppose," he said, "you could help me check one phase of your alibi?"

"What do you mean, Mr. Mason?"

Mason said, "I want you to do something which is going to be a nerve strain. I hate to inflict it upon you, but it's necessary. There's one point we want to establish, immediately."

"What?" she asked.

"I think I know the real reason for that original substitution of parrots," Mason said. "I remarked a while ago that we'd probably never know just what caused Sabin to make that switch. Now I think we can get the real reason. If what I suspect is true, there's an angle to this case so vitally important that . . . Do you think you could stand a drive to Santa Delbarra? Do you think you could point out to me the exact room in the hotel where you last saw your husband?"

"I could," she said, "but I don't understand why."

Mason shifted his eyes to meet the steady inquiry in those of Sheriff Barnes. "We've been talking quite a bit about becoming hypnotized by circumstantial evidence. After a person once gets a fixed belief, he interprets everything which happens in the light of that belief. It's a dangerous habit to get into, and I'm afraid I haven't been entirely innocent, myself. I've been so busy pointing out the trap to others that I've walked into one myself without noticing what I was doing."

Sheriff Barnes said, "I don't know what you're after, Mason, but we'll rush things through. I have the matron coming over with all the personal property taken from Miss Monteith. . . . Here she is now. Check this property and pay particular attention to the contents of your purse, Miss Monteith. Then, sign this receipt on the back of this manila envelope."

Helen Monteith had just finished signing the receipt when Della Street entered the room and nodded to Mason. "All ready, Chief," she said.

Mason shook hands with the sheriff. "I may give you a ring later on, Sheriff," he said. "In the meantime, thanks a lot."

He took Helen Monteith's arm, and, with Della Street on the other side, piloted her out into the fresh air of the warm night.

Twice while they were riding up the long stretch of moonlit road to Santa Delbarra, Helen Monteith tried to find out from Perry Mason what he expected to find at the end of their journey. In both instances Mason avoided the inquiry.

Finally, in response to a direct question, Mason said frankly, "I don't know. I do know that on one side of this case there's an inconsistency, a place where the loose threads fail to tie up. I want to investigate that and make certain. I'm going to need you to help me. I realize it's a strain on you, but I see no way of avoiding it."

Thereafter he drove in silence until the highway swung up over a hill to dip down into the outskirts of Santa Delbarra.

"Now," Mason said to Helen Monteith, "if you'll tell me how to get to the hotel where you stayed . . ."

"It's not particularly inviting," she said. "It's inexpensive and . . ."

"I understand all that," Mason told her. "Just tell me how to get there."

"Straight down this street until I tell you to turn," she said.

Mason piloted the car down an avenue lined with palm trees silhouetted against the moonlit sky, until Helen Monteith said, "Here's the place. Turn to the right."

He swung the car to the right.

"Go two blocks, and the hotel is on the left-hand corner," she said.

Mason found the hotel, slid the car to a stop, and asked Helen Monteith, "Do you remember the room number?"

"It was room 29," she said.

Mason nodded to Della Street. "I want to go up to that room, Della," he said. "Go to the room clerk, ask him if the room is occupied. If it is, find out who's in it."

As Della Street vanished through the door to the lobby, Mason locked his car, and took Helen Monteith's arm. They entered the hotel. "An elevator?" Mason asked.

"No," she said. "You walk up."

Della Street turned away from the desk and walked toward Mason. Her eyes were wide with startled astonishment. "Chief," she said, "I . . ."

"Let's wait," Mason warned her.

They climbed the creaky stairs to the third floor,

162

walked down the long corridor, its thin carpet barely muffling the echoing sound of their footfalls.

"This is the door," Helen Monteith said.

"I know," Mason told her. "The room's rented . . . isn't it, Della?"

She nodded wordless assent, and Mason needed only to study the tense lines of her face to know all that she could have told him.

Mason knocked on the door.

Someone on the inside stirred to life. Steps sounded coming toward the door.

Mason turned to Helen Monteith. "I think," he said, "you're going to have to prepare yourself for a shock. I didn't want to tell you before, because I was afraid I might be wrong, but . . ."

The door opened. A tall man, standing very erect on the threshold, looked at them with keen gray eyes which had the unflinching steadiness of one who is accustomed to look, unafraid, on the vicissitudes of life.

Helen Monteith gave a startled scream, jumped back to collide with Mason who was standing just behind her. Mason put his arm around her waist and said, "Steady."

"George," she said, in a voice which was almost a whisper. "George!"

She reached forward then with a tentative hand to touch him, as though he had been vague and unreal and might vanish like a soap bubble into thin air at her touch.

"Why, Helen, sweetheart," he said. "Good Lord, what's the matter, you look as though you were seeing a ghost . . . why, dearest . . ."

She was in his arms, sobbing incoherently, while the older man held her tightly against him, comforting her with soothing words in her ears, tender hands patting her shoulders. "It's all right, my dearest," he said. "I wrote you a letter this afternoon. I've found just the location I want."

CHAPTER FOURTEEN

GEORGE WALLMAN sat in the creaking rocking chair in the hotel bedroom. Seated on the floor by his side, her cheeks glistening with tears of happiness, Helen Monteith clasped her arms around his knees. Perry Mason was seated astride a straight-backed, cane-bottomed chair, his elbows resting on the back; Della Street was perched on the foot of the bed.

George Wallman said in a slow drawl, "Yes, I changed my name after Fremont made such a pile of money. People were always getting us mixed up because I looked like him, and word got around that I had a brother who was a multimillionaire. I didn't like it. You see we aren't twins, but, as we got older, there was a striking family resemblance. People were always getting us mixed up.

"Wallman was my mother's maiden name. Fremont's son was named Charles Wallman Sabin, and my middle name was George, so I took the name of George Wallman.

"For quite a while Fremont thought I was crazy, and then, after he'd visited me back in Kansas, we had an opportunity for a real good talk. I guess then was when Fremont first commenced to see the light. Anyway, he suddenly realized that it was foolish to set up money as the goal of achievement in life. He'd had all he wanted years ago. If he'd lived to be a thousand he could still have eaten three meals a day.

"Well," Wallman went on, after a moment, "I guess I was a little bit foolish the other way, too, because I never paid enough attention to putting aside something that would carry me through a rainy day. . . . Anyway, after Fremont had that first visit with me, we became rather close, and when I came out here to the West, Fremont used to come and see me once in a while. Sometimes we'd go live together in a trailer; sometimes we'd stay up in his cabin. Fremont told me that he was keeping the association secret from his business associates, however, because they'd think perhaps he was a little bit cracked, if they found out about me and my philosophy of life.

"Well, that suited me all right. And then, shortly after I was married, Fremont came down to San Molinas to talk with me."

"He knew about your marriage?" Mason interrupted.

"Of course. He gave me the keys to the cabin and told me to go up there for my honeymoon. He said I could use it whenever I wanted to."

"I see," Mason said, "pardon the interruption. Go ahead."

"Well, Fremont showed up with this parrot. He'd been up to the house and picked him up, and the parrot kept saying, 'Drop that gun, Helen . . . don't shoot. . . . My God, you've shot me.' Well, that didn't sound good to me. I'm something of an expert on parrots. I gave Casanova to Fremont and I knew Casanova wouldn't say anything unless someone had been to some trouble to repeat it many times in his presence—parrots vary, you know, and I knew Casanova. So I suggested to Fremont that he was in danger. Fremont didn't feel that way about it, but after a while I convinced him. I wanted to study the parrot, trying to get a clue to the person who had been teaching him. So I got Fremont to buy another parrot and . . ."

"Then it *was* Fremont who bought the parrot?" Mason asked.

"Sure, that was Fremont."

"Go ahead," Mason said.

"Well, Fremont bought the parrot, so that no one would suspect I was studying Casanova, and I wanted a gun to give him, so I got Helen to get me a gun and some shells, and I gave that to Fremont. Then, he went on up to the cabin, and I came here to Santa Delbarra to look things over and find out about getting a place for a grocery store. I didn't read the papers, because I never bother with 'em. I read some of the monthly magazines, and quite a few biographies, and scientific books, and spend a good deal of time around the libraries."

"Well," Mason said, "I'm afraid you're going to have to readjust your philosophies of life. Under your brother's will, you've inherited quite a chunk of money."

George Wallman meditated for a while, then looked down at his wife. He patted her shoulder comfortingly, and said, "How about it, Babe, should we take enough of it to open up a little grocery store, or shall we tell 'em we don't want any?"

She laughed happily. When she tried to speak, there was a catch in her throat. "You do whatever you want to, dearest," she said. "Money doesn't buy happiness."

Mason got up, nodded to Della Street.

"You going?" Wallman asked.

Mason said, "I've done everything I can here."

Wallman got up from the chair, bent over to kiss his wife, then came over to grip Mason's hand. "I guess," he said, "from all I hear, you did a pretty good job, Mr. Mason."

"I *hope* I did," Mason told him. "and I don't mind telling you, I never had a more satisfactory case, or a more satisfactory client. Come on, Della."

They walked down the creaking staircase to the street. As Mason climbed in his car Della Street said, "Chief, I'm so happy, I'm b-b-bawling."

Mason said thoughtfully, "He does leave a clean taste in your mouth, doesn't he, Della?"

She nodded. "It must be wonderful to have happiness like that, Chief."

They drove through the moonlight, along the ribbon of road, lined with palm trees on either side. They were silent, wrapped in thought, bathed in that perfect understanding which comes to people who have no need for words.

At length Mason turned on the car radio. "Della," he said, "I don't know about you, but I'd like to find a nice waltz program somewhere . . . or perhaps the tinkle of some Hawaiian music, with . . ."

The radio screamed into violent sound in the midst of a news report. Mason heard the tail end of an announcement concerning himself, as the announcer said, ". . . Perry Mason, the noted trial attorney." There was a short pause, then the flash news reports continued, "Sheriff Barnes said merely that he had been covering dozens of places, that finding Richard Waid up at the mountain cabin which he had used as headquarters when listening in on Sabin's telephone was partly routine, partly luck. Sergeant Holcomb, of the Metropolitan police, gave a long interview to newspaper reporters. 'I knew Waid would head for that cabin,' he said. 'I can't tell you all the evidence which pointed to that conclusion, but there was enough to send me up there. Waid put up a terrific fight, but he was taken alive.' "

Mason switched the radio into silence. "We've had enough of police and murders and evidence for a while, Della. I can't get Wallman and his philosophy out of my mind. . . . I should have suspected the truth long before I did. The evidence was all there. I just didn't see it. . . . That's quite an idea, to go through life doing your best work and letting the man-made tokens of payment take care of themselves, Della."

"Yes," she said, then added after a moment, "Well, that's about what you do, anyway, Chief." She slid down on the seat so the cushion was against her neck. The reflected moonlight bathed her features with soft illumination. "Lord, think of the people who live to bless you!"

He laughed. "Let's think of moonlight instead, Della."

Her hand slid over to the steering wheel, rested on his for a moment. "Let's," she said.

The Case of
the Beautiful Beggar

FOREWORD

FOR MANY YEARS I cherished a desire to meet and talk with Dr. T. Furuhata of Tokyo, Japan.

Almost from the beginning of my interest in legal medicine, I have heard of Dr. Furuhata, the discoveries he has made, the painstaking work he has done in the field of serology, in the field of legal medicine and police science.

When I wrote Dr. Furuhata about arranging an appointment in Tokyo, not only did he reply in the affirmative, but his treatment on our arrival was indicative of the innate courtesy and consideration of his race.

In the course of our correspondence, Dr. Furuhata suggested we come to his office in the National Research Institute of Police Science. We set the time when we would be there and tried to be punctual, but because of a heavy schedule of appointments and congested traffic, we were a few minutes late.

Despite the fact that it was a cold, windy day in Tokyo, we found two of Dr. Furuhata's assistants standing bareheaded by the sidewalk waiting for us to drive up. They had probably been there for at least a quarter of an hour.

They made ceremonial bows from the waist after the fashion of the Japanese, then shook hands with us after the fashion of Westerners; then we were ushered in to see Dr. Furuhata.

I knew enough about the statistical information concerning this man to know that he was past seventy. I knew something of the prodigious amount of work he had done in his lifetime, and the energy he had expended overcoming prejudices, pioneering new fields, promoting research, encouraging new discoveries. I therefore expected to see a man who was at least trying to take life easy; who would be a little weary, and more than a little blasé.

To my surprise I found a keen-eyed individual who

had all the energy of a tennis ball bouncing on a cement court.

The preliminaries over, Dr. Furuhata started talking about legal medicine, about blood grouping and about police science, and once he was embarked upon discussion of his favorite subject, his mind went racing over such a broad field that I confess he left me far behind.

From time to time we made an effort to catch up and managed to get a general understanding of what he was talking about, but it was impossible to keep up with the technical details.

For a long period doctors had felt that human blood was restricted to certain limited classifications. Then serologists began to find factors in those classifications and such men as Dr. Furuhata began to explore the field of subclassifications of these various factors.

The progress that has been made is amazing.

Dr. Furuhata, moving as swiftly as a professional athlete, began pulling down various and sundry tables, all carefully worked out on charts which, like window shades, could be rolled down from the ceiling and then rolled up out of the way.

Dr. Furuhata is bilingual. He speaks English and writes English as fluently as he talks and writes Japanese; but his charts, of course, were in Japanese, and while his explanations were in English he was soon racing into such technical fields that he left my mind tagging along, trying to catch up. I sat there nodding my head, getting as many points as I could, even more interested in the remarkable man than in the scientific principles he was expounding.

Then he took us into the police laboratory and museum, and started explaining the cases on which he had worked, cases represented by gruesome human remains pickled in formaldehyde, various weapons, bits of rope, bloodstained garments, all quite frequently illustrated by police photographs.

I was more at home here, but my main purpose in visiting Dr. Furuhata had been to find out something about the man as a man. His stature is so great in his profession that it needs only one word to describe it: Tops.

Dr. Furuhata, like so many first-class scientists, is completely, absolutely impartial. His devotion is to science, not to the prosecution, not to the defense, but to the science of investigative work, of legal medicine, of serology, and of proof.

He keenly probed my thinking. When we went into the police laboratory and museum he knew exactly when I had grasped the point he was making and the significance of the object he was pointing out.

They say that the definition of a good salesman is one who knows when to close the sale, and, by the same token, the definition of a good teacher is one who knows when he has explained his point.

Dr. Furuhata always stopped at the right moment, neither too soon nor did he keep on talking after we had grasped the point he was making.

Time ran on unnoticed. When I finally looked at my watch, I felt embarrassed because I knew how busy Dr. Furuhata was and how important his time.

Dr. Furuhata is internationally known, internationally respected. He is a Japanese scientist who has all the painstaking thoroughness which characterizes the Japanese, who, for this reason, have made so many interesting discoveries in the field of medical research. But, in addition to all this, Dr. Furuhata is a dynamic personality who gets all the material together before reaching a conclusion; and then when he reaches a conclusion, knows that it is the right one.

Because legal medicine is so important in our lives; because Dr. Furuhata's knowledge has been of such great value in the investigation of so many crimes; because of the discoveries he has made and the pioneering work he has done in the field of serology, I wish to take this opportunity to dedicate this book to my friend,

TANEMOTO FURUHATA, M.D., M.J.A.
Professor Emeritus Tokyo University

ERLE STANLEY GARDNER

CAST OF CHARACTERS

The Case of
the Beautiful Beggar

CHAPTER ONE

DELLA STREET, Perry Mason's confidential secretary, regarded the lawyer with pleading eyes.

"*Please* see her, Chief."

Mason frowned. "I have this ten-thirty appointment, Della, and before I see this man I want to—Oh, well, I don't want to ruin *your* day. What's it all about?"

"She's just arrived in Los Angeles from the Orient. She came by way of Honolulu. She has a letter from her uncle telling her to get in touch with you immediately upon her arrival here and before she goes home."

"And she didn't send a wire asking for an appointment?" Mason asked.

"She isn't that kind," Della said. "She's about twenty-two, naïve, demure, quiet-spoken and very much disturbed."

"She was told to see me immediately on arrival?"

"That's right. Her uncle, Horace Shelby, wrote her a letter and—"

"What's in the letter?"

"I don't know. She said that her uncle had told her not to show it to any living mortal except Perry Mason."

Mason sighed. "Show her in. I'll hit the high spots, get rid of her and—"

Like a streak Della Street went through the door to the outer office before he had finished the sentence.

Mason grinned and rose as Della ushered in a beautiful young woman.

"This is Daphne Shelby," she said, and then, smiling brightly at Daphne, "and this is Mr. Mason."

Daphne shyly mumbled a greeting, opened her purse, took out a letter, said, "Thank you very much for seeing me, Mr. Mason. I guess I should have sent a wireless but I was too upset. . . . I'll try and be as brief as possible."

Della passed the letter and envelope across to Mason.

The lawyer held the envelope in his hands for a moment while he sized up Daphne.

"Won't you sit down?" he asked.

She seated herself somewhat tentatively in the straight-backed chair across from his desk, rather than in the comfortable overstuffed leather chair usually selected by clients.

Mason regarded her thoughtfully. "How old are you?"

"Twenty-two."

"You wanted to see me about your uncle?"

"Yes. Horace Shelby."

"How old is he?"

"Seventy-five."

"He's your uncle?" Mason asked.

"Yes," she said, noticing Mason's uplifted eyebrows. "I'm the daughter of Robert Shelby who was eighteen years younger than Horace."

"Is your father living?" Mason asked.

"My father and mother were killed in an automobile accident when I was one year old. Uncle Horace sent for me and raised me."

"He's married?" Mason asked.

"No, he's a widower, but he had a wonderful woman keeping house for him. She was like a mother to me."

"Is she still with him?"

"She died two years ago. . . . Please, Mr. Mason, I feel that after you read that letter, you'll see the urgency of all this."

Mason unfolded the letter addressed to Daphne Shelby care of the steamship at Honolulu and marked *Urgent*.

The letter was in pen and ink and in the cramped, wavering handwriting of a person whose reflexes are somewhat impaired by age.

The letter began,

Daphne dear,

Don't come home until you have done what I am asking. Don't let anyone know you have heard from me. I won't be able to meet the boat. Take a cab and go as fast as possible to the office of Perry Mason, the attorney. Get Perry Mason to go to the bank with you; cash the enclosed check and have Perry Mason take charge of the money for you so that it can't possibly be found by anyone.

After you have done this, come home and try to keep your temper. Be prepared for a shock.

Tell Perry Mason to prepare a will leaving everything to you. I want a short will and I want it prepared just as fast as he can do it. Have Mr. Mason come to the house when the will is ready for my signature. Tell him to have the necessary witnesses with him. At the very first opportunity he's to hand me the will. I'll sign it and give it back to him to keep. No one except Mason and the witnesses must know he has a will ready for my signature, or that it has been executed. The greatest secrecy is necessary.

Please remember, Daphne, that no matter what happens I love you very much indeed.

Your Uncle Horace.

Mason read the letter, frowning thoughtfully. "Sounds like an emergency. Do you have any idea what it is?"

"The letter is all I know. It was sent to Honolulu. I had been in Hong Kong for a three-month vacation. They thought I needed a rest."

"Who is the 'they'?" Mason asked.

"The brother, Borden, and his friend."

"Borden Shelby?" Mason asked.

"No, his name is Finchley. He's a half brother. He and his wife came to visit Uncle Horace. He brought his friend, Ralph Exeter, and since Aunt Elinor was there it was suggested—"

"Aunt Elinor?" Mason asked.

"That's Borden's wife. She said she'd take charge of things. They agreed that I was rundown and needed a good long rest; that I was to go on an ocean voyage and forget about everyone except myself."

"And you've been away several weeks?"

"Nearly three months."

Mason extended his hand casually. "There was a check in the letter?" he asked.

She passed over a slip of paper. "Here it is," she said.

Mason looked at the check, suddenly straightened in the chair, frowned, looked at the check again and said, "This check is for *one hundred and twenty-five thousand dollars!*"

"I know," she said. "I couldn't understand it at all."

Mason pursed his lips. "Quite evidently there's something bothering your uncle." The lawyer looked at his watch. "All right," he said, "let's go to the bank and cash this check. Are you known there?"

"Oh, yes, I've always done my uncle's banking business."

"And he has a balance sufficient to honor this check in his commercial checking account?"

"That's right. There was around a hundred and forty-five thousand dollars in it when I left. I keep his books and make out his checks, you know."

"But he signs them?" Mason asked.

"Oh, yes."

Mason gave Della Street a troubled glance. "That ten-thirty appointment," he said, "explain that I've been unavoidably detained for just a few minutes. . . . Now, what do you want done with this money, Daphne; you can't go around carrying a sum like that."

"No, no, the letter says you are to take charge of it and fix it in such a way that I can have it but nobody can find it."

Mason frowned. "I don't think I care to undertake something of that sort, but I can certainly arrange to keep the money for you until we can find out what this is all about.

"You have some cash with you?" he asked as they started for the door.

"Actually I don't. Uncle Horace saw that I had traveler's checks when I started on the trip. But everything was a lot more expensive than we had expected. I cashed my last traveler's check in Honolulu. I had just enough money for taxi fare here. I'll have to take taxi fare home out of the money we get on this check.

"You see," she added apologetically, "I hadn't expected

4

anything like this, and the cost of the taxi here was a lot more than—Well, I'm broke."

"I see," Mason said. And then as they started down the corridor to the elevator added, "Your Uncle Horace is wealthy?"

"Quite wealthy," she said. "That is, I consider him so. He has some real estate holdings and stocks and bonds, and he keeps a large amount of liquid cash."

"I can see that he does," Mason said. "Why?"

"He likes to have cash on hand that he can use whenever he wants to for quick investments without bothering to sell stocks or bonds."

They went down in the elevator, walked two blocks to the bank, and Mason said to Daphne, "You know one of these gentlemen at the teller's window?"

"Oh, yes," she said, "I know several of them. There's Mr. Jones over there. There's a short line in front of his window."

She took her place in the line. Mason stood beside her.

The line thinned out at the window, and Daphne endorsed the check, then pushed it through the wicket.

"Why, hello, Daphne," the teller said, reaching for the check. "A deposit?"

"No, I'm cashing this check," she said.

The teller opened a drawer. "All right, how do you want it? You—" He looked at the check, paused in stiff arrested motion, said, "Excuse me for a moment, please."

He left the window, and a few moments later was back with the cashier.

The cashier glanced at Daphne, then at Perry Mason.

"Why, hello, Mr. Mason," he said.

Mason acknowledged the greeting.

"Is he with you?" the cashier asked Daphne.

She nodded.

The cashier handed back the check. "I'm sorry, Daphne," he said, "but there isn't any money to cover this check."

"No money?" she asked. "Why, I'm sure there is. When I left there was—"

"The account has been cleaned out by a Court order," the cashier said. "It's been transferred to a conservator—I think you'd better see your uncle. Mr. Mason can explain to you what has happened."

"I'm not sure I can," Mason said. "What's the exact status of the account?"

"A Court order appointing a conservator. The conservator asked for the balance in the account and wrote a check for that exact amount, transferring funds to an account in the name of Borden Finchley as conservator."

"When did all this happen?" Mason asked.

"Day before yesterday."

"I think I see," Mason said.

The cashier's eyes were sympathetic as he handed the check back to Daphne. "I'm sorry," he said, and then added, "but that's rather an unusual check."

"I know it is," she said. "That's the way Uncle Horace wanted it."

"Well, you'd better have a talk with him, and have a talk with this Borden Finchley. Do you know him?"

"Oh, yes," she said, "he's my uncle, too—that is, he's a half brother to Uncle Horace. He's staying there with Uncle Horace."

The cashier flashed a sharp glance at Mason, then turned back to Daphne. "You've been away?" he asked.

"Yes, I went on a vacation nearly three months ago."

"Apparently a good deal has happened while you've been gone," the cashier said, and then glanced at the line that was forming behind Daphne. "Mr. Mason will take care of you, I'm sure."

He gave a reassuring smile and turned away.

Mason took Daphne's elbow. "I think you'd better give me that check, Daphne," he said, "and perhaps you'd better let me keep the letter for you. Now, I have an appointment which I simply can't break. The person is waiting for me up in my office right now, but I think you'd better take a cab and go right out to the house and,

6

if possible, talk with your Uncle Horace. If you can't talk with him, get in touch with me and—"

"But why shouldn't I be able to talk with him?" she asked.

"I don't know," Mason said. "He may have had a stroke or something. You know, a person at that age is getting to a point where those things do happen. I feel certain that there's been a very drastic change in the situation while you were gone, and if for any reason you can't see your uncle, I want you to come right back to my office. You can telephone first and let my secretary, Miss Street, know that you're coming."

Her eyes were dark with alarm. "You think Uncle Horace has—?"

"I don't know," Mason said. "Your Uncle Horace was all right when he wrote that letter, but evidently something has happened. Perhaps he is not getting along well with his half brother."

"Well," she said, "I can understand that. He didn't want them to come and see him in the first place."

"All right," Mason said, "here's twenty dollars for cab fare and expenses. Run along now, get a cab. I'm going back to the office. You give Miss Street a ring. You be sure to let us know what the situation is out there."

The lawyer gave her shoulder a reassuring pat, held up his hand for a cab which was waiting, put Daphne in it, then strode down the street toward his office building.

CHAPTER TWO

IT WAS JUST BEFORE Mason was leaving for lunch that Della Street said, "She's back, Chief."

"Who is?" Mason asked.

"Daphne Shelby."

"I'll see her," Mason said.

Della nodded and brought Daphne into the office.

"What is it, Daphne? Bad news?" Mason asked.

7

Her eyes showed that she had been crying. She seemed numb with shock.

"They've done something terrible, Mr. Mason."

"Who has?"

"Borden Finchley, Ralph Exeter and Elinor."

"And what have they done?"

"They've put Uncle Horace away."

With that, she burst out crying.

"Now, take it easy," Mason said. "Keep yourself in hand. Let's find out about this. What do you mean, they put him away?"

"They had him declared incompetent or insane, or something, and they've taken over the house and they've locked up my room and told me that I have until tomorrow night to take all my things out. And they won't tell me what's happened."

"All right," Mason said grimly, "sit down. Let's get this thing straight."

Mason picked up the telephone. "Tell Paul Drake to come in, if you will, Gertie. I have a case for him."

Mason said, "Now, just try to relax for a minute, Daphne. Paul Drake is a private detective and a good one. He has his offices on this floor and he'll be in here within a minute or two.

"In the meantime, I want you to fill me in with a little background."

"What do you want me to tell you?"

"You've been in the Orient for three months?"

"Well, in the Orient, and on shipboard. I took a long cruise. I went to Honolulu, to Japan, to Hong Kong, then to Manila and then back."

"You had letters from your uncle while you were gone?"

"Oh, yes."

"What kind of letters?"

"Nice cheerful letters."

"And then when you got to Honolulu, you received this letter?"

"Yes. If I hadn't been in such a hurry to get ashore, I would have had it when the boat docked, and then I could have telephoned or taken a plane or done something. But I had made some friends in Honolulu on the trip over. They were waiting for me and I hurried off the ship as soon as we were cleared to land. I didn't get back until just before the ship sailed.

"So I stood on deck saying goodbye to friends before I went down to my stateroom. The letter was there, waiting for me.

"By the time I had read the letter, the ship was well out past Diamond Head.

"Somehow, the letter itself didn't mean so much to me. I thought that Uncle Horace was a little dispondent and he wanted me to have some money that that—Well, frankly, Mr. Mason, I thought it was some kind of a tax deal. I thought perhaps he was leaving me money in his will, but wanted me to have some money that wouldn't be subject to inheritance tax."

Mason shook his head, said, "It would have been a transfer in contemplation of death. He didn't send you that check for that purpose—the question is, why *did* he send it?"

"I don't know."

"His letters were cheerful?"

"Well, yes, but come to think of it, there was a little something strained in his letters as though he—Well, now that you mention it, I begin to think of certain things. The letters were sort of stereotyped and—perhaps he wanted me to keep on having a good time and not bother me with anything until I got back."

"Now, when you went out there this morning," Mason said, "what did . . ."

The lawyer broke off as Paul Drake's code knock sounded on the door.

Mason nodded to Della Street, who opened the door.

Paul Drake, tall, loose-jointed, deceptively mild of manner, gave a comprehensive grin by way of greeting.

Mason said, "Paul, this is Daphne Shelby. Sit down while I find out just what has happened. After I get this information from Daphne, we'll make plans, but right now getting this information is too important to justify any interruption."

9

Mason turned back to Daphne. "Tell me what happened when you went to the house," he said.

"Well, of course," she said, "I was worried and I was in a hurry to see Uncle Horace, so I didn't wait for anything but just used my latchkey and ran right in and yelled, 'Whoooo-hoooo! Here I am!'

"No one answered. I looked right away into the room Uncle Horace has and it was vacant, both his study and his bedroom. So then I ran up to my room and my room was locked."

"You had a key to it?" Mason asked.

"Heavens, no. When I left there was a key on the inside of the bedroom door, but I never kept it locked."

"But it was locked just now?" Mason asked.

"That's right. So I went looking for Uncle Borden or Ralph Exeter or Aunt Elinor or somebody."

"And who did you see?"

"Aunt Elinor."

"And what happened?"

"Aunt Elinor smiled and said, 'Oh, hello, Daphne. Did you have a good trip?' And I said, 'Yes. What happened? Where's Uncle Horace?' And she said, 'Your Uncle Horace had to be taken away. He's in a home where he'll be given the best of care. And we suppose you, of course, will want to move out just as soon as you can get your things together.'

"So then she smiled at me, a cold, frosty smile, and said, 'We've locked up your bedroom so that your things will be safe. We'd like to have you out by tomorrow night because Borden is figuring on renting the house furnished. It will bring in a very tidy sum.' "

"Go on," Mason said.

"Well, I just looked at her in consternation and said, 'Why, this is my home. It's been my home ever since I was a baby. I'm certainly not going to move out. I'm going to see Uncle Horace and find out what this is all about.'

"Then suddenly Aunt Elinor got hard. I'd never seen her get hard before. She was just like cold granite. She said, 'Indeed, you're *not* going to stay here, young lady! You've sponged off your uncle long enough.' And I said,

'What do you mean, I've sponged off him? I've been taking care of him and getting all rundown doing it. Why you, yourself, told me that I had been working too hard and I needed to take a three months' vacation.' "

"What did she say to that?" Mason asked.

"She said that she had found out a lot of things about me since I had left and that her husband had been appointed conservator of Horace Shelby's property and he certainly intended to conserve the property and keep it from being wasted and dissipated, or given to shrewd and designing persons. She said that she had evidence I was intending to play Uncle Horace for a good thing and get all of this money and that I had been too greedy even to wait for his death, but had been milking him right along and that his housekeeper, prior to her death, had been milking him and I had been standing in with her and helping her do it."

"Then what?"

"By that time I was in tears. I guess I just made a horrible scene. I couldn't stand up to her and I couldn't listen to those awful things she was saying. I turned and ran out of the house and she called after me that I had until tomorrow night to move my things out of the house. Otherwise, she would move them herself."

"And then?"

"I'm afraid I was hysterical. I—All I could think of was getting to you just as fast as I could, because . . . because something horrible has happened.

"I know now that they are just schemers, that they moved in on Uncle Horace, took advantage of his generosity and good nature and got me out of the place on the pretext that I needed a rest and a vacation and then, just as soon as I was gone, they ganged up on Uncle Horace in such a way that they irritated him past all endurance. And Uncle Horace, of course, knowing that I needed a rest and a vacation, thought too much of me to tell me anything about it in his letters, but tried to act as though nothing was happening."

Mason frowned thoughtfully and said, "The fact that your uncle sent you that check indicates that he thought he had a little more time than he did—or perhaps he felt you could take a plane back. In any event, they moved in more rapidly than he had anticipated and evidently had a court hearing."

Mason turned to Della Street and said, "Della, get hold of the clerk of the court, find out what department the Shelby hearing was in day before yesterday, what judge granted the order, and the status of the case at the present time."

He turned to face Paul Drake. "Paul, I want you to find out where Horace Shelby is now. They probably moved him by ambulance. They have some doctor who may or may not be in on the conspiracy, and they've probably been using dope of some kind."

Mason said to Daphne, "Have either of your uncles or your aunt had any experience with medicine, or any medical education?"

"Why, yes," she said, "Aunt Elinor was a trained nurse."

"I see," Mason said grimly. "There are some drugs that can calm an elderly person when he gets excited and there are some that throw him entirely off his mental balance. I'm afraid you have been the victim of a rather deep-seated conspiracy. . . . How much is your Uncle Horace worth? Do you have any idea?"

She frowned thoughtfully and said, "Well, at least a million dollars. Probably more, what with his real estate, his stocks and bonds."

Mason was thoughtful for a moment, then said, "Paul, I want you to find out something else. You have a pipeline into banking circles. They won't give you confidential information, but they will give you all the information that isn't confidential, everything that's a matter of record.

"Now, I want you to get to this bank and find out just what happened to the account of Horace Shelby."

Della, who had been on the phone, said to Mason, "The order appointing Borden Finchley as conservator for the estate of Horace Shelby was made by Judge Ballinger day before yesterday. Borden Finchley qualified with a bond and immediately proceeded to take charge."

"All right," Mason said, looking at his watch, "I happen to know that Judge Ballinger's secretary stays in his chambers until twelve-thirty. Ring the secretary and see if I can make an appointment with Judge Ballinger for one-thirty, if possible. In any event, I want to see him before he goes on the bench this afternoon. Tell him it's very important."

Della Street nodded, got busy on the telephone, and after a few moments said to Perry Mason, "He isn't expected in until just before court, but if you'll be there at one-forty-five, you can at least see him for a few minutes before he goes on the bench. The judge had a luncheon engagement today and may not be back until just before court."

"All right," Mason said, "I'll go to see him."

He turned to look at Daphne Shelby's forlorn face.

"Where's your baggage?" he asked.

"Right in the taxicab," she said. "I never did get it unloaded from the cab because I have no place to put it. . . . I know all this is horribly expensive. I'm living on borrowed money and I guess I don't have a cent to my name."

"That's all right," Mason said. "We'll see that you're taken care of temporarily."

She said, "I . . . I suppose I can get a job somewhere, but this is such a shock to me."

Mason turned to Della Street. "Della, go down and help Miss Shelby get a room in one of the downtown hotels. Go to the cash drawer and get a couple of hundred dollars so that you'll have plenty of money and leave her with enough to cover expenses."

"Oh, Mr. Mason," Daphne said, "I can't do that. I don't want to be a . . . a beggar."

Mason smiled at her and said, "Quit crying, Daphne. If all beggars were as beautiful as you are, it would be a wonderful world. . . . But you're not a beggar, you're a client and I'm a lawyer."

"But I can't pay you anything, and the way things look now, I don't know if I ever can. Tell me, if Uncle Horace left a will in my favor and they have found it and just burned it up, what could be done?"

Mason's face was stern. "Probably nothing," he said,

"unless we can prove that such a will was in existence and they had burned it. Do you know if he made such a will?"

"He told me that he was going to."

"His letter," Mason said, "indicates that he hadn't done it. I may as well prepare you for the worst, Daphne. You've been the victim of a very clever conspiracy. Also it's a conspiracy that is as old as the hills. A wealthy man has relatives. Some of the relatives are close to him; some of them are not. The relatives who aren't close to him come to visit, get themselves established in the house, get rid of the relative who is close to the old man, then take advantage of the absence to claim the old man is mentally weak and subject to being exploited by shrewd and designing persons. They have themselves appointed conservators, tear up any will they may find and so put themselves in a position of sharing in the estate."

"But can't . . . can't he make a new will?"

"Not after he's been declared incompetent," Mason said. "That's the beauty of the scheme."

"But how can they get a person declared incompetent when he's really in full possession of his faculties?"

"That," Mason said, "is the diabolically clever part of it. You take any man who is past a certain age, who is accustomed to love, devotion and loyalty, then surround him with people who are willing to commit perjury; who constantly irritate him and perhaps are willing to use drugs, and the first thing you know you have a man who seems to be incompetent.

"But what I'm afraid of is that he may have walked into a trap."

"What do you mean, a trap?" she asked.

"That letter to you," Mason said.

"Why, what about it? He just wanted me to be taken care of no matter what happened."

"Of course he did," Mason said, "but if they walk into court and say, 'Here is a man who gives his niece a check for a hundred and twenty-five thousand dollars and tells her to put the money where it can't be found—well, such a person needs a conservator of his estate.' "

14

Daphne's eyes grew large and round. "Do you mean that they used this letter——"

"I think perhaps they did," Mason said. "I don't know, but I think perhaps they did.

"However, you go with Della Street. I'll fill Paul Drake in on some of the details. He'll start work, and before two o'clock I'll have seen Judge Ballinger. By that time, we'll know a lot more about this."

"And what about my things out at the house?"

"You leave your things right there for the moment," Mason said, "unless there is something that you need."

"But they told me I had only until tomorrow night."

"By tomorrow night," Mason said, "you may be in the house and they may be out."

"But Mr. Mason, I . . . I don't know how I'm ever going to pay you."

"We'll work that out," Mason said. "Right at the moment, remember that I'm an officer of the court, a high priest at the temple of justice. You're a naïve individual who has been the victim of a very great injustice. As a matter of principle, I'm going to try to rectify it.

"Now, you go with Della."

Mason nodded to Della Street and said, "Be sure she has some lunch, Della, and you get some, too."

CHAPTER THREE

JUDGE BALLINGER came bustling into his chambers at twelve minutes of two.

"Hello, Perry," he said. "Come in. I'm sorry I'm cutting things so fine as far as time is concerned, but I had a rather important luncheon appointment."

Mason followed the judge to his chambers and watched while the judge put on his robe.

"Got to go on the bench at two o'clock," the judge explained. "I can hold it off maybe a minute or two. What's the problem?"

Mason said, "I think perhaps I'm going to appear

before you in your court on a contested matter and I don't want to jeopardize your position or mine by discussing it, but I do want to get some history and, if possible, find out the reasoning back of an order you made in the case."

"What's the case?"

"The matter of the Horace Shelby conservator."

"Why, I handled that just a couple of days ago," Judge Ballinger said.

"I know you did."

Judge Ballinger looked at him shrewdly. "You think there's anything wrong with the case?"

Mason said, "Let's not either of us discuss anything except the history, but I would appreciate your thinking."

"I'll discuss any guardianship matter any time," Judge Ballinger said. "In those cases the Court wants all the information it can get.

"Mind you, I don't want you to tell me anything you feel should come before me by way of evidence in a contested matter, but I'm certainly willing to tell you how I felt.

"Horace Shelby is an old man, and he's confused, there's no question about that, and he was incoherent. He was excited, emotional and apparently he'd made a check for a hundred and twenty-five thousand dollars to some young woman who had been living in the house with him.

"Now, when you get a combination like that, you figure that something needs to be done. I appointed the conservator on a temporary basis with the statement that the Court would review it at any time any additional facts came up."

The judge stopped talking and looked at Mason. "You feel that you have some other facts?"

"I think it's possible," Mason said.

"All right," Judge Ballinger said. "The order is subject to review with additional facts. Tomorrow morning at ten o'clock too early for you to present your facts?"

"I think not," Mason said.

"Tomorrow morning at ten o'clock—No, wait a minute, I've got another case on at ten. We'll convene court early. Make it nine-thirty. Tomorrow morning at nine-thirty we'll have another hearing.

"I'm not going to ask to have Horace Shelby brought into court, because I think the court hearing upset him. I'll take a look at any additional facts that are presented and then if I want to amend, suspend, modify the order I made, I'll do it. That suit you?"

"Fine," Mason said.

"Prepare notice to the other side with an order shortening time and all the rest of it," Judge Ballinger said. "I'm two minutes late now."

He shook hands with Mason and walked from chambers into the courtroom.

Mason left Judge Ballinger's chambers, hurried back to his office and entered through the reception room.

He nodded to Gertie, the receptionist, and asked, "Is Della back?"

"Back about twenty minutes ago," she said.

Mason went in to the inner office.

"How did you do, Della?" he asked.

"Everything's okay," she said. "The poor child could hardly eat a bite. . . . Isn't that the darnedest thing you ever heard of?"

"It happens more frequently than we like to contemplate," Mason said.

"How did you do with Judge Ballinger?"

Mason grinned and said, "Make an order shortening time and an order for an additional hearing tomorrow morning at nine-thirty. See that it gets served on opposing counsel. By the way, who is the attorney in the case?"

"Denton, Middlesex and Melrose," she said. "The junior partner, Darwin Melrose, was the one who appeared in court."

"That's a good firm," Mason said. "They wouldn't any of them be mixed up with anything that was off-color—not if they knew it, and they'd be pretty apt to look into it before they went into a case.

"Have you heard anything from Paul Drake?"

"Not yet. He's trying to get something from the bank."

"Well, get those orders out," Mason said, "and arrange to get them served. Also, ring up Daphne and tell her that we're going to court tomorrow morning at nine-thirty; that I want her here at the office at nine o'clock; that she can go to court with me. . . . You'd better look in on her this evening, Della, and keep her from getting too upset."

Della nodded and asked, "How was Judge Ballinger?"

"Well," Mason said, grinning, "the judge doesn't want to discuss anything which may come before him where there's a contest, but the judge wasn't born yesterday and he knows as well as anyone the manner in which relatives can act like the proverbial camel in the tent—first put in a head and then gradually get the whole body in and squeeze the occupant of the tent out into the cold."

"He didn't say so, did he?" Della asked, smiling.

"No, he didn't *say* so," Mason said, "but the judicial mind was working rather rapidly, I thought."

"This should be quite a hearing tomorrow morning," she said.

"Could be."

Drake's code knock sounded on the door.

"There's Paul Drake now," she said. "I'll go out and get those orders ready and get them served."

She opened the door and said, "Come on in, Paul, I've got a rush job to do. The boss just came in. He has a rehearing for tomorrow morning at nine-thirty."

"Not a rehearing," Mason said, "a hearing to take additional evidence."

"Well, I've got some evidence for you," Drake said.

"What is it?"

"Stanley Paxton, vice-president of the bank," Drake said, "is pretty much worked up about this. He wants to do anything he can."

"Will he testify?"

"Sure, he will. If he knows there's a hearing tomorrow morning, he'll be there."

"Go on," Mason said, "tell me about Paxton."

"Paxton is the vice-president of the bank who keeps an eye on all the active accounts, particularly the large ones."

"How well does he know Horace Shelby?"

"He knows him mostly through his business transactions. Most of the personal contact that he had was with Daphne."

"What does he think of Daphne?"

"Thinks she's one of the nicest young women he's seen in a long time. He thinks she has a good business head on her shoulders, and he thinks Horace Shelby is being railroaded into a position where he can't make a will that will stand up in court, and these relatives, the Finchleys, are moving in on the estate just for the purpose of seeing what they can get out of it."

"And just what will Paxton testify to?"

"That every time he saw Horace Shelby, the old man seemed to know exactly what he was doing; that he has talked with him about investments on the telephone several times; the conversations have been just what one would expect in dealing with a normally sharp businessman and that Horace Shelby has the greatest love and affection for Daphne; that he relies on her for virtually everything and that she has been loyal to his interests all the way through.

"He'll also testify that he never heard of Borden Finchley or Elinor Finchley or their friend, Ralph Exeter, until Daphne went on her trip; that while Daphne was on her trip, Borden Finchely was offensively curious. He was trying to pump Paxton to find out the extent of Shelby's holdings, his net worth and all the rest of it. He tells me that Borden Finchley gives him the impression of being a chiseler, a sharpshooter and that if anyone has selfish and ulterior motives, it's this same Borden Finchley."

"Well, of course, he can't testify to that," Mason said.

"Not in so many words," Drake said, "but Paxton is a pretty shrewd individual. You get him on the stand and start asking him questions about Horace Shelby and he'll find some way of letting the judge know how he feels about Borden Finchley."

"What about Ralph Exeter?" Mason asked.

"Exeter seems to be a kind of a barnacle on the ship,"

Drake said. "No one knows his exact connection with Finchley. Of course, he doesn't have any with Shelby."

"You're sure of that?"

"Reasonably. Remember that I've been working at pretty high speed and haven't had a chance to check everything I want, but apparently Finchley is indebted to Exeter for a rather large sum of money and Exeter was pressing for collection, so Finchley brought him along to visit his rich brother so Exeter could see for himself that Finchley was going to run into a big sum of money one of these days."

Mason's eyebrows lowered slightly as he became thoughtful. "That," he said, "would make quite a picture. And, of course, Exeter would have found that Horace Shelby intended to leave everything to Daphne and . . ." A slow grin spread over Mason's face.

"Paul," he said, "Exeter is the weak link in the chain. I want to find out everything you can about the indebtedness of Borden Finchley to Ralph Exeter. Get everything you can about Exeter's background. When Finchley gets on the stand, I won't cross-examine him about Shelby, I'll cross-examine him about Exeter. . . . How did you get this information, Paul?"

"There's a housekeeper who comes in six hours a day."

"Who does the cooking?"

"Elinor Finchley is doing the cooking now. Before the Finchleys came Daphne did the cooking. Shelby's wants are rather simple, and Daphne knew exactly what he wanted and how to prepare it. She was doing a whale of a job, but she was working herself to death.

"Then after the Finchleys and Exeter moved in, why Daphne was simply floored. They had this housekeeper in and had a catering service send in many of the meals. That's how they were able to get Daphne to take this long ocean voyage. She was doing the best she could to be a hostess as well as taking care of her uncle's personal needs and cooking his food for him the way he wanted it."

Mason grinned and said, "Paul, I'm not making any promises but I think tomorrow morning at nine-thirty

20

we're going to have a court hearing that will be very, very, very interesting.

"However, in the meantime, you'll have to get a line on Ralph Exeter. I want his background. I want the basis of his relationship to Borden Finchley; and, if Borden Finchley owes him money, I want to find out about it."

"He owes him money all right," Drake said. "The housekeeper heard Exeter telling Finchley that he didn't intend to wait forever and that he wasn't going to sit on the sidelines and wait for somebody to die; that he wasn't built that way; that he wanted to get his money and get a turnover on it.

"Then they saw the housekeeper was standing by the doorway and they changed the subject abruptly."

Mason nodded. "Get Exeter's background," he said, "and I don't care how many men you have to put on the job."

CHAPTER FOUR

PROMPTLY AT NINE-THIRTY, Judge Ballinger ascended the bench and said, "This is the matter of the conservator for the estate of Horace Shelby. The Court stated at the time of making the order that the Court might require additional evidence from time to time and was keeping the matter open.

"The Court now wants to hear additional evidence. Mr. Mason, you have something to present?"

"I do," Mason said.

"Do you wish to present a witness or affidavits?"

"I have an affidavit," Mason said, "from Daphne Shelby, the niece of Horace Shelby, stating that up to three months ago, when she was persuaded to take a long ocean voyage, leaving Horace Shelby in the house where Borden Finchley, his wife and Ralph Exeter were visiting, Horace Shelby was in good mental health and in possession of all of his faculties.

"I have an affidavit from Stanley Paxton of the Investors National Bank, where Horace Shelby has kept his account for many years, stating that Shelby is, in his opinion, thoroughly competent; that Shelby has shown good business judgment in handling all of his affairs; that his properties have grown in value over the years; that he has made shrewd business investments; that Daphne Shelby has always had his best interests at heart and has made a very efficient manager.

"This affidavit further states that from the moment Daphne Shelby was persuaded to take a trip Borden Finchley started nosing around, trying to get information about Shelby's personal financial affairs, trying to wheedle information out of the bank on the pretext that Shelby was ill.

"The affidavit states that Paxton called Shelby on the phone and that Shelby's manner was perfectly normal and his business judgment very sound.

"On the strength of the showing I am about to make, Your Honor, I suggest that the conservatorship be vacated; or, if there is any necessity for a conservator, that Daphne Shelby, who has now returned from her trip, is much better qualified to act as conservator than is Borden Finchley.

"And as a part of my showing, I desire to call Borden Finchley as a witness."

Judge Ballinger frowned down at Finchley. "Come forward and be sworn, Mr. Finchley. You've already been sworn in this matter, but I think I'll have you sworn again just so there can be no misunderstanding."

Borden Finchley, a stocky, rather thick-necked individual in his late fifties, held up his hand, took the oath, then occupied the witness stand and glowered at Perry Mason from rather small, cold, blue eyes.

"Now, your name is Borden Finchley. You're a half brother of Horace Shelby and you were the moving spirit in asking for the appointment of a conservator?" Mason asked.

"That's right," Finchley said.

"You are visiting at Shelby's house?"

"Yes."

"How long have you been visiting there?"

"About six months."

"In other words, you were there for about three months before Daphne Shelby left on her vacation?"

"Yes."

"Who is in the house at the present time, Mr. Finchley?"

"My wife, Elinor, and Ralph Exeter."

"Ralph Exeter?" Mason said, putting just the right element of apparent surprise in his voice. "And is Ralph Exeter a relative of Horace Shelby?"

"He is not."

"A close friend, perhaps?"

"Not of Horace Shelby. He is a close friend of mine. He came to the Pacific Coast with us. In fact, we were driving in his car."

"And you moved right in with Horace Shelby?"

"We stopped to visit Horace and when we saw that he was weakening mentally, we stayed long enough to size up the situation."

"And Ralph Exeter helped you size up the situation?"

"He was with us and we were in his car. We couldn't very well ask him to move on. We imposed upon his good nature by holding him here while the situation was coming to a head."

"And when you say 'coming to a head,' you mean that it was getting to a point where you could ease Daphne Shelby out of the picture and put yourself in charge of the Shelby finances?"

"I mean nothing of the sort. I mean that Ralph Exeter was good enough to forego his own personal plans in order to stay with me until the situation was clarified."

"And what do you mean by 'until the situation was clarified'?"

"Until my brother wouldn't be taken advantage of by some young woman who was flaunting her charms, wheedling him for money and finally using her powers of persuasion to get him to turn over to her a hundred and twenty-five thousand dollars in the form of a check on his account, and asking her to go to an attorney to see that the

23

money was handled in such a way that it couldn't be traced."

"I see," Mason said. "You knew about that letter?"

"I knew about it."

"And how did you find out about it?"

"I saw the letter before it was mailed."

"And where did you see it?"

"On my brother's desk."

"You thought the letter was addressed to you?"

"No, I knew it was not addressed to me."

"Did you know to whom it was addressed?"

"I most certainly did."

"And yet you read it?" Mason asked, his voice showing a degree of incredulity that made it appear that the reading of a letter was a heinous crime.

"I read it!" Finchley snapped. "I read it. I called in my wife and had her read it, and I saw the check for a hundred and twenty-five thousand dollars which was to go in the letter, and right then and there I made up my mind that I was going to put a stop to having my brother's estate exploited by a total stranger."

"A total stranger?" Mason asked. "Are you referring to his niece, Daphne Shelby?"

"I am referring to Daphne Raymond, who has been going by the name of Daphne Shelby and who has represented herself to the bank and to my brother's business associates as being his niece. Actually, she is the daughter of his housekeeper and is no blood relation to Horace Shelby."

Mason, veteran courtroom lawyer that he was, managed to keep his face from showing any element of surprise, but simply smiled and said, "You have, I believe, heard your half brother, Horace Shelby, repeatedly refer to Daphne as his niece?"

"I have," Finchley said grimly, "and every time I heard it I knew it was another indication of the fact that Horace's mind was weakening and that the blandishments and wheedlings of this young woman had had their effect."

"But he *is* my uncle," Daphne exclaimed. "He is—"

24

Judge Ballinger tapped his pencil. "You will be given ample opportunity to state your side of the case, young woman. Just please refrain from making any statements."

Judge Ballinger turned toward the witness. "You have made certain statements, Mr. Finchley. I presume you are in a position to prove them?"

"Certainly, Your Honor," Finchley said. "I didn't care to bring the matter up because I didn't want to blacken the young woman's name, but of course if she insists, we will have to get the facts before the Court."

"What are the facts?" Judge Ballinger asked.

"Marie Raymond was a rather attractive woman who had an unfortunate love affair in Detroit. She came to Los Angeles looking for employment and was penniless, without friends, and had had but little experience and no training in any form of work. She therefore had no alternative but to take up housework. She advertised for a job as housekeeper and it happened that Horace Shelby saw that ad in the paper.

"He arranged an interview. The interview was satisfactory and Marie Raymond went to work for him.

"At that time Marie Raymond rather suspected that she might be pregnant but didn't know for sure. Later on, when she found out that she was pregnant, she confided in Horace Shelby.

"Shelby, at that time, was generous enough to suggest that she go ahead and have the child and continue her employment.

"Later on, when Horace Shelby's younger brother and wife were killed in an automobile accident, Horace Shelby suggested to Marie Raymond that they let the young Daphne think that she was the daughter of the deceased brother and his wife. In that way, Daphne would be given a name and her illegitimacy would not be known to her schoolmates.

"This was done."

"You can prove all of this?" Judge Ballinger asked.

"Certainly, I can prove it. I have letters written by Horace Shelby to my wife and me, letters in which he tells the whole story."

"How did Daphne get her passport?" Judge Ballinger asked.

"On the affidavit of Horace Shelby," Borden Finchley said. "The courthouse at the county seat of the eastern state where the brother and sister had resided had burned, and the birth certificates in the courthouse were consumed in the fire.

"I may state that Horace, while he never remarried after his wife died, had always been very susceptible to feminine charms—that is, to wheedling and importunities. We have no reason to believe that there were any relations between Shelby and Marie Raymond other than that she persuaded him to give her daughter a name and that the daughter used the opportunity to insinuate herself into the affections of Horace Shelby. There is no question but that he regards her with deep affection and there is no question in my mind but that this young woman, being fully aware of the situation, deliberately took advantage of it."

"Where is Marie Raymond now?" Judge Ballinger asked.

"She died a little over two years ago. It was at that time my wife and I decided to look into the situation because we felt that Horace was being imposed upon."

"So you came out here with the deliberate intent of looking into the situation?" Judge Ballinger asked.

"Yes," Borden Finchley said. "Horace is an old man. We didn't intend to have him imposed upon."

"And you wanted to protect *your* interests?" Mason asked.

Before Finchley could answer the question, Darwin Melrose got to his feet.

"If the Court please," he said, "we have been patient in this matter because we felt that, if possible, we would like to keep from bringing out the matters which relate to the illegitimacy of this young woman; but in view of the circumstances which have now been disclosed, we respectfully submit that there is nothing before the Court; that Daphne Raymond, sometimes known as Daphne Shelby, is a complete stranger to the controversy; that Perry Mason, as her attorney, has no status before the Court

26

and is, therefore, not entitled to question the Court's decision or ask questions of the witnesses."

"Well, now just a minute," Judge Ballinger said. "This is certainly a peculiar situation. I'm not going to rule on the objection for the moment, but I am going to ask this witness some questions myself. Regardless of whether anyone except a close relative is in a position to question the decisions of the Court in a matter of this sort, the Court certainly has the right to be fully advised in the premises."

"We have no objection whatever to a most searching examination by the Court," Melrose said, "but we are simply trying to forestall a long hearing in which a total stranger insinuates herself into litigation where she has no interest and no right."

Judge Ballinger nodded, said to Borden Finchley, "You realized, of course, that your brother had, as you express it, been victimized by this young woman?"

"We thought it was a distinct possibility. We decided to look into it."

"By we, you mean Ralph Exeter and your wife?"

"My wife and I. Ralph Exeter knew nothing about it until after we arrived here."

"And you realized, of course, that this young woman had, in your opinion, so insinuated herself into the affections of your half brother that it was quite possible he would make a will leaving her his entire estate?"

Finchley hesitated, shifted his eyes. "We hadn't really considered that point," he said.

"It had never entered your mind?" Judge Ballinger asked.

"No."

"But you did realize that if you could have a conservator appointed, if you could make it appear to a Court that the subject of the Court's order was incapable of carrying on his own business and was in danger of being influenced by shrewd and designing persons, you could prevent his making a will which would stand up in court?"

"Why, no! That didn't enter our minds."

Perry Mason said to Daphne, "Give me that letter."

She handed him the letter which she had received from Horace Shelby.

Mason said, "I am not entirely certain of my status in the case, Your Honor, and I don't want to interrupt the Court's examination. However, in view of the fact that the witness has stated that he saw this letter which Daphne received in Honolulu, I think it is advisable for the Court to read the letter."

Mason took the letter up to Judge Ballinger.

Judge Ballinger read the letter carefully, then turned to Borden Finchley.

"You say that it hadn't occurred to you that your half brother might make a will disinheriting you?"

Finchley hesitated, then said, "Well . . . no."

"That's right," Judge Ballinger said, "you answered that with a flat 'no' without hesitation a short time ago. You have hesitated now but your answer is still 'no'?"

"That's right."

"You don't want to change that answer?"

"No."

"Yet in this letter which I have in my hand," Judge Ballinger said, "the letter which apparently was sent to Daphne and which letter you have stated you read, the writer specifically states that he wants Perry Mason to draw up a will leaving his entire estate to Daphne.

"Now then, Mr. Witness, in view of the fact that you have testified that you saw that letter, do you still insist that the thought never entered your mind that he might make a will disinheriting you?"

"Well, of course, after I saw that letter I realized there was that possibility," Finchley said.

"And it was after you saw that letter that you took steps to have yourself appointed as conservator?"

"Well, I had been thinking about it for a long time and—"

"Just answer the question 'yes' or 'no,'" Judge Ballinger said. "It was after you saw that letter that you decided to and did start proceedings to have yourself appointed conservator of Horace Shelby's estate?"

"Yes."

"Where is Horace Shelby at the present time?"

"He is in a private sanitarium," Finchley said. "It became necessary to take him there. He is quite disoriented and rather violent and we were simply not in a position to care for him. We felt that he needed professional care."

Finchley pointed to his wife. "My wife is a trained nurse—that is, she was a trained nurse. She has seen many of these cases and she unhesitatingly states that Horace Shelby is suffering from senile dementia."

"That's right," a woman's deep voice boomed, as Elinor Finchley arose. "I'm in a position to verify everything my husband has said."

Judge Ballinger said, "You're not a witness as yet, Mrs. Finchley. You haven't been sworn. I would like to ask you, however, if you saw this letter Horace Shelby had written Daphne?"

"Yes, I saw it."

"Who showed it to you?"

"My husband."

"Before it was put in the envelope?"

"I didn't see it put in the envelope."

"The letter was signed?"

"Yes."

"Folded?"

"I can't remember."

"Your best recollection?"

"I have no recollection."

"What did you do with the letter after reading it?"

"Borden put it back in the env—" She bit the word off.

"In the envelope?" Judge Ballinger asked.

"Yes."

"You had then steamed open the envelope?"

"Yes."

"You put it back in the envelope. Did you mail it?"

"No. We put the envelope back on Horace's desk after he asked what had happened to it. He mailed it himself."

"I haven't time to go into this matter at this present hearing," Judge Ballinger said, "because there is another matter heretofore set which comes on the calendar, but I am going to look into this with great care. This matter is continued until—" He turned to the clerk. "When is the first day that we have—Wait a minute. I understand this case of Johnson versus Peabody is going off calendar. That will give us a half a day tomorrow?"

The clerk nodded.

"I'm continuing this matter until tomorrow at two o'clock," Judge Ballinger said. "At that time I want to have Horace Shelby in court; and, in the meantime, I am going to have him examined by a doctor of my own choosing. What is the private sanitarium where he is now located?"

Finchley hesitated.

"The Goodwill Sanitarium at El Mirar," Darwin Melrose said.

"Very well," Judge Ballinger said. "I'm going to continue the matter until tomorrow afternoon at two o'clock. I want it understood that a physician appointed by the Court will examine Mr. Shelby at the sanitarium. I want Mr. Shelby in court and I want it understood that the Court is not going to rule upon the objection disqualifying Perry Mason from appearing in the matter as attorney for Daphne Shelby—or Daphne Raymond, whatever her name may be—from appearing as an interested party until after I have given the matter further consideration.

"I may state that I will probably rule upon the objection at the conclusion of the hearing tomorrow afternoon, and that I will permit the examination of witnesses by Mr. Perry Mason until the Court has made its ruling.

"It is the offhand impression of the Court that the public is sufficiently a party to inquiries of this sort so that the Court can have the assistance of any interested party or interested counsel, and in the event the Court decides that Mr. Mason is not entitled to appear and interrogate witnesses on behalf of his client, the Court will probably welcome the services of Mr. Perry Mason as *amicus curiae*.

"The matter is continued until tomorrow afternoon at two o'clock."

CHAPTER FIVE

DAPHNE CLUNG to Mason's arm as a drowning person
clutches a bit of floating wood.

Borden Finchley gave her a vague smile and stalked
out of the courtroom.

Darwin Melrose, walking up to Mason, said, "I didn't
like to jerk the rug out from under you, Mason, but it was
the only way I could play it."

"You haven't jerked any rug out from under anyone as
yet," Mason replied, smiling affably.

He put an arm around Daphne's shoulders. "Come on,
Daphne," he said, and led the way into an adjoining
witness room.

"You sit down here," he said, "until the others have got
out of the courtroom. And after that, you're going to find
reporters will be hunting you up—probably the sob-sister
type of columnists who like to do the Poor-Little-Rich-
Girl articles."

"Mr. Mason, this is absolutely incredible," she said.
"My whole world has come crashing down around my
ears. Good heavens, do you realize what I've been
through the last—"

"I know," Mason said. "I understand, but you're a big
girl now; you're out in the world. You'll have to learn to
take wallops and to come back fighting. Now, let's take
stock of the situation and see where we can start
fighting."

"What can we do?" she asked.

"Well," Mason said, "we can check for one thing.
Although I feel pretty certain they're sure of their facts or
they wouldn't have brought them out in this way. Otherwise, it would have been suicidal."

"I still don't understand it," she said.

"The relatives thought they were going to be disinher-
ited but felt that, if there was no will, they could control
the estate.

31

"So they arranged for a visit, contrived in some way to get left alone with the aged testator, then manipulated things so they could claim his mind was failing, that he needed someone to protect him from shrewd and designing persons. . . . And, of course, the shrewd and designing person they always pick is the person they think is going to be the beneficiary under the will.

"If they can get the Court to appoint a guardian or a conservator, they're that much ahead. If they can't, they have at least established a record so that they can claim undue influence and a lack of testamentary capacity when the will is finally brought up for probate."

"I can't imagine people being like that," Daphne said.

Mason looked at her sharply. "Do you mean you're as innocent as all that?"

"No," she said, "I just can't imagine people being that low—particularly where Uncle Horace was concerned. Uncle Horace is the best, the most bighearted man in the world."

"How did he feel toward Borden Finchley?"

"I don't know, Mr. Mason. I do know that he thought they were staying in the house altogether too long; but then when Uncle Borden suggested that I needed a good rest and a trip somewhere on an ocean steamer, Uncle Horace chimed right in with the idea.

"I know that it meant a lot to him. I know that he knew he would have to put up with a lot of inconveniences, but he wanted me to have the rest and relaxation and have a good time.

"I told you Aunt Elinor had been a nurse, and she told Uncle Horace that I was simply working myself to death and taking altogether too many responsibilities for a young girl—that I should be out having a good time."

"All right," Mason said, "I'm going to scout around and see that the coast is clear of reporters and get you out of here. Don't tell anyone where you are staying and try not to talk with reporters. If you do, tell them that you have no comment to make unless I am present at the time of the interview; that, under instructions from your attorney, you are making no statement.

"Can you do that?"

"Of course I can do that," she said. "It will be easy for me. I just don't want to talk about things, but—I just can't understand how anything like this can take place."

"Our system of justice isn't absolutely perfect," Mason said. "But the case isn't finished yet. They may have letters from your Uncle Horace telling them about your parentage, but those letters are hearsay except for the purpose of impeachment. You just sit tight and keep a good grip on yourself."

She shook her head. "I'm finished," she said, the corners of her mouth drooping. "I'm illegitimate, I'm nobody. I'm going to be forced to go out in the world and try and make a living and I haven't anything to offer. I have no skills. I've been too busy taking care of Uncle Horace to ever learn anything that will help me make a living."

"You type, don't you?" Mason asked.

"Sure," she said, bitterly, "I type, but I don't have any shorthand and I haven't had any experience with taking dictation on any kind of a machine. I just compose the letters and bring them to Uncle Horace to sign. That is, I did compose. I guess those days are all over now."

"You use the touch system?" Mason asked.

"Yes, thank heavens, I taught myself that. I was just using a hunt-and-peck system with two fingers on each hand, and I realized that if I didn't break myself of that habit, I'd never be a really finished typist so I started practicing on the touch system and finally mastered it."

"Well," Mason said, "you're doing all right. You can get a job that will keep you going if you have to and if worse comes to worst."

She said, "The worst has already come. I've been batted around . . ." She suddenly squared her shoulders. "No, I haven't either," she said. "And I'm not going to be a beggar. I'm going to make my own way in the world— but first I'm going to see what I can do for Uncle Horace. I'm not going to let those horrid people manipulate him just any old way they want to."

"That's the spirit," Mason said.

She smiled at him and said, "And I'm *not* going to be a beggar."

Mason said, "You endorsed that check for a hundred and twenty-five thousand dollars when you tried to cash it at the bank?"

She nodded.

"That," Mason said, "leaves you with a hundred-and-twenty-five-thousand-dollar check, endorsed in blank, which may not be too good; and that letter which your uncle sent is evidence that—"

"Mr. Mason," she interrupted, "I just can't believe that he isn't my uncle. Oh, this is terrible, some sort of a nightmare that I'll awaken from."

"It may be at that," Mason said, smiling reassuringly. "My experience has always been that these things look much worse than they actually are. In fact, I tell my clients that nine times out of ten they can say to themselves, 'Things are never as bad as they seem.' "

"Thank you for trying to reassure me but I just don't know what to do next. How am I going to live until I can get a job? How can I go and get a room and—

"No, no," she interposed hastily, as Mason started to speak, "don't tell me that you'll finance me. I can't just live on your charity."

"It isn't charity," Mason said. "It's a business investment. Give me that check and the letter. I'm going to keep them in my office safe."

She said, "That letter, I'm afraid, shows that Uncle Horace—or should I say Mr. Shelby—never made a will in my favor and suddenly realized that he hadn't made a will."

"Don't be too sure," Mason said. "Many times a person makes a will entirely in his own handwriting—which is perfectly legal and valid—but then wants to have it supplemented by another will executed in the presence of witnesses."

"A will in handwriting is good without witnesses?" she asked.

"In this state, yes," Mason said. "The holographic will, entirely written, dated and signed by the testator, is valid.

34

"There are, of course, several catches or legal pitfalls. There can't be anything on the sheet of paper except the handwriting of the testator. In other words, if part of the date is printed and the testator only has to fill in the day and month, then the will is considered as not being entirely of the handwriting of the testator. The testator should start with an absolutely blank piece of paper on which there is no writing or printing of any sort. He should set forth that he is making a will. He should be sure to state the date. He should make a clear disposition of his property and sign it. Now, I have a feeling that your Uncle Horace, being a pretty shrewd businessman, did make such a will."

"But if they are in charge of his papers, they can find it and destroy it," she said. "Probably they have already done that."

Mason shrugged his shoulders. "I can't answer that as yet. It is always a possibility. However, remember that we have seriously impeached Borden Finchley by this letter; having sworn that he had no thought about the possibility of his half brother executing a will which would disinherit him; and then having admitted he had seen this letter, he put himself in a very questionable position.

"You could see Judge Ballinger turn against him the minute he made that statement.

"Well, Daphne, I admit things look black, but we're going to keep fighting; and don't you get discouraged. . . . You have enough money for your present needs?"

She nodded. "Thanks to your generosity," she said.

"It's all right," he told her. "I repeat, I'm just putting up a little money as an investment. After I collect some money for you, you can repay me and pay me a fee as well."

Her smile was wan. "I am afraid that your chances of getting a good fee are just about as slim as your chances of ever getting repaid. I suppose after I get a job I can pay you ten or fifteen dollars a month—something like that."

Mason patted her shoulder. "Let me give you some good advice, Daphne. Quit worrying about the future."

Mason left her and went to his office, fitted his latchkey

to the door of his private office, and shook his head at Della Street.

"The poor kid," he said. "I felt so sorry for her—her whole world crashing about her ears."

"What chances does she have?" Della Street asked.

"I don't know," Mason said. "If we can get the order appointing a conservator set aside and if Horace Shelby is the type of man I think he is, we can do some good. But remember that Horace Shelby has been through a whole series of devastating experiences and these have probably been complicated by some medication which is contra-indicated in his condition. There may be some permanent damage there.

"You can see their strategy," Mason went on. "They got rid of Daphne for the longest possible period of time. While she was gone, they did everything they could to undermine the mental health of Horace Shelby. Then when they didn't dare to wait any longer, they went to court. Of course, the fact that he was trying to give his niece—who it now seems is actually a stranger to the blood—one hundred and twenty-five thousand dollars, which virtually wiped out his checking account, was a big factor in the mind of the Court.

"You put yourself in the position of a judge and find a set of circumstances like that and you're pretty certain to feel that the man needs protection."

Della Street nodded, said, "Mr. Stanley Paxton is waiting in the office for you."

Mason nodded. "Let's have him in," he said. "In the meantime, Della, remember that I have this check for one hundred and twenty-five thousand dollars made to Daphne Shelby and endorsed by her, and also the letter that Horace Shelby sent her. I want to put them in our safe and I'd like to have a photographer make photographic copies of them."

Della Street reached out her hand.

"I'll keep them for the moment," Mason said. "Let's not delay seeing Mr. Paxton. His time is valuable."

Della Street went to the outer office, returned with Stanley Paxton.

"Mr. Mason," the banker said, "I find myself in a peculiar situation."

Mason raised his eyebrows in silent inquiry as he gestured to a chair.

Paxton seated himself, ran his hand over his high forehead, looked shrewdly at Mason and said, "We have had a little experience in these matters from time to time and we can size people up. Our primary interest as a bank is in protecting our clients."

Mason nodded.

"Horace Shelby is our client," Paxton went on. "As far as we are concerned, the conservator is a stranger—an intruder, an interloper."

"Under an order of Court," Mason pointed out.

"Under an order of Court, to be sure," Paxton conceded. "That's what I want to talk to you about."

Mason nodded. "Go right ahead."

"Of course, it's unusual because you are attorney—not for Horace Shelby but for his niece."

Mason was silent, waiting for the other to continue.

Paxton put the tips of his fingers together, looked steadily at a spot on the floor about five feet in front of him. He spoke in the tone of voice used by a man who is accustomed to dealing in precise figures and wants to express himself in such a way that he conveys exactly the thought he wants to convey.

"In dealing with the conservator," Paxton said, "the general custom is for the conservator to file with us a certified copy of the order of Court and have us transfer the account to the conservator."

"That custom wasn't followed in the present case?" Mason asked.

"In the present case," Paxton said, "I remember the wording of the Court order very clearly because I have had occasion to look it up. It said that Borden Finchley, as conservator, was to take possession of all funds on deposit in the Investors National Bank in the name of Horace Shelby, and safeguard those funds as conservator. An order was made to the bank ordering the bank to turn over every credit existing in the bank as of the date of that order to the conservator.

37

"Then Borden Finchley—apparently not trusting us—drew a check on us for the exact amount of the balance on hand in the account of Horace Shelby."

"And opened a new account as conservator?" Mason asked.

"He did that temporarily. He opened a new account as conservator but, within two hours, went to another bank, opened an account in the name of Borden Finchley, conservator for the estate of Horace Shelby, and cleaned out the account."

Mason grinned. "He evidently didn't want to antagonize you until you had transferred the money to his account, then he went out of his way to give you a deliberate slap in the face."

"Probably," Paxton said, "he realized that our attitude was somewhat unsympathetic. We considered Horace Shelby a rather elderly but very shrewd individual. Some people are old at seventy-five, some people are alert at ninety."

"And Horace Shelby was mentally alert?"

"We considered him a very lovable old gentleman. I'll be frank with you, Mr. Mason, he would get a little confused at times and he knew it, and he relied implicitly on Daphne."

"And what's your opinion of Daphne?"

"She's a jewel. She's just a sweet, loyal girl who sacrificed her entire life for her uncle; and she did it out of affection and not because she was looking to see which side of the bread had the butter."

Mason nodded, said after a moment, "Well, the money was taken over under a Court order and it's out of the bank."

"That is true," Paxton said. "It might have been better if Finchley had handled it in the ordinary way and simply taken over everything in Shelby's account at the bank and served us with an order that only the signature of the conservator was to be recognized."

"What do you mean?" Mason asked.

"Simply this," Paxton said. "Yesterday afternoon a deposit of fifty thousand dollars was made to the credit of Horace Shelby."

"What?" Mason exclaimed.

Paxton nodded. "It was a payment due under a contract of purchase," he said, "and the contract provided that the money could be paid by depositing it to the credit of Horace Shelby in our bank. A grant deed had already been executed by Horace Shelby and placed in escrow with a title company with instructions that whenever the purchaser showed a deposit slip showing that the final fifty thousand dollars had been paid to the account of Horace Shelby at our bank, the deed was to be delivered.

"The purchaser knew nothing of the appointment of a conservator and insisted on depositing the money to the account of Horace Shelby and receiving a duplicate deposit slip, which he took to the escrow company."

Mason pursed his lips.

"Now then," Paxton went on, "we are in a peculiar situation. If we notify Borden Finchley of this extra fifty thousand dollars, he will simply have another order prepared and have that account transferred to his name. But do we need to notify him?"

"Certainly," Mason said. "I think it's your duty to notify him."

Paxton's face showed his disappointment.

"You should write him a letter immediately," Mason said, "and explain the circumstances to him."

Paxton got to his feet. "Well," he said, his manner showing disappointment, "I was hoping that perhaps you could suggest some other means of handling it."

Mason shook his head. "That's the only ethical thing to do," he said. "Go to the bank and write a letter. In fact, I'll walk down to the bank with you. I have some business in that direction. We can walk together."

"If Horace Shelby knew about this money," Paxton said, "I think he'd contrive in some way to take care of Daphne."

"There's nothing he can do," Mason said. "Your attorney would advise you that you couldn't take chances."

"Yes, I suppose so," Paxton said, with a sigh. "But you have the reputation of being very ingenious, Mr. Mason, and I thought I'd let you know."

"I'm glad you did," Mason said. "The bank's only a few doors down the street, I'll go on down with you."

"And you feel I should write Borden Finchley a letter?"

"Immediately," Mason said.

They walked down to the elevator, then strolled down the street. Paxton seemed to be dragging his feet.

"Of course," Paxton pointed out, "you can see what Shelby was trying to do. He was *trying* to take care of Daphne financially. That's what *he* wanted. If he hadn't been so anxious to take care of her, the Court might have been more hesitant about appointing a conservator."

"I suppose so," Mason said. "How's my credit at your bank, by the way?"

"*Your* credit?" Paxton asked in surprise. "Why, absolutely A-1."

"I'd like to borrow seventy-five thousand dollars," Mason said.

"Why, I think that can be arranged. You have some security?"

"No security," Mason said. "I would give my note."

Paxton started to shake his head, then frowned. "How long would you want the money, Mr. Mason?"

"About ten minutes," Mason said.

Paxton looked at him incredulously. "Seventy-five thousand dollars for ten minutes?"

"Yes," Mason said.

"Good heavens, what do you intend to do with it?"

Mason grinned. "I thought I would deposit it to the account of Horace Shelby."

"Are you crazy?" Paxton asked. "Are you . . ." Suddenly he stopped dead in his tracks, regarded Mason in a bewildered manner, then broke out laughing.

"Come on," he said, "let's get to the bank just as fast as we can."

He started walking more rapidly, and Mason lengthened his strides to keep up with the banker.

They entered the bank. Paxton called in a secretary. He said, "If you don't mind, Mr. Mason, I'll dictate a letter to Borden Finchley telling him—"

"I think," Mason interrupted, "the better procedure

would be to make the letter to Horace Shelby, care of Borden Finchley, Conservator."

Paxton grinned. "I get the point," he said. "It's a legal distinction, but an important one."

Paxton turned to the secretary. "Take a letter to Horace Shelby, care of Borden Finchley, Conservator.

"Dear Mr. Shelby, The $50,000 final payment on the purchase of the Broadway property was deposited to your account by the purchaser, who took a duplicate deposit slip to deliver to the escrow department. Paragraph. That money is now on deposit in your name. Very truly yours, etc."

Mason nodded. "Now," he said, "could we visit the Loan Department?"

"Right away," Paxton said.

Paxton went on, "I think, Mr. Mason, under the circumstances, I'll okay this loan myself. You want seventy-five thousand dollars?"

Mason nodded.

"I'll make it for thirty days," Paxton said.

"Any time you like," Mason said. "I won't want it that long but if you'd like to have your records so show, why, it will be for that period."

Paxton made out the note. Mason signed it.

"How do you want this?" Paxton asked.

Mason said, "I think, under the circumstances, cash would be preferable—seventy-five one-thousand-dollar bills."

Paxton went to the vault and returned with the seventy-five one-thousand-dollar bills.

"I think," he said to Mason, "that from here on you had better handle this through regular channels."

"Exactly," Mason said, and shook hands.

Mason put the money in his pocket, walked out to the window of a teller, made out duplicate deposit slips, and shuffled his way along in the line of customers.

When he reached the window, he pulled out the seventy-five one-thousand-dollar bills and the duplicate deposit slip.

"Please deposit this to the account of Horace Shelby," he said.

The teller looked at the seventy-five thousand dollars in surprise. "A cash deposit for seventy-five thousand dollars?" he asked.

"Exactly," Mason said.

"I think that account has been transferred," the teller said. "I'm sorry but—"

"Can't the bank take a deposit?"

"Yes, I guess we could."

"Then, please deposit this to the account of Horace Shelby."

The teller said, "Just a moment. I'm going to have to ask someone about this."

He was gone a few minutes, then returned and said, "If you insist on making the deposit, Mr. Mason, we have no alternative but to accept it."

"Very well," Mason said. "I want to make the deposit."

The teller stamped and signed the duplicate deposit slips.

"Now then," Mason said, taking the endorsed check of Daphne Shelby from his pocket, "I have a check here that I would like to cash. A check for a hundred and twenty-five thousand dollars."

"You want to *cash* a check for one hundred and twenty-five thousand dollars?" the teller asked.

"That's right," Mason said, and handed the check through the window.

The teller looked at the check in frowning incredulity; then, suddenly, a light dawned on his face.

"Just a minute," he said. "I'll also have to check on this."

He left the window and was back in a few moments. "It happens," he said, "that there is just enough money in the account to pay this check."

"I'm not interested in the amount of the account," Mason said. "I only want to cash the check."

The teller said, "This is a most unusual situation, Mr. Mason."

Mason yawned. "Perhaps it's unusual for you," he said, and glanced significantly at his wrist watch.

The teller said, "How do you want this, Mr. Mason?"

"In thousand-dollar bills," Mason said.

The teller opened his drawer, carefully counted out the seventy-five thousand that Mason had deposited, then counted out twenty thousand more bills, summoned the messenger to go to the vault, said, "Just a moment, please," and a few minutes later, handed Mason the balance of the money in thousand-dollar bills.

"Thank you," Mason said.

He put the money in his pocket, walked over to the enclosure in which Stanley Paxton had his desk and said, "Mr. Paxton, I borrowed seventy-five thousand dollars from the bank a short time ago."

"Yes, indeed," Paxton said. "It was a short-term thirty-day note on your personal security, Mr. Mason."

"Exactly," Mason said.

"I find that I have no further use for the money," Mason said, "and would like to pay off the note."

"Why, that's most unusual!" Paxton said.

"I know it is," Mason said. "As I figure the interest for one day, it amounts to about twelve dollars and thirty-two cents."

The lawyer gravely put seventy-five thousand-dollar bills, a ten-dollar bill, two one-dollar bills, and thirty-two cents on the banker's desk.

"Well, this is most unusual!" Paxton said. "However, if you insist on paying off the note, I guess we have no alternative but to accept it. Just a moment, please." Paxton took the money, put it in the drawer of his desk, picked up an interoffice telephone and said, "Send me in the Perry Mason note for seventy-five thousand dollars, please. Mark it 'Paid.' . . . That's right, I know it just came in. . . , That's right. *Mark it 'Paid'!*"

After some three minutes, a young man approached the desk with the promissory note.

"Here you are," Paxton said. "I'm sorry you didn't have further use for the money. We like to put our money out at interest on a good security."

"Oh, I understand," Mason said. "Now, I have one other request. I have fifty thousand dollars in cash. I would like to buy ten cashier's checks for five thousand dollars each, payable to Daphne Shelby. I believe you are acquainted with Miss Shelby."

"Oh, yes," Paxton said, "we know her quite well. She does all the business for her uncle. You wanted ten cashier's checks for five thousand dollars each?"

"That's right."

"If you can wait for just a few more minutes," Paxton said.

He took the fifty thousand dollars, left his desk and within a matter of fifteen minutes returned with the ten cashier's checks.

"Thank you very much," Mason said.

The banker stood up.

"I've shaken hands with you once, Mr. Mason," he said. "I'm going to shake hands with you again, and I hope you'll forgive me for my momentary doubts as to your ingenuity. When I really violated a confidence to give you information in your office, I was hoping against hope that you'd find some way of handling the matter, and then I felt my hopes dashed to the ground. I realize now that I should have had more confidence."

The banker gripped the lawyer's hand firmly, then patted him on the shoulder. "Good luck, Mr. Mason," he said.

"Thanks very much," Mason said. "And thanks to the Investors National Bank for the interest it takes in its clients. I can assure you that this action will eventually rebound to your benefit."

"Thank you. Thank you very much," Paxton said.

The lawyer, with the ten cashier's checks in his inside pocket, left the bank, went to Daphne Shelby's hotel.

"Daphne," he said when he confronted the young woman, "you're no longer a beautiful beggar."

"What do you mean?" she asked.

Mason took the ten cashier's checks from his pocket.

She looked at each one incredulously. "What in the world!" she asked.

Mason said, "Just endorse this one check 'Pay to the order of Perry Mason.'"

"That's your fee?" she asked.

"We're not talking about a fee yet," Mason said. "I'm

having you endorse this so I can get five thousand dollars in cash and send it over to you. That's all you should have on your person at the present time. In fact, you'd better get traveler's checks for about forty-five hundred dollars with it. The other checks you should hold against a rainy day."

CHAPTER SIX

MASON HAD BEEN BACK in his office less than an hour when Paul Drake's code knock sounded on the door.

Della Street admitted the detective and Drake said, "Well, I've got Ralph Exeter pegged."

"What about him?" Mason asked.

Drake said, "Exeter's real name is Cameron. His first name is a queer one—Bosley, B-O-S-L-E-Y. He's from Las Vegas. He's a gambler, and he's holding Borden Finchley's IOUs for over a hundred and fifty thousand bucks."

"So that explains a lot," Mason said.

"There's more to it than that," Drake went on. "Cameron became involved himself and, until he can get the money on those IOUs of Finchley, Cameron can't get back in good standing with his own crowd. So Cameron is hiding out. That's why he has taken the name of Ralph Exeter of Boston, Massachusetts."

Mason said, "That's darned good work, Paul. You did a wonderful job."

Drake shook his head and said, "I didn't really do anything. I just happened to cross the back trail of people who are trying to find Cameron."

"How?"

"Well, it was just a combination of circumstances. Finchley gave a rather synthetic background of where he had been and what he had been doing, but the person that comes in to do the housecleaning noticed that there were Las Vegas stickers on his baggage when he first came there, and that Finchley was at great pains to scrub them off the second day he was there.

"You remember Finchley said they were driving in Exeter's car. I traced the license plates on Exeter's car. They were Massachusetts license plates all right, but I used the long distance telephone, got some quick action, and found the person who was registered as owning that car when it left Massachusetts.

"He went to Las Vegas, became involved in a gambling game, and this man Cameron, to whom he owed a little over a thousand dollars, offered to trade automobiles and give him the difference. The fellow had no alternative but to make the deal so they simply traded possession of the cars without going through the formality of getting registrations transferred. They felt they could do that later on when they applied for new licenses.

"Once I had that lead, I did a little telephoning in Las Vegas and found that Cameron was one of those big-shot gamblers who will be way up in the clouds one day and way down in the depths the next.

"He got wiped out in a poker game and had some IOUs floating around. He told friends that he had a pigeon who owed him a hundred and fifty grand and that the pigeon had it all made, but it was going to take a little while to cash in; that he was going to ride herd on his pigeon until the money came in.

"Then Cameron disappeared.

"At first, the people who held Cameron's paper were willing to wait but now they're getting a little restless and they'd like very much to know where Cameron is."

Mason grinned, said, "Now then, Paul, we're beginning to get someplace. This is the sort of ammunition we can shoot."

"It's a shame we didn't have it for the hearing," Drake said.

"We'll have it for the next round," Mason told him.

The phone rang.

Della Street answered it, then looked inquiringly at Mason. "Will you talk with Mr. Darwin Melrose?" she asked.

"Certainly," Mason said, and picked up the telephone. "Hello, Melrose. What can I do for you?"

Melrose was so excited he talked with machine-gun rapidity. "What the devil have you been up to? The title company tells me that an escrow was terminated, that a man made a final payment on property to Horace Shelby —a payment of fifty thousand dollars."

"Yes?" Mason asked as Melrose stopped for breath.

"So we get at the Investors National and they said there wasn't any money in the Shelby account. We asked them about that fifty-thousand-dollar deposit and they said it had all been checked out, that there had been two deposits made—one of fifty thousand and one of seventy-five thousand, and they had a canceled check payable to Daphne Shelby for one hundred and twenty-five thousand, which had wiped the account out."

"Why, that's right," Mason said. "There's no secret about that. We discussed that check in court. Your own client knew all about it."

"Knowing about the check is one thing; getting it cashed is another."

"Well," Mason said, "the check was left in the possession of Daphne Shelby. There was money in the bank to cover the check. The bank had a right to cash it and she had a right to present it."

"But the bank knew a conservator had been appointed."

"The bank had been advised that a conservator had been appointed for the account of Horace Shelby as the account stood at that time. Nothing was said about any future accounts or any future deposits."

"Well, we didn't think it was necessary since we were cleaning out the entire account."

"I'm sorry if you misunderstood the situation," Mason said. "But your order to the bank was very specific. It was ordered to turn over to the conservator the exact amount that was on deposit in Shelby's account at the date the order was served."

"I don't like this," Melrose said. "I don't think the Court is going to like it either. It's sharp practice."

"I beg your pardon!" Mason said.

"I said it was sharp practice."

"I think you misunderstood the situation," Mason said with a grin. "It wasn't sharp practice on my side; it was dull practice on yours. Go into court, if you want to, and see what the judge has to say about it."

"That's exactly what I intend to do," Melrose said. "I'm going to ask the judge to make an order to show cause why you shouldn't be found guilty of contempt of Court and an order demanding that you turn all of the money you received on that check over to the conservator."

"That's certainly your privilege," Mason said. "Go ahead and make the motions in court and I'll be there to answer them. . . . Was there anything else you had in mind?"

Instead of answering the question, Darwin Melrose slammed the telephone back in place.

Mason grinned at Paul Drake and said, "You know, Paul, it's a long worm that has no turning."

Drake said, "I gather from your conversation that you slipped over a fast one?"

"Well, I don't know," Mason said judicially. "Darwin Melrose is one of those attorneys who wants to be specific. If he wants to describe a horse with a white, right hind leg, he makes the description read 'a horse with *one* white, right hind leg.'

"Of course, he knew just what the balance was in Shelby's account, so he made the order which he served on the bank specific—that they were to turn over to the conservator Shelby's account consisting of exactly so many thousand dollars, so many hundred dollars and so many cents—right around a hundred and fifty-six thousand dollars.

"Of course, it never occurred to him that someone might make a deposit in Shelby's name."

"And someone did?" Drake asked.

"Someone did," Mason said.

"Did you have anything to do with it?"

"Oh, a little," Mason admitted, with a grin. "We have carried out Horace Shelby's wishes in part and, thanks to the information you have, we may be able to carry them out the rest of the way."

"Your client?" Drake asked. "I take it you've seen she's provided for?"

"She's provided for."

"Don't you think she's a little bit too naïve?" Drake asked.

"What do you mean?"

"For a girl who's been handling her uncle's business affairs, writing all of his correspondence, more or less doing his thinking for him in matters running into a good many thousands of dollars, she seems just a little bit synthetic in her unsophistication."

Mason regarded the detective with thoughtful eyes. "You know, Paul, I've been thinking the same thing. I've been wondering if back of that schoolgirl naïve character there isn't a pretty smart mind. But remember, the bank has been doing business with her for a long time. They've known the connection between her and her uncle and they're for her all the way."

"Oh, I think she's all right," Drake said, "but—I don't know. Do you suppose she's suspected the true relationship and just kept playing demure so that Horace Shelby would never know she suspected?"

Mason shrugged his shoulders. "I'm darned if I know, Paul. But—What do you think, Della?"

Della shook her head. "You don't get me to express my opinion," she said.

"You have one?"

"Yes."

"And why don't you want to express it?"

"I'm not sure of my grounds," she said thoughtfully.

"Well," Mason said, "we're doing the best we can for her. She's had a whole series of jolts but I think, in the long run, we're going to come out all right.

"Who's the doctor the Court is appointing, Paul?"

"I don't know as yet," Drake said, "but I've got a line out so I can find out just as soon as—" He was interrupted by the telephone.

Della Street picked up the phone, said, "It's for you, Paul. Your office is calling on the unlisted line."

Drake took the call, said, "Give me that name again," said, "thanks," hung up and turned to Perry Mason. "Okay, Perry," he said, "the question is answered. The Court has appointed Dr. Grantland Alma as the Court's doctor."

Della Street immediately started riffling through the pages of the phone book, then furnished the supplemental information. "Here he is," she said. "His office is 602 Center Building and his phone is Lavine 2-3681."

"And," Mason said, "any attempt to influence him will make him mad but there's no reason why I, as an attorney, can't try to see Horace Shelby before the doctor does."

"You stand absolutely no chance," Paul Drake said.

Mason grinned. "If they've got him shut off from all of his friends, it might be a good thing to know."

The lawyer looked at his watch. "It's a cinch the doctor is in his office now. He probably won't try to see Shelby until tomorrow morning. Give his nurse a ring, Della."

"The nurse?"

"Yes. One should always communicate with a doctor through his nurse."

Della Street put through the call and nodded to Mason.

Mason said, "Hello, this is Perry Mason, the attorney, talking and I would like very much to talk with Dr. Alma on the telephone. If that is not possible, I would like to ask a question which he could answer. It is a matter of some urgency."

The feminine voice at the other end of the line said, "Well, this is his nurse. Perhaps you'd better give me the question. The doctor is busy now and has an office full of patients."

Mason said, "Dr. Alma, who's been appointed by Judge Ballinger to examine Horace Shelby sometime before a court hearing which is to take place—"

"Oh, I'm sure the doctor wouldn't discuss that with you or with anyone," the nurse said.

"I don't want him to," Mason said. "I am simply trying to find out if it would interfere with the doctor's plans in

50

any way if I went out to the Goodwill Sanitarium to visit Mr. Shelby."

"Oh, I'm sure it wouldn't," the nurse said. "Just so you don't do anything to upset him or alarm him. You're one of the attorneys in the case?"

"In the general case, yes," Mason said.

"Just be careful not to disturb him in case he should be excitable."

"Thank you," Mason said. "What room is he in, by the way?"

"He's in one of the isolation units, I believe. Just a minute . . . Unit 17."

"Thank you very much," Mason said.

"You're entirely welcome."

"Please tell Dr. Alma I called."

"I will."

"Well," Mason said, grinning as he hung up the phone, "if you want information, the way to go about it is to get it openly."

Drake grinned. "A good private detective could have put in two days at fifty dollars a day getting you that information, Perry. . . . You want me to go with you?"

"No," Mason said, "I think I'll go alone."

"The party may get rough out there," Drake warned.

"Under proper circumstances," Mason said, "I have been known to get rough myself."

CHAPTER SEVEN

THE GOODWILL SANITARIUM AND REST HOME at El Mirar was apparently the combination of a reconverted motel and a large old-fashioned three-story dwelling on an adjoining lot.

The properties had been united, a board fence put around the property, and on the windows of the motel units as well as on the windows on the lower floor of the big building were unobtrusive iron work—either ornamental grillwork or straight rectangular bars.

Perry Mason sized up the property, then made no effort to be surreptitious but walked through the gate, up the wide driveway and through the front door where a sign said OFFICE.

The lawyer noticed a sign on the gate reading, "Wanted: Young, well-adjusted woman with agreeable personality for general work." There was a similar sign in a frame on the side of the office door. Since these signs had been hand-lettered by a professional, it was apparent that the institution had quite a turnover in domestic help and experienced considerable trouble in getting replacements.

Mason entered the office.

There was a long counter across the room dividing it into two parts. Behind this counter was a switchboard and a chair; to one side, a desk littered with papers, a tilting swivel chair, two straight-backed swivel chairs; and a shelf of square cubbyholes, with room numbers over each partition.

A light was on at the switchboard and there was the customary loud buzzing sound indicating an incoming call.

Mason walked to the counter.

A middle-aged woman came hurrying through a door which opened from the back of the office. She hardly looked at Mason but went to the switchboard, picked up the headset and said, "Yes. Hello. This is the Goodwill Sanitarium."

She listened for a minute, then said, "Well, he isn't in now. I've left word with his secretary. He'll call as soon as he gets back. . . . No, I don't know just when he'll be back. . . . Yes, I hope so. Yes, sometime today. . . Yes, he'll call you, Doctor. As soon as he gets back, he'll call. . . . Goodbye."

She pulled out the plug, turned wearily and somewhat truculently to the counter.

"What can I do for *you?*" she asked Mason.

"You have a Horace Shelby here," Mason said.

Instantly, the woman stiffened. Her eyes grew wary.

"What about it?" she asked.

"I want to see him," Mason said.

© Lorillard 1975

Come for the filter...

A PRODUCT OF
Lorillard

KENT
WITH
THE FAMOUS MICRONITE FILTER

DELUXE LENGTH

18 mg. "tar," 1.2 mg. nicotine av. per cigarette, FTC Report Oct. '74.

...you'll stay for the taste.

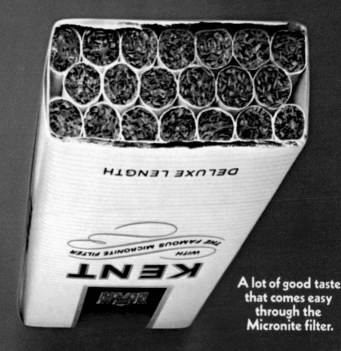

DELUXE LENGTH

KENT

WITH THE FAMOUS MICRONITE FILTER

A lot of good taste that comes easy through the Micronite filter.

18 mg. "tar," 1.2 mg. nicotine av. per cigarette, FTC Report Oct. '74.

"You a relative?"

"I'm a lawyer."

"You representing him?"

"I'm representing a relative."

"It's past visiting hours today," she said.

"But it's rather important that I see him," Mason said.

She shook her head firmly. "You have to come during visiting hours."

"And when are they?"

"Two or three in the afternoon."

"You mean I can't see him until tomorrow afternoon?"

"I'm not certain you can see him then. You're going to have to talk to Doctor. He's been having a little trouble. There's been a 'No Visitors' sign on his door. . . . What did you say your name was?"

"Mason. Perry Mason."

"I'll tell Doctor you called."

"Doctor who?" Mason asked.

"Doctor Baxter," she said. "Tillman Baxter. He runs the place."

"He's a medical doctor?" Mason asked.

"He has a license to run the place," she said. "That's all I know and I don't think it's going to do you any good to come back. I don't think Horace Shelby is going to be in any condition to receive visitors."

She abruptly turned her back on him and walked through the door leading from the office into the back room.

Mason turned away, made a quick survey of the place, and walked back to where he had parked his car.

A man was standing by the car. "You're the Court-appointed doctor?" the man asked.

Mason regarded the man thoughtfully. "What Court-appointed doctor?" he asked.

"The Shelby case."

"Why?" Mason asked.

"I want to talk with you," the man said.

"May I ask what about?"

53

"You didn't answer my question. Are you the Court-appointed doctor?"

"No," Mason said. "I'm Perry Mason, an attorney. Now, why did you want to talk with the—"

The man didn't wait for him to finish the sentence, but walked rapidly to a car which was parked ahead of Mason's, jumped in, said something to the driver of the car, and the car took off down the street.

Mason tried to make out the license number but the car had been parked too far ahead. He could see that it was a Nevada license and that was all.

The lawyer pretended to return to the sanitarium, but doubled back and, pulling the key for his own car from his pocket, hurried around to the street side to jump in behind the wheel. He started the motor and drove rapidly down the street.

He didn't see the car with the Nevada license plates. It had evidently turned off on one of the side streets.

The lawyer drove around several blocks trying to spot the car so he could get the license number but was unable to find it.

He drove back to his office.

"There's a call from Dr. Alma," Della Street told him. "He says he'll talk with you any time that you come in. I told him I expected you shortly."

Mason nodded.

"Gertie's closed up the office and gone home," Della Street said. "I'll put the call through."

Her fingers were a blur of motion over the dial on the telephone and she said, "Dr. Alma, please. Mr. Mason calling."

She nodded to Perry Mason.

Mason picked up the telephone. "Hello," he said, "Perry Mason talking."

"Dr. Grantland Alma, Mason. You wanted to talk with me?"

"Yes. I understand you've been appointed by Judge Ballinger to talk with Horace Shelby and make an appraisal of his physical and mental condition."

"That's right."

"Do you expect to see Horace Shelby soon?"

"I can't see him before tomorrow morning," Dr. Alma said, "but I have told the sanitarium I'll be there at ten o'clock in the morning."

"Is it wise to let them know exactly when you'll be there?" Mason asked.

"I think so," Dr. Alma said, "because I've told them that I want him to have no sedation after eight o'clock tonight; that I want a complete chart showing every bit of medication that has been given and that I don't want anyone from the sanitarium present when I examine him; that I'll have my own nurse with me."

Mason grinned and said, "Thank you, Doctor. I can see why the Court decided to appoint you as the examining physician. . . . I just wanted to ask you if ample precautions would be taken to see that the patient had a fair chance."

Dr. Alma said, "I know what you're thinking. I may also tell you that there are certain sedatives which, when given intravenously, put a patient into a deep sleep; but in some cases the individual becomes disoriented and a little erratic for several days. There are also other drugs which, when given to a person who has arteriosclerosis, can cause quite a bit of mental impairment."

"Can you test for those drugs?"

"Yes and no. I can make a blood test which will be of some help if I think they have been administered, but I can pretty well tell whether a person is his normal self or whether he is recuperating from the influence of drugs.

"I know all about you and your reputation, Mr. Mason. I understand you're representing the niece or the young woman who thought she was the niece—in any event, the young woman who's been taking care of the patient and who has been very devoted to him. I can also tell you in confidence that the sanitarium gave me an argument when I said I didn't want any medication after eight tonight. They told me the patient was restless, highly irritable, unable to sleep, and that he would have to be given heavy sedation.

"I asked what they meant by heavy sedation and we had an argument over that. I finally gave them a limit of

55

a sleeping medicine that could be given the patient tonight.

"I don't mind telling you, Mr. Mason, that I'm going to check this thing carefully. That's what I was told to do and that's what I'm going to do."

"Thanks a lot," Mason said. "I just wanted to find out what you had in mind."

"And I think I know what you have in mind," Dr. Alma said, chuckling. "Don't worry, Mason, I'm going to be fair but I'm going to be very, very thorough."

"Thanks a lot," Mason said. "And I certainly appreciate your co-operation."

The lawyer hung up and said to Della Street, "I guess there's no reason we can't close the office and go home. I think everything is taken care of. Dr. Alma knows what he's doing. He evidently knows all of the angles. Daphne is out of circulation. The sanitarium is on the defensive and I wouldn't be too surprised if tomorrow wasn't a day with plenty of action, as far as the sanitarium is concerned."

"How did it impress you?" she asked.

Mason made a gesture with his hand. "It's one of those things," he said. "I think the man they call 'Doctor' who is in charge of it is not a licensed physician although he probably has a license to run a nursing home.

"Some of those places are all right; some of them aren't. In fact, in some of them—heaven help the poor guy who gets put in there! All too frequently, relatives don't want to be bothered with an old man who is getting a little forgetful and a little unsanitary in his habits, so they bundle him off to a nursing home, wash their hands of him, and practically forget about him.

"The nursing home doesn't care just as long as they get a regular monthly check.

"Then there are some of those nursing homes which are pretty foxy. They know when the old man is supposed to be incompetent; and when they know the patient hates them but the person who has been appointed guardian or conservator of the estate is making the check every month, it doesn't take long for them to decide which side of the bread has the butter."

"And you think this sanitaruim is one of those places?"

Mason said, "I wouldn't be the least surprised, Della. However, I think things are working all right now. Let's call it a day and go home."

CHAPTER EIGHT

PERRY MASON entered the office at nine o'clock the following morning to find Della Street opening mail and segregating it into three piles: Urgent, Important, and Unimportant.

Mason casually glanced through some of the letters on the Urgent pile, said, "Well, I guess we may as well do a little catching up, Della. . . . Have you heard anything from Daphne?"

"Not yet."

Mason glanced at his watch. "In an hour, Dr. Alma will be out at the sanitarium to examine Horace Shelby. I imagine there'll be some action about that time."

"What sort of action?" Della asked.

"I don't know," Mason said. "Several things are possible. Either they've drugged the old man, ignoring Dr. Alma's orders; or they'll try to invent some reason why Dr. Alma can't see him."

"And what will Dr. Alma do?" Della Street asked.

"From the way he talked," Mason said, "I imagine he'll tell the sanitarium people he's going to see Horace Shelby or they're going to be hauled into court for contempt."

"And if he's drugged?" she asked.

"Dr. Alma will find it out and so report to the Court."

"And if he isn't?"

"If he isn't," Mason said, "I'm betting ten to one that Horace Shelby is as bright as a dollar. Probably rather the worse for wear as a result of his experience but he'll be logical and coherent and I think we'll get the Court's order appointing a conservator set aside. And the minute that happens, Shelby will order the Finchleys out of his house, make a will in favor of Daphne Shelby, and everything will end happily."

"What about the business you did of cashing the check? Won't they make trouble over that?"

"They'll try to," Mason said, "but my guess is that they're going to have their hands full with other things. In a matter of this sort, the best defense is a counter-offensive. . . . All right, let's get some of these letters out of the way."

The lawyer dictated until ten o'clock, then stretched and yawned.

"That's enough for the time being, Della. I can't get my mind off the Goodwill Sanitarium and what's apt to be happening out there. . . . Give Daphne a ring. Let's tell her to stand by. There's just a chance the whole opposition may collapse."

"You're optimistic this morning," Della Street said, reaching for the telephone.

"Had a wonderful night's sleep," Mason said, grinning, "a good breakfast, and—Hang it, Della, just the way Dr. Alma talked over the telephone made me feel that he knows what he's doing. The minute a doctor of that caliber who knows what he's doing enters a case of this kind he strikes confusion into the other side.

"If the so-called sanitarium and rest home is in danger of losing its license or thinks it is, they're very apt to swing right around to the other extreme."

Della said into the telephone, "Miss Daphne Shelby, please. She's in Room 718."

She held the phone for a while, then frowned, looked at her watch and said to Mason, "There's no answer."

"All right," Mason said, as Della waited, "leave a message for her. Tell her to call Mr. Mason when she comes in."

Della duly transmitted the message, then hung up the telephone.

"I have an idea she slept late and is in the dining room eating breakfast," Mason said.

"Or perhaps out shopping," Della said. "After all, she

came into quite a windfall, thanks to your financial skulduggery."

"No skulduggery about it," Mason said, grinning. "Darwin Melrose is the kind of attorney who goes into so darned much detail he sometimes lets the general issue slip through his fingers.

"Melrose was so specific about the fact that the exact amount of the balance which was in the account that day was to be turned over to Borden Finchley, as the conservator, that he entirely forgot to mention that the Court had appointed Finchley as conservator of all of Horace Shelby's property; and that any accounts, credits, or other tangibles which the bank held in its possession or which might come into its possession were to be turned over to the conservator. He simply made a specific demand for that one account and then had Finchley check the account out to the last penny, opening a new account at another bank in the name of Borden Finchley, conservator."

Mason chuckled. "If the guy wants to get technical with me, I'll get technical with him."

"What will Judge Ballinger say about it?"

"I don't know," Mason said. "I think the judge is rather broadminded and I think he has a pretty shrewd suspicion there's something in this case that won't stand scrutiny. Of course, the fact that Daphne is no blood relative is the thing that puts us behind the eight ball. If it weren't for that, I'd walk into court and start shooting off fireworks. As it is now, I have no official standing the Court can recognize."

The telephone rang. Della Street picked up the instrument, said, "Yes, Gertie," and to Mason said, "That's probably Daphne calling now."

Mason nodded, started to reach for the telephone, then paused at the expression on Della's face.

She turned and said, "It's Dr. Alma and he says it's very important that he talk to you immediately."

Mason nodded, picked up the phone, said, "Yes, Mason talking."

Dr. Alma's heavy masculine voice came over the wire.

"Mr. Mason," he said, "I'm down here at the so-called Goodwill Sanitarium and Rest Home. As you know, I came here under court order to examine Horace Shelby."

"What about him?" Mason asked. "Nothing's happened to him, has it?"

"A good deal has happened to him," Alma said.

"Good heavens, he isn't dead!"

"We don't know," Alma said. "He isn't here."

"He isn't there?"

"That's right."

"What happened? Did they let Finchley take him out somewhere?"

"I don't know and I'd like very much to find out," Dr. Alma said. "The man is gone. They say he's 'escaped.'"

"Before anyone has a chance to clutter up the evidence any more, I'd like to find out. . . . You have a private detective who works with you, who has quite a bit of experience in investigation, I believe."

"That's right," Mason said.

"And you yourself are a legendary figure. I wonder if you and your detective could get out here?"

"Will they let us in?" Mason asked, winking at Della Street.

"Let you in?" Dr. Alma exploded. "*I'll* let you in! I'll turn this place wrong side out if they don't put all of their cards on the table and play ball right down the line!"

"I'll be right out," Mason said.

Mason slammed up the telephone receiver, grabbed his hat, said to Della Street, "Call Paul Drake. Tell him to take his car and join me at the Goodwill Sanitarium in El Mirar. Call Daphne Shelby again. Get her alerted to what has happened. Tell her to sit tight and wait for word from us—not to leave the hotel room."

"If she doesn't answer?" Della Street asked.

"Have her paged," Mason said. "I'm on my way."

The lawyer dashed out of the door and sprinted down the corridor.

It took Mason thirty-four minutes' fast driving to reach El Mirar.

He slammed his car to a stop at the parking place near

the gate and noticed, without attaching any significance to the fact, that the signs asking for help had now been removed and that the door to the office was standing wide open. The woman who had been so curt the afternoon before was now effusive in her greeting.

"Doctor is expecting you, Mr. Mason. They're down in Unit 17. It's right down this walk to the right."

"Thank you," Mason said. "A private detective by the name of Paul Drake will be out here any minute. When he comes, send him down to Unit 17."

"Yes, indeed," she said, and her hard mouth twisted into what was intended as a cordial smile. Her eyes, however, were cold, blue and hostile.

Mason hurried down the walk to Unit 17, a small cottage standing in a row of similar cottages.

The lawyer heard angry voices from inside.

He walked up to the porch and jerked the door open.

The tall man who whirled to face the lawyer as he entered the room was somewhere in his forties—alert, slightly stooped, almost as tall as Mason, and, quite obviously, very indignant.

The other and older man was a head shorter—an apologetic, cowed individual who was very much on the defensive.

Mason seized up the situation at a glance.

"Dr. Alma?" the lawyer asked of the tall man.

Dr. Alma's indignant smoldering eyes focused on Perry Mason, then softened. "You're Perry Mason," he said.

"Right."

The two men shook hands.

"And this is 'Dr.' Tillman Baxter."

Mason didn't offer to shake hands with Dr. Baxter.

"*Dr.* Baxter," Dr. Alma went on, "is licensed as a naturopathic physician in another state. He has theories about diet."

"I'm licensed to run this rest home," Baxter said.

"Doubtless you are," Dr. Alma said, "but how much longer that condition is going to exist is anyone's guess. Now, I want to know everything there is to know about Horace Shelby. You say you don't keep charts."

"This isn't a regular hospital," Baxter protested. "This is a rest home."

"And you don't keep records of treatment?"

"We keep records of the important things."

"What do you consider important?"

"Anything which indicates a change in the physical or mental condition of the patient."

"You've told me you don't keep a record of drugs that are administered?"

"We do not administer drugs. That is, as a rule."

"What do you do?" Dr. Alma asked.

"We give our patients rest, privacy, and healthful food. We—"

"I was told that Horace Shelby was under heavy sedation," Mason said. "Who gave it to him?"

"Heavy sedation?" Dr. Baxter asked lamely.

"That was my understanding," Mason said.

"An outside private physician had been prescribing for Mr. Shelby," Dr. Baxter said. "We, of course, honor prescriptions given by the patient's own doctor."

"Who is this doctor?"

"I can't remember his name right now."

Mason looked around the room, taking mental inventory of an iron frame hospital bed, washstand, chest of drawers with a mirror, worn linoleum on the floor, drab lace curtains on the window.

"Where does this door go?" Mason asked.

"The bathroom," Dr. Baxter said.

Mason jerked the door open, looked at the old-fashioned bathtub, the toilet, the worn linoleum, the crowded cubicle, the wavy mirror over the shallow medicine cabinet.

"This other door?" the lawyer asked.

"The closet. That's where the patient keeps his clothes."

"I looked in there," Dr. Alma said. "The clothes are gone."

Mason looked in the closet at the row of clothes hooks along the wall.

"He took everything?" Mason asked.

"As nearly as we can tell, everything," Dr. Baxter said.

"Of course, the man had virtually no personal possessions. An attendant shaved him. The man had a toothbrush and toothpaste and those are left in the medicine chest in the bathroom. Aside from that, he had virtually nothing except the clothes he wore when he was received."

"In other words," Mason said, "the man had no idea he was being taken to a sanitarium when he was railroaded in here."

"I didn't say that," Dr. Baxter said, "and I couldn't say it because frankly I don't know."

"A man going to a sanitarium carries at least a suitcase of clothes," Mason said. "Pajamas, underwear, shirts, socks, handkerchiefs."

"A *normal* man does," Dr. Baxter said.

"And Horace Shelby wasn't normal?"

"By no means. He was irritable, nervous, excited, aggressive and refused to co-operate."

"Who brought him here?"

"His relatives."

"How many?"

"Two of them."

"Borden Finchley and Ralph Exeter?"

"Finchley was one; I don't know the name of the other person. There was a nurse with them, too."

"Mrs. Finchley?"

"I believe so."

"And the three of them strong-armed Shelby into this room?"

"They registered him in the sanitarium. He was disturbed at the time, but the nurse gave him some sedation."

"You know what the sedation was?"

"It was a hypodermic."

"Did she tell you what it was?"

"She said it had been prescribed by his regular physician."

"Did you see a copy of the prescription? Did you know who the physician was?"

"I took her word for it. She was a registered nurse."

"In this state?"

"I believe in Nevada, I don't know."

"How do you know she was a registered nurse?"

"She told me so—and, of course, from the way she handled the situation I could see that she had had training."

Mason suddenly backed into the room, picked up one of the straight-backed chairs, carried it into the closet, climbed up on it and reached back into the dark recesses of the closet shelf.

"What are these?" he asked, bringing out a set of straps.

Dr. Baxter hesitated, coughed, said, "Those are straps."

"Of course, they're straps," Mason said. "They're web straps. What's their purpose?"

"We use them to restrain patients who are inclined to become physically unmanageable—they use them in all hospitals which treat mental cases."

"In other words, you strap a man in bed?"

"When his condition requires."

"And Horace Shelby was strapped in bed?"

"I am not sure. He may have been at one time."

"And how long was he strapped in bed?"

"I would assume a very brief interval. We only use those straps when the patient becomes entirely unmanageable, and at times when we are somewhat short-handed. You can see yourself that the straps have been removed, Mr. Mason."

"They've been removed, all right," Mason said, holding out two pieces of the strap. "They've been cut with a sharp knife."

"Dear me, so they have!" Dr. Baxter exclaimed.

"Then," Mason said, "if Horace Shelby escaped, as you claim, he must have had outside aid. Somebody must have cut those straps. A man who has been strapped in bed and has no knife can't very well cut the straps which are holding him."

Baxter said nothing.

Mason glanced at Dr. Alma.

Dr. Alma said, "I'm going to give this place a good airing. I'm going to find what it's all about. Did you start this place, Baxter?"

"*Dr.* Baxter," Baxter said.

"Did you start it?" Alma said, raising his voice.

"No. I am buying it from the man who had started it."

"He's a licensed M.D.?"

"I didn't inquire particularly into his qualifications. I saw the license to operate the place and I had that license assigned to me."

"By whom?"

"By the person who sold it to me."

"You'd better be in court at two o'clock this afternoon," Dr. Alma said. "I think Judge Ballinger is going to want to talk with you."

"I can't be in court. It's a physical impossibility. I have many patients and I am shorthanded. We have been doing everything in our power to attract competent help but we simply can't get them."

"Nurses?"

"We have practical nurses," Baxter said. "And we have one trained nurse, but much of our trouble is in getting competent household help. We are all of us doing double duty at the present time."

There were steps on the porch.

Paul Drake's voice said, "Hello, Perry."

"Come in," Mason said.

Drake entered the room. Mason said, "Dr. Grantland Alma, Mr. Drake; and *Dr.* Baxter."

"You're the detective?" Dr. Alma asked.

"Right," Mason said.

"I think Mr. Mason has uncovered the key clue," Dr. Alma said.

"Key clue?" Drake asked.

"To the disappearance of Horace Shelby."

"The escape of Horace Shelby," Dr. Baxter corrected.

"As far as I am concerned," Dr. Alma said, "the man is gone and I don't know how he went, where he went, or who took him."

"He took himself," Dr. Baxter said.

"You believe that?" Dr. Alma asked.

"Yes."

"All right," Dr. Alma said, "I'm going to quote you on that."

"What do you mean?"

"You've been holding him here as an aged incompetent," Dr. Alma snapped, "a man who was disoriented, who couldn't take care of himself, who was incapable of managing his affairs.

"When he resented that treatment, you strapped him down to the bed. You wouldn't allow visitors to see him. You wouldn't allow any attorney to consult with him.

"Now then, you adopt the position that this man was shrewd enough to find some way of cutting the straps that held him, getting up out of bed, dressing, getting out of the gate, out to the street—an aged, infirm man without enough money to get on a bus and, yet, he's vanished.

"Now then, you just come into court and say that you thought he was aged, infirm, senile, and unable to take care of himself, and let's see what the Court has to say."

"Well, now, wait a minute," Dr. Baxter said hastily. "Of course, he could have had help. What I meant to say was that he didn't have any help from this institution. In other words, we weren't trying to spirit him away so that the process of the court couldn't be used in his case."

"It isn't what you *meant* to say; it's what you did say," Dr. Alma said. "As far as I am concerned, I'm finished. I'm going back and make my report to the Court. . . . How about you, Mason?"

"I can't see where there's anything to be gained by staying here," Mason said, looking at the unhappy and frustrated Dr. Baxter. "Particularly, since we're all due in court this afternoon. . . . I take it Dr. Baxter has been subpoenaed?"

"If he isn't, he will be," Dr. Alma snapped. "I'll see to that."

"Now, just a minute, just a minute," Dr. Baxter said. "I can't be running around going to court. I am short-handed as it is and—"

"I know," Dr. Alma said with mock sympathy. "I have the same thing happen from time to time myself. They subpoena me to come to court and I lose a day at the office. It's one of the duties of the *profession*, eh, *Doctor?*"

Mason moved to the door, led Drake to one side. "You have the car that has the telephone in it?" the lawyer asked.

Drake nodded.

"All right," Mason said, "put men on the job. I want everybody you can pick up put under twenty-four-hour surveillance."

"What do you mean 'everybody'?"

"Exeter, Finchley, Mrs. Finchley, Dr. Baxter here—and stick around and see if you can get any clue as to how Horace Shelby left here."

Drake nodded.

Mason said, "I have a hunch someone pulled a fast one. I noticed yesterday that there were two signs asking for help to run the place. Those signs have now been taken down. That means that someone applied for a job last night and got the job—probably a night job. See if you can find out anything about that person because that could well have been a plant—someone that Borden Finchley put in here to get Horace Shelby out of sight so that Dr. Alma couldn't examine him.

"If you can get a line on that person—in case some person was hired last night—spare no expense to get all the information possible."

Drake nodded. "Will do. It's going to cost money."

"Let it cost money," Mason said. "We're in a fight and we're going for the jugular."

CHAPTER NINE

PROMPTLY AT TWO O'CLOCK, Judge Ballinger took his place on the bench.

"This is the time heretofore fixed for a continued hearing in the matter of a conservator for the estate of Horace Shelby.

"I see that Dr. Grantland Alma, the physician appointed by the Court to examine Horace Shelby, is in court. Dr. Alma is the Court's own witness, and the Court would like to have you come forward and be sworn, Doctor."

Darwin Melrose was on his feet.

"If the Court please," he said, "before Dr. Alma is examined, I would like to make a statement to the Court."

"What is it?" Judge Ballinger asked.

"Mr. Perry Mason, attorney for Daphne Shelby, has used a device to circumvent the Court's order appointing a conservator for the estate and preventing Horace Shelby from being imposed upon by shrewd and designing persons.

"He has so manipulated things that fifty thousand dollars of the money in the estate has been turned over to Daphne Shelby, no blood relative of Horace Shelby and the very person from whom Horace Shelby was supposed to be protected by Court order."

"How did he do that?" Judge Ballinger asked. "Didn't you serve a copy of the Court's order on the bank?"

"If the Court will remember," Melrose said, "I had special orders made for the bank—orders which turned every penny of the account in Shelby's name to Borden Finchley, as conservator."

"Didn't the bank do it?" Judge Ballinger asked.

"The bank did it."

"Then how did Mason get possession of fifty thousand dollars of that money?"

"Not of that money, but of other monies."

"Covered in the order?" Judge Ballinger asked.

"Well," Melrose said, and hesitated.

"Go on," Judge Ballinger snapped.

"They were not covered in that specific order—not by the letter of the order; they were, however, covered by the spirit of the order."

"Well, before we go into that, let's find out how incompetent Horace Shelby is," Judge Ballinger said. "I know how busy Dr. Alma is. I know that this is his busy time of the afternoon when he has an office full of patients and I would like to have him on the stand now, have him examined and cross-examined and then permit him to return to his office."

Judge Ballinger turned to Dr. Alma, leaving Darwin Melrose uncomfortably aware that the initiative had been taken from him.

"Did you see Horace Shelby, Doctor?" Judge Ballinger asked.

"I did not."

"Why not?"

"He was no longer at the so-called sanitarium and rest home."

"Where is he?"

"I don't know."

"How did this happen?"

"Again, I don't know. I have my own idea from certain things I discovered."

"What things?"

"This so-called sanitarium is nothing but a rest home. It is under the management of a man who uses the title of a doctor but is, in my opinion, completely inexperienced in psychiatric medicine.

"We found evidence that Horace Shelby had been strapped to a bed—perhaps ever since he had been placed in the institution. We found that the institution keeps no charts on patients, no hospital records. In my opinion, it is a very poor place to keep a person who is quite evidently held against his will.

"I tried to find out whether Mr. Shelby had, in some way, made an escape by himself or whether he had been removed by people in the institution who wanted to keep me from examining him.

"In connection with my inquiries, I received a very remarkable statement from the man who manages the institution. He said that, in his opinion, Mr. Shelby had contrived to effect an unaided escape.

"I asked him if that meant that this man, who was claimed incompetent to handle his own affairs and who had to be strapped into a bed to restrain him, had sufficient intelligence and ingenuity to get hold of a knife to cut the straps, to dress, to make his escape unseen from the institution without sufficient funds to summon a taxicab or even to pay fare on a bus, and vanish so that he couldn't be found. I pointed out that there was no other construction which could be placed upon his statement."

"If the Court please," Darwin Melrose interposed, his face red, "I respectfully insist that this is not proper testimony from a psychiatrist, even if he has been appointed by the Court. He is giving conclusions, not from an examination of the patient but from surmises which he made as to the actual meaning of Dr. Baxter's statement that the patient had escaped."

Judge Ballinger frowned thoughtfully. "A very logical interpretation, certainly," he said. . . . "Does *anyone* know where Horace Shelby is at the present time? And I am asking this question particularly of counsel. I intend to hold counsel responsible for the actions of their clients in this matter."

Melrose said, "I want to assure the Court that I have no idea where Horace Shelby is, and my client, Borden Finchley, and his wife, Elinor Finchley, have assured me that they have no information; and Ralph Exeter, who has been visiting in the house with them, tells me that he has no information.

"I understand, however, that Daphne Shelby, the young woman who tried to establish relationship, is absent from her hotel; that messages have been unclaimed; and, despite the fact she knew that this hearing had been continued to this hour, she is not present. And I feel further that her counsel doesn't know where she is."

Judge Ballinger frowned. "Mr. Mason?" he asked.

Mason got to his feet slowly, turned as he heard the

door open and said, without changing his expression by so much as the flicker of an eyelash, "Since Daphne Shelby has just walked into court, I suggest that she can speak for herself."

Daphne came rushing forward. "Oh, Mr. Mason, I am so sorry. I got caught in a traffic jam and—"

"That's all right," Mason said. "Just be seated."

Mason turned to the Court and said, "As far as I am concerned, Horace Shelby's disappearance came as a big surprise to me. I was summoned to the sanitarium by Dr. Alma and that was the first intimation I had that Mr. Shelby was no longer there."

Judge Ballinger said, "The Court isn't going to try a moot case. If it is impossible for Dr. Alma to examine Horace Shelby, the Court is going to continue the case until he can examine the man."

"But what about this manipulation of property so that fully fifty thousand dollars of the ward's estate has been spirited out from under control of the Court by Mr. Mason's subterfuge?"

Judge Ballinger looked at Mason, then at Melrose. There was a trace of a smile on his countenance. "Did Mr. Mason specifically violate any order of this Court?" he asked.

"No order that had been served on him—no, Your Honor."

"Did the bank violate any order of this Court?"

"Well . . . I believe the bank had notice that a conservator had been appointed."

"And the bank paid out funds which had been taken over by the conservator?"

"No, Your Honor. The bank paid out funds before the conservator had an opportunity to take them over."

"Didn't the order served on the bank specifically cover any and all accounts, credits, monies on deposit? And didn't the conservator order the account of Horace Shelby to be changed to the account of the conservator?"

"Not in exactly that way," Darwin Melrose said. "The order was that the bank pay over the entire sum that was in the account of Horace Shelby to the conservator."

"And where did this other money come from?"

"It was other monies that came in and were whisked out of the account before the conservator knew anything about them."

"But they were not specifically covered in the order served on the bank?"

"Not those funds, no."

Judge Ballinger shook his head. "The better practice would have been to have anticipated such a situation," he said. "We will take that up with the bank at a later date but certainly, as far as Mr. Mason is concerned, no order had been served on him. Mr. Mason's position is that the man was fully competent to carry on and transact his own business and, if this man had sufficient ingenuity to escape unaided from the institution where he was strapped to a bed, he would hardly seem to be disoriented, confused, senile and incompetent."

"We don't know that his escape was unaided," Darwin Melrose said.

"We certainly do not," Judge Ballinger pointed out, "and that is the thing which concerns the Court. It opens up rather sinister possibilities. If it should appear that Shelby was spirited out of that sanitarium so that Dr. Alma couldn't examine him, the Court is going to take very drastic steps.

"The matter will be continued until next Wednesday afternoon at four o'clock. In the meantime, court is adjourned."

Mason beckoned to Daphne to join him and once more led the way into the witness room.

"You've got to keep in touch with me, Daphne," he said sternly. "I've taken all sorts of chances on your behalf and I've been trying to get you. My office repeatedly has called, left messages at the hotel, and—"

"Oh, I'm sorry," she interrupted. "Mr. Mason, you'll have to forgive me just this once. I became involved in a matter and—I just can't explain now. I'd have been here in plenty of time if it hadn't been for that horrible traffic jam. Traffic on the freeway is getting so it's absolutely impossible!"

"I know all about that," Mason said. "But I want you to keep in touch with my office. You have my telephone number; you can pick up the telephone and call me from time to time."

Her eyes refused to meet his. "Yes, I know," she said.

"Look here," Mason asked, "what have you been up to?"

Her eyes wide, innocent and naïve, raised to his. "What do you mean, what have I been up to?"

"I thought you were acting a little guilty," Mason said.

"Guilty of what?"

"I wouldn't know. You knew that your uncle had disappeared from the sanitarium?"

She said bitterly, "That's no surprise to me. They didn't dare to let a physician appointed by the Court examine him."

"That's the way it looks, all right," Mason said. "But sometimes the obvious deduction isn't the only deduction or the correct one.

"Now, I want you to keep in touch with my office, and I want you to keep in touch with your hotel so if I leave any messages for you, you can pick them up. Is that clear?"

"Yes. I'm very sorry, Mr. Mason."

"You said you'd been having trouble with traffic," Mason asked. "Were you riding with somebody?"

"No, oh no. I—Well, in a way. . . . I was using a friend's car."

"What friend?" Mason asked.

"Uncle Horace."

"His car?" Mason said. "Why, Finchley took over his car at the same time he took over the bank account and all that."

She lowered her eyes again and said, "This was one that Mr. Finchley didn't know about."

Mason said, "Look here, young lady, I've got to get back to my office. I have two or three lines out. I think you'd better come up there in about an hour and let's find out a little more about this."

"But what is there to find out?"

"I don't know," Mason said. "That's what I want to

investigate. How did you get hold of another car belonging to Horace Shelby?"

"It was one he had."

"That they didn't know about?"

"Yes."

"A good car? Any good?" he asked.

"Practically new," she said.

Mason regarded her in frowning contemplation.

There was a knock on the door.

Mason opened it.

A court attaché said, "There's a telephone call for you, Mr. Mason. They say it's most important and that you're to take it right away."

"All right," Mason said. "Excuse me for a moment, Daphne."

Mason followed the attaché into the courtroom.

"You can take the phone on the clerk's desk," the officer said.

Mason nodded, picked up the telephone, said, "Hello," and heard Paul Drake's voice sharp with excitement.

"Did Daphne show up in court, Perry?"

"That's right."

"Tell you anything about where she had been?"

"No."

"Are you giving her a detailed examination as to where she's been and what she's been doing?"

"I've just started," Mason said.

"Forget it," Drake told him. "Let her go. Tell her to get in touch with you tomorrow morning. Let her go."

Mason said, "She's acting rather strangely, Paul, and she says there's another automobile that Finchley doesn't know about—"

"I'll say there is," Drake interrupted. "There's a lot no one knows about. Now, I haven't time to explain, but for heaven's sake let her go. Get her started. I want her on her way. I'll see you at your office shortly after you get there and explain."

"Wait a minute," Mason said. "I'm beginning to get the glimmer of an idea. You checked on the tip I gave you that some woman might have applied for a job and got a job at the sanitarium last night?"

74

"Right."

"Is there," Mason asked, looking over his shoulder to make certain that no one was listening, and lowering his voice, "any chance that—"

"Don't mention it over the phone," Drake said. "There's all the chance in the world. Meet me in your office and don't let Daphne know you're suspicious."

"Okay," Mason said, "I'll be there in twenty minutes."

The lawyer hung up the telephone and returned to the witness room.

There was no sign of Daphne.

Mason left the witness room, went to the outer office of Judge Ballinger's chambers and said to the judge's secretary, "Will you ask the judge if I can see him for a few moments on a matter of some importance?"

The secretary picked up the phone, relayed the message, said to Mason, "Judge Ballinger says for you to come on in."

Mason nodded, walked past the secretarial desk, and into the judge's private chambers.

"Judge," he said, "I made a statement in open court which was entirely true at the time I made it, but the situation has changed somewhat."

Judge Ballinger regarded him with not unfriendly eyes. "You understand, of course, Mr. Mason, that this is a bitterly contested matter and that I don't want you to say anything which would embarrass you or which might tend to disqualify me from hearing the case."

"I understand," Mason said. "This was in connection with a statement I made in open court, that I had no idea as to the whereabouts of Horace Shelby."

Judge Ballinger's eyes grew hard. "That statement was not correct?" he asked.

"That statement was entirely correct," Mason said.

"But since you have made it, you do know where Horace Shelby is?"

"No," Mason said, "but I think it is only fair to tell you that I have unearthed a clue which may lead me to Mr. Shelby before the hearing in this matter is resumed."

Judge Ballinger thought that over, then said, "I think i will be all right for you to tell me what the clue is becaus the Court is *most* anxious to have Dr. Alma get in touch with Shelby at the earliest possible moment. In fact, with out committing myself in any way, I think I may say tha it is quite important that the contact be made as soon a possible."

"I understand," Mason said. "I can, if you wish, tel you the clue."

"I think it will be all right for you to tell me tha much," Judge Ballinger said.

Mason said, "There is a possibility that Daphne Shelb knows where her uncle is."

Judge Ballinger raised his eyebrows. Human curiosit struggled with judicial prudence, and human nature wo out.

"What makes you think so?" Judge Ballinger asked.

"There is evidence," Mason said, "that Daphne Shelb purchased a car and took immediate delivery, that sh may very well have gone to the Goodwill Sanitarium at E Mirar where she was not known and secured a position a a night nurse."

"That was last night?" Judge Ballinger asked.

"That was last night."

"Have you asked Daphne Shelby about this?"

"I haven't had an opportunity. I only learned it mysel just a minute or two ago."

Abruptly Judge Ballinger threw his head back an laughed.

Mason stood silently waiting.

Judge Ballinger controlled himself, said, "Mason, can't say anything without putting myself in a compromis ing position. However, if it's any satisfaction to you, thi Court wasn't born yesterday.

"I'm glad you told me what you did because it puts m mind at ease about a matter which was causing me con siderable concern. I think this conversation, however, ha gone quite far enough and it is, of course, just betwee the two of us. I think it was your duty to tell me. I wil also say this, that in the event you do have any persona contact with Horace Shelby, I want Dr. Alma to examine him at once. For reasons which I am not going to mention and which I don't think I need to go into at this time, I think it is highly important that the examination take place at the earliest possible moment."

Mason nodded. "I think I understand you."

"I'm quite certain you do," Judge Ballinger said, and then added, "and you yourself weren't born yesterday."

CHAPTER TEN

PAUL DRAKE was waiting in Mason's office when the lawyer fitted his latchkey to the door of the private office and entered.

Mason glanced at Della Street. "Any calls, Della?"

She shook her head.

Mason turned to Drake. "What happened, Paul?"

"I can't tell you for sure," Drake said, "because I have been afraid to tip my hand by asking too many direct questions, but here's the story in a nutshell.

"Yesterday afternoon, a girl who answers the description of Daphne Shelby stopped a brand-new-looking car in front of the sanitarium and said she had noticed the sign that they wanted domestic help.

"It seems the sanitarium is pretty well filled and they were badly in need of help. They wanted someone to go to work making beds, sweeping, cleaning, and doing a general job of practical nursing.

"The girl who had been on the shift from ten o'clock at night until seven o'clock in the morning had quit, and our friend Dr. Baxter was desperate. This girl—I'm going to call her Daphne because I'm satisfied that's who she was—said she'd be back at ten o'clock to start work.

"No one got the license number on her car. She gave the name of Eva Jones, and said she'd had some nursing experience caring for aged people.

"Dr. Baxter didn't waste any time examining her credentials. He just needed someone in the worst way and he took her on.

"She worked during the entire night; was alert, intelligent, and on the job. Dr. Baxter got up and checked her a couple of times and everything seemed to be running fine.

"They had a cook and two more so-called nurses who came on duty at six o'clock in the morning to prepare breakfast; and then, after breakfast, to make beds.

"Those were experienced people who had been with the institution for some time and knew the ropes. The big trouble they had was keeping someone on night duty—the so-called 'graveyard shift' from ten until seven o'clock in the morning.

"This new girl was last seen about five-forty-five in the morning. When the cook came to the sanitarium, the new girl was there. She was supposed to stay until seven and help get the breakfast ready, but no one saw her after the cook greeted her.

"For a while, everyone was busy with breakfast and getting things started, and then they went into Unit #17 to make up the bed and see what could be done for the occupant who had been giving them a lot of trouble. They'd had to forcibly restrain him.

"They found the bed empty. Horace Shelby had vanished and the new girl had vanished.

"They didn't think too much about the significance of the girl not being on duty. Everyone thought she had misunderstood the hours she was to work, and they still feel that she'll be on duty tonight at ten.

"I followed up your lead about the 'Help Wanted' signs, found out Eva Jones had been employed, and pretended that I was a credit man trying to get a credit rating on Eva Jones, asked about what they knew about her background, got her residence address, and—most important of all—the physical description.

"I went to the residence address. It was phony—a rooming house. They'd never heard of Eva Jones. What's more, they didn't have anyone who answered the physical description of Eva Jones living there.

"Now then, Perry, you can put two and two together.

She bought a car; she went out and parked it at the sanitarium; she didn't duck out during the night because that would have been too much of a coincidence; she waited until the cook came on duty in the morning and then slipped in, cut the straps that were holding Horace Shelby to the bed, using a sharp butcher knife she had picked up from the kitchen. She got Shelby's clothes on him, got him across the yard, through the gate and into the automobile."

Mason nodded thoughtfully. "What about the car?"

"I've traced the records through the bank and the Motor Vehicle Department. Daphne Shelby bought a Ford automobile from a downtown agency yesterday and wanted immediate delivery. She paid for the car with a cashier's check drawn on the Investors National Bank and signed by the cashier.

"Because she was in such a hurry, the automobile agency people were a little suspicious, but they took the check to the bank and cashed it, rushed through the registration and delivered the car.

"The license is LJL 851—but, as I mentioned, no one got the license number of the car the so-called Eva Jones had when she drove up to the sanitarium. Apparently, it was a new Ford."

Mason, who had seated himself with one hip on a corner of his desk, one leg swinging back and forth, frowned thoughtfully.

"Our little naïve, unsophisticated girl seems to have a head on her shoulders and a lot of intiative."

"What's the Court going to say about all that?" Drake asked.

"That depends," Mason said thoughtfully.

"On what?" Della Street asked.

"On just what the facts are. If Horace Shelby is being railroaded into incompetency, that's one thing.

"On the other hand, *if* Borden Finchley was acting in good faith and believed that Daphne had been wheedling Horace and insinuating herself into his good graces so that she could make away with a large chunk of money, that's something else.

"Once Horace Shelby is interviewed by Dr. Alma, he'll tell the true story of how he was treated at the sanitarium, about being strapped to a bed, and all the rest of it.

"If the conspirators are railroading him, they can't afford to have *that* happen. They'll put a stop to it at all costs."

"What do you mean 'at all costs'?" Della Street asked.

"Murder," Mason said.

"Murder?" Della exclaimed.

Mason nodded.

"But how will murder help?" Della Street asked.

"Murder in itself won't help," Mason said. "They'll have to commit a murder that they can blame on Daphne Shelby. Their story will be very simple, that Daphne got Horace out of the sanitarium; that she got him to make a will leaving everything in her favor; that he died during the night. His death will seem to be from natural causes, but those causes were helped along by Daphne. We've got to find Daphne in order to protect her from herself and from the others."

Drake said, "I've got men shadowing Daphne from the time she left the courthouse. We've got the license number of the automibile she's driving, and we should know where she's holed up within the next few minutes."

Mason looked at his watch. "She may have decided not to go directly to the hideout."

"What do we do when we get her located?" Drake asked.

"Notify Dr. Alma, take him out there and let him examine Horace."

"And if Shelby is confused and disoriented?"

"Then we'll put him in a good hospital under the care of Dr. Alma, go to court and see what we can do about getting another conservator appointed."

"And if he isn't confused?"

Mason grinned. "Then we accuse the Finchleys of criminal conspiracy, get them thoroughly discredited, get Horace Shelby declared competent and then—if he wants to, and apparently he does—let him make a will leaving all of the property to Daphne. And by that time, the show will be over."

"The Finchleys are gambling for high stakes," Drake said.

Mason nodded.

The unlisted telephone rang.

Della Street answered it, said, "It's for you, Paul."

Drake picked up the instrument, said, "Drake speaking. . . . Yes, hello, Jud—What? . . . How did that happen?"

Drake listened for a full minute, then said, "Where are you now? . . . Okay, wait there for instructions."

Drake hung up the telephone, turned to Mason and said, "I'm sorry, Perry, but they lost her."

"Lost her!" Perry Mason exclaimed.

"Well, they didn't lose her; she gave them the slip."

"How come?"

"I had to work fast," Drake said. "I had a man waiting at the courthouse to pick her up when she came out. There was a parking problem and she got a little head start. But I don't think that was what caused it. What really caused it was that she knew she was being tailed and was smart enough so she never let on."

"What makes you think that?"

"Because she took elaborate precautions to see that no one could follow her."

"What sort of precautions?"

"She was moving along with traffic, apparently entirely oblivious of her surroundings. She turned into a side street and suddenly whipped the car into a U-turn which was illegal, right in the middle of a busy boulevard—not a freeway, but a pretty important through boulevard.

"Of course, when you pull a maneuver like that you're able to pick the time and the place where you can make a quick U-turn without giving any signal. If an officer happens to pick you up, you're hooked. But if you get away with it, you're pretty apt to be in the clear because the maneuver takes the person who is following entirely by surprise. But if the boulevard is reasonably busy, by the time he gets his own car in a position where *he* can make a U-turn, it's too late.

"That's what happened in this case. Daphne made a U-turn right in front of a whole stream of cars that were bunched up because they'd been held up by a traffic signal a couple of blocks down the street. By the time my operative managed to make a U-turn, fifteen or twenty cars were between him and Daphne. And Daphne swung down a side street, went around the block, came to an intersection where she could have either gone straight ahead, to the right or the left. My man assumed she hadn't gone straight ahead because he couldn't see her. He had a choice of right or left. He chose right because usually a person trying to get away from someone will make a right-hand turn if it's clear.

"Well, it's the same old story. Once you've lost a person you're very lucky if you get them back in your sights. He came to another intersection, had the same choice to make, and somewhere along the road he made the wrong choice."

"Now," Mason said, "Daphne has really got herself in a jam. If she isn't on the square, the Court is going to feel that she is deliberately interfering with the process of the Court; and if she is acting in good faith and Borden Finchley can find her before we do, she's in danger and Horace is in danger."

"You really think they'd resort to murder?" Della Street asked.

"I don't know," Mason said. "All I know is it's a big possibility in the case, and it's up to a lawyer to look at possibilities.

"Paul, round up every man you can get on short notice. Put them on the freeway leading into El Mirar. Watch for Daphne Shelby's car."

"She wouldn't be in El Mirar," Paul Drake said. "She wouldn't dare."

"I think that's the only place she does dare to be," Mason said.

"Put yourself in her position. She went out to the sanitarium at El Mirar to see if she could get a job. In the event she could get a job, she intended to make an escape with Horace Shelby, and she was smart enough to figure out the details of that escape so she could pull it at a time when it wouldn't attract too much attention.

"On the other hand, she couldn't be certain that someone wouldn't see them leaving the place or that, through some circumstance she hadn't anticipated, the escape would be discovered before they had been gone very long.

"Therefore, the smart thing for her to have done was to have driven out to El Mirar in the afternoon, gone to some motel, explained that she wanted twin units, that her uncle was going to join her later.

"Then, when she had the stage all set, she simply showed up with the uncle.

"I was interested in the statement she made to me about being late for court. She said that traffic on the freeway was terrible and it had taken her longer than she had anticipated.

"At the time, I didn't know she was driving a car and I wondered just what she meant.

"I think it was a case of blurting out the simple truth before she realized what a statement of that sort would mean."

Drake nodded. "Okay, Perry," he said. "Let me go down to my place. I can get better action on the men I want to put out down there."

Mason said, "Cover the motels at El Mirar. See if you can't find Daphne Shelby's new car parked in front of one of the units."

CHAPTER ELEVEN

IT WAS JUST AS Perry Mason and Della Street were closing the office that Paul Drake's code knock sounded on the door.

Della opened the door and Mason said, "Hi, Paul, we've been waiting to hear from you but had decided to go out and have a cocktail and a little dinner—thought we'd drop by your office and give you an invitation. Since you're here, we'll give you the invitation in person."

Drake grinned. "You're dangling temptation in front of my nose," he said, "but I'll probably be sending out for hamburger sandwiches and drinking coffee out of a paper cup."

"What gives?" Mason asked. "Have you struck pay dirt?"

"We've not only struck pay dirt, we've got Daphne Shelby."

"The deuce," Mason said. "Where?"

"Your hunch paid off," Drake told him. "I started men looking for automobiles parked in motels around El Mirar, and we finally located the car at the Serene Slumber Motel. She's in Unit 12 and she's all alone."

"Alone?" Mason asked.

Drake nodded.

Mason walked back to the desk, sat down in the big swivel chair and started drumming softly on the edge of the desk with the tips of his fingers.

"And what has happened to Horace Shelby?" Della Street asked.

Mason said, "She may have him hidden out. He's probably in another unit and—"

"Not in the Serene Slumber," Drake interrupted. "My men are thorough enough for that. They checked every unit and quizzed the people who are running the place. There's no single, unattached elderly man in the place, and Daphne Shelby has just the one unit and she's alone in there."

"What name is she registered under?" Mason asked.

Drake grinned. "Her own name."

"Thank heavens for that," Mason said. "It will give us something to work on when they catch her."

"They'll catch her?" Drake asked.

"Probably," Mason said. "But the person we're interested in right at the moment is Horace Shelby. They'll certainly be trying to corral him, and if the Finchley crowd get him before Dr. Alma can have a chance to examine him, you can't tell what's going to happen.

"I'll tell you what you do, Paul, keep a tail on Daphne

and let's see if she isn't keeping him hidden in some other motel."

"What would be the object of that?" Drake asked.

"Darned if I know," Mason said, "but I have a hunch she's trying to cover her trail so that if anyone locates her they can't automatically put their hands on Horace Shelby.

"Come on, Paul, put your men out on the job and leave word where you can be reached. Have a cocktail and then a nice thick steak, a baked potato filled with butter, some French fried onion rings and—"

"Don't, you're killing me," Drake said.

"Those hamburgers will be soggy by the time you get them sent up to the office," Della Street said. "The coffee will taste of the paper cup, and—"

"Sold!" Drake exclaimed.

"Come on," Mason told him. "We'll stop by your office and leave word where they can catch you on the telephone."

Drake said, "Something seems to tell me the case is going to get hot all at once and I *should* be where I can get on the phone and put out men."

"We'll go someplace reasonably close," Mason promised.

"I've already succumbed to the temptation," Drake told him, "so you can ease off on the sales talk. Let's go."

They stopped by Drake's office on their way to the elevator. Drake left minute instructions with the switchboard operator in charge, said to Mason, "All right, let's hurry. I'll bet you that I get my appetite sharpened with a cocktail, that we order our steaks and just as they are put on the table the phone will ring with an emergency that will send me scampering and I'll wind up with—"

"A steak sandwich," Della Street said. "We'll get the waiter to bring you a bowser bag as soon as you order and you can have some French bread all buttered and waiting."

"You may think you're kidding," Drake said, "but as a matter of fact, that's exactly what I'm going to do. You've got an idea."

They went to the Purple Lion Restaurant which was

one of Mason's favorites and was within easy cab distance of the office.

They had a cocktail and ordered their dinners at the same time they ordered the cocktail.

"Now then," Mason told the waitress, "bring a bowser bag, bring the freshest sourdough French bread you have in the place, and lots and lots of butter, both for the baked potato and for the steak sandwich."

"Steak sandwich?" the waitress said. "Why, I have orders for three extra thick steaks, but——"

"This man may have to make his into a steak sandwich and leave in a rush," Mason told her.

"Oh, I see," she said, smiling. "All right, we'll have the cocktails immediately. I'll have the steaks put on the fire and the bread and the bowser bag will come while you're drinking the cocktails."

Drake grinned and said, "Not a bad idea. If necessary I could eat a steak sandwich in the taxicab on my way to the office——What the deuce do you suppose she's doing sitting out there all by herself?"

"She's awaiting developments of some sort," Mason said. "But you can gamble on one thing—she isn't going to let Horace Shelby go wandering around unchaperoned, even if he's in a fit condition to do so."

"So?" Drake asked.

"So," Mason said, "somewhere along she's going to see that he has dinner. After all, the guy has to eat, you know."

"Well, let's hope she didn't give him a hamburger," Drake said. "Those things are fine when you eat them while they're fresh, but when you put them in a paper bag the bread gets soggy and——Oh, I guess they're all right, but I've eaten so darned many of them sitting up there in the office with a telephone at my ear that I just don't like the idea."

"Why don't you get something else?" Mason asked.

"What else can you have sent in?" Drake asked. "What takes the place of a good old hamburger sandwich with lots of onions?"

"Well, when you put it that way," Mason said, "you make it sound appetizing."

The waitress brought their cocktails and the French bread, butter and the bowser bag for Paul Drake.

Drake made a ceremony out of buttering two thick slices of French bread.

They finished the cocktails and after a few minutes the waitress brought the steaks.

Della Street waived her feminine prerogative; pointing at Paul Drake she said, "Serve him first. He's apt to be called out."

The headwaiter approached the table. "One of you is Mr. Paul Drake?" he asked. "I have a call for you. Shall I plug the phone in here?"

Paul Drake groaned.

Mason nodded. "Bring the phone," he said.

Drake picked the steak off the plate with a fork, put it between the two slices of French bread.

As the waiter brought the telephone, Drake sliced a piece off the steak, started chewing on it; then, still chewing, picked up the telephone, said, "Yes, this is Drake."

The receiver made noises. Drake listened for a while, said, "Just a moment."

He turned to Mason, said, "The tail is reporting on Daphne Shelby. She went to a Chinese restaurant and ordered food to take out—chow mein, fried rice, barbecued pork and chicken pineapple. I'll get back to the office and—"

"Stay right here," Mason interrupted. "You won't have time to get to the office. What's she doing now?"

"She waiting for the food. My man slipped to a telephone."

"She doesn't know she's being tailed?"

"No, apparently not. She looked around a bit when she started out, but apparently she feels pretty safe."

"Tell your man to keep on her tail," Mason said. "Don't take any chances of losing her. We've got to know where she goes. She's taking food to Horace Shelby right now."

"You mean I eat?" Drake asked with mock incredulity.

"You eat," Mason said. "Tell your man not to lose her under any circumstances."

Drake gave instructions in the telephone, slipped the thick steak out from under the pieces of buttered French bread, noted especially the stained surfaces of the bread where the steak juices had soaked in mingling with the melted butter.

He heaved an ecstatic sigh and said, "Sometimes, Perry, I think you're a slave driver, but this time I'm for you a million per cent. I thought you'd want to have me get Horace Shelby located, bolt my food and get out there."

Mason shook his head. "I want to find out what Daphne Shelby is up to first, Paul. There's something cooking and I don't know what it is."

"You don't think there's any chance the guy really is off his rocker and Daphne is keeping him stashed away?"

"I doubt it," Mason said. "If he were confused and disoriented, she wouldn't want to leave him alone and— After all, Paul, the guy's only seventy-five and the way we're living nowadays with vitamins and people being conscious of diet and cholesterol, a guy at seventy-five is just coming into the prime of life."

"Some of them get a little woozy at that age," Drake pointed out. "You know you have the testimony of the doctor who said he found him disoriented and confused."

"And, by the same token," Mason said, "we don't know what medication he had had before the doctor saw him."

The headwaiter took away the telephone. Drake attacked his steak, wolfing it down with swallows of hot coffee between bites.

Mason and Della Street ate more leisurely but without wasting time.

The waitress, sensing the urgency of the situation, hovered over the table.

Paul Drake dug out the last of the baked potato, rich with golden butter and red paprika on the top.

"That's the first time I've really enjoyed an evening meal in a long time. You'd be surprised how exacting this job is, Perry. And when *you* get a case, everything seems to go bang all at once."

"I'll admit I want lots of fast service," Mason said. "Somehow my cases seem to develop at high speed."

Drake said, "You're the high speed factor. Once you start on something you whip it through to a conclusion. The other attorneys I work for keep office hours, go home at four-thirty or five o'clock, forget about business until eight-thirty or nine-thirty the next morning."

"They don't have my type of work," Mason said.

"No one does," Drake told him, grinning.

The headwaiter was apologetic as he returned with the phone the second time.

"For you, Mr. Drake," he said.

Drake grinned affably. "It's all right now," he said, "I've had my dinner. No hamburger tonight."

Drake picked up the telephone, said, "Drake speaking . . . Go ahead, Jim, what do you know?"

Drake was silent for a moment, then cupped his hand over the mouthpiece and said to Mason, "She took the food to the Northern Lights Motel, parked the car directly in front of Unit 21, gave a perfunctory knock on the door, then opened the door which was unlocked and went in with the food in two big bags."

"Then what?"

"Closed the door. She's there now. There's a phone booth at the corner and my man is in the phone booth."

"Tell him to keep an eye on the situation," Mason said, "and particularly notice the time element. I want to know what time she went in; I want to know what time she comes out; and I want to know where she goes when she leaves there. . . . How about some more coffee, Paul?"

"Are you kidding?"

"No, I'm serious."

Drake relayed Mason's instructions into the telephone, settled back in his chair with a grin. "Paul Drake," he announced to no one in particular, "is dining high on the hog tonight. I think I'll have a hot fudge sundae as well."

"May as well have whatever you want," Mason said. "I

have an idea Daphne is going to be in there for some time and we have to wait here."

They had a leisurely dessert.

"Now what?" Drake asked when they had finished.

"We still wait," Mason said.

"We can go to my office," Drake suggested. "My men all call the office, and the office relays the call to wherever I happen to be."

Mason nodded. "Call your office. Tell them we're on our way back," he said.

"I hope you know what this is all about," Drake said. "It's all mixed up as far as I'm concerned."

"It's mixed up as far as *I'm* concerned," Mason admitted. "But I want to get a few high cards in my hand before I start calling for a showdown."

"You're calling for a showdown?" Drake asked.

"I'm going to have to," Mason said, "somewhere along the line."

"Tonight?"

Mason nodded, summoned the waiter, signed the check, gave the waitress an extra ten-dollar tip and said, "I just want you to know how much we appreciate the friendly service that you gave us."

Her face lit with pleasure. "Why—thank you *so* much. You're *so* nice!"

Mason detoured past the headwaiter, handed him another bill, said, "Thanks ever so much for keeping an eye on us and, incidentally, the waitress who handled our table did a wonderful job, the sort of job that makes people want to come back."

The headwaiter bowed. "She's one of our best. I assigned her to your table, Mr. Mason."

"Thanks," Mason said.

Driving back to the office, Drake said, "Why all the flowery talk, Perry? The money would have been enough. That's what they care about."

Mason shook his head. "They like appreciation."

"You show it with money."

"No you don't," Mason said. "It takes both money and words. Money without words is vulgar. Words without money are cheap."

"I never thought of it exactly that way," Drake said. "But perhaps that's why you always get such good service in restaurants."

"Don't you?" Mason asked.

Drake grinned. "Sure, I send my secretary down to the restaurant for a couple of hamburgers with mustard and onion, and a pint of coffee. She always smiles when she brings it in. That's what you call service with a smile."

"We're going to have to do something about your eating," Mason said.

"You can say that again," Drake told him. "Now that I've found out how the other half lives, I'm ruined."

They dropped Paul Drake at his office. Mason and Della Street went on down to the lawyer's office.

"She's having dinner with Horace Shelby?" Della asked.

Mason nodded.

"And you're worried about the case, aren't you?"

Again Mason nodded.

"Why?"

"In the first place," Mason said, "my client has started taking shortcuts. I don't like that. In the second place, she isn't confiding in me and I don't like that. In the third place, the fact that she's taking such elaborate precautions to keep Horace Shelby out of circulation either means that he's pretty far out in left field or that both of them are afraid the Finchleys are going to put him back in that sanitarium and restrain him by force."

"Well," Della said, "after a man has been strapped to a bed; after he's been taken against his will and thrown into what is virtually a mental institution and all of that, he's going to dread any possibility of returning."

"That probably accounts for it," Mason said, "but the situation may be a lot more complicated than appears on the surface. . . . What do you suppose Borden Finchley and his wife are doing? What do you suppose Ralph Exeter is doing?"

"Doesn't Drake have men on them?"

Mason shook his head. "After his men picked up Daphne Shelby, I concentrated on her. The others are relatively unimportant, and I don't want Finchley reporting to the Court that I had him shadowed."

"Do you think he'd know that he was being shadowed?" Della Street asked.

"He's pretty apt to find it out. A skillful shadow can tail a person for a while, but when you have three people to shadow, someone's going to get wise. And then, of course, if that one communicates his thoughts to the others and they begin to look around, it isn't too difficult to spot a shadow.

"Of course, it *can* be handled if you have the money to spend. You can alternate shadows, you can put several shadows on one suspect; you can have them behind him, ahead of him, and generally do a pretty good job. But I didn't want to take chances in this case, and therefore once we've found Horace Shelby that's what we're playing for. When we get him, we've hit the jackpot."

"And what are you going to do then?"

"It depends on the condition he's in," Mason said. "I'm going to play fair. As soon as we're dead certain we have him located, I'm going to get in touch with Dr. Alma and arrange for an interview. If Shelby is okay, I'm going to see what we can do for Daphne. If he isn't—if he's really in need of having someone look after him, then, of course, we're in a different situation.

"However, I am going to try and get evidence that will make the Court change his order in regard to Borden Finchley. I think we'll have some other conservator."

Mason walked around the office aimlessly, working off his restlessness while he was waiting.

Della, knowing that Perry Mason did much of his intensive thinking while pacing the floor, settled herself in the big, overstuffed leather chair, remaining motionless so as not to disturb the lawyer's thoughts.

The silence of night settled upon the big office building.

The sound of the unlisted telephone ringing shattered the silence.

Only three people had the number of that unlisted telephone—Perry Mason, Della Street and Paul Drake—

so Mason scooped up the instrument and said sharply, "Yes, Paul."

Drake said, "My man just telephoned. She's back at the Serene Slumber Motel. He didn't have a chance to telephone when she came out of the Northern Lights. She just jumped in her car and started moving and he had to follow. He's at a phone now, waiting instructions."

"Tell him to wait until we get there," Mason said. "Unless, of course, she goes out. If she does, he's to follow her and report at the earliest opportunity. We can't afford to lose her now."

"Your car or mine?" Drake asked.

"Both," Mason said. "We may want to separate later. You take your car and lead the way. Della will go with me. We'll pick you up at your office and start out at once."

Mason hung up the telephone, nodded at Della Street, who already had her hand on the light switch.

They hurried down the corridor, stopped at the illuminated oblong of Paul Drake's door. Mason was reaching for the doorknob just as the door was opened from the inside and Drake emerged.

"All ready?" Drake asked.

"All ready," Mason said. "Let's go."

They rode down in the elevator, crossed to the parking lot, got in their respective cars, and Drake led the way out to the freeway, then along to the turnoff at El Mirar.

The lawyer knew that Drake had the telephone in his automobile and saw the detective using it once in a while, apparently getting directions as to the best way to get to the Serene Slumber Motel.

Drake drove unerringly, making good time, then blinked his brake lights a couple of times to call Mason's attention to the illuminated sign ahead which read, "Serene Slumber Motel" and, down near the street, a red illuminated sign reading, *Sorry. No Vacancies*.

Drake pulled his car into the parking lot and usurped a vacant place. It took Mason a few seconds to find a place where he could leave his car. Since the marked parking stalls were all filled, it was necessary for the lawyer to leave his car down at the curb at the far end of the lot.

Mason and Della walked to join Paul Drake, who, by that time, was standing close to the shadowy figure of a tall, young man.

"I think you know Jim Inskip," Drake said, by way of introduction; and then added, "this is Della Street, Mr. Mason's secretary."

Inskip bowed. "I've met you before, Mr. Mason, and I'm very glad to meet you, Miss Street. Our party's in Unit 12."

"Any sign of leaving or turning in for the night?"

"Neither. Her car's here. You can see the lights on in the unit—that's the one with the light right over there."

The detective pointed.

"What do we do, Perry?" Drake asked.

Mason said, "Inskip stays here and keeps the place covered. He is to stay with Daphne Shelby no matter what happens. If we come out and drive away, Inskip is not to come anywhere near us but is to sit in his car and wait, because Daphne might be smart enough to turn out the light and look out of the back window. We'll arrange our communication system by phone later on."

"You want me to come with you?" Drake asked.

"I think I do," Mason said, "but I may have to ask you to leave. Anything that a client says to a lawyer is a privileged, confidential communication; anything that a lawyer says to a client is a privileged, confidential communication.

"That privilege also applies to a lawyer's secretary, but if the lawyer takes along someone else as an audience, that person can be called to the stand to relate any conversation which took place. I may want to have certain parts of the interview confidential. A great deal will depend on just what she's trying to do and just what she hopes to accomplish."

The three of them separated from Inskip, moved around to the walk which went around the front of the units, and Mason tapped gently at the door of number 12.

There was no answer from within, although a faint illumination shone through the curtains.

Mason tapped again.

Again, there was no answer.

The third time, the lawyer's knock was loud and peremptory.

After a moment, the knob turned, the door opened a crack and Daphne Shelby said, "Who . . . who is it? . . . What do you want?"

Mason said, "Good evening, Daphne."

Daphne, light-dazzled eyes failing to penetrate the semidarkness, flung herself against the door, trying to close it, but Drake and Mason pushed their weight against the door and Daphne slid back along the carpet.

Mason held the door open while Della Street entered.

Daphne, apparently recognizing him for the first time, was wide-eyed with surprise.

"*You!*" she exclaimed. "How in the world did *you* get here?"

Mason said, "Daphne, I want to ask you some questions. I want you to be very careful how you answer them. Anything that you say to *me* is a privileged communication as long as only you, Della and I are in the room. But with Paul Drake, a detective, present, the communication is no longer privileged. Drake can be called as a witness. Now, if there are any questions I ask which are going to embarrass you, or anything you want to tell me which you don't want known just speak up and Paul Drake will either step outside or step into the bathroom. Is that clear?"

She nodded wordlessly.

"All right," Mason said, "just what do you think you're accomplishing?"

"I'm trying to save Uncle Horace's sanity," she said. "He would have gone stark, staring, raving mad if I hadn't got him out of that place. Or did you know that I had got him out of the place?"

"I knew," Mason said. "Why didn't you tell me what you were intending to do?"

"I didn't dare. I was afraid you would stop me."

"Why?"

"Your ideas of professional ethics."

Mason regarded her thoughtfully.

She said after a moment, "I presume you know all that I've done."

Mason said, "You went out to the sanitarium. You saw from the sign that they were very anxious to get someone to do domestic work. You applied for the job."

She nodded.

"You bought a new car."

Again she nodded.

"All right," Mason said, "you went out and went to work. What happened?"

She said, "I'll never forget what I saw when I got out there. I started work. It took me a couple of hours before I dared to slip into Unit 17 where they were keeping Uncle Horace.

"There was that poor man strapped to a bed—absolutely strapped—and the straps were stretched so tight that they were holding him motionless."

"What was his mental condition?"

"What would your mental condition be in a situation like that? Here the poor man had been taken away from his home, had been stripped of his property. And they intended to leave him there until he died, and to do everything they could to hasten his death.

"Uncle Horace has always had claustrophobia—a fear of being rendered helpless where he couldn't move. And he was tied down there, he was moving his head and trying to get at his straps so he could bite them. He was wild and disheveled and—"

"Did he recognize you?" Mason asked.

She hesitated a moment and then said, "I don't think I'd better talk any more about that phase of it until you and I can be alone, Mr. Mason."

"All right," Mason said. "What else can we talk about now?"

"Well," she said, "I went back in the morning after the night's work had all been done and just before the morning shift came on—right after the cook came in. I had picked up a very sharp butcher knife in the kitchen and I cut through those straps. I found Uncle Horace's clothes in the closet and I got some clothes on him and got him out into the automobile and drove away."

"Did you think they would follow you?"

"Yes."

"Why didn't you keep Uncle Horace here with you?"

"I thought it would be safer to park him off by himself."

"Did he recognize you in the morning when you took him out?"

"Oh, heavens, yes," she said.

"What's his mental condition now?"

"Pretty nearly normal, except when you mention something about the sanitarium he just goes all to pieces. He's on the verge of a complete nervous breakdown because of the things he's had to put up with."

"You knew they'd find out about what you did?" Mason asked.

"I felt they probably would, yes."

"You knew that they'd come looking for you?"

"That's why I got Uncle Horace where no one could ever find him."

Mason raised his eyebrows.

"No one will find him where he is," she said. "He's going to stay there until he's got his nerves back in shape and until we can get Finchley shown up for the type of man he is.

"Uncle Horace tells me that no sooner had I left for the Orient than they started doing all sorts of little things that they knew would irritate and annoy him. They treated him like a child. They wouldn't let him do what he wanted to. They started making him nervous. He thinks Aunt Elinor was giving him some drug that overstimulated him. He couldn't sleep, and when he told her he couldn't sleep, she said she'd give him some sleeping pills.

"Within a week or ten days, he was so dependent on those sleeping pills that he had to have them in order to get a night's sleep. Otherwise he'd lie there and toss and get nervous, sleep for an hour or two, then lie awake for the rest of the night."

"Didn't it occur to him that Mrs. Finchley was deliberately drugging him?"

"Not at the time. She handed him a great line of talk

97

about how he was upset because he was accustomed to having me around, but that the trip was the best thing on earth for me and that I was going to crack up if I didn't have some recreation and some help. And she pointed out to him that he was pretty much of a nuisance and needed altogether too much attention for one person to give it to him. And then she kept giving him more and more medication.

"Finally, he realized what they were trying to do. That was when he wrote that letter to me."

"Just what was his idea in writing that letter?"

"He wanted me to get enough money out of the bank account so that if they did start proceedings for a guardianship, he wouldn't be absolutely helpless."

"He realized what they had in mind?"

"By that time, yes; it was very obvious. . . . That's a horrible thing, Mr. Mason. They suddenly drag a man into court and claim that he's incompetent to manage his affairs and strip him of every cent he has in the world.

"How would you feel if you'd saved up enough money to be independent, and then relatives suddenly moved in and took all that money away from you and put you in some kind of an institution where—"

"I'd feel pretty bad," Mason said, "but that's not the point. Just what are your plans now?"

"I was intending to get in touch with you."

"You took long enough doing it."

"Well, I had to make arrangements to see that Uncle Horace would be safe and comfortable."

"Where is he?" Mason asked.

She clamped her lips together and shook her head.

Mason smiled. "You're not telling me?"

"No. I'm not going to tell a soul. That's why I have him where people can't get at him until he's ready to step into court and go in there fighting. And this time, he's not going to be drugged."

"He was drugged when he went to court?" Mason asked.

"Of course," she said scornfully. "You don't think that they could ever have pulled a fast one like that unless they had him drugged in such a way that he didn't have his normal responses."

"The judge didn't detect that he was drugged and the doctor that examined him didn't."

"They were rather clever but they had been brainwashing him for three months. Don't ever forget that! And with a man of that age, a very clever person can do a lot of brainwashing in three months."

"How is he now?" Mason asked.

She hesitated for a long moment, then said, "Better."

"And you gave him money?" Mason asked.

"I gave him forty thousand dollars of his money."

"Forty thousand dollars?" Mason asked.

She nodded. "I bought the car, and I'm keeping enough money so I can do the things that have to be done. I gave him the rest."

"Did you," Mason asked, "tell him about the evidence that had been brought out in court, that you weren't actually related to him?"

She said, "I don't think I want to talk about that for a while, but I can tell you this, he's made his will now."

Mason's eyes narrowed. "I was afraid of that," he said. "I wish you'd got in touch with me. That was the one thing he should never have done."

"Why?"

"Don't you see," Mason said, "you're playing right into their hands. They claimed that if you could ever get him where he was under your control, you'd have him make a will and you'd get his property.

"That letter he wrote with the check for a hundred and twenty-five thousand dollars was just the sort of thing they needed; and, if they can show that you had him make a will in your favor as soon as you got him out of the sanitarium, that also will be ammunition they can use."

"But this was his own idea," she said. "He wanted to do it. He insisted on it. He'd been trying to make a will so there couldn't be any question."

"Then he should have done it through an attorney and in the regular way," Mason said. "The document should have been formally witnessed. . . . What kind of a will did he make?"

"He said that in this state a will is good if it's entirely written, dated and signed in the handwriting of the testator; and you had told me the same thing, so that's the sort of will he made."

"Who has it?" Mason asked.

"I do."

"Give it to me."

She hesitated a moment, then opened her purse, took out a folded document and handed it to Mason.

Mason read the will. "This is all in his handwriting?"

"Yes."

Mason checked the points: Dated . . . Signed . . . Purporting to be a last will and testament . . . "You'd better let me keep this, Daphne."

"I want you to."

"And," Mason said, "say nothing about it unless you're asked. I want to get hold of Horace Shelby; and in the event he's competent, I want him to make a will setting forth whatever he wants to put in it, and I want to make certain it will be a valid will.

"Now then, let's go and see Horace Shelby."

She shook her head. "I am not going to tell you where he is."

"Suppose," Mason said, "that you just take a little ride with me and we'll go to see him."

She smiled. "And you can't bluff me, Mr. Mason. I know you regard me as a naïve child but I'm not as green as some people think."

"I'll say you're not," Mason said. He nodded significantly to Della Street and gestured toward the telephone directory.

Della moved quietly behind Daphne's chair to consult the directory and then, when she had the address she wanted, made a surreptitious note and nodded to Mason.

Daphne Shelby, in the meantime, had been glaring at Mason defiantly.

"I'm not going to tell you," she said. "And you're not going to bluff me by making me think you know so that I'll say something that will be a giveaway. I know all about that technique of getting information."

Mason smiled. "I'm sure you do," he said. "Well, get your hat and coat and we'll take a little ride."

"I'll ride with you," she said, "but I'm not going to give you any information about where Uncle Horace is. He needs rest; he needs to have the assurance that he's his own man once more. You just can't imagine what a devastating experience this has been for him."

"You gave him forty thousand dollars?" Mason asked.

"Yes."

"How?"

"I endorsed seven cashier's checks for five thousand dollars over to him and I gave him five thousand dollars in cash."

"A man in his condition shouldn't be carrying that money around with him," Mason said. "In fact, nobody should carry that much, but particularly your Uncle Horace shouldn't have it."

"It's his money!" she blazed. "And that's the only way he's ever going to snap out of it—is to feel that he's his own master, that he can do what he wants to with his own money."

"All right," Mason said, "let's get in the car. Perhaps you'd better follow us in your car, Paul."

"Will do," Paul Drake said.

"Perhaps you'd be so good as to tell me where you're taking me?" Daphne asked.

Mason grinned. "Just down the road a piece. We'll bring you back in due course. There's a man down there I want to see."

Her head held high, she stalked out to Mason's car.

Mason, Della Street and Daphne got into the front seat. With Paul Drake following, they drove down the thoroughfare, turned to the right, cruised past the Northern Lights Motel. Mason frequently glanced at Daphne's face.

The young woman kept looking straight ahead, not even her eyes turned as they cruised slowly past the motel.

Paul Drake, in the car behind Mason, snapped his

lights on and off, gave two quick taps on the horn button.

Mason swung to the curb, rolled down the window on his side and waited.

Drake's car pulled alongside.

"What is it?" Mason asked.

"Cops," Drake said tersely.

"Where?"

"Other end of the motel. Two cars."

"Oh-oh," Mason said.

"What do we do?" Drake asked.

Mason said, "We pull around the corner and wait. You go ask questions. Not pointed questions but adroit questions."

"Will do," Drake said.

As the detective pulled away, Mason turned to Daphne and said, "That's what comes of trying to give your own attorney a double cross and taking things into your own hands.

"Now you can see what's happened. Finchley has found out where your Uncle Horace is. He's charged him with escaping from a sanitarium where he was confined under a Court order and has probably brought in police to take him back."

Daphne, who had been bravely silent, suddenly started to cry. "If they take him back to that sanitarium and strap him in bed, it will kill him," she said.

"We'll *try* not to let it happen," Mason told her. "We'll get out of the way and park and see what we can do."

The lawyer eased the car into motion, came to the cross street and started to turn. A police car, with siren moaning a low but peremptory message for the right-of-way, came around the corner. Mason pulled to the curb.

The police car, traveling at slow speed, started past the lawyer's car, then suddenly stopped. The beam of a red spotlight illuminated the interior of Mason's car.

"Well, well, well," Lieutenant Tragg's voice said. "Look who's here!"

"Why, hello, Lieutenant," Mason said. "What are *you* doing here?"

"I think I'll ask you first and make the question official," Tragg said. "What are you doing here?"

"I had been out to see a client on a probate matter," Mason said, "and—"

"Your client live at the Northern Lights Motel?" Tragg interrupted.

Mason grinned and shook his head. "Why?"

"We're investigating what seems to be a homicide," Tragg said.

"A what?" Mason asked.

"Some fellow out here in Unit 21," Tragg said. "Evidently somebody fed him some Chinese food that was drugged with a barbiturate; and then, when he went to sleep, turned the gas stove on and didn't light it. Occupants of an adjoining unit smelled the gas, called the proprietor, the proprietor got in the door, opened the windows, shut the gas off. It was too late."

"Dead?" Mason asked.

"As a mackerel!" Lieutenant Tragg said. "You wouldn't know anything about it, would you?"

"About the man's death?" Mason asked. "Heavens, no! I had no idea there had been a death until you told me just now."

"Well, I was just checking—that's all," Tragg said. "Sort of a coincidence, you being here."

He nodded to the driver of the car. "Let's go," he said.

When the police car pulled away, Mason turned back to look at Daphne Shelby.

She was sitting white-faced and frozen, her eyes wide with terror.

"Well?" Mason asked.

She looked at him, tried to say something, then collapsed to the floor of the car.

Mason said, "Inskip will be trailing us because we have Daphne in the car with us. Let's see if we can spot him."

The lawyer made a U-turn, circled back to the corner, suddenly spotted a car parked at the curb, braked his own car to a stop and motioned.

Inskip started the agency car he was driving and pulled alongside.

"Tell Paul we're going back to the Serene Slumber Motel," Mason said. "Tell him to come back there as soon as he finds out what's cooking."

The lawyer drove back to the motel where Daphne had her room. He and Della Street helped Daphne from the car. Daphne handed him the key with cold numb fingers. The lawyer opened the door, escorted Daphne inside.

"All right," Mason said. "Pull yourself together, Daphne. Let's have it straight from the shoulder. Did you have anything to do with your uncle's death?"

She shook her head. Her lips quivered. "I loved him," she said. "He was a father to me. I've sacrificed most of my life trying to make him comfortable."

"That's right," Mason said. "But that's not the way the evidence is going to point."

"What evidence?"

"Let's look at the evidence," Mason said. "You aren't related by blood to Horace Shelby. You can't inherit without a will.

"Shelby's half brother has filed affidavits stating that you are a shrewd and designing person; that you have planned to ingratiate yourself with Horace Shelby and get him to turn his wealth over to you. The records show that Shelby gave you a check for a hundred and twenty-five thousand dollars.

"The Court ordered Shelby to have a conservator for his estate. You smuggled Shelby out of the rest home where he was placed on the orders of a physician, took him to the Northern Lights Motel. You got him to make a will leaving everything to you. And, within hours after he made that will, the man was dead."

"I suppose," she said, "he was so despondent that he *could* have committed suicide, although I would never have thought of it."

"We'll wait until Paul Drake comes," Mason said. "Evidently, the police have reason to believe that barbiturates entered into it. You bought him a Chinese dinner tonight?"

"Yes."

"Brought it in in cardboard containers?"

"Yes."

"And had spoons and ate it from the containers?"

"He liked to use chopsticks," she said. "I bought two pair of chopsticks. We ate it with chopsticks."

"And what did you do with the empty containers?"

"They weren't quite empty," she said. "I had to leave, but Uncle Horace promised he'd flush what was left of the food down the toilet, wash the containers out so they wouldn't smell, and put them in the wastebasket. After all, it isn't a housekeeping unit—just a bedroom—and I thought they might make trouble if he used the wastebasket as a garbage pail."

"There was food left over and he promised to flush it down the toilet?"

"Yes."

"Looking at it from the standpoint of the police," Mason said, "they'll claim you did the flushing and it will be considered an attempt to conceal the evidence. Then you weren't content with that, they'll say you washed the cardboard containers out with hot water. You told your uncle to do that?"

"Yes."

"That and the will you let him make out in your favor can send you to the penitentiary for life," the lawyer said.

Drake's code knock sounded on the door.

Della Street let him in.

Drake looked serious.

"How bad is it, Paul?" Mason asked.

"Bad," Drake said.

"Give us the lowdown."

"Someone in Unit 22 had been out to dinner, came home and smelled gas coming from Unit 21. They notified the manager of the motel. He got a passkey and opened the door. The gas just about knocked him down. He opened the door, ran to the windows, opened them, and dragged the man's body out into the open. He notified the police. Police arrived and tried resuscitation. It didn't work."

"Why did they figure homicide instead of suicide?" Mason asked.

"The gas stove is vented," Drake said. "Someone had unscrewed the feed pipe so the gas could escape directly into the room. The guy had been eating Chinese food. The doctor who is riding with the deputy coroner suspected barbiturates. He made a quick test. Apparently, the food was loaded. I think they also found evidence of drugs in the bathroom."

Mason looked at Daphne Shelby.

Her eyes refused to meet his.

"You stayed with your uncle while you both ate Chinese food?" he asked.

"I left before he was finished."

"Did you," he asked, "give him any barbiturates?"

"I—I don't know."

"What do you mean, you don't know?"

"I told you he couldn't sleep without these sleeping pills. He has developed such a need for them that he had to have them. I knew that, so when I left him I gave him the sleeping pills that I had."

"Where did *you* get them?"

"They were given me by a doctor—the same doctor who treats Uncle Horace. You remember when I went away, I was all rundown and nervous. The doctor gave me some sleeping medicine in case I had any trouble sleeping.

"I never needed to use it. From the time I got on that boat, I slept like a log. I felt that Uncle Horace might need those pills, so I gave them to him to use if he needed them."

Mason said, "You have put yourself in a beautiful spot for a first-degree murder rap."

Drake said, "The proprietress of the motel got a little suspicious that everything wasn't quite on the up-and-up. This young woman rented Unit 21 and said her uncle was going to occupy it; that she would bring him in later. She got the license number of her automobile—it was a new Ford."

Mason turned to Daphne and said, "And there you are, Daphne!"

Paul Drake caught Mason's eye; jerked his head, indicating he wanted a private conference.

"Excuse us a moment," Mason said, and walked over to the far corner of the room with the detective.

Drake lowered his voice to a half-whisper. "Look, Percy," he said, "you're in a spot. Your client is in a spot. The minute she produces that will, she's convicted herself of murder.

"That girl isn't any sweet, innocent, naïve rosebud. She's shrewd, scheming and clever.

"She located her uncle. She spirited him out of the institution. She was too smart to put him in the motel where she was staying, but she took him to another motel.

"Everything that she's done indicates that she's quick-thinking and ingenious.

"Now then, she found out that she wasn't actually related to Horace Shelby. She can't get any of his money unless she has a will.

"So she spirits him out from under the hand of the authorities and the guardianship of the Court, gets him to make a will, and then the guy promptly dies.

"Now then, if *you* want to forget about that will, *I'll* forget about it."

"What do you mean?" Mason asked.

"It's the strongest single fact against her," Drake said. "Just take that will and burn it up. Have her refrain from mentioning it to anyone, and we can refrain from mentioning it. In that way, we can dispose of some of the worst evidence against her."

Mason shook his head.

"Why not?" Drake asked. "I'll stick my neck out. I'll put my license on the line to give your client a break."

"It isn't that," Mason said. "In the first place, as an officer of the court, I can't tamper with evidence. As a licensed detective, you can't. In the second place, I've always found that truth is the strongest weapon in the arsenal of any attorney. The trouble is lawyers quite frequently don't know what the truth is. They get half-truths from the evidence or from their clients and try to get by on those half-truths.

"As far as we are concerned, we are——"

Mason stopped talking abruptly as heavy steps sounded on the wooden porch of the motel, then knuckles pounded on the door.

Mason said, "Permit me, Daphne." He walked across the room and opened the door.

Lieutenant Tragg, accompanied by a uniformed officer standing on the threshold, had a hard time hiding his surprise.

"What the devil are *you* doing *here?*" Tragg asked.

"Talking with my client," Mason said.

"Well, if your client is the owner of the new Ford automobile out in front, she's going to need an attorney in the worst way," Lieutenant Tragg said.

"Come in," Mason invited. "Daphne, this is Lieutenant Tragg of the Homicide Department. Lieutenant Tragg, Daphne Shelby."

"Oh ho," Tragg said, "I'm beginning to see a great light. Headquarters tell me they've been looking for Horace Shelby, who was spirited out of the Goodwill Sanitarium despite an order of Court."

Tragg turned to the uniformed officer and said, "Bring in the woman. Let's see if we make an identification."

"Let me point out that that's hardly the best way to make an identification," Mason said.

"Well, it is in this case," Tragg said. "We're working against time."

The officer left the porch, a car door slammed, then there were steps on the porch, and the officer escorted a woman into the motel unit.

"Look around," Tragg invited, "and see if there's anyone here you know."

The woman instantly pointed to Daphne Shelby.

"Why, that's the woman who rented Unit 21," she said. "She told me that her uncle was going to be occupying it."

Tragg turned to Mason with a grin. "This," he said, "is your exit line, Counselor. We can get along without you from here on."

Mason smiled. "I think you're forgetting about the recent Supreme Court decisions, Lieutenant," he said.

"Miss Shelby is entitled to have an attorney representing her at *all stages* of the investigation."

Mason turned to Daphne and said, "Before you answer any questions, Daphne, look at me. If I shake my head, don't answer; if I nod my head, answer it and *tell the truth*."

"That's going to be one hell of a way to interrogate a witness," Lieutenant Tragg said.

"It may be a poor way to interrogate a *witness,* but it's the only way you can interrogate a prospective defendant," Mason said. "Perhaps I can make some stipulations which will make things easier for you, Lieutenant."

"Such as what?" Tragg asked.

"This is Daphne Shelby," Mason said. "Until a short time ago, she believed in good faith that she was the niece of Horace Shelby.

"However, whether there is any blood relationship or not, Daphne is very fond of the man she has always regarded as her uncle. She lived in the house and took charge of his rather restricted diet. She was on the verge of a nervous breakdown from trying to nurse him, do the cooking, and supervise the housekeeping problems.

"When Horace Shelby was sent to the Goodwill Sanitarium by a conservator and a doctor who was employed by the other relatives, Daphne obtained employment at the sanitarium. She found Horace Shelby strapped to a bed, she took a knife, cut the straps, took Horace Shelby to the Northern Lights Motel and established him in Unit 21.

"Now then, Lieutenant, that's as far as we are going to go at the present time."

Tragg whirled to Daphne. "Did you bring him some food tonight?"

Mason shook his head.

Daphne remained quiet.

"Chinese food in particular," Lieutenant Tragg said. "We know you did so you might just as well make it easy on yourself. After all, Miss Shelby, we're trying to get at the truth in the case; and, if you're innocent, you have nothing to fear from the truth."

Again Mason shook his head.

"Shucks," Tragg muttered, then turned to Mason. "Any objection to letting her identify the body?"

"None whatever," Mason said.

Tragg turned to Daphne Shelby and held out his hand. "Would you mind giving me those sleeping pills you have, Miss Shelby?" he asked. "The ones you've got left."

She started to reach for her purse, then caught Mason's eye.

"No dice, Lieutenant," Mason said. "We don't want to have you resort to subterfuge because, under those circumstances, we might quit co-operating."

Lieutenant Tragg said bitterly, "It's one hell of a note when the Court takes the handcuffs off the defendant and puts them on the wrists of honest officers who are trying to enforce the law."

"I don't see any handcuffs," Mason said.

"Well, I can *feel* them," Tragg snapped.

"We were going to identify a body," Mason reminded him.

"All right, come on," Tragg said; and then added, "We're going to have to deprive you of that Ford automobile for a while, Miss Shelby. It's evidence, and we've got to have it identified."

"That's all right," Mason said. "We're co-operating in every way we can in the investigation."

"Yes," Tragg said, drawing his extended forefinger across his throat. "I can feel the cordiality of your co-operation."

Tragg turned to the officer, said, "Call in on the radio. Have a fingerprint expert come out and check that Ford car for fingerprints."

He turned to Daphne and said, "You come with me."

"I'll ride in the car with you," Mason said.

Tragg shook his head.

"Then Daphne rides with me," Mason announced.

Tragg thought things over, then said, "All right, Daphne rides with you. You follow me."

"I'll tag along behind to make the procession complete," Drake added.

"Come on, Della, you and Daphne sit in the back seat of my car," Mason instructed.

"Daphne, you're not to answer any questions by anyone unless I am present and advise you to answer. Do you understand?"

She nodded.

"Now, you're in for a shock," Mason said in a low voice. "They're going to take you to identify your uncle's body. You can make the identification, that's all. I don't want you to volunteer any information or answer any questions, do you understand?"

She nodded in a tight-lipped silence.

"This is going to be a very harrowing experience," Mason said, "and you've had plenty of them within the last twenty-four hours. But you're going to have to brace yourself and bear up.

"All right, Lieutenant, let's go."

The cars made a procession down the road until they came to the Northern Lights Motel.

A stretcher wagon was waiting to take the remains to the morgue for autopsy.

Lieutenant Tragg walked over to the stretcher, took hold of a corner of the blanket and said, "This way, please, Miss Shelby."

She came to stand by the officer. Mason stood at her side, holding her arm.

Tragg jerked back the blanket.

Suddenly, Mason felt Daphne stiffen. She clutched at the lawyer, then gave a half scream.

Mason patted her shoulder.

"That isn't Uncle Horace," she said. "That's Ralph Exeter!"

Lieutenant Tragg was puzzled. "Who's Ralph Exeter?" he asked.

Daphne's numb lips made two futile attempts before words came. "A friend of Uncle Borden."

"And who's Uncle Borden?"

"A half brother of Horace Shelby."

"Then how did Exeter get in this unit of the motel and where is Horace Shelby now?"

Mason said, "Those are two questions, Lieutenant, which you are going to have to answer all by yourself."

The woman who had identified Daphne Shelby came over to the officers. "Want to take a look?" Lieutenant Tragg asked her.

She nodded.

Tragg drew back the blanket.

"I don't think that's the man who's supposed to be in Unit 21!" she said. "It looks like the man who rented Unit 20 about three hours ago."

"How did he come here?" Tragg asked.

"He had his own car. It had a Massachusetts license. There may have been someone with him—a woman. I can get the registration card."

"We'll get it," Tragg said.

He accompanied her to the office, came back holding the registration card.

"That's right," he said. "He registered under his own name. He gave the license number of his car—a Massachusetts license number.

"Now then, where's his car? What became of it? It isn't here."

There was an interval of silence, then Tragg said, "Let's take a look in Unit 20 and see what we find in there."

He turned to Mason. "Since you aren't of any help in this phase of the investigation, you and your client can go, but I want both of you to be available where I can reach you on short notice."

Mason said, "Excuse me a minute, Daphne. It will only take a moment."

The lawyer moved over to Paul Drake, lowered his voice, said, "Paul, Horace Shelby was in that cabin. He isn't there now. He left under his own power' or he was taken away.

"If he was taken away, we're in trouble. If he left under his own power, I'd like to make sure that he's on his own and see if we can take steps to keep him on his own."

Drake nodded.

"Start your men covering the taxicab companies right away," Mason said.

Again Drake nodded.

"Now then," Mason went on, "it would be fatal if the police managed to implant in the proprietress' mind the idea that Ralph Exeter was the man Daphne brought to the motel.

"She's seen Daphne. She identified the license number of the car Daphne was driving, and she's identified Daphne.

"Get to work on her in advance of the police. Get her to state that she can't identify the woman who was with Exeter in the car in which Exeter arrived at the motel. And be darned sure to tie her up so that she can't testify later on that the more she thinks of it, the more she believes Daphne was the one who was in Exeter's car.

"You know and I know that personal identification evidence is just about the worst, the most unreliable type of evidence we have—not when a person identifies someone he knows but when he gets a glimpse of an individual and then later on makes an identification—either from a photograph or from personal contact."

"Sure, we all know that," Drake said. "I'll do what I can. Anything else?"

"That's all," Mason said. "Get your men working. Use that telephone in your car. Put your men out and get busy on that woman while Lieutenant Tragg is searching Unit 20 for clues."

"On my way," Drake said. "Which comes first?"

"The talk with the proprietress of the motel," Mason told him. "We don't know how long Lieutenant Tragg is going to be in Unit 20. You can telephone the taxicab companies shortly after that."

CHAPTER TWELVE

MASON PUT AN ARM around Daphne Shelby, drew her over to his car, felt her trembling like a leaf beneath her coat.

"Take it easy, Daphne! Take it easy!" the lawyer warned. "We're running up against something that may be pretty complicated. This man was found in Unit 21. Now, that's the unit you rented for your uncle?"

She nodded.

The lawyer escorted her into the back seat of his car, had Della Street move in on the other side, said to Daphne, "You went to the Chinese restaurant and got Chinese food to take out?"

"Yes."

"Who waited on you?"

"Heavens, I don't know. It was some girl."

"Not Chinese?"

"No. The cook was Chinese."

"How did you happen to go to that restaurant?"

She pointed and said, "You can see the sign there— right over there."

Mason followed the direction of her finger and saw the big illuminated sign in green letters reading CHINESE COOKING.

Mason said, "When Lieutenant Tragg asked you for the sleeping pills you had, you started to open your purse."

She nodded.

"You have sleeping pills in there?"

"No, it was because he extended his hand and acted the way he did. I forgot for the moment that I had given the sleeping pills to Uncle Horace."

"Keep on forgetting it for the time being," Mason said. "Don't answer any questions about the sleeping pills.

"Now then, Exeter checked into this motel sometime this afternoon. That means that they knew where you had placed Uncle Horace and were just biding their time."

"Then why didn't they get officers and take him back to the sanitarium?" she asked. "That's what both Uncle Horace and I were afraid of."

"Probably because they were afraid that the Court-appointed doctor would then examine him, and they wanted to work him over a little bit before they let Dr. Alma get in touch with him."

"Then you think they have Uncle Horace with them?"

"It's a very distinct possibility," Mason said.

"What will happen now?" she asked.

Mason said, "They'll get him all doped up. They'll terrify him. They will then return him to the sanitarium and notify Dr. Alma."

"Is there any way of counteracting that?" she asked. "Is there anything we can do? Any way we can find Uncle Horace?"

"I really don't know," Mason said, "but we have two alternatives to consider."

"What are those?"

"One," Mason said, "is that your Uncle Horace left here with Borden Finchley. But somehow I don't subscribe to that theory."

"What's the other alternative?"

"That he left here under his own power and of his own volition."

"But why would he leave here?" she asked.

Mason looked her straight in the eyes. "Because he had killed Ralph Exeter."

"Why, Uncle Horace wouldn't . . ." Her voice trailed off into silence.

"Exactly," Mason said. "You don't know *all* the details about how your Uncle Horace has been treated. You don't know his mental condition. You gave him sleeping pills. Suppose Exeter had the adjoining room; then, after you had left the motel, Exeter walked into Horace Shelby's room and started making demands on him.

"Remember that Exeter wasn't really Borden Finchley's friend. He was only interested in getting money, and the money had to come from Horace Shelby.

"So suppose Exeter demanded a hundred and twenty-five thousand dollars from Horace Shelby as the price of his co-operation. Suppose Exeter said he hadn't had anything to eat and started to help himself to the rest of the food in the containers.

"Horace wanted to get rid of the man. He simply dumped the sleeping medicine into the Chinese food. He could have mashed the pills up into a powder while Exeter was talking.

"Perhaps his original intention was to drug Exeter into insensibility and then escape. But after he saw Exeter lying there helpless, he may have decided to make a permanent job of it."

She shook her head. "Not Uncle Horace. He wouldn't do anything like that. He wouldn't kill a fly."

"Then," Mason said, "unless we can involve Borden Finchley, there's only one other suspect."

"Who?"

"You," Mason said.

"Me?"

Mason nodded.

She shook her head and said, "This is what Uncle Borden would have done, but not what I would have done and not what Uncle Horace would have done."

"We'll also investigate your Uncle Borden," Mason said.

"When?" she asked.

"Now," Mason said and, putting his car into gear, drove out of the motel parking lot.

"What am I to do?" Daphne asked.

"You," Mason said, "are going to go back to your hotel and stay there. If you cut any more capers or have any more unauthorized absences, you're going to find yourself charged with murder."

"Ralph Exeter?"

"Yes."

"But why in the world should I have murdered him?"

"I can think of half a dozen reasons," Mason said. "One of them is that he is the moving force against your

Uncle Horace. He was the one who was putting on the pressure. And if I can think of one good motive, the police can think of a dozen.

"You aren't out of the woods yet, young lady. You're suspect right now. There *are* those who think that underneath that shell of cherubic innocence you're a shrewd, scheming individual trying to look out for your own future at all costs."

She said, "I've been perfectly frank with you, Mr. Mason."

"Yes, I know," the lawyer said. "You've told me all the things you wanted me to know. You've put all the cards on the table that you wanted me to see. But I'd feel a lot better about you, Daphne, if you hadn't sneaked out of that hotel, shown such ingenuity in going to that sanitarium and getting a job, then spiriting your uncle out of there.

"I don't know whether you're doing it for you or doing it for him, but you certainly aren't being very considerate of me.

"I stuck my neck out getting some money for you, and I'm entitled to your co-operation."

"I know," she said quietly. "And don't think I don't appreciate all you've done."

"If you gave that money back to your uncle," Mason said, "it's one of the good things to be put on the credit side of the ledger as far as you're concerned. But don't kid yourself, before the night is over the police are going to be hot on your trail.

"If they call on you, I want you to insist that you telephone me. I'll give you a night number where I can be reached. Don't answer any questions, under any circumstances, until I get there.

"And, in the meantime, don't question anything that I do."

"Why should I question anything that you do?" she asked.

"Because," Mason told her, "if I have the chance, I'm going to use your Uncle Horace as a red herring."

"What do you mean 'a red herring'?"

Mason said, "I'm going to let the police get the idea that your Uncle Horace murdered Ralph Exeter, and that he was medically if not legally insane at the time he did it."

CHAPTER THIRTEEN

IT WAS WELL after ten o'clock that evening when Paul Drake's code knock sounded on the door of Mason's office.

Della Street opened the door.

A bedraggled Paul Drake, his face oily with weariness, came in, slumped into a chair, said, "I tried to make it sooner. I knew you people wanted to go home, but it's been one hell of a job."

"What did you find out?" Mason asked.

"Something that the police have been suppressing," Drake said. "I found out how they really knew about the barbiturates."

"How come?"

Drake said, "In the bathroom in the apartment where they found the man lying dead—Unit 21 of the motel— they found a tumbler, one of those heavy glass tumblers that go with motel rooms, you know the kind they wrap up in a wax paper package with an antiseptic label."

Mason nodded.

"Inside the tumbler was the glass tube of a toothbrush case and a little white powder," Drake said. "Lieutenant Tragg treated the glass for fingerprints."

"Did he get any?"

"He got some prints. Probably those of Horace Shelby, but they don't know for sure."

"Go ahead," Mason said.

"Someone had used the glass tube of the toothbrush case to grind up some sleeping pills, using the tumbler as an impromptu mortar, and the toothbrush case as an improvised pestle."

"How do they know about the toothbrush case having been used as a pestle?"

"Some of the powder had been ground into the rounded end of the glass case hard enough so it stuck there."

"Tragg's a thorough cuss," Mason said.

Drake nodded.

"What was the powder?" Mason asked.

"It's a barbiturate preparation called Somniferone. It's a combination preparation that is very quick in its action and is combined with another barbiturate derivative which is more lasting. The result is a combination which takes effect quickly and lasts a long time."

"How'd they get it identified?" Mason asked.

"One of these X-ray analytical machines. Tragg got fingerprints from the glass and then rushed the whole thing up to the police laboratory."

"All right," Mason said, "I can see you're leading up to something. Hand it to me."

"Somniferone," Drake said, "is the barbiturate that was prescribed for Horace Shelby by the doctor who was called in by Borden Finchley after they moved in. He is the same doctor who prescribed the sedative for Daphne to take with her on her long ocean voyage—and just before she left they filled the prescription for her. She had a whole three months' supply of Somniferone."

"Go on," Mason said.

"The police don't know it yet, but they're investigating," Drake said. "They're getting on the right track."

"What's the right track?"

"Your client," Drake said. "That girl certainly can put on an act. She poses as little Miss Sweetness, little Miss Innocence, but she's a deep one."

"What did she do?" Mason asked.

"She went to a Chinese restaurant. She got some Chinese food. She went to Unit 21. She took her sleeping pills and ground them up in the glass tumbler with the toothbrush case. She invited Ralph Exeter in for a conference. She drugged his food, dumped all the food that was uneaten down the toilet and washed out the pasteboard containers. After he slipped into a drugged sleep, she disconnected the gas pipe so the gas was on, and left. She knew that, one way or another, she wasn't going to be bothered any more with Ralph Exeter."

Mason shook his head. "I won't buy it, Paul."

"You don't have to buy it," Drake said. "The police are going to buy it."

"She bought the Chinese food for Horace Shelby," Mason said.

"No she didn't," Drake said. "Shelby was long gone."

"What do you mean?"

"We've found a cabdriver who received a call to pick up a passenger at the street corner where the Northern Lights Motel is located.

"He went there. An elderly man, who seemed somewhat confused, was waiting. He got in the cab and seemed a little uncertain about where he wanted to go. He started for the Union Station; then changed his mind and said he'd go to the airport. The cab took him to the airport. The man seemed to be loaded with cash. He took a roll of bills from his pocket. A hundred-dollar bill was the smallest he had. The cabdriver had to go with him into the airport to get the bill changed.

"That man was Horace Shelby. The description fits."

"The time element?" Mason asked.

"The time element was a good hour before Daphne went to the Chinese restaurant, got the food in pasteboard containers; then went to the Northern Lights Motel."

"All right," Mason said, "that's circumstantial evidence, but we haven't got all the evidence yet, Paul. Daphne didn't have any motive for killing Ralph Exeter."

"Don't kid yourself," Drake said. "She was more resentful of Ralph than of anyone in the crowd. She regarded Borden Finchley as her uncle and Borden's wife as her aunt. Exeter was the one who was making the trouble, putting on all the pressure, and she knew it."

"What about Borden Finchley?" Mason asked. "Where was he while all this was going on?"

"Borden Finchley has an alibi. So does his wife, Elinor."

"You've checked?"

"I've checked. Of course, it's a husband-and-wife affair in part, but there's some independent corroboration. The Finchleys were moving all of Daphne's things out of her room, taking an inventory of every garment, every jar of toilet preparations, every paper. They were at it for three hours.

"The housekeeper was downstairs most of the time, crying over what was happening. Mrs. Finchley came downstairs for something and gave the housekeeper a tongue-lashing and sent her home."

Mason said, "There were men from Las Vegas who were interested, Paul. When I made my first visit to the Goodwill Sanitarium, a man came up to the car and asked me if I was the doctor the Court had appointed to examine Horace Shelby. I told him I wasn't. The man hurriedly walked away, got into a car which was parked some distance ahead and drove off.

"I couldn't make out the license number but I could see it was a Nevada license plate. I could tell by the colors. I didn't want to be too obvious about trying to follow him, because I felt they might be watching in the rearview mirror, so I made a play of starting to go to the sanitarium; then changing my mind. I took out after them to try and get the license number. I never did find them. I must have lost them at an intersection."

"Could be, all right," Drake said, "but at the time your client was in Unit 21 at the Northern Lights Motel apparently taking food to Horace Shelby, Horace Shelby had been long gone."

"No question about the time element?"

Drake shook his head. "No question."

Mason said, "All right, Paul, we're going to have a showdown with Daphne. She's held out on me too often and too much."

Mason nodded to Della Street. "Get her on the phone," he said.

Della Street checked the number on the card she had, sent her fingers spinning over the dial, gave the number of Daphne's room and said, "I'd like to speak with Miss Shelby, please."

She waited a moment, then said, "The poor kid's probably asleep. She's certainly had a day."

"Poor kid, my eye," Drake said. "That girl is probably up to some skulduggery right now."

The three of them sat waiting in tense expectancy.

After a while, Della Street said, "Are you certain you're ringing the right room, Operator? Would you mind trying it again just to make sure?"

Again there was a period of silence and Della Street said, "Thank you, we'll call later. No message."

She hung up the telephone and said, "No answer. She's either not in her room or . . ."

Her voice trailed away into silence.

Perry Mason got up from his chair, nodded to Drake. "Okay, folks," he said, "let's go."

"One car?" Drake asked, as they descended in the elevator.

"Taxicab," Mason said tersely. "I don't want a parking problem when we get there, and we can get plenty of cabs in front of the hotel when we want to come back."

They emerged from Mason's office building, found a cab parked at the cabstand a few steps from the entrance and the three of them piled in.

Mason gave the driver the name of Daphne's hotel, and the driver made a quick run, getting there within a matter of seven or eight minutes.

The lawyer gave him a liberal tip, entered the hotel and with complete assurance walked to the elevator, said, "Seventh floor," to the elevator operator, and when they left the elevator the lawyer turned to the left, strode down the corridor.

The elevator doors closed.

Mason waited until the operator had moved the cage from the seventh floor before looking at the numbers of the rooms, then turned abruptly. "Wrong direction," he said. "I didn't want the elevator boy to know we weren't oriented."

"What's the number?" Drake asked.

"Seven eighteen," Mason said.

They retraced their steps, found 718.

There was a sign on the door, DO NOT DISTURB.

Della Street said, "Let's take one thing into consideration. The poor kid was up all last night, working in that sanitarium. She's gone for thirty-six hours without sleep. It's only natural she should put a *Do Not Disturb* sign on the door and go to bed."

"Also it's only natural that she should wake up to answer the telephone," Mason said.

"Perhaps not if she's sleeping the sleep of exhaustion," Della Street said.

Mason's knuckles banged on the door.

The lawyer waited for a moment; then knocked loudly for a second time. There was no answer.

Mason said, "Della, I hate to ask you to do this, but I want to see the inside of that room.

"Go down on the elevator, leave the hotel; then re-enter, walk boldly up to the clerk's desk and ask him for the key to 718.

"If you have just the right amount of assurance, just the right poise, he'll hand the key to you. If he asks you your name, tell him Daphne Shelby. If he goes any further and asks for identification, tell him who you are, tell him I'm waiting up here; that Daphne is my client; that I'm afraid she's been drugged or perhaps murdered and is not answering the door because she can't answer the door.

"If it comes to that, ask the house detective to accompany you up here."

"Chief, do you really think she's—"

"How do I know?" Mason said. "We've had one murder. We could have two. What I'm telling you now is the attitude you're to adopt with the house detective if necessary. Tell him I'm waiting up here with a private detective. That will take you off the spot for trying to get the key to another person's room."

Della Street nodded.

"Think you can do it?" Mason asked.

"I can make one of the best attempts that you ever saw," she said, smiling.

"Try to leave the lobby unostentatiously so the clerk won't notice you going out. When you come in, just ask for the key."

"But suppose Daphne has the key with her?"

"These hotels nearly always have two keys to a room in the pigeonhole, and a third key in a drawer that they can open in case the other keys are lost."

Della Street said, "You'll be here?"

"We'll be here," Mason said.

Della Street walked to the elevator, rang the button, and a moment later was taken down.

Mason, simply as a matter of precaution, tapped on the door again. When he had no answer, he turned, leaned against the wall with his shoulders and hips, elevated his right foot so that it was flat against the wall and said to the detective, "We have more damned complications."

"Depending, of course, on what has happened," Drake said.

"No matter what's happened," Mason said, "we've got complications. If she's in and doesn't answer the door or the telephone, we've probably got a corpse—or perhaps someone who has been drugged with a barbiturate. In that case our only hope is that we can rush her to the hospital and save her life.

"If she *isn't* in her room, we've got real problems."

"Such as what?"

"Suppose Lieutenant Tragg wants to question her. He told her not to leave town, to keep herself available for questions. If she's not in her room, Tragg will regard that as flight, and in this state, flight is evidence of guilt."

"Oh, oh!" Drake said.

They waited for some four or five minutes, and then the elevator stopped again at the seventh floor. The doors slid back, and Della Street nodded her thanks to the operator and started walking rapidly toward them.

"Do any good?" Mason asked.

By way of answer, Della Street exhibited the key with the metallic oval tag fastened to it by a ring.

She fitted the key in the door.

"Better let me do this," Mason said, stepping forward. "If the door is bolted from the inside, it means we've got a major problem. If it isn't bolted, I'm her attorney and I'd better be the one that opens the door."

The key clicked back the latch. Mason tentatively tried

the door, turned the knob, pushed against the door, then put his shoulder against it.

Mason turned to the others.

"That does it," he said. "It's bolted from the inside."

"That means she's in there?"

The lawyer nodded.

Drake said, "Let's get the house detective."

"We'll try one more time," Mason said.

This time his knuckles pounded a double tattoo on the panels of the door.

"All right," Mason said, "we've got to get the detective and force the door. We . . ."

The lawyer broke off as there was the sound of a bolt being moved on the inside of the door.

The bolt on the inside of the door slid all the way back, and the door opened.

Daphne Shelby in a sheer nightgown stood sleepily regarding them.

"What . . . I'm dizzy . . . Help." She collapsed to the floor.

Della Street ran to her side.

Mason said, "There's a house physician here. Let's get him. But first, keep her from going to sleep. Paul, get some cold compresses. Put them on her head and neck."

Drake said, "Okay, let's lift her back into bed and——"

"Not bed," Mason said. "That's the worst place for her if she's been drugged. Keep her walking. I'll take one side, Della can take the other. Keep her moving. Get some cold towels."

"I'll get a wrap of some sort," Della said.

She hurried to the closet, came out with a wrap, and the three of them managed to get the garment around the girl. Then Mason and Della started her walking. Drake hurried into the bathroom.

Daphne took one or two steps, then suddenly slumped, moaned and said, "Oh, I'm so sleepy . . . so, so . . . so sleepy."

Drake came hurrying out of the bathroom with a cold towel. He put it on Daphne's neck; then on her head. "Come on, Daphne," he said, "keep walking."

Mason said, "What happened, Daphne?"

"I think I'm poisoned," she said sleepily.

"I know. What makes you think you're poisoned?"

"I stopped at the lunch counter. I had some chocolate. That was all I wanted, just a big pot of hot chocolate and some toast. I was so tired. I'd been up all night."

"I know," Mason said, "go on."

"The chocolate tasted funny," she said, and then added, "I had gone to the telephone and left it there for a minute. I asked the waitress not to take it away. There was a funny-looking woman sitting next to the end . . ." Abruptly Daphne ceased talking and became a dead weight.

Mason and Della Street got her to her feet. Drake appeared with another cold towel. Mason said, "Get on the phone, Paul. Get the house doctor up here on the double. Tell him we have a sleeping pill case."

Mason pulled back the robe, shoved the cold towel down Daphne's spine.

"Ooooh," she exclaimed, giving a little jump. "That's cold."

"It'll do you good," Mason said. "Keep walking."

"I . . . can't . . . walk . . . I want to lie down and go . . . sleep."

"Keep walking," Mason said. "Keep walking."

Drake turned from the telephone. "A doctor will be on his way up here inside of a few seconds."

Mason nodded to Della Street. "Get Room Service, Della, tell them to send up two pots of strong black coffee."

"Please let me . . . go . . . ," Daphne said.

"Keep the towels coming, Paul," Mason ordered.

"No, no," she protested listlessly, "I'm sopping wet!"

Mason said, "You'll *be* wet when *we* get done here. . . Paul, fill the bathtub full of water that's just a little bit warmer than lukewarm. Della Street can see that she gets a tepid bath—just enough to give her a little stimulation and keep her from getting chilled. We want it just a few degrees warmer than body temperature."

Drake handed Mason two more cold towels, said, "I wish I had four hands."

Mason kept Daphne walking. Della Street ordered black coffee. From the bathroom was the sound of running water.

Daphne sighed. Her head fell over on Mason's shoulder and again she slumped.

The lawyer elevated her to her feet.

"Walk," Mason said, "walk, Daphne. You've *got* to help. You've got to walk. I can't just carry you by your arms. Walk!"

"I can't feel the floor," she said. "My feet aren't touching anything."

"Do you think the woman sitting next to you put something in your chocolate?"

"It tasted funny, sort of bitter, but I put more sugar in it."

"Can you describe her? Do you know what she looked like?" Mason asked.

"No . . . I can't concentrate . . . I'm sorry to let you down like this, Mr. Mason."

Again her legs seemed to buckle.

Mason and Della lifted the dead weight.

Mason pulled back his left hand, and with the palm gave Daphne's rump a sharp slap.

Her back arched as she jerked her hips out of the way.

"Don't you ever do that again!" she blazed, and then suddenly moaned and again collapsed.

This time neither the lawyer nor Della Street could get her to make any effort to stand on her feet. She simply remained a dead weight.

Mason stood looking down at her with thought-slitted eyes, then said to Della Street, "Let's put her over on the bed."

"But she'll just go into unconsciousness," Della Street said. "You told us that yourself, Perry."

"I know," Mason said. "Get her over on the bed."

There was a knock at the door.

Drake opened it.

A professional-appearing man with a black medical bag said, "I'm Dr. Selkirk."

Mason said, "This young woman seems to have been given an overdose of barbiturates."

"All right," Dr. Silkirk said, "we'll pump her stomach out."

"And let's save what we get," Mason said. "I'm interested."

"Any container around here?" Dr. Selkirk asked.

Mason said, "There's a water pitcher."

"Well, that'll do if we have to use it."

Dr. Selkirk said, "We need some coffee."

"It's been ordered," Mason said.

"And we'll cover her up and keep her warm."

The physician pumped out the contents of the stomach; then listened with a stethoscope at the girl's chest. He frowned, took her pulse, then went over to the pitcher containing the contents of the stomach.

Mason stepped into the bathroom, said to Paul Drake, "Get that water just as ice cold as you can get it, Paul."

"What?" Drake asked, incredulously.

"Just as cold as you can get it."

Dr. Selkirk motioned to Perry Mason. "May I see you a minute?" he asked.

Mason moved over to him. Dr. Selkirk lowered his voice, glanced apprehensively over his shoulder to where Della Street was smoothing Daphne's wet hair back from her forehead.

"There's something funny about this," Dr. Selkirk said. "Her pulse is strong and active, her respiration is normal and regular, but there are remains in the stomach contents that are pills, all right."

"You mean the pills haven't digested? Did she swallow them in the chocolate?" Mason asked.

"She's had chocolate within the last hour or so," Dr. Selkirk said, "but I doubt if the pills were ingested at the same time as the chocolate. I think that they were taken later."

Mason said, "Would it be all right if I tried an experiment, Doctor?"

"What sort of an experiment?"

Mason raised his voice. "I've instructed Mr. Drake

here, a private investigator, to fill the bathtub with warm water. I want to . . ."

Dr. Selkirk started shaking his head.

"I want to keep her from getting chilled by putting her in this warm water," Mason said.

Dr. Selkirk started to say something.

Mason raised a finger to catch Dr. Selkirk's attention; then closed his eye in an unmistakable wink.

"Come on, Della," Mason said, "get her in the bathroom. We'll help you if necessary. Let her soak in that water for about ten minutes."

"She'll relax and go right to sleep, probably into a deep stupor," Dr. Selkirk said.

"Let's try it, anyway," Mason said. "We can always pull her out."

"I'm not going to strip the clothes off her," Della said angrily. "You should have a nurse if you want—"

"That's all right," Mason said, "leave her clothes on, that is, *both* the robe and the nightdress, just dunk her in that warm water."

Della said, "You'll have to help me."

"I'll help you," Mason said.

They picked Daphne up, carried her to the door of the bathroom, swung her around over the bath water.

"Are you awake, Daphne?" Mason asked.

The eyelids fluttered, but there was no other motion.

"All right," Mason said, "drop her, Della.

Mason let go of the shoulders, and Della Street let go of the feet. The girl splashed into the bathtub.

There was a shrill scream. Daphne exclaimed, "What the hell do you think you're doing!" and came up out of the bathtub, pushing, clawing, fighting mad. "That water's ice cold!" she screamed. "You son of a—"

"All right, Daphne," Mason interrupted. "It was a good try but it didn't work. Della will stay in here with you and help get you dry and bring you some clothes from the closet; then perhaps you can come out and tell us what this is *really* all about."

Mason stepped out and closed the door.

"I'm freezing," Daphne said as the door closed.

"Get those things off," Della ordered.

"Put some hot water in that tub. Get me a hot shower. I'm frozen to the bone."

Drake said, "How the hell did you know, Perry?"

Mason said, "The first two steps she took when we started walking her were perfectly normal steps; then she suddenly remembered and took all the spring out of her legs. A moment later, she was a dead weight. Then she came to again and tried it some more. She did a pretty fair job, but she didn't know just what she was doing."

"What about these stomach contents?" Dr. Selkirk asked.

"Forget them," Mason said. "Flush them down the toilet and send me your bill, Doctor. I'm Perry Mason, the lawyer. I've found out all I want to know."

"That was pretty strenuous treatment, a girl who expects to be immersed in warm water suddenly finding herself plunged into a bathtub full of ice cold water . . ."

"I felt there'd be a reaction." Mason grinned. "But I didn't think it would be quite as . . ."

He broke off as knuckles sounded on the door.

Dr. Selkirk looked questioningly at Mason.

"This is the girl's room," Mason said hastily. "I don't think we should answer the door."

The knocking became peremptory. Lieutenant Tragg's voice called out, "Open up. This is the law!"

Mason shrugged his shoulders.

Dr. Selkirk said, "I'm house physician here at the hotel. We have to recognize a summons of that sort."

He walked across and opened the door.

Tragg showed surprise. "Is a Miss Daphne Shelby in here?" he asked. And then, suddenly catching sight of Perry Mason, said, "Well, for heaven's sake, what are *you* doing here?"

Mason said, "Miss Shelby is ill. She's been poisoned with barbiturates. Della Street is with her in the bathroom. I want to talk with her when she comes out."

"And I want to talk with her," Lieutenant Tragg said.

He turned to Dr. Selkirk. "Who are you?"

"I'm Dr. Selkirk, the house physician."

"What's the matter with her?"

Mason said, "You have treated her as a professional man, Doctor. You should have the consent of the patient, I believe, before answering that question."

Dr. Selkirk hesitated.

Tragg said, "Don't let that sharp lawyer bamboozle you. Did she call you?"

"Somebody called me from this room," Dr. Selkirk said.

"You're the house physician?"

"Yes."

"You're representing the hotel," Tragg said. "What's the matter with her?"

"I . . . I'm not prepared to state at this moment."

Tragg walked over to the pitcher which was on the floor by the bed.

"What's this?" he asked.

"Contents we pumped out of her stomach."

"What are these pink things?" Tragg asked.

"Pills. Pills which have become partially dissolved."

"Somebody tried to give her a drug?" Tragg asked.

"That was the reason I had the stomach contents pumped out," Dr. Selkirk said, then hesitated.

"Well, I'll be darned," Tragg said.

"However," Dr. Selkirk went on, "I would say that those pills had been ingested within the last fifteen minutes. We've been here almost that long. It is my considered professional opinion that those pills were ingested just before she opened the door to let these gentlemen in."

A triumphant smile spread over Tragg's face.

"Now that," he said, "is exactly the type of evidence I was looking for. I didn't know whether we'd find it so easy, but—"

"Well, *what* do you know!"

Mason said, "Are you absolutely certain of your diagnosis, Doctor?"

Dr. Selkirk grinned. "You seemed to be absolutely certain of yours."

Mason stepped to the door of the bathroom, said, "Lieutenant Tragg is here. He's going to ask some questions, Daphne, and I don't want you to answer a single question, not a word."

"Now, wait a minute," Tragg said, "tactics such as those are going to be responsible for making a lot of trouble for this young lady."

"What sort of trouble?"

"I'll take her up to Headquarters."

"Under arrest?"

"Possibly."

"You won't take her from here unless you do arrest her," Mason said; and then added, "And if you arrest her, your face is going to be awfully red if you have to back up in the light of subsequently discovered evidence."

Tragg thought things over for a moment, then walked over to the most comfortable chair in the room and seated himself.

"Doctor," he said to Dr. Selkirk, "I don't want you to talk with anyone until I've had a chance to ask you some questions about this case. You may as well go now, if you think there's no danger."

"No danger whatever," Dr. Selkirk said. "Her pulse is strong and regular, just a little rapid. Apparently she's under some excitement. Her heartbeat is strong and clear. Her respiration is perfect. The pupils of her eyes react normally. Her stomach has been pumped out, and any barbiturates she may have taken will perhaps help her to get a good night's sleep, but they aren't in the least dangerous."

Tragg went over to the writing desk, folded a piece of stationery so it came to a sharp point and started fishing the pills out of the liquid in the water pitcher.

"Rather a dirty job," he said, "but I think this is going to be evidence, the sort of evidence I've been looking for."

Della Street called out from the bathroom, "Will you hand me in the clothes that are on the chair by the bed?"

Mason crossed over to the chair, picked up the clothes which had been piled helter-skelter on the chair, knocked on the bathroom door.

132

Della Street opened it a crack, and Mason passed the clothes in.

Tragg said, "Perry, I'm going to take this girl down to Headquarters. If I have to, I'll arrest her on suspicion of murder. I have enough evidence to justify what I'm doing."

"Go right ahead," Mason said, "but I'll instruct her to answer no questions unless I'm present. This girl has been up all night. Why don't you let her have a night's sleep and interrogate her tomorrow?"

"We will," Tragg promised, "but she's going to have that night's sleep where we can be pretty darned sure she doesn't gobble another dose of sleeping pills."

"Have it your own way," Mason said.

Tragg looked at him thoughtfully and said, "There's something going on in that brain of yours, Perry. What is it?"

Mason said, "Simply the feeling that you're making trouble for yourself, taking irrevocable steps before you're sure of what you're doing."

"You worry about your problems and I'll worry about mine," Tragg said.

After a few minutes, Della Street and Daphne emerged from the bathroom.

"I'm sorry, Daphne," Lieutenant Tragg said, "but you're going to have to go up to Headquarters. I'm going to keep you tonight where I can be sure I can put my finger on you in the morning. I've promised Perry Mason that I'm going to let you get a night's sleep and I will, but I'm also going to see to it that you don't take any more sleeping pills.

"Now, how many did you take?"

"Don't answer any questions," Mason said.

Tragg sighed. "All right," he said, "bring your things. I'm not going to try to search your purse here, but I warn you that when we get to the detention ward all of your possessions will be searched. Then you'll be given prison clothes and no sleeping pills."

Daphne, her head erect, her eyes flashing, marched toward the door, turned to Perry Mason and said, "Mr. Smarty Pants! You with your cold water!"

Mason warned, "Be your age, Daphne. I'm trying to help you. Your own efforts are amateurish."

"Well, yours are *thoroughly* professional and disgusting," she snapped.

Lieutenant Tragg listened curiously. "All right, Daphne," he said, at length, "let's go."

They left the room.

Perry Mason said in a low voice, "Keep your key, Della."

They all rode down in the elevator. Tragg hustled Daphne across the lobby and into a police car.

Mason said hurriedly, "Let's go back up to Daphne's room. Hurry!"

"Why?" Drake asked.

"Why do you think Daphne took those sleeping pills?" Mason asked.

"To arouse sympathy; to make it appear someone else was passing out the drugs?"

Mason shook his head. "We trapped her when we knocked on the door. She didn't dare come to the door until she'd jumped out of her clothes into a nightie, gulped down some sleeping pills and decided to put on the act."

"Why?" Della Street asked.

"To keep us from speculating on what she'd been doing while we were knocking on the door and waiting."

"What had she been doing?"

"Unless I miss my guess very much indeed," Mason said, "she had been visiting with her Uncle Horace Shelby in the adjoining room.

"She had to get out of that room, lock the connecting door, get her clothes off, get on a nightie, get into bed, gulp down a few sleeping pills and then come staggering to the door and put on the act of being drugged so no one would suspect the real reason she didn't answer the door when we first knocked."

"That's a *wild* hunch," Della Street said.

Mason grinned. "Perhaps it is, but we're going back to Daphne's room, knock on the connecting door leading to the next room and see what happens. And while I'm

134

knocking on that door, Paul, you're going to be standing in the corridor so in case Uncle Horace tries to slip out, you'll be in a position to nab him. . . . Come on, let's go."

CHAPTER FOURTEEN

MASON WENT AT ONCE to the door at the side of Daphne Shelby's room, a door which apparently communicated with the adjoining room.

The lawyer tried the door. It was bolted.

He twisted the knurled knob so the bolt came open and quietly opened the door. Then he gently pressed against the door leading to the other room.

The door silently opened. The room was empty.

Mason hurriedly looked in the bathroom and the closet, and then ran to the hallway door and jerked it open.

Paul Drake was standing in the corridor.

"No one came out," Drake said.

"Quick!" Mason said. "He's smart. He checked out while we were in there with Daphne. She put on an act, not only to protect herself, but also to give him time for a getaway. Come on, let's go."

The lawyer raced down the corridor to the elevator, jabbed frantically on the button, and when the cage stopped, handed the operator a five-dollar bill. "All the way to the lobby, quick!" he said.

The cage doors clanged shut. The grinning operator dropped the cage to the lobby. Mason hurried to the cashier's desk.

"You had a check-out in 720?" he asked.

"Why, yes, just a few moments ago."

"What did the man look like?"

"Rather elderly, slender, distinguished-looking, but nervous—There he goes now!"

"Where?"

"Just through the revolving door to the street."

Mason raced across the lobby, out of the door, said to the doorman, "Get us a cab, quick!"

Again a five-dollar bill worked magic.

Mason, Della Street and Paul Drake jumped in the cab.

"Where to?" the cabby asked.

"Follow that man who's walking down the street," Mason said, "and don't let him know you're following. This is entirely legal but it's a ticklish matter. Here's twenty dollars to ease your conscience."

"Hell," the taxi driver said, "for twenty dollars I don't have any conscience to ease."

He pocketed the bill with a grin.

"That's in addition to the meter," Mason told him.

"Don't we want to stop him?" Drake asked.

"Hell, no," Mason said. "Let's see where he's going."

The man went to the hotel garage.

"He'll come out driving a car," Mason said to the cabdriver, "and we've got to follow him. . . . Paul, there's a telephone booth there. Get your office on the line, tell a couple of operatives to stick around. . . . How many cars do you have with telephones?"

"Two."

"Get them both in action," Mason said. "Start one east, one south."

Drake put through the calls.

It was a matter of nearly ten minutes before the man they were following emerged, driving a car with Massachusetts license plates.

Mason took one gleeful look at the license plates; then grabbed Drake by the arm. "That's Ralph Exeter's car."

Mason turned to the cabdriver. "You're going to have to follow him. It'll be difficult once he gets out of town, but do the best you can."

The cabdriver said, "I can beat him all to pieces in traffic, but if he gets out on the freeway and puts it into speed I'm going to have a hard time keeping up. These buses are geared down for city traffic, fast stops and starts, but not any great speed on the freeway."

"I know," Mason said, "do the best you can."

The elderly man drove the car cautiously, taking no chances, keeping well under the speed limits. The cab had no difficulty keeping up. The car ahead turned on the Santa Ana Freeway, began to gather speed.

The cabdriver had some difficulty keeping up, but the driver ahead kept in the outside right-hand lane and drove cautiously.

After ten minutes, the car stopped at a service station for gasoline.

"Need any gas?" Mason asked the cabdriver.

"I can use some."

"Pull in," Mason said.

"Isn't that dangerous?" Della Street asked.

"He doesn't know what *we* look like," Mason said.

The driver of the car with the Massachusetts license plates went to the restroom.

Mason approached the attendant, gave him a twenty-dollar bill, "We're in a hurry," he said. "Could you get us serviced before the other car?"

The attendant grinned. "I can stall around a bit on that other car."

"Do that," Mason said.

Paul Drake was at the telephone.

"Get the number of your cruising car that's headed south," Mason said. "He's probably on the freeway here somewhere. Tell him where we are; give him the time and tell him to try and pick us up."

The lawyer paced back and forth on the hard surface in an ecstasy of impatience.

At length, the driver emerged from the restroom, and Mason had a good look at the man's face. It was an aristocratic face, a high thin nose, a stubby gray mustache, high cheekbones, blue eyes.

The man kept looking back over his shoulder, his eyes darting around nervously. He seemed to pay almost no attention to the taxicab, and Mason kept in the background as much as possible.

Drake emerged from the phone booth and nodded. "The man is about five miles behind us," Drake said. "He should catch up with us by the time we leave here."

"Good work," Mason said. "Those car phones are well worth the price, Paul."

Drake said, "These taxicabs are so darned conspicuous, Perry. He'll get wise if *we* follow him."

"That's why we're going out first," Mason said. "He's committed himself to the freeway now. There's not much chance he'll turn off."

"If he does, we're licked," Drake said.

"That's okay," Mason said. "It's a chance we've got to take. In this business every once in a while you have to take a real chance."

The attendant nodded to Perry Mason. "You're all filled," he said.

Mason paid the bill, said to the cabdriver, "Straight on down the freeway and go slow. Let that other car pass us if it will."

"It's hard to recognize cars coming from behind," the driver said. "All headlights look alike."

"I know," Mason said, "we've got to wait until he passes us."

"Hold everything!" Drake exclaimed. "Here's my agency car!"

A big sleek, black sedan drove alongside. The driver tapped the horn a couple of times.

"Pull off to the side and stop," Mason said to the cabdriver. "Here's twenty dollars. That'll cover your fare out here and back. Let me have your number so I can get you as a witness if I want you."

"You're Perry Mason, the lawyer, aren't you?" the cabdriver asked.

"That's right."

"It'll be a pleasure to be a witness for you, Mr. Mason. Here's my card."

The cab came to a stop. The passengers jumped into the big sedan.

A few moments later, Drake, who had been looking out of the back window, said, "Here comes our man, Perry."

"How much gas you got?" Mason asked the driver of Drake's car.

Drake grinned. "Don't worry, Perry. He starts out with

a full tank. Every one of these agency cars is filled to the brim whenever we park it."

Mason sighed with relief. "Okay," he said, "this should be easy."

The Massachusetts car drove on past. The agency car fell in behind.

"Jockey around a bit," Mason said. "Don't keep a fixed distance behind him."

Drake grinned, and said, "Practice law, Counselor, this man has forgotten more about shadowing than you'll ever know. It's a highly specialized profession and he can do it to perfection."

Mason settled back with a sigh. "I'm nervous as a cat," he admitted.

"I don't get all this," Drake said. "What's Horace Shelby doing driving Ralph Exeter's car, and why did Daphne have him put in the adjoining room and—"

"Hold the questions," Mason interrupted. "We're getting the answers."

Della Street said, "This is no life for a working girl. We're apt to be in Tucson by the time I have to open the office in the morning."

"More likely Ensenada," Mason said.

They settled back for a long job of following, but to their surprise the car ahead stopped at a motel at San Diego, and the driver rented a room under the name of H. R. Dawson.

Mason himself gave instructions to the operative.

"We'll get you relief just as soon as possible," he said. "We need two or three operatives on the job. You report to Drake's office by telephone. You're going to have to stick it out to put the finger on the subject, but we should have someone to help you within an hour."

"It's all right. I can take it all night if I can get a cup of coffee once in a while," the operative said. "And I keep some pills here to keep me awake if it gets too rough. I can take it."

"Keep in touch by phone," Mason said; then to Paul Drake, "Get on the phone. Have your San Diego branch send an operative."

Drake nodded, said to the operative, "Phone the office and get two more relief cars sent down."

"Preferably another car with telephone," Mason pointed out.

"The other one started out on the San Bernardino Freeway," Drake said. "I phoned the office to call him back. He can be down here by three o'clock in the morning."

"You'll get some immediate relief," Mason promised the driver. "Now, we've got to get a car and get back."

The driver used his phone to summon a taxicab. Mason had the cab take him to a car rental agency, and within half an hour the attorney, Della Street and Paul Drake were headed back north in the rented car.

"Do you know what this is all about?" Drake asked.

"Not for sure," Mason said. "But I'm beginning to have an idea."

"Don't we have to report what we've been doing?"

"Why?"

"If that's Horace Shelby, he's suspect in a murder case the minute he drives the car belonging to the murdered man."

"Suspect by whom?" Mason asked.

"The police."

"But not by me," Mason said. "Heaven forbid! *We* know that he wouldn't do anything like that!"

"How do you know?"

"Because Daphne herself said so. She said that Uncle Horace wouldn't harm a fly."

"Perhaps there's been a personality change," Drake said dryly. "—I just don't feel comfortable not advising the police that we've located the car of the murdered man."

"The police haven't asked us anything about it," Mason said. "We've got to give Horace Shelby a break."

"What kind of a break?"

"We're going to let him be his own man for a while and have a chance to recover his poise. We're also going to give him a chance to outwit the police just as much as possible. If his half brother tries to show that he's incompetent again, we can show that he was outwitting Lieutenant Tragg, and that calls for rather a high I.Q."

"I thought you were going to try and make him the murderer and prove that he was legally insane," Della Street said.

Mason grinned. "The good campaigner changes his battle plans in accordance with changing facts."

"And facts have changed?" they asked.

"Greatly," Mason said. "Now, here are some things we need to do, Paul.

"First get an operative to check into the Northern Lights Motel. You can phone in instructions from the next pay phone. Have him check in tonight."

"Why?"

"Because the place will be filled up," Mason said. "The only vacancy will be Unit 21. The police have removed the body, photographed the room, and by this time have released it for rental.

"If your man checks in now, he'll get Unit 21.

"Now then, have *another* man use his official I.D. card and go to the motel early in the morning. Have him ask to see the registration cards and have him get the numbers of all cars with Nevada license plates.

"Run down these registrations, if there are any, and run a preliminary check on the owners, who they are, what they do."

"Will do," Drake said. "How about letting me drive awhile? It's a long way home."

"Wait another half an hour," Mason said, "I'm jittery as a cat in a thunderstorm and I've got a lot of thinking to do."

"That," Della Street announced in a tone of finality to the detective, "is an invitation to us to keep quiet."

CHAPTER FIFTEEN

A RATHER EXHAUSTED Della Street entered the office at ten o'clock the next morning to find Perry Mason already on the job.

"Perry!" she exclaimed in surprise. "How long have *you* been here?"

"About half an hour," Mason said, grinning. "Get any sleep?"

"Just exactly half enough," Della Street said. "Man, how I hated to get up."

"Things are moving," Mason said. "Paul Drake's man from San Diego telephoned. Horace Shelby has crossed the border, gone through Tijuana and is on his way to Ensenada. Apparently, he doesn't have the faintest idea that anyone is following him, and he's breezing along as happy as a lark, driving faster and with more assurance. But he's no longer in the Massachusetts car."

"He isn't?"

"No, he parked that one in San Diego, purchased a used car for cash at one of the car lots which was open early in the morning."

"What about Daphne?"

Mason grew serious. "They don't have a thing in the world against her," he said, "but the district attorney's office has had a complete report from the police, has read a lot of unwarranted meaning into the evidence and wants to try her. They think they've got a case."

"What do you think?"

Mason closed his right eye in a wink, said, "I'm playing both ends against the middle, but I'm only representing Daphne, not anyone else. No matter what *she* wants me to do, I'm protecting *her* interests."

"What have you done?"

"Demanded a preliminary hearing," Mason said.

"Do they have enough evidence to bind her over?"

"They think so. They are absolutely convinced that Ralph Exeter was in that motel unit after Horace Shelby had left, that Daphne bought the Chinese food for him, and that Daphne and Exeter are the two who ate the food."

"In which case, she gave him the barbiturates?" Della Street asked.

Mason nodded.

"How do they know Horace Shelby wasn't there?"

"They've found the taxi driver that Paul Drake uncovered."

"Do we have anything new?"

"Drake's man is already planted in Unit 21 at the motel."

"Any trouble?" she asked.

"None whatever. Now, Della, we've had some dealings with Bill Hadley, the physicist detective."

"The one who specializes in automobile accidents?"

Mason nodded. "He knows metallurgy and all that stuff and can tell how fast cars were going because of the degree of impact and all that. I just have an idea that he might take a look at that disconnected gas pipe and come up with some answers the police don't have as yet.

"They've accepted the gas pipe as just one of those things, but actually you don't disconnect a gas pipe with your fingers. It takes tools, and regardless of what the police may think at the present time, no jury is going to feel that a girl like Daphne would have been carrying a bunch of tools with her to disconnect gas pipes."

Della Street's face lit up. "Why, *that's* a thought," she said. "That had never occurred to me."

"I don't think it's occurred to Hamilton Burger, the district attorney," Mason said, grinning.

"Get Bill Hadley on the telephone."

A few moments later when Della Street had the physicist on the line, Mason said, "Bill, you've worked for me in a few automobile accident cases. This time I want you to work in a murder case. Get over to the Northern Lights Motel; get into Unit 21. A murder was committed there—at least the police think it was a murder. A gas pipe was disconnected and a man who had been put to sleep with barbiturates was asphyxiated."

"What do you want me to do?" Hadley asked.

"Find out what happened," Mason said.

"Am I supposed to be clairvoyant or something?"

Mason said, "Take a look at that gas pipe. You don't disconnect a gas pipe with fingers."

"Can I get in?" Hadley asked. "Do I have to show any authority or——"

"None whatever," Mason interrupted. "Go there as soon as possible. You'll find the occupant will be very courteous as soon as you identify yourself. The pipe has been reconnected. See what you can find out."

"I take it I am to bring cameras and take pictures?"

"Bring cameras, floodlights, microscopes, the works."

"Okay," Hadley said, "anything else?"

"Don't let anybody on the outside know what you're doing," Mason said. "The man in the unit is all right."

"Okay," Hadley told him, "I'll start getting things together right now. I'll be there early in the afternoon."

"Don't arouse suspicions," Mason warned.

"Shucks, I'll be a tourist from the country," Hadley promised, "a regular shutterbug."

Mason hung up, said to Della Street, "Now, I'm going down and see Daphne and see what kind of a night *she* had."

"The poor kid," Della Street said.

"Well, it depends upon how you look at it," Mason told her. "You have to admit she pulled a fast one getting her uncle to take that adjoining room and then pulling that sleep medicine gag."

"I suppose they'll use that against her," Della Street said.

"Oh, sure, Tragg fished every last pellet out of the stomach contents."

The lawyer chuckled. "I can't get over remembering the squawk she made when she hit that cold water in the bathtub, thinking it was going to be lukewarm."

Mason left the office, went to the detention ward and muttered expressions of sympathy as a bedraggled Daphne Shelby, who had quite evidently passed a sleepless night, was brought into the consulting room by the matron.

Mason said, "Somehow it seems impossible to impress upon you that you should play fair with your lawyer."

"What have I done now?"

"It's what you haven't done. You forgot to tell me about your Uncle Horace having been registered in the hotel in that room right next to yours—720—and the fact that you had been in there talking with him which was the reason you didn't hear me when I first knocked on the door of your room."

"Mr. Mason," she said, "let's have one understanding. I'm going to be fair and play fair with you except for one thing. I'm not going to tell you anything that might hurt Uncle Horace."

"You know by this time he isn't related to you?"

"I can't help it, I have a feeling for him. I've been like a daughter to him. I've watched over him and guarded him, and now he's an old man and he's sick and I'm going to protect him in every way that I can."

"Do the officers know anything about his being in the adjoining room?" Mason asked.

She shook her head. "I don't think so."

"Then you haven't told them?"

"Heavens, no!"

"Their questions haven't indicated that they have any idea he was there?"

"No."

"Did you know that he was driving Ralph Exeter's car?"

She looked him defiantly in the eyes, took a long breath, and said, "No!"

"All right," Mason said, "we're playing games, Daphne. You're playing games with me to protect your uncle. Now, *I'm* going to tell *you* something. I'm representing you. I'm going to try and get you acquitted on this murder charge.

"I'm not representing your uncle. I'm not representing anyone except you. I'm going to try every legal and ethical strategy that I know of to get you acquitted. That's my duty. Do you understand that?"

"Yes, I guess so."

"You're going to have to stay here for a while," Mason said.

"I'll get accustomed to it."

Mason got up to go.

Suddenly her hand was on his arm. "Please, Mr. Mason, I can take it. I'm young. I'm resilient. I can stand it; but if Uncle Horace got in one of these places, if he had bars over the windows and guards and cells and things of that sort, he'd go absolutely crazy."

Mason smiled down at her. "Daphne," he said, "I'm protecting you. A lawyer doesn't have room for more than one allegiance. You'll have to get accustomed to that.

"And," she said, "I'm protecting Uncle Horace. You'll have to get accustomed to *that*."

Mason grinned. "I've learned to accustom myself to that," he said, and then added, "the hard way."

Mason returned to his office to find that Paul Drake had a significant report. A Nevada car had been registered at the Northern Lights Motel. The owner had registered as Harvey Miles of Carson City, but the car was registered in the name of Stanley Freer of Las Vegas.

"Get a rundown?" Mason asked.

"On Freer, yes," Drake said. "Miles seems to be simply a name, but Freer is a collector."

"A collector?"

"Yes. They use him when some tinhorn tries to squirm out of paying a gambling debt."

"Methods?" Mason asked.

"Since gambling debts are illegal in most states," Drake said, "the methods used by Freer are reported to be illegal—but highly successful.

"Now, if Exeter owed a gambling debt and Freer called on him and perhaps told him Horace Shelby was hiding in Unit 21 at the Northern Lights, it's a cinch Exeter would have gone there to try a shakedown.

"At least that's the way I figure it."

Mason was thoughtfully silent. At length he said, "That figures, Paul. Some men from Nevada were watching the sanitarium. They were anxious to talk with the doctor the Court appointed.

"That means the gamblers were getting tired of waiting, and it also means they were very much on the job.

"They could have discovered when Horace Shelby left the place and where he went. Then they told Exeter they weren't going to wait for Shelby to die, that it was up to Exeter to get the money *or else*.

"Then a 'collector' would have tagged along to see what Exeter was doing—and if Exeter bungled the job, the collector *might* have lowered the boom on him."

"It's a possibility," Drake agreed. "Those collectors are willing to write a debt off every once in a while in order to throw a scare into the pigeons. If word gets around a man who gets too delinquent in payments doesn't stay healthy, it helps with collections everywhere.

"Usually, however, they get some muscle men to give a guy a beating first."

Mason thought the situation over. "A jury might buy that theory, Paul. I might even buy it myself."

CHAPTER SIXTEEN

Marvin Mosher, one of the leading trial deputies of the district attorney's office, addressed Judge Linden Kyle, who had just taken the bench.

"May I make an opening statement, if the Court please?"

"It is not usual at a preliminary hearing," Judge Kyle said.

"I understand, Your Honor, but the purpose of a preliminary opening statement is so that the Court may understand the purpose of the testimony which is being elicited and co-ordinate that testimony into the whole picture."

"We have no objection," Mason said.

"Go ahead," Judge Kyle said, "but I suggest you be brief. A trial judge becomes rather adept at co-ordinating testimony."

"Very well," Mosher announced, "I will present the matter in a very brief summary.

"The defendant, Daphne Shelby, thought until a few days ago that she was the niece of Horace Shelby, a man of some seventy-five years of age.

"She had acted as this man's niece and, as the evidence will show, had ingratiated herself with him and was on the point of using that relationship to secure a very material financial advantage.

"It was at this point Shelby's half brother, Borden Finchley, and his wife, Elinor, accompanied by a friend, came to call on Horace Shelby. They were shocked at what they found, the extent to which this young woman had ingratiated herself and the extent to which Horace Shelby had become dependent upon her."

"Now, just a minute," Judge Kyle interrupted, "you say that the defendant *thought* she was the niece of Horace Shelby?"

"That is correct, Your Honor. I am coming to that, if the Court will bear with me."

"Go right ahead. The Court is interested in this."

"The Finchleys suggested that the defendant take a three-month vacation, that they would take care of Horace Shelby while she was gone and take charge of the household affairs. The defendant was quite rundown, and, in fairness to her, we should state that she had been very solicitious in her care of the man with whom she was living as a niece, a very devoted niece.

"The defendant was given ample funds to take a trip to the Orient on shipboard. She was to be gone three months.

"While she was gone, the Finchleys learned not only that Horace Shelby intended to make her the sole beneficiary under his will, but that he had been giving the defendant large sums of money and was preparing to give her even larger sums of money."

"What do you mean, large sums of money?" Judge Kyle asked.

"The last amount, the one which triggered the action on the part of the Finchleys, was a check for one hundred and twenty-five thousand dollars."

"For *how* much?" Judge Kyle asked.

"A hundred and twenty-five thousand dollars."

"Was this woman his niece?"

"She was not, Your Honor. She was a complete stranger to the blood. She was the daughter of Horace Shelby's former housekeeper, a daughter by an affair which had taken place at the other end of the continent.

"I will state in the defendant's favor, however, that she, in good faith, thought Horace Shelby was her uncle. He had led her so to believe."

"And the mother?" Judge Kyle asked.

"Her mother had passed away a relatively short time ago. She had been Horace Shelby's housekeeper for some twenty years.

"The Finchleys found that Horace Shelby had deteriorated mentally, that he had exaggerated ideas as to what he considered his duty toward the defendant, that the defendant was carrying on a course which could well strip this rather elderly man of every cent he had in the world. And when the Finchleys found that Horace Shelby was giving this young woman a check for a hundred and twenty-five thousand dollars, they went to court and asked that a conservator be appointed."

"That is quite understandable," Judge Kyle said, looking curiously at Daphne.

"When Daphne returned from the Orient," Mosher went on, "and found that the furtune that she expected to inherit within a short time was being placed beyond her grasp, she became furious. Horace Shelby, at the time, had been placed in a sanitarium for treatment.

"Daphne Shelby secured employment in that institution, using an assumed name and taking a job as a domestic for just long enough to surreptitiously aid Horace Shelby in making an escape. She took him to a motel known as the Northern Lights Motel. She placed him in Unit 21.

"From that day on, if the Court please, none of the real relatives of Horace Shelby have seen him or heard from him. The police were and are unable to find him. Horace Shelby, with the connivance of this defendant, vanished into thin air *after making a will leaving every-thing to this defendant.* He may well be dead.

"Moreover, and by the use of an ingenious fraud perpetrated upon the Court, and despite the appointment of a conservator, the defendant managed to get her hands on fifty thousand dollars of Horace Shelby's funds.

"The decedent, Bosley Cameron, alias Ralph Exeter, was a friend of the Finchleys, and as such, familiar with the facts. It appears that in some way Exeter traced Horace Shelby to the Northern Lights Motel. The evidence will indicate that the defendant lured Exeter into the room occupied by Horace Shelby at a time shortly after Horace Shelby had left the place.

"The defendant went to a nearby Chinese restaurant, secured food in containers and, using the bottom of a glass toothbrush container as a pestle, and a tumbler in the motel as a mortar, ground up sleeping pills which had been given her to take on her trip in case she became unduly nervous.

"She placed this barbiturate in the food which was given Exeter, and after Exeter became unconscious, left him in the motel after first deliberately unscrewing the gas feed pipe which went to a vented heating appliance in the unit.

"Exeter's body was found when a neighboring tenant smelled gas. He was quite dead. Death had apparently been due to the gas, but he had first been rendered unconscious by the barbiturate.

"This young woman then went to the Hollander-Heath Hotel, and when officers traced her there, hurriedly swallowed some barbiturates of the same brand as those which had been administered to Ralph Exeter, telling the officers a concocted story about how some chocolate she had taken had been poisoned.

"The obvious purpose of this was to lead the officers to believe that some third person had administered the poison to Ralph Exeter.

"Now, I would like to state to the Court that the reason this case is being prosecuted at this time is because of recent decisions of our higher courts aimed at protecting he innocent, but which unduly complicate the duties of a prosecutor and of the police.

"This young woman has refused to co-operate with us. She has refused to answer questions without her attorney being present. Her attorney has advised her to make no statement in regard to certain key matters, and, as a result, we are left with no alternative but to marshal the evidence that we have and present our case to the Court.

"We wish to call the Court's attention to a matter which is, of course, elemental. At this time we only need to show that a crime has been committed and to show reasonable grounds for believing that the defendant perpetrated the crime. In that event, the Court is duty bound to hold the defendant for trial in the higher court."

Mosher sat down.

Judge Kyle said, "If the proof bears out the statement, there is certainly no doubt that the Court should bind the defendant over for trial.

"This court has frequently announced that some of the recent decisions protecting the rights of defendants sometimes boomerang and force the authorities to take official action, whereas if the authorities had more time for a detailed investigation such formal action might have been spared.

"However," and here Judge Kyle smiled, "this Court has no authority to overrule decisions of our higher tribunals. You may proceed with the case."

"May I make an opening statement?" Mason asked.

"Why, yes, if you desire," Judge Kyle said, "although this is entirely unusual."

Mason said, "The evidence will show that the Finchleys had for years taken no interest in Horace Shelby. When they learned, however, that Shelby had become comparatively wealthy, they came to visit him; and on finding that Shelby had made a will, or intended to make a will, leaving his property to the defendant, they hustled the defendant off to the Orient and in the three months that they had Horace Shelby under their control, exasperated him to such a point that the man was desperate.

"Learning of their intentions to railroad him into a sanitarium, Shelby tried to get a substantial part of his fortune in the form of cash out from under the control of the Finchleys so that he would have some money with which to fight the case as he saw fit. He therefore asked the defendant to take charge of that money.

"She tried to do so, but was prevented by an order of the Court appointing a conservator.

"As to the fifty thousand dollars which the prosecutor would have the Court believe the defendant had secured by artifice and fraud, the money was secured legally and through my efforts. It was given to the defendant, and she, in turn, gave the bulk of that money to Horace Shelby so that he would be able to spend his own funds.

"We expect to show that Ralph Exeter was a professional gambler indebted to other gamblers; that the Finchleys were, in turn, indebted to him, and that Exeter was the driving force behind this situation, suggesting to the Finchleys that they use their connection and relationship to Horace Shelby to raise immediate money.

"We expect to show, at least by circumstantial evidence, that Ralph Exeter found where Horace Shelby was located; that Exeter made demands upon him, offering to let Shelby keep his liberty in return for a substantial cash payment.

"We expect to show that Shelby mashed up some sleeping pills which had been given him by the defendant, put them in food which was given Exeter for the sole purpose of enabling Shelby to escape from the clutches of his oversolicitous relatives.

"It is our contention that after the defendant had left the motel; after the departure of Horace Shelby, while Ralph Exeter was asleep in the room, someone disconnected the gas pipe and asphyxiated Exeter."

"You can prove this?" Judge Kyle asked.

"We can prove it," Mason said.

Judge Kyle was thoughtful for a few moments, then said to Mosher, "Very well, put on your proof."

Mosher called witness after witness, building an iron-clad case of circumstantial evidence.

Dr. Tillman Baxter identified Daphne; told of how she had applied for a job; how she had enabled Horace Shelby to escape.

He described Shelby's condition in technical terms. He was, he explained, suffering from the first definite stage of senile dementia; that the Court had appointed a doctor, Dr. Grantland Alma, to examine Horace Shelby; that that examination was to have taken place on the afternoon of the day when Shelby had been spirited from his institution.

Dr. Baxter said he had been looking forward to having his diagnosis confirmed by an independent psychiatrist, but that the action of the defendant in enabling Horace Shelby to escape had foreclosed any opportunity to learn of the man's actual condition.

Lieutenant Tragg told of finding Ralph Exeter, also known as Bosley Cameron, dead in the motel unit at the Northern Lights. He had found in the room a glass tumbler. In the glass tumbler was the glass container in which new toothbrushes are sold. This had been used as a pestle in grinding up pills which were identified as sleeping pills of a trade name known as Somniferone; that these were the same pills which were subsequently taken by the defendant in the hotel at a time when her attorney visited her, apparently to warn her of the impending visit of the officers.

Lieutenant Tragg gleefully described the manner in which the malingering of the defendant had been exposed by her own attorney, who was putting her in what she thought was a tub of lukewarm water but was actually ice cold.

Tragg was temporarily withdrawn. A clerk in a drugstore near the Northern Lights Motel identified the glass toothbrush container as being similar to the container in which a toothbrush of a certain standard brand was marketed. He identified the defendant as having stopped in his store earlier that day and purchasing a toothbrush and toothpaste, a hairbrush and comb, a safety razor and shaving cream, and a small plastic bag in which they could be carried. She had explained that her uncle had lost all of his baggage and needed these articles immediately.

The waitress at the Chinese restaurant identified Daphne as being the person who had purchased Chinese food in containers to take out, explaining that she was getting the food for her uncle who was very fond of Chinese food.

The waitress described the manner in which Daphne had waited while the food was being prepared. She was, the waitress said, exceedingly nervous.

Mason listened to these witnesses with a detached air of idle curiosity, as though their testimony not only related to some matter in which he had no interest, but that the testimony itself was immaterial. He didn't bother to cross-examine any of the witnesses until Lieutenant Tragg had returned to the stand and finished his testimony. Then Mason arose and smiled affably at the police officer.

"You say the pipe which connected the gas heater to the gas supply had been unscrewed, Lieutenant?"

"Yes."

"And you gave it as your conclusion that this had been done after the decedent had become unconscious from the barbiturates?"

"As an investigating officer, I felt that was a reasonable interpretation," Lieutenant Tragg said. "The autopsy bears this out with indisputable proof.

"I took into consideration that the unscrewing of such a pipe would be accompanied by considerable noise, and Exeter could hardly have been expected to sit idly by while the preparations for his death were being carried out."

"Unless, of course, he had committed suicide," Mason said.

Lieutenant Tragg smiled a triumphant smile. "If he committed suicide, Mr. Mason, he disposed of the weapon, and when we find a missing weapon we usually discount the theory of suicide."

"Weapon?" Mason asked.

"A small pipe wrench," Lieutenant Tragg said. "The gas pipe had been joined to the heater so that there would be no leak, and it took a pipe wrench to loosen a three-inch section of the connecting pipe. There was no wrench in the room."

"Ah, yes," Mason said, affably, "I was coming to that, Lieutenant. You've anticipated the point I was going to make. It took a pipe wrench to loosen the gas feed line?"

"Yes, indeed."

"In order to prevent leaks, these lines are customarily screwed up very tight?"

"Yes, sir."

"Sometimes with a compound which furnishes a seal and prevents leakage?"

"That's right."

"And in order to loosen this pipeline, it took considerable force, did it not?"

Tragg avoided the trap. "Quite a bit of force," he admitted, "but nothing that a reasonably strong young woman in good health couldn't have done, if that's what you're getting at."

"That's not what I'm getting at, Lieutenant," Mason said. "The point is that a pipe wrench has to bite into the pipe in order to get a firm enough hold in order to unscrew the pipe."

"That's right."

"Now, these pipe wrenches have jaws with sharp ridges on them so that when pressure is applied to the handle the jaws tighten and the corrugations or ridges on the jaw bite into the pipe enough to keep the pipe from slipping. Is that right?"

"Yes, sir."

"And it is because you found indentations in this pipe that you knew it had been loosened with a pipe wrench?"

"Yes, sir."

"Now then, did you photograph these marks on the pipe, Lieutenant?"

"Photograph them?"

"That's right."

"No, sir, why should I have photographed them?"

"Did you then disconnect the pipe so that it could be used as evidence?"

"Certainly not. Gas was escaping. We reconnected the pipe just as promptly as possible."

"But you did notice these marks on the pipe?"

"Yes, sir."

"Didn't it occur to you, Lieutenant, that those marks which were on the pipe might be very significant?"

"Certainly, it did. They were significant in that they showed a pipe wrench had been used, and that's the extent of their significance."

"Did you," Mason asked, "examine those marks under a microscope?"

"I did not."

"Under a magnifying glass?"

"No, sir."

"You knew, did you not, Lieutenant, that in the case of chisels or knives being used on wood it quite frequently happens that some blemish in the blade leaves an imprint in the wood so that the instrument used can be identified?"

"Certainly, anyone knows that."

"But did you also realize, Lieutenant, that on some of these pipe wrenches one of the ridges on the jaws becomes damaged or nicked so that that wrench leaves an indelible identifying mark upon any pipe on which it may be used?"

Lieutenant Tragg's face showed that he suddenly realized the point that Mason was making and its significance.

"We didn't remove the pipe," he admitted. "It's still there in its original condition."

"It has, however, been screwed back into the appliance?"

"Yes, sir."

"And as of this date, Lieutenant, you don't know whether there were any distinctive markings in the indentations on that pipe which would give an indication of the wrench that had been used in unscrewing it?"

Lieutenant Tragg shifted his position, then finally said, "I will admit, Mr. Mason, that you have a point there. I don't know. I will also admit that perhaps the better practice would have been to have examined those markings carefully under a microscope. I have always tried to be fair. The investigation of a crime is frequently a scientific matter. I will admit in this case it would have been better practice to have examined those indentations with a magnifying glass, and in the event any distinctive marks had been found, to have photographed them."

"Thank you very much for a very impartial statement, Lieutenant Tragg. I have always appreciated your integrity, and I now appreciate your fairness. I have no further questions."

Judge Kyle said, "Well, gentlemen, it seems we have covered a lot of ground today. I assume that the case can be finished in a few hours tomorrow?"

"I would think so," the deputy district attorney said.

"Very well," Judge Kyle said, "it's the hour of the evening adjournment and Court will adjourn until tomorrow morning at nine-thirty o'clock. The defendant is remanded. Court's adjourned."

CHAPTER SEVENTEEN

BACK IN HIS OFFICE, Mason found Paul Drake with a supplemental report on Horace Shelby.

"The guy's doing pretty good," Drake said. "He's down there in Ensenada soaking up sunlight, walking around with a lot more assurance than when he first arrived, and he seems to be enjoying himself."

"Anybody talk with him yet?" Mason asked.

"Not as an interview. But one of my men managed to engage him in conversation when Shelby was taking a stroll down on the wharf, and he reports the man is bright as a dollar."

Mason sighed. "All right, I guess he can stand another shock by this time."

"You going down?"

"I'm going down," Mason said. "I'll have 'Pinky' fly me by fast twin-motored plane to San Diego, then pick up

Francisco Munoz at Tijuana and—Instruct your man to be looking for me. I'll meet him in front of the motel."

"Will do," Drake said.

"Now then," Mason said, "I want to be sure that you don't lose either Borden Finchley or his wife tonight. I want a shadow on them every minute of the time. Put on two or three operatives with cars if you have to."

"I've already got them," Drake said.

"What are the Finchleys doing?"

"Living normally. They went up to court to hear the evidence and then they went back home."

"Watch them carefully," Mason said. "Della and I are going to Ensenada. Come on, Della."

"No dinner?" Della asked.

Mason said, "A wonderful dinner. Genuine turtle soup, fried quail, a little venison steak on the side, if you'd care for it, some Santo Tomas wine and—"

"You mean we're eating in Mexico?"

"I mean we're eating in Mexico," Mason said. "Ring up 'Pinky' and Francisco Munoz and let's go. The sooner we get started, the sooner we eat."

Della Street sighed. "A girl can't keep on a diet in Ensenada. It would be a crime to order a cottage cheese salad under such circumstances."

Her fingers started flying over the telephone dial.

Mason turned back to Paul Drake.

"Now then, Paul," he said, "do you know anything about the technique of taking a pipe wrench, putting a piece of chamois skin around the jaws so that you can get a tight enough grip on a bit of metal so you can unscrew it but so the jaws don't leave any mark in the metal?"

"I've seen it done," Drake said.

Mason handed Paul Drake a section of pipe.

"Have your man at the Northern Lights get the section of pipe which connects the gas feed to that heating stove out of there and replace it with this pipe."

Paul Drake took the piece of pipe which Mason handed him.

"Will this fit?" he asked.

"This will fit," Mason said. "Very careful measurements have been taken."

Drake turned the piece of pipe over slowly in his hands. "This has deep marks on it," he said, "the marks of a pipe wrench and—there's a nick in one of the jaws."

"Exactly," Mason said.

"Now, look here," Drake said, "This is substituting evidence."

"Evidence of what?"

"You know what I mean. Evidence of murder. At least, evidence in a homicide case."

Mason said, "Carefully remove the piece of pipe that's now in there and be careful you don't leave any marks on it. Use chamois skin to enable you to get a grip on the pipe without leaving any marks from your pipe wrench or obliterating any marks now on it. Take that piece of pipe into custody and hold it until Tragg asks you for it."

"It's still concealing evidence."

"Concealing evidence, my eye," Mason said. "You're taking the evidence into your custody. It's evidence that Tragg didn't want. Now, get busy and get this thing done fast before somebody raises a question about it."

Drake sighed. "You can skate faster and on thinner ice than anybody I ever worked with."

"You'll get a man on the job right away?"

Drake nodded.

"It has to be right away," Mason said. "A lot may depend on it. I want it done within an hour, while Tragg is reporting what happened in court."

Della said, "Pinky will have the plane waiting for us, all gassed up and ready to go."

"Let's go," Mason said.

"We'll be back tonight?" Della Street asked.

"We'll be back tonight," Mason said, "and in court in the morning."

CHAPTER EIGHTEEN

THE TAXICAB came to a stop at Casa de Mañana Motel.

Mason assisted Della Street from the cab, paid off the driver.

"No wait?" the driver asked.

"No wait," Mason said, smiling. "Thank you very much. *Gracias!*"

The driver thanked Mason for the tip, started the car and drove on.

Mason and Della Street stood where he had left them.

Inskip, Paul's detective, gave a low whistle from a parked car, and Mason and Della Street crossed over to that car.

"Unit five," Inskip said. "He's in there."

The lawyer said, "Wait here, Inskip, you'll be taking us to the airport and then your job will be over."

The lawyer and Della Street walked under some banana trees, past the office down a wide corridor, and Mason knocked on the door of Number 5.

There was no answer; no sound of stirring within.

Mason knocked again.

The door opened a tentative crack.

Mason surveyed the anxious face, smiled reassuringly and said, "I'm Perry Mason, Mr. Shelby, and this is my secretary, Della Street. We thought it was time to have a talk with you."

"You . . . *you're* . . . Perry Mason?"

"That's right."

"How did you—Oh, well, never mind, come in."

Shelby opened the door.

"I was getting ready to retire for the night," he explained apologetically, putting on his coat.

Mason patted him reassuringly on the shoulder, walked over and sat down on the edge of the bed. Della Street seated herself in one of the heavy leather chairs, and Horace Shelby took the other chair.

"It's been a long, hard battle for you," Mason said.

Shelby nodded. "You're the attorney representing Daphne."

"Yes."

"That poor kid."

"She's having troubles," Mason said.

Shelby looked up. "*She's* having troubles?"

"That's right."

"Why? She shouldn't be having any trouble!"

"I know she shouldn't."

"What sort of troubles?" Shelby asked.

"She's being tried for the murder of Ralph Exeter," Mason said, and stopped talking.

Shelby's face showed a succession of expression—surprise, consternation, anger.

"You said murder?"

"I said murder."

"Ralph Exeter," Shelby said, spitting out the words. "A cheap, blackmailing, gambling fourflusher—so he's dead!"

"He's dead."

"You say it's murder?"

"Yes."

"Who killed him?"

"The police say Daphne did."

"She couldn't have."

"The police think she did."

"Where was he killed?"

"In Unit 21 at the Northern Lights Motel."

Shelby was silent for a long thoughtful period.

Della Street surreptitiously extracted her shorthand notebook from her purse and started taking notes.

Shelby said, at length. "Well, I guess I'd better face the music."

"The music?" Mason asked.

"If he was found dead in the room I occupied at the Northern Lights Motel, I killed him."

"How?" Mason asked.

"I gave him an overdose of sleeping pills," Shelby readily admitted.

"Suppose you tell me about it?" Mason asked.

"There's not much to tell. I have been through hell, Mr. Mason, absolute hell. I don't even want to think about it, much less to describe it."

"I know something of what you went through," Mason said.

"No, you don't. You see my experience from the light of a robust man in full possession of his faculties.

"I'm not a young man anymore. I know that my mind wanders at times. There are times when I'm all right, and there are times when I feel—well, I feel sort of half asleep. I don't co-ordinate the way I should. I go to sleep when people are talking. I am not young.

"On the other hand, I'm not old. I'm able to take care of myself. I know what I want to do with my money. I know how I want to handle my business. You have no idea what it means to suddenly have the rug jerked out from under you; to be left without a five-cent piece in your pocket, not a dime that you can put your hand on that belongs to you; to have others telling you what to do; to have people giving you hypodermics, strapping you down in a bed.

"I wouldn't go through that again if I had to commit a dozen murders."

Mason nodded sympathetically.

"Daphne got me out of it," Shelby said, "bless her soul. She used her head. She got me down at that room in the Northern Lights."

"And then what?"

"She told me to stay under cover; that she'd come and bring me food."

"And she did?"

"Yes, she went to a Chinese restaurant and brought in some Chinese food."

"Then what?"

"After she left," Shelby said, "—and she hadn't been gone over two minutes, there was a knock at the door.

"I sat tight for a while, but the knock was repeated and I didn't want to attract attention to the unit by not answering the door. So I went to the door and opened it, and there was Ralph Exeter, smiling that nasty, oily smile

162

of his and he said, 'I'm coming in, Horace,' and pushed his shoulder against the door and literally pushed his way into the room."

"Tell me what happened," Mason said. "I want to know about Ralph Exeter. Just what happened?"

"Exeter pushed his way into the room and put it right up to me," Shelby said. "He said that he was the one who controlled my future; that if I wanted to pay him a hundred and twenty-five thousand dollars I could go my way; that he'd see that Borden Finchley and his wife cleared out; that I could have what was left of my own money to do what I wanted to do with it; that if I didn't play ball with him he was going to turn me in to the authorities; that he was going to swear I was completely incompetent and that I'd spend the rest of my days in a sanitarium under the influence of dope or strapped to a cot."

"Go on," Mason said.

"You don't know what I'd been through, Mr. Mason. If it hadn't been for that experience, I'd have laughed at him and gone to the telephone and called the police. But the way it was, no one would have taken my word for anything. I'd have been considered crazy. I was desperate."

"What did you do?"

"Daphne had given me some sleeping pills to take in case I needed them. I stepped into the bathroom, ground up some of those sleeping pills in a glass, and came back into the room. I was going to try to slip them into a drink or something.

"But the guy played right into my hands. When I came back he was looking around at that Chinese food. He asked me, 'You got a plate and anything to eat this with?'

"I told him we had some chopsticks; that this food had been left over from stuff I'd been eating. He wanted the chopsticks. So I got them, and as I handed them to him, took the opportunity to dump the ground-up sleeping pills into the food.

"He cleaned it up.

163

"I told him that I'd have to try and figure things out a bit; that I'd agree with him on principle, but getting a hundred and twenty-five thousand in cash would wipe out my cash reserves. I told him I'd have to do some figuring.

"The sleeping pills began to take effect. It wasn't long before he stretched out on the bed, yawned, and went to sleep."

"And what did you do?"

"I washed the containers, took his car, went to the Hollander-Heath Hotel and managed to get the room next to Daphne's."

"Why did you take his car?" Mason asked.

"I had to," Shelby said. "I'd tried calling a taxicab earlier in the day. I had to go out and stand on the street corner to wait for it. That was dangerous."

"What did you do with the taxicab?"

"I went uptown and—Well, first I was going to the Union Station; then I decided to go to the airport. I had money and I wanted to rent an automobile.

"I got to the airport and tried to rent a car and neither one of the places there would let me have one unless I had my driver's license."

"You didn't have your driver's license?"

"I didn't have anything. I had a toothbrush, some pajamas, a hairbrush and comb, only the few little things that Daphne had bought for me."

"So what did you do?"

"I took a bus back to El Mirar and walked four blocks back to the motel."

"Go on," Mason said. "What happened after you got to the Hollander-Heath Hotel?"

"Daphne was in the room with me. She didn't hear people pounding on the door. She had a *Do Not Disturb* sign on her room, but she'd made the mistake of bolting the door from the inside, and that way people knew she was in there. She had to do something quick. She gulped the rest of the sleeping pills I had, jumped out of her clothes, put on a nightie and climbed into bed. Then she got up to open the door. She was going to put on an act until the sleeping pills began to take effect. She said they'd pump her stomach out and that this would mix things up enough so I'd have a chance to escape."

"Then what did you do?"

"She went through her end of it. I had to wait for a while to get just the right opportunity. I put the things she'd bought for me in that little plastic bag, went down to the desk, checked out; went over and got Ralph Exeter's car out of the garage, drove down to San Diego, parked the car, spent the night in a motel, went to a used car lot where they weren't so darned particular about my driving license and got a used car.

"I wanted to go farther down in Mexico, but this is as far as I could go without a tourist permit, and I couldn't get a tourist permit without proving citizenship and showing a driving license and all that sort of stuff."

"Is it true," Mason asked, "that Daphne is the daughter of your housekeeper?"

Shelby looked him square in the eyes. "It's true," he said, "and it's also true that I'm her father."

"What!" Mason exclaimed.

"That's the truth," Shelby said. "I wanted to marry Daphne's mother, but she hadn't been divorced and she couldn't get a divorce. Then my other brother and his wife got killed in an auto accident, and I felt we could bring Daphne up as my niece.

"But of course Borden Finchley would know that wasn't the truth, so I told Borden Finchley that Daphne was the daughter of my housekeeper and that the housekeeper had been pregnant when she came from the East to work for me.

"Borden Finchley never cared anything about me. I never let him know that I'd put by a goodly bit of money. I guess Ralph Exeter was the one who found out that I was fairly well-heeled.

"Borden was indebted to Ralph Exeter on a big gambling debt. Exeter was putting the screws on him. They came down to make a visit.

"The first time Borden and his wife had visited me in twenty-odd years. Then they got this devilish idea of getting rid of Daphne and started irritating me until I went off my rocker.

"You've no idea the things they did, the little things. And then they started giving me dope and the first thing I knew I was all mixed up. . . . Well, I've got over that now, I'm my own man. I'm going back and face the music. If I gave Ralph Exeter too much drug and he died, why that's a responsibility I've got to take. But all I was trying to do was to get him to go to sleep so I could get out of there, and that's the truth."

Mason said, "The sleeping pills didn't kill him. Somebody unscrewed the gas pipe and he was asphyxiated by gas."

"What!" Shelby exclaimed.

Mason nodded.

Shelby paused for a moment, then sighed, "Well, I guess I've got to take the rap," he said. "No one's ever going to believe it the other way."

"The police found out that you took a cab from the motel earlier. They knew that Daphne bought Chinese food for someone, and they thought that it must have been Ralph Exeter because they learned that you had left earlier."

"I left and then I came back," Shelby explained. "And when I did that I broke my promise to Daphne. She wanted me to stay right there, but I just wanted to have the means of escape, and I wanted to have a car so I could go places."

Mason looked at his watch. "I have planes waiting," he said.

Horace Shelby sighed, took a new suitcase from under the bed, started packing clothes.

"Okay," he said, "it'll take me ten minutes to be ready."

CHAPTER NINETEEN

COURT RECONVENED at nine-thirty. Judge Kyle said, "People versus Daphne Shelby."

Marvin Mosher was on his feet. "If the Court please," he said, "I wish to recall Lieutenant Tragg for further direct examination."

Lieutenant Tragg returned to the stand.

Mosher said, "There was some question yesterday about the evidence of tool marks on the pipe in the motel. You stated that you had not taken that pipe as evidence. I will ask you, Lieutenant, if there has been any change in the situation since yesterday."

"Yes, sir."

"What is the present situation?"

"I went to that unit in the motel this morning and removed the section of the connecting pipe. I have it here."

Lieutenant Tragg handed the deputy prosecutor a section of pipe.

"We object, if the Court please," Mason said, "on the ground that no proper foundation has been laid."

"Just what do you mean by that, Mr. Mason?" the judge asked. "It was, I believe, your suggestion that because the police had *not* removed this pipe, they had not preserved the evidence."

"That is true," Mason said, "but the police can't prove that this is *now* the same pipe that was in the unit at the time they discovered the body."

"Oh, I think that's a technicality," Judge Kyle said. He turned to Lieutenant Tragg. "Was there any evidence that the pipe had been tampered with from the time you first saw it until you secured this section of pipe, Lieutenant?"

"None whatever."

"Were the tool marks which appear on this pipe the same as the ones which were on the pipe when you first saw it?"

"They seem to be entirely similar."

"Very well, I'll admit the pipe in evidence," Judge Kyle said.

"Cross-examine," Mosher snapped to Mason.

Mason arise and approached Lieutenant Tragg. "Have you," he asked, "exmained these tool marks on the pipe through a magnifying glass?"

"No, sir, I haven't. I just secured the evidence before coming to court. I thought if you wanted it, we'd have it."

Lieutenant Tragg's smile was almost a smirk.

Mason produced a magnifying glass from his pocket, studied the tool marks on the pipe, handed the glass and the pipe back to Lieutenant Tragg.

"I invite you to study the tool marks now," he said. "Study them carefully."

Lieutenant Tragg adjusted the magnifying glass, rotated the pipe in his hand. Suddenly he seemed to stiffen.

"See anything?" Mason asked.

"I believe," Lieutenant Tragg said cautiously, "that there *is* evidence here that one of the tool marks is distinctive. One of the sharp edges on the jaws of the pipe wrench seems to have a flaw in it, a break."

"So that the tool with which this pipe was disconnected can be identified?"

"Possibly so," Lieutenant Tragg said.

"Then you admit that you overlooked a material piece of evidence?"

Tragg fidgeted uneasily, said, "Well, the evidence is now before the Court."

"Thank you," Mason said. "That's all."

"That concludes our case," Mosher said.

"Is there any defense?" Judge Kyle asked. "It would certainly seem that there is at least a *prima facie* case against this defendant."

"There will be a defense," Mason said. "And I call as my first witness, Horace Shelby."

"What!" Mosher exclaimed.

"My first witness will be Horace Shelby," Mason repeated.

"If the Court please, this comes as a very great surprise

to the prosecution," Mosher said. "May I ask a fifteen-minute recess? I would like to report to the district attorney, personally."

"I will give you fifteen minutes," Judge Kyle said. "The case seems to be taking an unexpected turn."

When the judge had left the bench, Mason turned to Daphne.

"Daphne," he said, "you're going to have to prepare yourself for a shock. I don't want to tell you anything that's coming. I want it to be a surprise to you. They're going to be watching your reactions. I want them to see your surprise."

"You actually have Uncle Horace where you can call him as a witness?" she asked.

Mason nodded.

"Oh, don't do that!"

"Why not?"

"Because they'll take him and put him back in the sanitarium. They'll—"

"You must think I'm an amateur, Daphne," Mason interrupted. "I've had three expert psychiatrists examine your uncle—one of them late last night, two of them this morning. Your uncle has had a good night's sleep. He feels fine. He's been pronounced absolutely sane and bright as a new silver dollar. You've no idea how *that* makes him feel.

"These doctors are experts. They're the tops in their profession. The most that Borden Finchley could use to support his contentions was the testimony of general practitioners and this man who runs the rest home or so-called sanitarium. The men who say your uncle is normal are experts."

"Oh, I'm *so* glad, so terribly glad!"

"You like him, don't you?"

"I don't know why, Mr. Mason, but I just respect and admire the man so much."

"Well," the lawyer said, "we'll wait a few minutes and I think things will start working out for the better."

"You sit here, Daphne, and don't talk with anybody. I'll be back in a moment."

Mason sauntered over to the place where Paul Drake

was waiting. "Got your men shadowing all the subjects, Paul?"

Drake nodded.

Mason stretched, yawned.

"You must know what you're doing," Drake said.

Mason laughed. "Do I look confident, Paul?"

"You look as though you were holding four aces."

"That's fine," Mason said. "Actually, all I have is a pair of deuces, and I'm shoving a stack of blues into the middle of the table."

Drake said, "Somehow I have an idea you're going to get away with it, too!"

"Let's hope," Mason said.

Suddenly Hamilton Burger, the district attorney, came striding into the courtroom, and Mosher promptly collared him for a conference.

"See what I mean?" Mason said. "They've telephoned the big boy himself to come down and see what this is all about."

Judge Kyle returned from chambers, took the bench, called court to order and said, "I see the district attorney himself is here in court. You are interested in this case, Mr. Burger?"

"Very much so, Your Honor. I'm going to watch developments with the greatest interest."

"May I ask why?"

"Because," Hamilton Burger said, "in the event the defendant did not murder Ralph Exeter, Horace Shelby did; and I want to see that every bit of legal procedure is handled in such a manner that we can't be jockeyed into a position of not being able to prosecute Horace Shelby."

"Very well," Judge Kyle said. "Proceed, Mr. Mason."

"Call Horace Shelby to the stand," Mason said.

Shelby took the oath and took his position on the witness stand, after smiling reassuringly at Daphne.

"Now just a moment," Hamilton Burger said. "First, Your Honor, I want this witness warned that he is suspect in a murder case, either acting alone or as an accessory with the defendant, Daphne Shelby. I want him warned that anything he may say may be used against him at a later date."

Mason, on his feet, said, "Your Honor, I object to this as a flagrant contempt of Court; as an attempt to browbeat a defense witness and frighten him so that he cannot give testimony."

"Furthermore," Hamilton Burger interjected, "I object to this witness giving testimony, on the ground that he is incompetent to testify; that he is suffering from a disease known as senile dementia."

Mason smiled and said, "I would like to have the district attorney make up his mind if he is certain the witness is incompetent to understand what he is doing. If that is the case, it would appear that having the Court instruct him that anything he might say could be used against him at a later date would be an empty act."

Judge Kyle smiled, then turned to the witness.

"The Court wants to ask you a few questions, Mr. Shelby."

"Yes, sir," Horace Shelby said.

"You understand that this is a courtroom?"

"Yes, sir."

"Then why are you here?"

"I'm called as a witness by the defense."

"You have been declared an incompetent by a Court in this county?"

"I don't know as to that. I was beset by greedy relatives who gave me drugs that I knew nothing about, who railroaded me into a so-called sanitarium where I was restrained against my will and strapped to a bed. I understand the Court that committed me has designated a doctor to examine me."

Mason was on his feet. "If the Court please," he said, "Dr. Grantland Alma, who was appointed by the Court to examine this man, has examined him and pronounces him absolutely competent, completely sane. Two other well-known psychiatrists have also examined him and pronounced him sane, as well as completely competent to conduct his own affairs. I can call these doctors if the Court wishes."

Judge Kyle smiled. "Does the district attorney continue to urge his point?"

Hamilton Burger held a whispered conference with Marvin Mosher, then said, "I understand, if the Court please, there are two doctors who will testify that he is suffering from senile dementia."

"Two general practitioners who could never qualify as specialists," Mason said. "The Court-appointed doctor pronounces him sane, and two outstanding psychiatrists so pronounce him sane and competent. If you wish to take up the Court's time having two general practitioners testify against three specialists, we can do so."

Hamilton Burger had another whispered conference, then said, "We will temporarily withdraw our objection, Your Honor, but we wish this witness warned."

Judge Kyle turned to the witness. "Mr. Shelby, the Court does not wish you to be intimidated in any way. The Court does, however, warn you that in accordance with a statement made by the district attorney of this county, you may be considered an accomplice, an accessory or a principal in connection with the crime with which this defendant is being charged. The Court, therefore, warns you that anything you may say may be used against you at a later date; that you are entitled to your own individual counsel at any stage of the proceedings.

"Now then, does Mr. Mason represent you as attorney?"

"Only to the extent of proving that I am sane and competent."

"He does not represent you in connection with possible charges which may be filed against you in connection with the death of Ralph Exeter?"

"No, sir."

"Do you wish to have an independent counsel advise you at this time as to your rights, duties and privileges in connection with that crime?"

"No, sir."

"Do you wish to go ahead and testify of your own free will?"

"Yes, sir."